Eos Books by
Sheri S. Tepper

THE FAMILY TREE
THE FRESCO
SINGER FROM THE SEA
SIX MOON DANCE

Available in Hardcover

THE VISITOR

SHERI S. TEPPER

THE FRESCO

An Imprint of HarperCollins*Publishers*

EOS
An Imprint of HarperCollins*Publishers*
10 East 53rd Street
New York, New York 10022-5299

Copyright © 2000 by Sheri S. Tepper
Excerpt from *Destiny* copyright © 2002 by Sharon Green
Excerpt from *Memory of Fire* copyright © 2002 by Holly Lisle
Jacket illustration by Jean Targete
ISBN: 0-380-81658-X
www.eosbooks.com

First Eos paperback printing: February 2002
First Eos hardcover printing: November 2000

Eos Trademark Reg. U.S. Pat. Off. And in Other Countries,
Marca Registrada, Hecho en U.S.A.
HarperCollins® is a trademark of HarperCollins Publishers Inc.

Printed in the U.S.A.

10 9 8 7 6 5 4 3

THE FRESCO

1

things that go bump in the night

Along the Oregon coast an arm of the Pacific shushes softly against rocky shores. Above the waves, dripping silver in the moonlight, old trees, giant trees, few now, thrust their heads among low clouds, the moss thick upon their boles and shadow deep around their roots. In these woods nights are quiet, save for the questing hoot of an owl, the satin stroke of fur against a twig, the tick and rasp of small claws climbing up, clambering down. In these woods, bear is the big boy, the top of the chain, but even he goes quietly and mostly by day. It is a place of mosses and liverworts and ferns, of filmy green that curtains the branches and cushions the soil, a wet place, a still place.

A place in which something new is happening. If there were eyes to see, they might make out a bear-sized shadow, agile as a squirrel, puckering the quiet like an opening zipper, rrrrip up, rrrrip down, high into the trees then down again, disappearing into mist. Silence intervenes, then another seam is ripped softly on one side, then on the other, followed by new silences. Whatever these climbers are, there are more than a few of them.

The owl opens his eyes wide and turns his head backwards, staring at the surrounding shades. Something new, something strange, something to make a hunter curious. When the next sound comes, he launches himself into the air, swerving silently around the huge trunks, as he does when he hunts mice or voles or small birds, following the pucker of individual tics to its lively source, exploring into his life's darkness. What he finds is nothing he might have imagined, and a few moments later his bloody feathers float down to be followed by another sound, like a satisfied sigh.

Near the Mexican border, rocky canyons cleave the mountains, laying them aside like broken wedges of gray cheese furred with a dark mold of pinon and juniper that sheds hard shadows on moon glazed stone, etched lithographs in gray and black, taupe and silver.

Beneath feathery chamisa a rattlesnake flicks his tongue, following a scent. Along a precarious rock ledge a ring-tailed cat strolls, nose snuffling the cracks. At the base of the stone a peccary trots along familiar foot trails, toward the toes of a higher cliff where a seeping spring gathers in a rocky goblet. In the desert, sounds are dry and rattling: pebbles toed into cracks, hoofs tac-tacking on stone, the serpent rattle warning the wild pig to veer away, which she does with a grunt to the tribe behind her. From the rocky scarp the ring-tailed cat hears the whole population of the desert pass about its business in the canyon below.

A new sound comes to this place, too. High in the air, a chuff, chuff, chuff, most like the wings of a monstrous crow, crisp and powerful, enginelike in their regularity. Then a cry, eerie and utterly alien, not from any native bird ever heard in this place.

The peccary freezes in place. The ring-tailed cat leaps into the nearest crevice. Only the rattler does not hear, does not care. For the others, staying frozen in place seems the appropriate and prudent thing to do as the chuff, chuff, chuff moves overhead, another cry and an answer from places east, and west, and north as well. The aerial hunter is not alone, and its screams fade into the distance, the echoes still, and the canyon comes quiet again.

And farther south and east, along the gulf, in the wetland that breeds the livelihood of the sea, in the mangrove swamps, the cypress bogs, the moss-lapped, vine-twined, sawgrass-grown, reptile-ridden mudflats, night sounds are continuous. Here the bull gator bellows, swamp birds call, insects and frogs whir and buzz and babble and creak. Fish jump, huge tails thrash, wings take off from cover to silhouette themselves on the face of the moon.

And even here comes strangeness, a great squadge, squadge, squadge, as though something walks through the deep muck in giant boots on ogre legs, squishing feet down and sucking them up only to squish them down once more. Squadge, squadge, squadge, three at a time, then a pause, then three more.

As in other places, the natives fall silent. The heron finds himself a perch and pulls his head back on his long neck, letting it rest on his back, crouching a little, not to be seen against the sky. The bull gator floats on the oily surface like a scaly buoy, fifteen feet of hunger and dim thought, an old man of the muck, protruding eyes seeing nothing as flared nostrils taste something strange. He lies in his favorite resting place near the trunk of a water-washed tree. There was no tree in that place earlier today, but the reptilian mind does not consider this. Only when something from above slithers sinuously onto the top of his head does he react violently, his body bending, monstrous tail thrashing, huge jaws gaping wide . . .

Then nothing. No more from the gator until morning, when the exploring heron looks along his beak to find an intaglio of strange bones on the bank, carefully trodden into the muck, from the fangs at the front of the jaw to the vertebra at the tip of the tale. Like a frieze of bloody murder, carefully displayed.

2

benita

It had rained a lot in August, warm wet air pouring up from the Pacific, across Mexico, into New Mexico, on north into Colorado and Wyoming. Another year of it coming, said the lady-with-the-graceful-hands, posturing in front of her weather map, bowing to the highs and lows, tracing the lines of cold and hot with balletic gestures. So simple, on the map. So simple on the TV. Not so simple when the rain came down two inches in half an hour and the arroyos filled up with roaring brown water, washing away chicken coops and parked cars, filling up the culverts and running over the road to deposit unknown depths of gooey brown.

Benita Alvarez-Shipton had negotiated two such mud flows in a fine frenzy, just not giving a damn, determined to make it up the canyon, but by the time she reached the third one, her fury had cooled, as usual. Her daughter Angelica told her that was her trouble—she couldn't stay mad. Angelica, now, she stayed mad. Something inherited from her grandma on one side or grandpa on the other, no doubt, and probably far healthier for her than Benita's continual doubts. Benita herself was plagued by voices, mostly Mami's, counseling prudence, counseling patience.

You made your bed, Bennie, now lie in it. God gives us strength to bear, Bennie. The stallion prances, but it's the mare that nurses the colt. You've wasted so much, daughter. You can't afford to waste another bit.

So, caution. The goo covering the road was suspiciously smooth and untouched. Things that were untouched might be so for a reason. *If it looks too good to be true, Bennie, it probably is. If it was possible, Bennie, somebody would have done it already.* Mami hadn't always been right, thank heaven, but she scored high, nonetheless. In this case she would have asked, *What if you get stuck, Bennie? What if somebody comes along, someone, you know, not a nice person?*

Not long after Angelica was born, Benita had begun to realize she'd made a major mistake. By the time the kids were in school, she was seeking hiding places from the ghosts in her head, learning ways to cope without money, without help. Solitude was easier to live with than people. Books were less threatening than relatives. The fewer things she said to them, the fewer things she did with them, the fewer mistakes she would make, the fewer hurtful memories there would be.

When the children were little, she'd taken them into the mountains, put up the tent borrowed from her father, and camped for a week at a time without any bad memories. In the mountains you walked, admired birds, smelled flowers, threw rocks in the river and picked up pretty stones. Nothing happened to come back and haunt you in the night. Sleeping on the ground wasn't Bert's kind of thing, especially not in the mountains, miles from the nearest bar. Back then, as now, the predator she feared most was the one she lived with. Other risks paled in comparison.

At the side of the road a slightly higher stretch of ground offered itself. She drove atop it and killed the engine. Even if another flash flood came down the arroyo, it wouldn't come as high as the wheels. She rolled up all the windows and locked the doors—not that it would stop anyone stealing the car if they were of a mind to, but no use wishing somebody would! The old wreck was beginning to cost more than it was worth, just to keep it going. Unlike Bert, who could cheerfully rob Peter to pay Paul, and then rob

Paul to bet on football, Benita's ghosts wouldn't let her risk it. In her life there were no discretionary expenditures. Every penny was committed.

She studied the clouds massing in the west, readying themselves for a full-scale downpour, checking to be sure she had both a hooded rain poncho and a sweater in her pack. She didn't plan to go more than a half hour away from the car. Gingerly, she placed one foot on the mud flow, which turned out to be a false alarm: only half an inch of clayey goo spread over silt that had settled into a bricklike mass.

Just ahead of her the road turned up the canyon between two groves of ponderosa pine. This world was empty, no people, no sounds of people talk or people machines. Saturdays people slept in, read the papers, did yard work, maybe had a barbecue or went to visit family. Since Mami died, she hadn't had any local family except Dad. Since she'd become a recluse outside of working hours, she hadn't had any real friends. Anyhow, she wouldn't want to see anyone, not for a few days.

Half a mile up the road the pines gave way to aspen and fir around grassy glades, and within a hundred yards she saw the first mushrooms gleaming from the dappled shade. She knew what they were. Mami had taught her what to avoid as well as what to pick, but she walked over to them anyhow, admiring the picture they made, like something out of a child's fairy tale. *Funga demonio*, Mami had said. *Amanita muscaria*, said the mushroom guide. Red with wooly white spots on the cap. Also *amanita phailloides*, white as a dove's wing, graceful and pure. She stood looking at them for a long time, pretending not to think what she was thinking.

With a heaving sigh, she left the death caps behind and wandered among the trees parallel to the road. One winy, plate-sized bolete crouched in a hollow among some aspens, a triple frill of tan *pleurotus* fringed a half-rotted cottonwood stump, half a dozen white domes of *agaricus* poked through dried pine needles in a clump, gills as pink as flamingo feathers. There wasn't a single wormhole in any of them. That was enough. She had learned a long time ago not to take more than she could eat in one day, unless she was drying them for winter.

Lately she hadn't been in the mood to do anything for winter, or for any future time. No more planning. No more preparation. No more dedication. Getting through each day was enough. No use drying mushrooms when she'd be the only one to eat them. Bert had never cared for mushrooms, not even on pizza, and the kids weren't here to eat them. Benita had always imagined the summers between college terms as a time of homecoming, but it had been only imagination, not thought. Thought would have told her that once they were gone, they would stay. Angelica had a job she couldn't leave. Carlos said he was getting a job. Cross your fingers and pray. He needed to work, at something, not to go on doing . . . whatever it was he did. Angelica begged her to come visit them, but somehow . . . it hadn't seemed to be the right time.

She glanced at her watch and went on upward, strolling now, relaxed by the quiet, the soft air, the bird murmur in the trees, keeping an eye on the shadows. When they said near enough to noon, she sat down on a flat rock and unpacked her lunch. Diet soda. Turkey sandwich. Two white peaches from the orchard behind the house—apricot trees, peach trees, plus plums, pear, apple, cherry. This year the peach trees bloomed even earlier than usual, but instead of the blossoms being killed by the April frost, they'd managed to set fruit before it happened. Pears, apples and cherries bloomed later. July was for pitting cherries, night after night, to freeze for pies. August and September were for making applesauce, apple jelly, and putting up pears.

That was then. Other years had been other years, and now was now.

She dallied with her food, small bites, little swallows, not wanting to think about going home, reluctantly packing away the scraps and the empty can in the pack with the mushroom bag on top. The clouds had moved swiftly from the west to make a dark layer almost overhead, and it was time to head back to town, go to the market, pick up some groceries. Maybe she'd stop at the bookstore for a couple of books. One nice thing about working there was borrowing new books freebies. Or, she had a free pass to the movies. Something light and fun with no chance it would make her cry. Lately, if she got started, it was hard to stop.

She left the trees behind and stepped out onto one of the parallel tracks in the grass that passed for a road, looked up at the sky once more, lowered her eyes and was confronted by the aliens.

Thinking it over later, she blamed the TV and movies for her immediate reaction. The media gobbled everything that happened or could happen, then spit it out, over and over, every idea regurgitated, every concept so mushed up that when anything remarkable actually occurred it was already a cliché. Like cloning or surrogate mothers or extraterrestrials and UFOs. The whole world had heard about it and seen movies about it, and had become bored with the subject before it even happened!

So, when the aliens walked out of the trees across the rutted road and asked her what her personal label was, her first thought was that she'd stepped into the middle of TV movie set. She looked around for cameras. Then she thought, no, she'd seen ET arrivals done better, far more believably, and certainly with better actors playing the abductee than herself, so it was a joke. A moment's consideration of the creatures before her, however, told her they couldn't be humans in costume. Entirely the wrong shape and the wrong size.

Her final reaction was that she'd wanted to get away from home, sure, but an alien abduction was ridiculous.

The lead alien, the slightly taller one, cocked its head and repeated in the same dry, uninflected tone it had used the first time, "Please, what is your identity description?" Then, as though recognizing her uncertainty, "My designation is mrfleblobr'r'cxzuckand, an athyco, of the Pistach people."

Benita had to clear her throat before she could speak. "I'm sorry, but I can't possibly pronounce your name. I am Benita, that is Benita Alvarez-Shipton of the . . . Hispanic people."

A rather lengthy silence while the alien who had spoken turned to the other alien and the two of them focused their attention on a mechanism the first one was holding in one of its pincers. Claws? No, pincers. Very neat, small, rather like a jeweler's tools, capable of deft manipulation.

The first alien turned to ask, "Are we mistaken in thinking this is America area? We are now in Hispanic area?"

She fought down an urge to giggle and almost choked instead. "This is the southwest part of *North* America, yes, but there are many Hispanic people in this area as well as Caucasian people and Indian people. This country also has Afro-American people, ah, Hawaiian people, Chinese people . . ." She caught herself babbling, and her voice trailed off as the two went back into their huddle. Could two huddle? She sucked in her cheeks and bit down hard, trying to convince herself she was awake. Half hidden in a grove of firs beyond the two aliens a gleaming shape hovered about two feet above the ground. The alien ship: a triangular gunmetal blue thing, flat on the bottom, rounded like a teardrop above. It looked barely big enough to hold the two beings, who were about her height, five foot six, though much lighter in build, each with four yellow arms and four green legs, and what seemed to be a scarlet exoskeleton covering the thorax and extending in a kind of kangaroo tail in back, like a prop. Or maybe wing covers, like a beetle. So, maybe they were bugs. Giant bugs. And maybe they weren't. The exoskeleton could be armor of some kind, and they had huge, really huge multifaceted eyes, plus several smaller ones that looked almost human. The mouths didn't look like insect mouths, though there were small squidgy bits around the sides. She couldn't see any teeth. Just horny ridges. They couldn't make words with inflexible mouths like that, so evidently they talked through the little boxes they had hanging around their . . . middles.

"Are you receptor person?" the taller one asked. "That is, provider of sequential life with or without DNA introduced by another individual or individuals?"

She thought about this, sorting it out, flushing a little as she thought, Oh, Lord, are they going to ask me about sex? She swallowed. "I'm a woman, female, yes, and I have two children." With DNA introduced by another individual. Which explained a lot, if one was looking for explanations.

"Are you recently injured?" the other, slightly shorter alien asked, reaching out with a pincer foot to stroke the swollen purple skin around her left eye.

It felt rather like being touched with a pencil eraser: not hard, but not soft, either. Possibly very sensitive, she supposed, and the gesture was delicately nonintrusive. "A small accident," she murmured, putting her hand protectively over the bruise. "It'll heal up very soon."

"Ah. You have our sympathy for being marred," this one said.

"Are you person of good reputation?" asked the taller one, with an admonitory glance toward its companion. "You have done no foolish or evil thing that would make others consider your words false or unbelievable?"

"All of us do foolish things," she said. "None of us are perfect. I've never done any purposeful evil . . ."

You didn't mean to, Benita, but you hung your life out on the line like an old towel, to get faded and ragged. I wish you could go back, daughter, but we can't do that.

". . . I don't think I've done anything too ridiculous." She sighed, and looked at her shoes.

"Will you help us make contact with your people, so we may do so peacefully, without injury to anyone?"

This was real! The idea went off like a roman candle, pfoosh, whap! Honest to goodness real! Good Lord, of course she would help avoid injury, though what could she do? "I will if I can," she equivocated, trying to wet her mouth and lips. They were dry, achingly dry.

"We ask only what you can," the tall one said. "We will first give you names you can pronounce. We will simplify our own names from our youth, our undifferentiated time. You may call me Chiddy, and my companion is Vess." Chiddy held out a bright red cube about six inches square. "This is our declaration. Our investigation shows that this America section is the section most interested in search for extraplanetary intelligence, so you will go to your authorities of this America section, and you will give them this. When it is in the hands of authority, it will automatically do all necessary convincing, advising, and preparing." It nodded, well satisfied with this exposition.

The other one, the smaller, softer-voiced one, held out a folder. "Here is money for your trouble, legal money, licitly obtained, not a replication, which we understand to be improper, plus we will do you a welcome reversal." The aliens stepped back, bowing, with their four hands or tweezers or whatever together, upper right to lower left, upper left to lower right, so their yellow sleeves (shells?) made a neat little X across their scarlet bellies.

Then the two of them, Chiddy and Vess, turned and went back to their ship, quad-a-lump, quad-a-lump, like a team of trotters. The ship liquified to let them in, then solidified again, which was fine because everyone knew about morphing ever since Arnold Schwarzenegger did one of those movies about time travel, only it was the other guy who morphed . . .

Benita stayed where she was, holding the cube and the folder, while she tried to find words to tell them they had the wrong messenger, that she didn't do things like this, that she didn't know how, couldn't possibly . . .

By the time her mouth was ready to say "Wait," the ship was well off the ground. It rose until it cleared the tops of the trees then soundlessly disappeared. The treetops moved as though hit by a strong gust of wind from the east. She stood stupidly staring from the empty spot in the sky to the enigmatic thing in her hands. It was warm. It hummed a little on her palms and she could feel the vibration. It also changed color, from bright red to deep wine, and finally to dark blue. She set it on the ground, where it turned red again and started to make an agitated noise, rather like a fussy baby. She looked in the folder they had given her, counted for a rather long time, took a deep breath and counted again. There were two hundred five-hundred-dollar bills. She put the money back in the folder and dropped it on the ground, staring at it, as though it was a snake.

We're often tempted to be foolish, Bennie. Often tempted to do wrong.

Mami had never said anything about being tempted to do right! So, if she was tempted by this money, did that mean it had to be wrong? Heavens, even children and puppy dogs received rewards for doing right!

The cube was now squealing for attention, but it quieted and began to change color when she picked it up and patted it, as she had done with her babies. After a moment's more confusion, she picked up the folder as well. Though her brain seemed to be having a fit, her feet started moving, carrying her body down the hill while her brain skipped here and there like a dud kernel of popcorn, badly overexcited but unable to explode. The best her legs could manage was a wavering stroll, but at least they kept going until she reached the car. The familiarity of it, the dents, the rust spots, the smell of the inside of it—fast food and dog, mostly—settled her a little.

She leaned on the open door, still trying to think. Lord. She couldn't just get in the car and drive off with no plan, nothing decided. And she couldn't just go home, either. Though it was remotely possible that Bert had crawled out of his boar's wallow of a bed and found someone to give him a ride to work, it was far likelier he'd stayed in bed, watching baseball and making his way through the rest of the case of beer he'd talked Larry Cinch into bringing him last night. Larry was an open-hearted man whose kindness used up all the room in his head, leaving no space for either evil intentions or good sense. One would think that since Bert had been convicted of DUI five times, his friends would begin to catch on that he'd be better off without beer!

And one would think when he did it five times, the last time killing somebody, they'd put him in jail! Other places, maybe. Not in New Mexico, where at least a third of the male population considered getting drunk a recreation and driving drunk an exercise of manly skill, something like bull fighting. The judge had put Bert on house arrest, sentenced him to an electronic anklet that set off an alarm at the station house if he wasn't within fifty feet of the monitor at home or at his so-called job in the Alvarez salvage yard. He was supposed to call the station before he went from one to the other and they gave him thirty minutes to arrive. Most of the time, Bert figured it wasn't worth a phone call to get to work, especially on weekends when Benita was home and he could get some fun out of bedeviling her.

The rest of the week was bearable. Ten to nine, Monday through Friday, she was at The Written Word, doing more than a bit of everything. Marsh and Goose, the owners, were casual about their own work hours and pretty much left it to her. She'd been there part time for two years, starting when Carlos was three and Angelica was one, then full time for fourteen. The first two years were mostly learning the job, stocking shelves, unpacking, doing scut work. Gradually she progressed, and after they put her on full time she read reviews and ordered books and paid the bills and sent back the unsold paperback covers and did the accounts. She took adult education literature courses so she could talk to customers about books, and computer courses so she could use bookkeeping systems and inventory systems. When she ran out of anything else to do, she read books. Considering the correspondence courses, the books and the Internet, PBS, Bravo and the History channel, she'd soaked up a good bit of education, maybe even a hint of culture, occasionally comforting herself with the thought she was probably as well read as some people who came into the store, people who had obviously not hung their lives out on the line like an old, ragged dish towel.

Sometimes it was hard to remember how she'd felt more than twenty years before, a kid, a high school senior madly in love with an older man. Among her friends, there'd been a little cachet in that, his being older. She'd been too naive to wonder why an older man, a self-described artist, would be interested in someone just turned seventeen. She was pretty, everyone said so, and artists were romantic, everyone knew that, and the label wasn't an actual lie. Bert had never claimed to make a living as an artist, and he had won a few third prize ribbons or honorable mentions at regional shows.

A man of minor talents and major resentments. The marriage counselor had said that, quietly, to Benita. It had been a revelation, not the fact that Bert had major resentments, she couldn't have missed knowing that after all these years. But the bit about the minor talent, yes, that was a revelation. Somehow, Benita had come to think of him as being too lazy to live up to his potential. After that, she'd fretted over it, wondering if he thought he had no potential, and if he drank rather than admit it. She felt sad for him and wanted to comfort him, and that coincided with a few days when Bert wasn't drinking so they had a weeklong second honeymoon, not that she'd ever had a first one. It made her feel better until the next time he got drunk and knocked her down.

It was really hard to be understanding or sympathetic with Bert. When he was sober, he would sit at the table listening as she begged him to talk to her. He would grunt or utter a monosyllable, or he'd grin, that infuriating grin that told her he was teasing her, goading her. She never got close! Oh, he had good points. He was always good to his mother. He wouldn't work to help her out with money, but he was always ready to help her out with advice or carrying stuff or taking her somewhere. He never once laid a hand on the children. If he was sober, he was delightful with them: he'd tell the tall stories about places he'd been, things he'd done. He'd take them to the zoo or the playground or the movies. Of course, if he was drunk, he could tongue-lash them raw, so she kept them out of his way when he was that way. But even sober, he never talked with her, and she tried to figure out why that was, what she could do differently. She bought books and tried everything they suggested. After that one try at counseling at the county mental health clinic, there didn't seem to be any point in trying again.

Even with his drinking cronies, he didn't talk much, and what little she overheard going on among them was totally predictable. Same stories. Same angers. Same jokes directed at the same targets: women, fags, foreigners, any racial or religious group except their own. Not that they were religious, but they had a common acceptance of what they'd honor and what they wouldn't. They wouldn't spit on a cross or the flag or a Bible, but they'd kick a small dog or hit a sassy woman without blinking.

At seventeen, she'd taken him at his own estimation, at his own word. He was an artist. He would have a great career. Besides he had brooding good looks, simmering glances, a line of compliments, used often enough with enough other women to sound sincere, though she didn't know that then. Benita had

had no defenses, and she'd very quickly become pregnant with Carlos and defiantly happy about it. Papa said she would be married before the baby was born, or else. He and Mami had a furious argument about it, one of the few Benita could remember. Mami said no, let the baby come, they'd take care of it in the family, Bert wouldn't be a good husband. Papa said no, Benita had to learn that actions have consequences, good husband or not, she would not have a bastard.

Surprisingly enough Bert wanted to marry her, and she thought marrying him was all she wanted. He even had a place for them to live, with his widowed mother. In fact, as it turned out, Mrs. Shipton had suggested to Bert that he get married so she'd have some company and help in the house, which was something else Benita didn't know at the time. Benita's giddy delirium carried her through Carlos's birth and Angelica's birth two years later, and partway through the year after that, by which time she had begun to perceive, though still dimly, just what it was she had done.

"You must go to work, Benita." Mami had said it calmly, as she said most things. "This is the fourth time you have come to me to borrow money for groceries."

"Mother Shipton . . . she's been paying for groceries, Mami, but her social security only goes so far . . ."

"If you have no money to feed your children, you must work. You have no choice."

"Mami, Bert's looking for work . . ."

"He quit his last job, Benita."

"He said they fired him for no reason . . ."

"He quit, Benita. The people gave him that job as a favor to your father, so he asked them why Bert left. He left because they expected him to work, actually do things. Bert prefers not to work. If he will not work, you must."

"But, the babies, and Mother Shipton . . ."

"I will care for the babies daytimes. Soon they can go to nursery school, and you must also pay for that. Bert's mother is Bert's concern, and her own. She is not an invalid, Bennie."

"I'm not qualified for anything . . ."

"You are a woman. *Hombres son duro, pero mujeres son durable.* I have found you a job."

After that, Benita had been so busy she had never had time to think, except about one thing.

"The mistake you made must stop with you," said Mami. "Your children must go to school! To college."

That was the start of the secret bank account. That was the start of Mami's little lectures to Carlos and Angelica. By the time Angelica was five, she was saying, "When I go to college, Mama."

Bert had a different idea. He played with Angelica and called her his cutie-pie, but since the time Carlos first grabbed a crayon and made marks on the bedroom wall, Bert decided that when Carlos graduated from high school, the two of them would start a gallery. Bert talked about it all the time, as though it were real. Carlos would bring his scribbles home from school for Bert to critique. Bert would put on his pontifical voice and explain art techniques. The two of them would huddle over the table while Angelica, Benita, and Mother Shipton fixed meals or washed dishes. Bert was an artist. Carlos would be an artist.

Before long he was saying, "Granny says I will be a great artist, Mama." Benita didn't contradict him or his granny. So long as he expected to succeed, she would help him. It was something to think about, to plan for, to work for.

Bert kept the idea alive, hugging his son. " 'At's my boy, we're gonna show 'em, huh, Carlos, when we open the gallery."

Carlos agreeing, "Right, Dad. When we open it."

The years were all the same, with only the sizes of their needs changing: extra large instead of medium for Carlos, size twelve instead of eight for Angelica, an old wreck of a car instead of a bike for Carlos, a computer instead of a TV for Angelica. Mother Shipton died when Carlos was eight; Bert inherited the house. The years accumulated in Benita's routine of buying books, supervising homework, making Carlos do better than he cared to, helping Angelica do as well as she wanted to. The years accumulated with the drinking bouts happening oftener, then very often, then every day or two. Benita couldn't figure out where he got the money! He never had any money for groceries or the gas payment. When the children were little, Benita had occasionally fled with them to the shelter when things got violent. When Carlos was as big as his father and at no risk of his father's temper, Benita and Angelica found a refuge in Benita's office, after the store was closed, sleeping on the floor on a spread sleeping bag, with no one knowing where they were.

Then, suddenly Carlos was out of school (low C average) and neither Bert's plans nor Benita's turned out to have been sure things. Carlos approached his father about the gallery idea.

"Well, we'll need a few thou, Carlos. Got to get together a few thou first. For rent, you know. Rent and making contacts with artists, all that."

"Where are we going to get that?" Carlos demanded. Carlos might not have done well in school, but he could add two and two.

"Mortgage the house," said Bert suddenly, out of nowhere. "We'll mortgage the house."

But he didn't mortgage the house. Not for a while.

Benita said, "Carlito, while you and your dad are figuring out the gallery business, why don't you enroll at UNM? I know your test scores and grades weren't great, but you can get student aid, and it's right here in town, and you can study art . . ." Benita, trying to move him but not telling him about the secret bank account, not until he, himself, was committed to going on. That had been Mami at her most succinct.

The bait only works if the fish is hungry.

Carlos was unresponsive. "Aw, Mom. Leave me alone. I need a break from school. I'm not ready for college. I need to, you know, give this gallery thing a chance! Have a time of self discovery!"

Three separate times Goose or Marsh or Benita herself found jobs for Carlos, but Carlos didn't want a steady job. He preferred to sleep until noon, to take long, long showers, eat like a lion and go out with friends most nights. He worked for his grandfather at the salvage yard every now and then, just long enough to earn money for his car, or when he needed money for gas or repairs. Now and then he'd get some odd job with his friends, moving furniture or bussing tables. The rest of the time he ate, watched television, slept, and drove around all night with several other young men who were doing pretty much the same thing.

The bait only works if the fish is hungry, Benita would say to herself, wiping her eyes, remembering Mami's face when she said it. You couldn't make a fish hungry. You just had to wait.

So long as Benita let Carlos alone, he seemed contented enough. If she tried to push him, he retreated into gloom. The sulks, her father said, who had no patience with the boy. Melancholia, Benita read in nineteenth-century books. Depression, Marsh said, but then Marsh had a family that reveled in despondency. The doctor prescribed antidepressants, but Carlos refused to take them.

"There's nothing wrong with me. Leave me alone."

Two years like that. He was nineteen going on twenty when Angelica graduated, proudly presenting her mother not only with her diploma but also a letter from a California university granting her a scholarship! One of her teachers had applied for her, and she had saved the news for a surprise.

"I didn't want to get your hopes up, Mama. Isn't it wonderful? I've always wanted to go to California. The scholarship won't be enough, all by itself, but I'll get a job, and maybe a student loan . . ."

That was when Benita held her close, crying happily, and told her about the secret bank account. Don't tell Daddy, dear. You know why. But shortly thereafter, Angelica, all unthinking innocence, told Carlos.

He was waiting for Benita when she came home from work, his nose pinched, his face haughty. "Angelica told me you'd been saving money for us. I think I deserve half of it!"

"I saved it for my children's education," she said, her own cheeks pink with resentment at his tone. "And if you're in college, you'll get half of it."

"I prefer to take it in cash, now. Dad and I can use it to help start the gallery." Haughty, that *I prefer*. Arrogant.

She swallowed deeply, hating his tone, his resentments, his pomposity, hating the fact she could not meet any of it without tears and pain. She hated the way he resented anything she did for Angelica, as though his sister were negligible, not worth the investment. He got that from his father. Bert was big on the worthlessness of women. The books said sibling rivalry was normal, that confrontation was an ordinary thing, a difference of opinion, it should not hurt like this!

"The gallery plans are between you and your father, Carlito. I was never part of them, so it's up to you and him to make those plans come true. My plan has always been for your education. The money will be used for that only, for one or both of my children. If you don't want to go on to school, if you aren't ready to do so, then Angelica can use the money."

He hadn't accepted this. Carlos never accepted *no*. He had done what he always did: badgered her, harassed her, talked her down, kept after her, but this time it didn't work as it always had before. There were too many years of hard work in that bank account. Too many years of doing without and making do and, more important, Angelica deserved the help and would damned well get it. And something else happened she hadn't counted on ever, hadn't even conceived of. She went inside herself looking for the love she'd always felt for both the children and wasn't able to find it for her son. He had done something to it, or she had, or it had dried up, all on its own.

Strangely enough, throughout it all, Carlos never told Bert about the money. He was smart enough to know that would have killed it for all of them. A month later, all his harassment unavailing, he had said he would go to college as well, but not to the state university. He wanted to attend the school in California, the one Angelica planned to attend. They should, he said, be treated equally.

Benita had cried, "I've always treated you equally, Carlos."

"No, you haven't. When Angelica needed help with reading, you had her read to you while you fixed supper. When I needed help, you had somebody at school do it!"

She stared at him, unbelieving. "Angelica was in the second grade, you were in fourth. All she needed was practice.

You had a problem with dyslexia. I can listen while someone practices, but I don't know anything about helping dyslexia. The school had a specialist who knew all about it. Equal doesn't mean identical! It's impossible to treat different people as though they were identical."

Again the sulks, the depression, the endless hating silences.

Goose asked what was the matter, and she told him. "He's digging up old, silly resentments from when he was seven or eight years old, Goose. And it's been two months. It's like breathing poison gas, being around him. He's perfectly capable of keeping it up for months, even years, and I can't take it."

"Well, I can't stand to see you this upset," Goose drawled in his lofty, patrician voice. "It's extremely enervating. I've got some family contacts in California. Let me see what I can do."

He came up with the name of a Latino foundation that provided loans, tutoring, and counseling for less-than-perfect Hispanic candidates for college. Carlos hyphenated his last name, charmed the committee—like his dad at that age, he could charm anyone when he tried—and was accepted. Since he was twenty, he chose to share a house with several other foundation beneficiaries, while Angelica, only eighteen, lived in a dormitory.

For Benita, it was the tape at the end of her race. She had a day or two of exhilaration, then she deflated slowly and inexorably, like a soufflé taken out of the oven. She had never considered what she would do when it was over, never planned for afterward when the thing was done. Mami hadn't ever mentioned what she would do then. The worst was the unforeseen fact that with Angelica gone, not just to college but *away* to college, Benita had no one to celebrate with or sympathize with or mourn with. With both of them gone, she couldn't stay busy enough not to think, and over all those mostly solitary years at the bookstore, she had learned to think.

It seemed to her that up until then, she had been two people, one at work, one at home. The work Benita was decisive, crisp, intelligent, capable. She spoke to people directly, simply, without strain and without later self-recriminations over wrong words, wrong emphases, wrong ideas. The home Benita, on the other hand, was tentative, common, an ignorant woman who used a small vocabulary and bad grammar, who ventured comments on nothing more complicated than the dinner menu, a sort of wife-mother-sponge to soak up Bert's rages and Carlito's sulks.

When the kids went away, however, there was no need for a mother-sponge anymore, no reason for that person to take up space. Perhaps it was time to let bovine Benita go. The planning that had kept her going all these years was over, so maybe it was now time to make another plan.

She joined a women's support group. She signed up for an aerobics class at the Y. She began going to work even earlier and—if it wasn't group night—staying even later. Half a dozen fast food places were within a few blocks of the store; her little office was quiet and private; she had a comfortable old recliner chair and a little TV back there. She continued putting money away, for her own use this time, for sometime three or four years from now, when she couldn't stick it anymore. She knew she would leave Bert eventually, the time just hadn't come yet. She managed to encounter him only over occasional breakfasts or sometimes very late at night when he staggered in and fell on the couch. She kept food in the refrigerator for him. She did his laundry. Up until the house arrest, they'd managed to get along without real damage.

And that was the story of her life, which had now taken this totally unexpected and ridiculous turn, leaving her miles from home with a screaming cube in her hands and nobody to ask for help. Though, sensibly, asking for help would be exactly the wrong thing to do! She turned to Mami's litany, instead. *Help yourself, Benita. You can if you will. Think for yourself, Benita. Make a life for yourself. Take a deep breath and figure out what needs to be done.*

She closed her eyes, trying to clear the fog in her head, then leaned forward, gripped by a sudden cramp in her middle, or in her chest, or somewhere she couldn't locate, all of her at once totally occupied by a spasm of pain that seemed to pull her apart, arms off in different directions, legs gone swimming away, head only vaguely attached, all the world going gray and hazy. She gasped, opened her mouth to scream, but was unable to make a sound, felt the gray go to black . . .

And then it all went away, all at once, the pain, the grayness, all of it, and she stood up, breathing deeply, wondering what in the hell had happened to her? Was that a faint? A swoon? How remarkable.

She climbed into the car and turned on the blower to air it out. The pain had filled her entire being, but now she could find no lingering evidence of it. Not the tiniest ache. Everything around her shone with an almost crystal clarity. She had never seen things so clearly. So. Figure out what came next.

First thing: hide the cube and the money. Bert must not get his hands on either the cube or the money. Just counting it had dried her mouth again. She had never had any money except what she'd earned, and she'd always cashed her regular paycheck and paid the bills in cash so there wouldn't be anything left for Bert to drink up. The other check, the secret check that included all her overtime and hourly wages above minimum wage, had gone into the secret bank account.

She took the remnants of her lunch out of the pack, put the cube and money on the bottom and covered them with the sweater, the poncho, the leftover wrappers, peels and crusts from lunch, plus the empty soda can along with a couple more she'd found lying near the road. The mushroom bag went on top. She turned the car and started back down the road, the way she'd come, reaching out every few moments to touch the backpack, just to be sure it was there. A hundred thousand dollars! Oh, what she could do with a hundred thousand!

Though maybe it wasn't right to take money for doing one's duty, which this thing probably was. It felt complicated and troublesome enough to be duty. If she was going to do what the aliens had asked her to do—well, actually hired her to do—then she would need some of the money to get to the right people, whoever they were. Not her senator, Byron Morse, with his new, sort-of-Hispanic wife and his far-right friends. Goose had worked for Morse's opponent during the last election, and he'd talked about the unethical stuff Morse had pulled. Her congressman, though he was also a hyphenated-Hispanic, would be a better bet.

The trip that had seemed a long one on the way out was all too short getting home. She saw immediately that she was not in luck. The studio-cum-garage door was open and Bert was perched on his so-called workbench drumming his heels against the paint cans on the shelf below. Neither they nor the dusty canvases against the end wall had been moved in years, but the beer cans scattered around him were new.

"Where the hell you been?" he demanded, leaning in the open car window, the smell of him filling her breathing space with a rank, sweaty, beeriness.

She tried not to breathe and kept her voice steady. "I felt like some exercise and fresh air, so I drove up to the mountains to hunt mushrooms and have a picnic lunch."

"Yeah, I'll bet," he sneered.

She opened the pack and displayed the contents of the mushroom sack. "Mushroom hunting, Bert. You used to go with me and the kids sometimes. I left you a note."

"Your note said you were going shopping."

"I plan to. I thought I'd do it on my way home, but I got rained on in the hills, so I decided to come home and change before I did the shopping."

"It'll have to wait. Give me the keys."

She became very still inside. Something clicked, like a relay switch. She said softly, "Bert, you know what the judge said. Now's not the time to get him down on you . . ."

He jerked the car door open. "Give me the goddamn keys. The judge won't do a damned thing, and you know it. I'm not drunk, I'm not going to drink, it's Saturday, and nobody's gonna be watching the goddam monitor on Saturday! I'm going over to Larry's place to watch the game with him and Bill. Now come on!"

He wore an expression she had learned to heed, one that

was a half-step from violence, one that begged her to cross
him and give him an excuse to go over the edge. Normally
at this point she dissolved into sludge, tears and whines, attempts to dissuade him. Today, amid this new clarity, she did
a much simpler thing. Leaving the keys in the ignition, she
edged away from him, across the passenger side and out,
taking the pack with her.

"They impounded your car, Bert. If you get picked up in
my car, they'll impound my car too." Without difficulty, she
kept her voice perfectly level, normally an achievement in
itself. "I won't have any way to get to work."

He jeered, "Moo, moo. Bossie-Benita the human cow!
You worried your hubby'll let you starve?" He climbed in behind the wheel and backed out into the street, wheels
screaming.

She stood where she was, not moving. The car was
stopped, half into the street, while he waited for her to do
something. Come after him, maybe. Make a face. Stamp her
foot. It wouldn't take much. Any little thing. She turned to
the trash barrel and took the empty cans from the pack, one
at a time throwing them away, paying no attention to the
beer cans, which ordinarily she would have gathered up immediately. Today she realized he would consider her throwing them away a comment on his morning's activities, so she
let them lie. Bert was always able to establish that she had
done something wrong, no matter what she did, and ordinarily she kept a wary eye on him. Today she ignored him as
she fiddled with the trash until the car went away too fast,
squealing before it got to the stop sign, only half stopping
before screeching around the corner and away.

Six months ago there had been two injured, one dead. A
trial date months in the future. And a judge with no more
sense than to accept that "don't lock him up, he's a working
man" argument. She had explained the situation to his
lawyer. Benita's father paid Bert when and if he showed up at
the salvage yard. Since he didn't often show up, he wasn't
really a working man. The public defender said his first duty
was to his client, and it would go easier on him if he were a
man with a job and a family to support.

"But he's not," she said.

The lawyer gave her a mulish stare. "Well, he must contribute something. The house . . ."

"Right. His mother left him the house when she died. Bert sold his last piece of art thirteen years ago. For the last ten years, I've paid the property taxes and maintenance, because that's the last time Bert worked for money. Last year Bert took out a mortgage on the house so he could pay cash for a new car, which he said he needed for a new delivery job he was taking. I don't know what happened to the job, but he borrowed on the car for drinking and gambling money. When he was picked up for drunk driving, they impounded the car and the finance agency repossessed it. I haven't made any of the mortgage payments and the house is about to be foreclosed. That's Bert's contribution to the family welfare."

"You didn't make the mortgage payments?" the lawyer had asked, as though she had done something unfamilial.

She had stared at him, making him shift uncomfortably. "It isn't my house, as Bert often reminds me. I didn't borrow on it. Foreclosure is sixty days away."

"And when they foreclose?"

"Bert won't have anywhere to live."

"Neither will you," he challenged.

"I'm moving in with my father," she said. "Alone. My father doesn't like Bert."

Actually, she planned to rent a small apartment when the time came, but that was no one's business but hers. As it turned out, nothing she had said made any difference, for the lawyer totally ignored it, as did la raza judge. Typical. As time passed, more and more of the elected magistrates were women, but they were still too few and far between.

She shut the garage door and went into the house, rubbing her forehead. If Bert followed his usual pattern, he'd spend the afternoon with his drinking buddies, maybe Larry, but just as likely that had been misdirection on his part. The police would show up sooner or later, and he wouldn't want her to know where he really was. During the afternoon he'd go through stage one, which was boisterous conviviality, and stage two, slightly morose nostalgia, and when they ran out of beer, he'd move on to stage three, which might bring him home to tear the house apart, looking for liquor or money he thought he might have hidden sometime in the past. He was always sure one of his old caches was still there and if he didn't find one, it was because Benita had stolen his money or thrown out his liquor. That's usually when he hit her, if she was around. Stage four involved belligerence and violence, and she had this cube-thing to protect. Bert had the car, however, and she had no way to go except, maybe, call a cab, and they were so expensive . . .

An audible click. Like that little relay switch. There was money. There, beneath her hand, was money. Quite a lot of money. She had planned to leave after the foreclosure, because that would focus Bert's belligerence on the bank rather than on herself. But here under her hand was the opportunity to do it now. So call a cab. Pack a bag. Take Sasquatch to a kennel so Bert couldn't take out his temper on the dog. The money was right there, and even though she hadn't earned it yet, she planned to earn it, she could start earning it!

Right away, here came the marching ghosts. Mami and Papa wouldn't approve. It wasn't fair to Goose and Marsh. The children might not like the idea . . .

She felt a flash of that same pain she'd felt up in the hills, momentary, fleeting, like a splinter being pulled out, a moment's pang, but then the ache went away, and so did the ghosts, leaving her mind even clearer than before. How very strange. Almost as though she were . . . emptied out. Like a garbage can, all emptied out and washed with hot water and soap. She'd never been able to banish the ghosts before!

Unbidden, a picture of the aliens came into her mind. They would do her a welcome reversal. A good turn. Yes. They would banish her ghosts. They would go down all her nerves and synapses and exorcise her. They would leave her in clarity. Delicately, as though handling fine crystal, she set the thought aside, knowing it to be true. Obviously, they didn't want a hag-ridden envoy. They wanted someone with her wits about her!

She had almost a month accumulated leave coming. As

she went up the stairs, she planned what to do next: first, call Marsh or Goose at home, tell them there was an emergency. She'd take her new suit she'd saved up for. Several pairs of slacks, the neat ones she wore to work, with clean shirts, underwear, the two new sleep tee's that Angelica had sent for her birthday. Her hands worked almost by themselves, opening drawers, taking down hangers, stuff from the medicine cabinet: hair dryer, curling iron, toothbrush, vitamins, allergy medicine. She always stuffed up in places with high humidity.

High humidity? Where?

Not here, stupid, a voice told her. Washington, D.C. Where else would she find people in authority?

Everything went into one suitcase plus a small carry-on bag. She'd get her ticket at the airport, the airline or route didn't matter. She'd learned to drive when she was sixteen and had never changed the name on her driver's license, so she could buy the ticket under her maiden name. There were X-ray machines. How would the cube react to an X-ray machine? And what about the money? She didn't dare carry that much money in her purse! Or her carry-on bag. What if she got mugged?

She got the sewing kit out of the linen closet along with a strip torn from the end of a worn bedsheet, spread the cloth neatly on the bed, arranged layers of money down the center of the strip, then folded it over twice and basted the cloth into a thick, flexible belt, finishing it off with two ribbon ties. The belt went around her waist to be double-tied in front, like a child's shoelaces. She had kept ten of the five-hundred-dollar bills separate, two in the bill compartment of her wallet and eight of them in the secret compartment of her purse, where they wouldn't show when she paid for anything.

She'd have to leave a note, though it didn't matter what it said. Any attempt at communicating with Bert in writing always made him furious. He liked to disagree or hit out if something annoyed him, and hitting a letter wasn't rewarding for him. In the end, she wrote, "Bert, I've decided to take some vacation time on my own. I'm taking the dog with me."

She thought a moment. If he was drunk, he would look for her at her father's. Well, nothing she could say would keep him from doing that, but she'd better let her father know she'd left.

The note to her father was brief. "Have to get away, have to do some thinking, I'll be in touch."

Mami had died years ago. No way to tell her anything. Not that she would have needed telling. Benita made two calls, one to the kennel, one to Goose.

"Goose, sorry to bother you at work, but this is Benita, and I have to tell you an emergency has come up and . . . No, the kids are fine. This is something else. . . . No, it isn't. Goose, just listen! I've got to take my accumulated vacation now. . . . No, I don't need checks in advance, but would you mind depositing them to my personal account until I get back? That's right, the one at First Bank. Thank you, Goose. Tell Marsh, okay?"

When the cab came, she was ready, everything counted six times and everything in the house locked up, put away, turned off. There was a house key on her car key ring, so if Bert came home, he could get in. Sasquatch was on the leash, eager to go anywhere.

As she went out the front door with her suitcase, a police car pulled to the curb. Officer Cain. She knew him all too well.

"Benita, sorry, but Bert's monitor went off . . ."

"He took my car," she said, without expression or apology. "He said he was going to Larry's, but I'm not sure he did."

"You try to stop him?" he asked, looking at her face.

"No. The bruise is a couple of days old."

"Sorry, Benita, but we have to look for him."

"I do hope you find him before he kills someone," she said sweetly, smiling briefly as she got into the cab.

"Head out toward the airport," she said, settling back in the seat with a slightly queasy feeling. "We'll make one stop, but it's on the way. I'm leaving the dog at a kennel."

Sasquatch put his front feet on the seat and looked out the window, while Benita ruffled the fur of his neck, taking a certain comfort from the solidity of him. She and the kids had named him Sasquatch. He'd never been away from home, anymore than she had. Except for the few times she had run to the shelter when the children were little, she had never in her whole life taken off like this. Even when Angelica had begged her to come visit them in California last winter, Bert hadn't wanted to go, and she hadn't wanted to go for fear . . . for fear of what?

Simple, really. If she'd gone to visit the kids last winter, she wouldn't have come back. At that time, she hadn't been ready to do anything final. Donkey-like, she'd been waiting for the stick to hit her. Well, the house arrest and the foreclosure had been two good whacks, one right after the other. The extraterrestrials and the money were more in the nature of a carrot. Take a bite. Go on, it's delicious!

Stick behind, carrot before, there was no point in waiting for anything. Besides, she'd given her word. She'd claimed to be a person of respect, and she'd given her word. It sounded stupid as all get-out, even to her, but it would just have to do.

3

incidents

On Pacific time, Rog Wooley's alarm went off, though softly, at four A.M., and he reacted almost at once to stop it before it woke Susan. She hadn't been sleeping well lately, none of the lumbermen's families had, and if she woke at this hour of the morning, she would only mess up his routine with her doubts and worries. His clothes were in the bathroom, and he dressed there, taking care with his socks and the warm layers of shirts and sweaters, being sure everything lay smooth against his body. Climbing a few hundred feet into the air lugging a heavy saw was enough to tire a man without adding socks or clothing that bunched and bound. By the time he'd topped the first tree, he'd be sopping wet and it would be warm enough to take off a few layers.

Outside, the world was dark and chill, with wisps of fog moving around like ghosts. He had backed the car up the driveway and parked outside the garage door, so he could release the brake and roll half a block before he started the engine. His climbing irons were in the car, along with his lunch. He'd fixed that last night after Susan went to bed. He checked his watch. The van would be at the edge of town by five, and it wouldn't wait for late arrivals.

He was on time, one more sleepy, aggravated timber cutter, trying to get to the work site on Sunday, when the damned tree-huggers wouldn't expect them. Later this morning, they would be there to block the road as they had yesterday, and the day before, and the day before that. Every time one judge signed an order to disperse, some other judge overrode it. Meantime, nobody was making any money, jobs were on the line, and rent payments were coming due. He stared out the window of the van, half dozing, as the jagged skyline emerged from the dark and the sky lightened in the east.

They joined up with several other vans as they crossed the bridge, and the convoy drove the last eight miles in absolute silence. The tree-huggers could be camped out there, and nobody wanted any more confrontations. The bosses were afraid somebody was going to get killed, the toppers and fellers were ready to do the killing, and meanwhile the trees just sat there, benefitting nobody! So they were old growth! That's why they were valuable! Why couldn't the idiot environmentalists see that? Trees that size had to be cut while they were still healthy. They wouldn't do the human race any good if they were left to rot!

They reached the site when the sky was barely light enough to see by, hours before the picketers were out, or the guys that made a big thing out of lying down in the road so the trucks couldn't get by. Steve Buck and Harry Rider were the other two toppers, the trees were already marked for selective cutting—and that was another gripe! No more clear cutting, even though that was the easier way to do it! No worry about topping, let them fall where they would! A man could sure as hell make more money that way, though, hell, something was better than nothing. Selective cutting meant they had to limit and clear the fall zones, so they were back to topping trees. While he was doing his thing, the other men would keep busy clearing fall zones until the first big ones were ready to come down. The tractor men wouldn't even arrive until around nine.

The first marked tree was a monster, so big around that he couldn't throw a line around it until he was thirty feet off the ground. Even then it took extreme effort just to heave the rope that held him to the trunk while he spiked his way up. A third of the way to the top he shifted around the trunk to avoid the sun, just poking over the horizon dead level with his eyes. The rope bound and rattled, almost as though something was fooling with it on the other side of the trunk. He hadn't seen any stubs from the ground, not this low on the trunk, but then it hadn't been light enough to see very well. He sidestepped to one side, then the other, but the trunk was clear almost all the way up and without many stubs to drop. Jase Steele was below, clearing away anything he dropped. Jase was a careful man, a good man to have on the ground, one who wouldn't take any chances that ended up getting him hurt and getting the man above him fired.

When he came to the first stub, he checked the area below, saw it was clear, jerked the saw into noisy action and took off the branch. It was short, but as big around as his leg. When it hit bottom, Jase came out of the brush and waved; Rog let the saw dangle at the end of its safety line and heaved himself up another ten feet. He was about eighty feet up and the damned tree was just now beginning to taper enough that it was halfway easy to climb. It smelled weird, too. Maybe because it was cold. Sun-warmed redwood, sun-warmed pine, they both smelled clean, but this smell was different. A real stink. Like something died up here.

Jase yelled something from below, but Rog didn't look down. He still had fifty feet to go to the point where he could top this monster. Now that the trunk was thinner, he could move faster. Jase yelled again, a kind of panicky scream, and Rog shifted to the side to block the sun and let him look down, but as he moved he caught a glimpse of something on the other side of the tree, just a quick look at something hairy and big and good lord God in heaven, look at those teeth . . .

In the Gila wilderness of southwestern New Mexico, a small pack of Mexican wolves, introduced the previous year by the Forest Service, lay in the midmorning sun on a rock shelf above a den still in use by the alpha female and her four half-grown pups. The alpha dog lay beside the bitch, licking his front paws and, occasionally, his mate's ear. Several others of the pack were nearby, and the pups were tumbling over and around him, but he ignored them, eyes half closed in the warmth of the sun and the stone.

The pups were weaned. They were almost big enough to join in the hunt, and this was the time Mack Cerubia had been waiting for. He'd spotted the den months before, a natural tunnel in solid rock that he couldn't dig out, and the mother had been too sly and shy for him to get a good shot at. Mack had killed the last of the former pack sixteen months ago. The Fish and Game people and the Forest Service had a ten-thousand-dollar reward posted for "information leading to arrest," but nobody had claimed it because nobody knew anything. Mack didn't talk about his intentions, unlike some idiots who stuck their faces on TV, making threats. If you knew wolves were vermin, and you knew they needed killing, but the vermin were protected by the damned greenies, you didn't talk about it. You just did it, making damn sure nobody saw you.

Nobody would have suspected him, anyhow. He didn't run cattle anymore. He wasn't getting rid of the wolves because they threatened his stock, he was getting rid of the wolves because his forefathers had killed every last wolf in the U.S. of A. because they'd needed killing! Right along with cougars and grizzlies and lesser vermin like wolverines, coyotes and eagles that picked off lambs. The country was Godgiven for the people who used and grazed it and hunted on it, and he'd be damned if some government official was going to tell him what was vermin and what wasn't.

He could have shot the bitch months ago, leaving the pups to starve, but it had been early enough in the season that another pair might breed. He'd figured he'd wait until the young ones were a bit grown and the pack was all together. Then he could get the bitch and the dog. Once the alpha animals were dead, the others would be disorganized, easier to kill. He'd made a new kind of silencer and he'd bought a new scope. Yesterday and the day before he'd used fifty rounds with both, sighting in the scope. With any luck at all, he'd have both alphas and some of the pups before the others knew what was happening.

Just now he was working his way up the slope to the ridge across from the den. It would be about a hundred-yard shot, easy with this weapon. When he neared the ridge, he dropped on his belly and crawled up, stopping once or twice when his sight blurred. He took off his goggles and wiped his eyes. The haziness came and went. He'd noticed it the last time he was here, too. Probably sun-warmed air rising off a rockface down the slope before him.

Raising his head slowly, he looked down on the den. The shelf above it was hip deep in dogs. He counted, eagerly. The four pups. The alpha bitch, the alpha dog, three others. He eased the muzzle of the rifle over the ridge, settled it firmly and applied his eye to the scope, put his finger to the trigger and began to tighten it . . .

And damn it, something screamed!

It was a sound so vehement, so near that he completely lost the target as he rolled and looked upward where the sound had come from. His first thought was eagle. Eagles screamed, though he'd never heard one as loud as that. Hell, it would take an eagle the size of a truck to scream like that, and besides there was nothing around! Just sky, and trees, and the line of the ridge, and across the canyon . . . not one damned wolf! Either down the den or gone, hell knows where!

He rolled into prone position again, cursing, staring at the trees around him. Except for the wavery air he saw absolutely nothing. His first clue that he wasn't alone came when something invisible grabbed him by both ankles and yanked him, yelling his head off, straight up into the sky.

A Forest Service officer climbed to the same spot later in the day, to check on the den as he'd been doing at weekly intervals ever since the female pupped. He found the rifle lying at the top of the ridge. All around and on top of it were torn fragments of denim and flannel and knit cotton and leather, some of them bloodstained, like feathers someone had plucked from a chicken. There was no sign of anyone, however. Not even any bloodstains on the ground.

*   *   *

Sunday was a working day at the Waving Palms Motel, or what would be Waving Palms when the twelve-acre site was drained. The trick was, so Bubba Miller claimed, to get the acreage drained over the weekend, and do it so fast nobody had time to know about it. That way there'd be no complaints, no EPA challenges, no outcries about endangered species. Besides, it wasn't any big deal, only twelve acres, and it had been in Bubba's family since Grampa Miller took it on account of an unpaid repair bill, back in the fifties. It was plenty big enough for a small motel, and there were no recent changes of ownership papers floating around, requiring surveys or confusing things. The permit to dig a foundation that was posted on the road had been issued for a dry piece of land a half mile away. The permit had a mistake on it indicating that other piece of property. Just two numbers twisted around was all. Nobody's fault, if anybody caught onto it. It just happened that way.

So, Bubba and his brother Quentin, who had fallen heir to the twelve acres along with their cousin Josh, all of whom had agreed to throw in their shares for the Waving Palms project, had Bubba's front loader and a backhoe they'd rented, and they were digging a nice big pond at the lower, western end of the ten acres and running a good-sized ditch into it along the swamp on the north. Bubba didn't own the ground on the north or the south side, where another good-sized ditch led into the swamp. Everything the backhoe dug out of the pond and the ditches got dumped on the eastern edge of the property, along the road, to raise it up. It'd be muddy as hell for a few weeks, fulla dead frogs and snakes and all the stuff that squirmed around down in that muck, but when the eastern end had a chance to dry out a little, they'd dump a few loads of fill dirt and gravel on it, grade it out and really dig the foundations. By that time, they'd be able to fool with the ditches some, make them look more natural, and plant some other stuff around.

"Hey, Bubba," yelled Quentin, when Bubba cut the engine for a minute to clear some brush from the bucket-teeth. "C'mon over here. See what Josh found!"

Trampling through a patch of rare and endangered orchids, Bubba stomped over to the other two men who were standing in a patch of ferns on a little hillock, one they hadn't planned to touch.

"Why the hell'd ya smash it?" he asked, more interested than irate. The patch of ferns looked as flat as a pool table, though it might be very slightly dished at the center.

"C'mon," Quentin admonished. "Look addit! We din do that."

It seemed to Bubba likely they hadn't. The general flatness had been accomplished through repeated pounding by something large, like a section of log, like the heavy tampers used to settle fill dirt around drainpipes, or foundations, stuff like that. Must be a big man or more'n one did it. Something that size would be a heavy ole bitch of a thing, almost two feet across.

"Whaddaya think?" asked Quentin.

"I think somuddy buried somethin," Bubba replied. "And when he set them ferns back on top, he smooshed the whole thing down tight. Probly, just did it. A week from now, they'd all be growed up again, and we wouldn'a seen it."

"You think maybe money?" asked Josh, thoughtfully.

Bubba looked around. "Nah. I think more likely a body. It's too wet here for money or paper. Most likely a body."

"We gonna dig it up?" asked Quentin.

"Why'n hell we do that?" his brother replied. "Get all messed up in somethin none of our binness! Let dead bodies lie, that's what I say."

They returned to their work, making considerable progress by early afternoon, when they stopped work, parked the machines, and got into Bubba's pickup to drive to the nearest town for sandwiches and beer. After some jollity between them and Dolly, the clerk at the convenience store, they took an extra sixpack, got into their car and drove back the way they'd come. At least so Dolly told the police when they came asking, having found a receipt with the store's name on it in the empty seat of the pickup.

That was the last she saw of them, she said, driving off down the road, waving at her.

"They were okay?" asked the police, "not fighting among themselves?"

"Oh, hell, no," said Dolly. "Those boys'd have to be sober to fight about anything, and they ain't been sober since high school. I've knowd 'em forever, since then, anyhow. They're just happy drunks."

If so, they'd died happy. The backhoe was right where somebody left it, and the front loader. The truck the men had arrived in was parked by the road. Scattered around the machines were six empty beer cans, two shoes (unmatching), one shirt sleeve, a pair of dark glasses and a blood-soaked item later identified as a hernia truss. Trodden into the muck were the missing men's bones, all three skeletons, the medical examiner said, when he'd had a chance to sort them out and reassemble them. No flesh. Just bones.

The local paper carried the sheriff's musings on the subject, which were largely focused on the likelihood of satanic rites or upon greens who had gone mad with enviro-rage and blood lust.

4

benita

First thing Monday morning, Benita phoned Congressman
Alvarez's office, then took a cab to the Congressional Office Building. The young woman at the desk in the outer office looked at her curiously, then invited her to sit while she
went into an inner office. The door wasn't shut all the way,
and through the crack Benita could see into the office
where her namesake representative sat behind his desk,
going through a stack of messages. The young woman
handed him a note, and he looked up, saying in an annoyed
voice,

"Who is this Alvarez woman, Susan?"

"She said she's your cousin, Congressman. Benita Alvarez,
Joe Alvarez's daughter. She says she's not a nut, not a hys-
teric, not looking for money or to get any kind of bill introduced, but she has something that was given to her to put
into the hands of *authority*, and she thought you would be
the one to decide who *authority* was because she is one of
your constituents, and even though she didn't vote for you,
you still represent her interests."

He barked laughter. "All that?"

Eavesdroppers never hear good of themselves. Benita flushed and turned her head away from the door, but she didn't stop listening.

The young woman went on, "When she called, I suggested she bring whatever it is by and leave it, and she said no. It had been entrusted to her to put into someone's hands, and she was going to put it into someone's hands she could trust and she didn't know me from Eve."

"Lord save us. She could have mailed it. That's a long way to come."

"She's waiting outside. What do I tell her?"

Benita could visualize him, looking up at the ceiling. He did that during debates, looked up at the ceiling, as though hoping for a sign.

He said, "I don't remember Joe Alvarez, though I don't doubt he was some kind of cousin, umpteen times removed, and so far as I can remember, I've never heard of Benita. Better err on the side of kindliness than go the other way and have her turn out to be the widowed sister of the state Democratic chairman. I can see her now. I should have about five minutes before the lumbermen get here, or is it the tree-huggers?"

"That's tomorrow. Today it's General Wallace and the Forest Service."

Benita straightened. She'd actually met General Wallace, well, heard him speak, at a conservation seminar she'd attended. He had made a big name for himself at the Pentagon before retiring to the family ranch in Arizona. Evidently he felt his years of service entitled him to be heard on a whole range of civilian topics. Range being the operative word among cattlemen. In Benita's part of the country, the people who ran cattle in the national forests did not like laws protecting the environment, or protecting endangered wildlife. If it wasn't something a human being could eat or make money off of, it wasn't important.

The congressman said, "Why don't retired generals fade away like they're supposed to? Why is he so involved in this grazing issue? He's working me into a real bind. If I vote to protect the land, my constituency will howl, because they prefer to do things the way they've done them for three hundred years, despite the fact that three hundred years ago there were only a few hundred people cutting timber and running cows where several thousands want to do it now!"

"I'm sure it's very difficult, sir."

"Oh, no, hell, as one recent visitor rancher told me, the world is coming to an end soon, so it won't matter whether there is any range or rivers left or not."

There was a long silence. Benita visualized the young woman standing patiently, saying nothing. She'd probably heard it all before.

"End of speech," said the congressman in a tired voice. "I'll see Ms. Alvarez."

He opened the door himself. The way he pushed it back, fully open, told Benita he didn't plan for her to stay long. If the door was open, he could walk people out, chatting, arm around the shoulders of whoever it was, casually reaching down from his six-foot-four-inch height to take a visitor's hand, to murmur something about nice of you to have come by, you take care now, have a nice day, bye-bye. She'd seen him do that at campaign rallies. Congressman Gregorio Alvarez was actually Greg Kempton on his birth certificate, but he ran for election on his mother's maiden name, and that side of the family had always called him Gregorio. He really was a sort of cousin, through a many times great-grandfather. His mother had been short, like most of the Hispanics of the Southwest, but his father, Brad Kempton, had been six foot five.

She got up, putting on her careful smile, wondering what he was thinking. She had taken pains to dress like a woman who deserved to be taken seriously. She'd gone to the hairdresser at the hotel first thing this morning, her suit was well made, and so were her shoes. The cube was in a shopping bag, so she could look like any ordinary shopper, except for the bruise greening one cheek, just under her dark glasses. She saw Representative Alvarez's eyes settle on it, just for a moment, and his lips tightened.

"Mrs. Alvarez?" He smiled very nicely and kept his voice gentle. Well, he'd sponsored a lot of anti-abuse legislation, and the public knew all about how his mother had died. "I'm intrigued by your message."

"Are you, really?" She was pleased. "I tried to make it intriguing. I know you must be pestered to death, and the last person you want to talk to is some *mujer loca* from back home." She looked around his office, a little flustered, summoning up her daytime, working-woman self, the one who dealt with people all the time.

She went to the chair he gestured toward and seated herself when he did, just across from him, with no desk between.

"Tell me about yourself," he asked, smiling. "You're from New Mexico? Married? With children?"

"Two. They're both in college in California."

He started to say something then caught himself. She guessed he was going to say she didn't look old enough. People often said that. The truth was, she wasn't old enough. There were still too many Hispanic girls like her, having babies at fifteen or sixteen, more among Hispanics than any other group. Among her people, *familia* had always been more important than anything, and babies born too soon, though grieved over, were accepted.

"Now, what brings you to Washington?" he asked.

She took a deep breath and said firmly, "I was hired. They paid me to bring this thing to someone in authority."

She bent toward the shopping bag, unwrapped the tissue and came up with the shiny cube, reached over and handed it to him. He took it as though it might be a bomb and almost dropped it when it immediately turned firecracker red. He was old enough to remember when kids played with firecrackers, and he held it, feeling it.

Benita knew it felt like leather. Not soft, precisely, but yielding. Not like plastic or wood. He turned it over, and it screamed at him. He almost dropped it.

She reached for it and turned it over, at which point it stopped yelping. "It has a right side up," she told him. "And it yells if you upset it or leave it alone. So long as you've got it near you, it stays quiet. When it turns blue, it's okay. You can feel it kind of buzzing? On your fingers?"

He stared at the thing. She knew he could feel the vibration, and the color had faded somewhat toward the purple. "What does it do?" he asked.

"They didn't say. They just said it would do all the convincing and explaining that was necessary. I kind of expected it to do it when I gave it to you. Maybe not, though. Maybe it won't turn on until it gets to the president or somebody like that?"

He snorted. "I can picture that. The Secret Service would just love it. A sealed container with who knows what in it!"

"I thought it might be a bomb," she agreed, nodding. "Except it went through all the machines at the airport. There was even a sniffer dog, and he didn't twitch."

"Probably looking for cocaine," he muttered. "Who gave this to you?"

"They were strangers to me," she said, using the phrase she had decided upon during the plane trip. Strangers were acceptable. Aliens might not be. "They came up to me in the mountains, where I was hunting mushrooms, and they gave me that cube and some money, and they asked me to take it to someone in authority over our country."

He started to ask the sensible questions, like where, and when, and how many of them had there been, when a loud voice in the outer office made him turn in that direction.

". . . never mind, I'll just go on in," the voice boomed, and in he came, tall and bulky, straight up and down as a post, white hair and broad shoulders, a drill-sergeant Santa Claus, seeming to take up all the air in the room just by saying hello. She recognized him at once, both from having heard him speak and from the constant news coverage he received. He crossed to the congressman, who was gaping, one hand holding the cube, the other raised in surprised greeting.

"Good to see you, son, and what the hell's that?" the general asked, grasping the congressman's free hand. He gave it one quick pump, then took the cube from the other hand, like a child finding a surprise . . .

And they all went somewhere else.

The three of them seemed to be standing in space, far, far out in space, with galaxies whirling and dust clouds gently surging and a godlike voice speaking from the center of the universe, saying, "Ladies and gentlemen of the human race, may we introduce ourselves. We are of the Pistach people, originally of a double star system toward the center of your galaxy and ours, long-time space farers, who have recently become aware of the interest your race has expressed in the discovery of extraterrestrial intelligence."

The scene changed abruptly to a mountain trail, where the three of them stood on an outcropping of rock watching two uniformed persons who looked only slightly exotic handing the cube to Benita, then bowing and departing. The godlike voice went on: "It is our habit to approach a single member of a new race to receive our initial contact. Despite your recent spate of fables concerning alien abduction, no one from your planet has been abducted. We can find out all we need to know about any creature without kidnapping or vivisecting it. We choose this method of introducing ourselves to limit the risk which always comes with surprise. We are happy that our message has been brought to (. . . click, click, click . . .) General Wallace and (. . . click, click, click . . .) Congressman Alvarez by (click, click) his kinswoman, Benita Alvarez, and we ask that you take this message to the highest authorities of your nation."

They were abruptly back in the congressman's office.

"What in the hell," breathed the general, staring down at the cube in his hands, which hummed softly inside its deep blue self.

"Don't ask me," cried the congressman, sinking into his chair. "She brought it!"

"I gathered as much," snapped the general. "I'm not blind."

He turned on Benita with his brows drawn together, obviously ready to pounce. "When, madam? And where?"

"Well, actually," she said weakly, "it was Saturday. Day before yesterday. And I thought of taking it to the governor, but he's really such a flake. And then I decided the congressman, only evidently he wasn't authority enough, because it didn't say a word to him . . ."

"I'd only held it for a moment," murmured the congressman defensively, flushing angrily.

". . . and they didn't look like that, either," she concluded, rather annoyed at the fact.

"What do you mean?" the general demanded.

"The ones who spoke to me didn't look like people, and their ship was in the background, and they had a reference machine they used all the time when they talked to me."

"What do you mean they didn't look like people," snarled the general.

Her annoyance grew. "The beings who spoke to me were not humans, sir. I think they must change their appearance to be acceptable to whomever they are addressing."

"Meaning *you* would accept nonhumans?"

She simmered down, thinking. "Well, I guess that's true, yes. I would. I watch a lot of crazy things on TV, so I've become used to the idea. And I've never been afraid of animals or bugs or things."

"Don't move," said the general, crossing to the congressman's desk, picking up the phone and punching in strings of numbers. He turned his back on them and mumbled into the mouthpiece, covering his mouth with his hand. The cube, left behind on the low table, began to squeal.

Benita picked it up and patted it into quiet.

"How much did they pay you?" asked the congressman.

"Five thousand dollars," she said, without a moment's hesitation. If they searched her purse or her hotel room, that's what they'd find, or what was left of it after she had paid for the airfare and the cabs and the hotel and three meals yesterday and one today. The other ninety-five thousand was in a safety deposit box rented first thing that morning, and the receipt and the key were hidden in her bra. It had occurred to her that all that money might be confiscated by the powers that be and she might not get it back.

The general turned away from the phone and seated himself in the congressman's chair. "They're on the way over."

"They? Who?" asked the congressman.

"People from the Pentagon. They'll call the president's office and the FBI."

"Well," Benita said, heaving a sigh, "since you've got it all in order, I think I'll go get myself some lunch. I was so worried about putting this in the right hands, I hardly touched my breakfast . . ."

"Sit down," said the general.

"I beg your pardon!"

"I'm sorry, ma'am. If you're starving, we can send out for some sandwiches or something, but I want you here when the others arrive. They're going to have questions. I have questions."

"The people said the cube would give you all the answers and explanations. Certainly I can't."

"We'll still have questions. Just sit."

He was a man very accustomed to being obeyed, and Benita sat, annoyed at herself for doing so, no matter how important he was. She got annoyed like this with her relatives who were always telling her what she ought to do or had to do, because sometimes she said things to them that were rude, or things she thought in retrospect might have been rude, and the memory of rudeness made her cringe inside even when no one else remembered whatever it had been. Where did all that come from? She hadn't a clue, but it was why she liked the bookstore, the routines she knew best, customers who didn't know her from Eve and wouldn't presume to order her around or comment on her daily life.

Now, however, she was evidently to submit to being ordered. People arrived in waves, most of them wearing suits, some of them wearing uniforms. Sandwiches were provided, along with coffee and iced tea. The questions went on for the rest of that afternoon, well into the evening, moving from place to place depending upon the number of simultaneous questioners. Where had she hunted mushrooms? Find the place on this map. What kind had she found? What time of day? Where had she found the *agaricus*? Was anyone else around? What had the ship looked like? Where did *pleurotus* grow? On and on. She drew maps of the place and sketches of mushrooms. Someone provided dinner, hastily catered in a meeting room.

Finally she was allowed to go back to the hotel to sleep, though they put someone on guard outside in the corridor.

They took away the money she had left, just as she'd suspected, though they gave her a receipt.

On Tuesday, the questions continued at an office somewhere on the outskirts of the city.

"The money is good," the general told her at one point. "Not counterfeit. We're keeping the bills you were given just in case the lab people can come up with anything, but here's replacement currency. Everyone seems to feel you're telling the truth. I don't suppose you'd mind taking a polygraph?"

"I would mind," Benita said belligerently. She had not slept well, and she had a headache. "I'm sure by this time you know all about me, where I work and what I do and who my family is. I hope you've honored my request not to tell my husband where I am, and if you've investigated me, you know why I ask that! You know I'm just an ordinary person, that I don't know anything special. I let people take blood yesterday just to prove I don't drink or smoke marijuana or take drugs or anything like that. Now I just want to do some sightseeing, and eat some good food and . . ." She paused, ending weakly, ". . . go home." Actually, she didn't mean that. Not that home, anyhow.

"The president would like to meet you."

"Oh, my," she mumbled, suddenly giddy. "Oh, my goodness. The president? Did you take the thing to him?"

"We did. It amplified its pronouncements, in case you're interested."

She whispered, "Are you allowed to tell me what it said?"

"It specified a place and a time for a personal meeting, which took place very early this morning. I wasn't there. Just the president and a few Secret Service people. The . . . people who showed up weren't the ones we saw on the cube. We think you're right. They change appearance depending on who they're talking to. You expected aliens, I would expect military personnel, the president would expect humanoids somewhat exotically dressed. Too much *Star Trek* in my opinion, but we're of different generations. They gave him another one of those cubes, for him to take to the Cabinet and the Congress, however the schedule works out. The president wants to ask how they struck you."

Her hand went to her cheek. The general looked away. "What impression they made on you," he said hastily.

She agreed, flushing. They took her in a stretch limousine. The Oval Office looked just like it did on TV. So did the president, and he was just as charming as she'd always thought, never mind all that other stuff that was nobody's business. Mami used to say, "Roosters crow and cocks doodle, and so long as they don't peck the hens, it's God's will." By the time he was through talking with Benita, she had told him all about the children being at school and what she did for a living, and how the aliens had seemed perfectly trustworthy.

"And they gave you money."

"I guess they figured it would take money for me to travel and stay in a hotel and buy meals and all."

"Ms. Alvarez, do you think they picked you at random?"

She started to say yes, then stopped. "No. Not really. I imagine they wanted someone without any ax to grind."

"In giving you money, were they hiring you to represent them?"

She didn't hurry with her answer. "That's what I told Congressman Alvarez. In a sense they did. They didn't ask me to *mis*represent anything. They could have known a lot about me before they picked me. They might have known I had a good reason to want to interrupt my life, the way it was. They told me they were ethical beings, and I think that was part of their ethic, not disrupting people's lives or forcing them to do anything against their will. They knew I couldn't get here to Washington without the money they gave me."

And an incentive to do it! Never mind the other ninety-five thousand dollars. She would think about that later. "If they wanted somebody just . . . ordinary, they'd almost have to provide the wherewithal, wouldn't they?"

"They didn't give you anything else?"

She furrowed her brow, remembering. "No . . . no, but they said they would do me a welcome reversal."

"What's a reversal?"

"Mr. President, I figured out they meant they'd do me a good turn. A good turn is a welcome reversal, isn't it?"

Which she figured they already had, if the way she'd been coping for the last two days was any indication.

He nodded and thanked her. As she was about to leave, she turned to say, "If this all comes out, like in the newspapers, will you have to say who it was that talked to them first?"

He cocked his head, making a gesture that could mean yes, no, maybe, why?

"If you can . . . if it comes out, if you can keep me out of it, Mr. President? That awful thing that happened to Princess Di. And then, that actor who killed himself, because of the terrible lies that paper told. Those men in Congress, the ones who'll spend more to destroy a political opponent than they will to feed the poor, you know who I mean, they'll probably try to use this against you, and that means they'll try to get hold of me. They're like leeches, those . . . people. Well, I'm having some family trouble of my own just now, and I'd just as soon not . . . not, you know, have my kids read about it in the newspapers."

He shook his head a little sadly, and she knew what he meant. He'd try. For what it was worth.

5

from chiddy's journal

Autumn. Thirteen. Stairs.

This is what the Pistach call a trialur, an evocative three-
ness. Autumn, because that is the season that best marks
both ending and beginning. Any gardener will understand
this. You will understand it, dear Benita. Though our ac-
quaintance has been brief, one finds in you something
charming, something one has not experienced before with
others the Pistach have helped. If you were one of us, one
would bring you worms from the home ground before one
leaves you. You are other than us, so one writes this journal
for you, instead, hoping, when the time comes, that you
may receive these squirming lines spelling renewal where
worms might not be welcome.

You and ton'i, we, met in autumn.

After autumn comes thirteen, because that is the age at
which Pistach people are both ended and begun. And the
last of the three is stairs, of course, seemingly endless flights
of stairs that one climbs over and over during the thirteenth
year, the year of selection. It is called a year, though it is occasionally shorter than that, or, as was true in to'eros case,
my case, much longer.

One's thirteenth year begins on the day of one's twelfth birthday and continues until selection. Selection takes as long as it takes, and one may not celebrate one's thirteenth year until the time of selection is done. Thereafter, that date becomes one's natal day, and at the end of the next year the count begins again at one. After one is selected, one no longer counts the years of undifferentiated childhood, only the years of being what one was meant to be.

The symbols of renewal were much emphasized the autumn ton—that is to say, I—began that year. (Since this account is meant for you, dear Benita, one who is unfamiliar with our language, ton, I, will use the tongue of you who will read except where our own is needed for clarity—or when one forgets. Even Pistach forget. We are not perfect.)

Perhaps the symbols that autumn were merely more noticeable than in previous years, but I seemed to see for the first time the shallow, woven-reed trays of flower bulbs before the gardener's kiosks; the piles of gnarled hisanthine roots wrapped in damp, green moss and tied with lengths of ever-life vine; the transparent jars of seed; the tools used to rake and chop fronds when they fall; the canvas sacks in which the mulch is kept until time for it to be spread around dry stems, covering the cold soil. Even perforated clay jars of worms, though it is considered slightly disreputable to buy worms. One has one's ancestral place, and after generations of dedicated care, one's land should have enough worms to share with the less fortunate. Still, some families have been selected away from the care of their home place for generations—though this speaks of negligence by the selectors—leaving the soil to impoverish itself and in need of a generation's attention before it can be returned to health.

It is customary for the far flung to return to home places in autumn, to visit the stelae of our loved ones and ancestors, to plant a corm of loral or a root of hisanthine in the soil where their ashes were spread, to spread sweet fern mulch there, and even, if one cannot go oneself, to send a worm or two from the home ground to the ground of those who were burned and spread far from home. Autumn wreaths are hung upon the stelae around which the ash-grounds are gathered, thus twining our departed ones into the circle that includes ourselves and those to come. One sees renewal wreaths everywhere in autumn, on doors and walls and over windows, always vine-shoots of evergrow twisted into a circlet and decorated with fruits, dried blossoms and leaves. Our family wreath that year was decorated with a traditional trialur: dried star-rays of spring hisanthine, dark green feathers of summer's fragrant loral, and the hard-skinned, silver-sheened autumn fruits of the red pomego. End and beginning. Beginning and end.

Since the thirteenth year is the one of selection, it is on the twelfth birthday that one is taken to the nearest stair of selection for the first time. The stairs are great slabs of polished igneous rock of crystalline texture, with a carved banister at either side and a railing up the middle. They are rather wide, though not particularly steep, and they are built, always, to rise along a hillside spiked with cupressa trees, for the slow-growing cupressa is a symbol of patience. The stairs go up to a terrace that stretches on either side in great widths of mosaic paving, balustraded on the downhill side and on the uphill side, on either side of the stairs, lined with the entryways and doors cast from an alloy of copper, one that has a lovely red-gold glow—the doors of the selectors. The stairs continue upward to another terrace, and another after that, and so on up to the final seventh terrace at the top of the hill. This apex is marked by an edifice, near ton'eros, my, home place, *the* edifice, the golden dome that stretches over the most sacred place of our people: the House of the Fresco.

Here, long ago, following our departure—some say expulsion—from our spiritual home, the aged Canthorel bid the masons among our people raise up a circular wall pierced on the east by three doors, and when they had done it, he set a crew to plaster the inner walls, beginning at the right side of the middle door and moving sunwise as he followed the plasterers with paints to illustrate the revelatory episodes of our history. The resultant work, we are taught, was inspired, infallible, and miraculously completed in a single day during which, some avow, the planet slowed its turning to lengthen the light. When Canthorel laid down his brushes, daylight was no longer needed and night fell. He then commanded a dome to be reared above the whole, and when the keystone of the dome was set, Canthorel died. It is said his spirit went into the work, and it is certain his ashes lie at the center point of the sanctuary, in an earthen plot planted with fragrant vine.

In those early times, the sanctuary was approached by means of a road that twisted back and forth across the hillside. The stairs and terraces came later, to meet the needs of a growing population. Still later came replicas of the whole structure, stairs, terraces and Fresco House—though it would have been blasphemy to copy the Fresco itself—in every region and on every world we occupy. One's family lands are and have always been, however, in the verdant valley near the true, the only original Fresco.

Though every child knows this story from infancy, though many of us have played follow-on or quick-ball on the green meadows at the foot of the Fresco hill, one's first formal approach to the stairs comes as an awful, even terrifying event. I was surprised at my own tremors as we set out. I was dressed in the customary green, symbolizing a new shoot, a new stem. My inceptor was in gold, the house historian in formal brown, the receptors were draped in silver, the nootchi were clad in festive reds and yellows, the household campesi wore their leather aprons. All the younger children had been left at home. Except for celebrants, only those who have climbed the stairs are permitted to climb the stairs, and only they may escort a celebrant on the first climb.

The choral finisi who habitually arrange themselves at the edges of the stairs all along the ascent were present in large numbers on my day. Since it was unlikely my parsimonious inceptor had paid them to sing, their presence indicated a busy day, with many candidates scheduled to ascend amid a consequent probability of largess. No matter how stingy, no inceptor would let an offspring ascend to the terrace without making some gift to the choristers, for they have jeering songs aplenty to direct at the niggardly. As it was, they sang me upward with our own nootch joining in the responses (ke had always fancied kerself a singer) while my inceptor handed out sufficient coin to sop their esteem. Though our climb was done with measured and dignified tread, as was proper, it was completed all too soon at the first terrace.

Inceptor and receptor gripped my arms; the proffe-historian readied licos, his, writing instrument; one nootch, one campesi marched behind as ton'i veered to the left and approached the first columned entrance out of a dozen or so, all of them surrounding massive doors leading into the mountain. My inceptor knocked, as was proper.

"Who comes?" cried the brazen voice I had been warned to expect.

"An undifferentiated one," my inceptor called in a firm voice. "A candidate for selection, now come to the age of reason."

"So we all hope, Chiddy," muttered the receptor clutching my other arm, giving me a firm look. Ke wasn't my own receptor. My own receptor (though one should really not say or write or even, if one is very observant, think the words, "my own") had left the family earlier in the year for a time of specialized training. Ke had licked my eyelids tenderly and left me to the care of the nootch, for ke was retiring from receptorhood to go on to something else. Unlike the nootchi or the campesi or many other categories, receptors and inceptors were often picked for genetics alone, even when they had no inclination for the task. Those without inclination were allowed to change category later on. If one was selected as a nootch or a campes, however, it was considered permanent except in those rare cases where everyone agreed the selector had made an error. It did happen. We all knew it, and we all regretted the tragedy it caused. My receptor had been selected, as ke often said, for genetics alone. Ke certainly was not inclined to be a carer, as everybody knew, including the ket. That's what my old nootch often said about it. Everybody including the ket knows Tithy's no carer.

Sounds came from behind the door, rattlings and bang-ings and long, ominous hummings, like gigantic engines. At last the door opened and the voice called, "Enter."

I looked helplessly at my family, but they merely made shooing motions, as though I were a flosti they were shooing from the garden. I would rather have been a flosti, flying away to the top of a tree or anywhere else, but there wasn't a chance. The family was a solid phalanx between me and the stairs; another family with another candidate was marching behind them toward the second door, and beyond them were still others headed farther down the terrace; the only comfort came from the nootch at the left, who gave me a little nod and a tiny smile. The open door was the only way out.

So, I did what every twelve-year-old has been doing since time immemorial. I entered.

Looking back on that time, the strangest part of it was that nobody seemed to care if I did well or not. At home, when I was a child, people did care. Foot coverings were meant to be polished and put away. Body covers were meant to be washed and smoothed and hung up. Sleeping and eating places were meant to be kept neat, and houses and people were meant to be kept clean. Animals were to be fed; persons were to be fed, in that order; and both persons and animals were to be kept healthy. All of this required attention and care, and it was important that one's tasks, whatever they were, should be done dependably and well. *Wanting* to do things had nothing to do with doing them. If things weren't well done, then one got a rap on the head from a proffe or inceptor, or one did without sweetness at meals, or one spent the whole day helping the campesi clean out the compost house.

Selection is different from that, as I soon learned.

The person behind the desk was clad in a dark brown robe. The person was to be referred to as selector, licos pronouns were third level, le and lic, and one was not to speak to lic until spoken to. So much I knew.

"Why is someone here?" selector asked.

"It is the time of selection," I said breathlessly.

"Is someone frightened?"

"I think so," I muttered. "A little."

"It will pass," said selector. "One may look back on this time as the easiest time of someone's life, for no one will discredit someone on teros behavior, no matter what it is. For this time, someone is to behave as someone likes, as someone is moved to do, as someone's inclinations guide. Understand?"

I did not understand, but I bowed, murmuring, "Mentor," to show I had heard. "Mentor" is a word that may be politely used to any older person of any caste who is instructing one.

The selector shuffled papers on the desk and came up with one that seemed applicable, for le looked at it as le said, "Tomorrow morning, someone will go to crèche central and assist the manager in caring for the infants. Be there at the beginning of work hour."

There was only one reply allowed, as I well knew. "Yes, Selector."

The door behind me opened. I bowed, turned, and went out. The family had departed except for my nootch, and it was ke who took my hand and walked with me down the stairs. "What is Chiddy's first duty?" ke asked.

"Help the crèche manager," I said, only then beginning to think how strange that was. Why the crèche manager? "Why . . . ?" I started to ask, only to have ker fingers laid gently across my lips.

"Why not?" ker said.

I was to think of that over and over in the time that followed. Why not? Why not anything, or everything?

I was at the central crèche when it opened in the morning. Family nootchi were leaving off babies, the crèche nootchi were dandling them or winding them in hammocks or hanging the fretful ones upside down and walking them. I was put to walking, which I did, a baby hung from my shoulder by his toes and my hand pat-patting it on the back, the way the others were doing. When it sicked on me, I washed up and was given a smock to wear. So the day went, dandling and walking and making frequent trips to the sandbox, with much changing of underwraps when we didn't make it in time. It did not seem like work, though it wasn't play, either. It was not unpleasant, not arduous, not enjoyable. Just . . . neutral. Since it was my inclination to ask questions, I did so. Many of them. After four days of this, the manager told me to return to the selector.

On the morrow, I did so. It was not the same selector, though the words and attitudes were similar.

"When someone leaves here, go to the agricultural school and see the field superintendent."

So, I did that, and for the next four days, I joined the school campesi and hoed weeds out of the grain rows. This was dirtier than the former work, and it was harder, too. It was so hot we all panted, water dripping from our mouth parts, but I enjoyed it more than the crèche, being out in the sun and hearing the birds arguing in the trees at the field side. On the fourth day, the superintendent sent me to the greenhouses, where I did similar work, pulling weeds out of beds of seedlings. Then I spent two days learning how the records were kept, and another few days helping the record keeper. It was interesting enough for the nine or ten days I was there, and I learned a lot from the things I asked people.

Then it was back to the selector again, who told someone to ascend one level and go to the fourth selector on the right, and I did that. It was like the first one all over again. Le gave me things to do, le watched closely while I did them, but le didn't seem to care how well I did them. I spent a cluster cleaning the laboratories. I spent a cluster at the theater, helping paint sets. I worked with a whole string of finisi, an artist in paint, a dancer, a designer of costumes. I was sent up another level and spent a long, long time directing a crew of ten-year-olds who were planting seedlings on the sanctuary hill as an autumn duty. As soon as their toe hooks fall off, when their wings begin to grow, around age six, all children have autumn duties and spring duties, things that are done for the community. I had planted my share of seedlings between ages six and eleven.

Sometimes when I had completed a stint of work, they'd let some time go by, then send me back to spend another cluster doing the same thing, so I ended up back at the agricultural center, helping with records a couple of times, and at the theater, doing all kinds of things. On the fifth level, I attended lectures on the confederation and the member races, the egg-differentiated Credons, the swamp-living Oumfuz, the fearsome Xankatikitiki and many others. When I got up to the sixth level, there were sessions I don't remember very well. They gave me juice to drink that made me dizzy, and then asked strange questions that made my head ache. Then there were other times when my body felt certain ways, and they measured what it wanted and what it needed. Some of that was embarrassing, for I could feel myself wanting and unwanting.

We are not supposed to want a specific role in life. Opinions of that kind are not considered useful. We are selected to live as what we are, body and mind. The whole process of selection is centered upon determining what each of us really is. One of the strangest things I have encountered on your world, dear Benita, is that many of your people have no idea who they really are but many ridiculous ideas about what they are expected to be, plus many religious convictions about what they should be, although nobody is! One should not want to be anything but what one is, because it creates unhappiness. If one cannot dance, one should not be a dancer. If one cannot paint, one should not be an artist. It defies good sense. One should not be sexual if one cannot enjoy both the process and the product, and if there is no place for the product, one should stop being sexual. One should want to do what one can do most easily and most happily.

Often I was allowed to go home for evening gathering, and afterwards I sometimes went down to the river. There was a patch of short grass there with a playswing to hang babies on, and a bench for others. My nootch used to hang me there in the evenings, while she rested on the bench with a glass or two of viber. It was a good place to sit and think about things. So, this one night I had just settled myself in the swing when my nootch came down the path and sat on the bench, looking at me.

"Well?" ke asked.

"Well what, Nootch?"

"How does someone think it's going?"

I laughed. "One hasn't a clue."

"What has someone liked the most?" ke said firmly. "Tell someone!"

"Most? The time in the theater, one supposes. One felt more useful there than anywhere else. And one likes the thought of acting."

"Ah," ke hummed between ker teeth. "And what has someone liked the least?"

"Cleaning the laboratories. One learned a lot, though. Just by listening. And of course, one asks questions."

"One day someone will question oneself into trouble," ke said darkly, frowning at me. "Ta, Chiddy, one has such hopes for someone."

This was not something a nootch should say. Hoping was like wanting. Inappropriate! "Nootch-isi," I said, "hei!"

Ke wiped ker ducts. "All right, all right. Someone shouldn't have said it. But still. Remember this, Chiddy. Someone will have learned to be wise when someone knows how to keep someone's mouth parts fastened."

That upset me more than anything that had happened with the selectors because it upset the equilibrium I'd managed to hold on to that far. We're not allowed to choose or want, but of course, we all do! Nootch-isi's leakings washed all my resolve away, and there I was, choosing! Wanting! Or not wanting! I did not want to be an inceptor. I did not want to be a receptor. I did not want . . . oh, certainly did not want to be a nootch. One may love one's nootch, but one can see how difficult it is to be a good one! Of the hundred or so other things one was allowed to be, there were only a few my soul leaned toward. I would not mind greatly being a worker, a campes, or a craftsman, a finis. I would not mind greatly being a proffe, a doctor or engineer. The one thing I wanted not to be was an athyco. Not that I'd ever met one, just that everyone said the life of an athyco was the hardest life one could have.

So, when on the morrow the selector told me to climb the stairs all the way to the top and report to the curator of the Fresco, it sent a thrill of trepidation all the way to my toes.

The selector was watching me closely, the way they always did. "What?" selector asked.

"Ah . . . one has heard . . . no one should go there except . . . someone who knows . . ."

"If a selector sends someone, someone can go there. Around back, door marked *Staff only*. Just walk in and ask for the curator."

At that point, I was on the sixth level, so it wasn't a long climb, but it felt like I was trying to scale Mount Ever-ice. I was actually gasping for breath when I got to the top, and I stood outside the staff door a long time, letting my gills stop fluttering and my hearts stop pounding before I walked in.

The curator was a tall person in a white gown with a blue apron and cowl. I bowed, muttering, "One regrets not knowing how to address someone."

"Call me Curator," it said. "My pronouns are fourth level, ai, ais, and aisos. Come, I will show someone the Fresco!"

Ai took me down a hall, and up a flight of stairs, and through a narrow little door into a gallery above the vast circular floor of the House. The gallery was a narrow ring above the Fresco and below the dome. Though other memories of that time may have faded, one remembers that experience clearly. The floor pave is of compact metamorphic limestone of a lucent ivory color, brought into golden or rosy flushes by the slightest light, the rays making radiant shadows that wander across the polished surface as though searching for the luminous realm from which they have come. Their motion is caused by the wind moving branches of the great trees above the high windows topping the dome, as I came to know later, but the first impression was of a clear stream in which living, questing, nondimensional beings swam. Or, that is how one later described what one then, wordlessly, saw.

Across from the tiny door through which we had entered stood the three great cast metal doors, each between its protecting columns and surmounted by its individual architrave, their surfaces brought into high relief by the same fugitive lights that wandered the floor. The metal was the dark brown of good soil, not shadowed but deliberately darkened to separate it from the room itself. Between the middle door and the right-hand one was the first section of the fresco, *The Meeting*. Though one had never seen it, one knew that it portrayed Mengantowhai leaning on his staff and reaching out to the Jaupati people, his angelic countenance lit from within as they held out their hands in awed wonder and incipient friendship. Beginning from that point and sweeping sunwise about the great hall, the sixteen other panels of the Fresco told the tale of Mengantowhai's labors on behalf of the people he had adopted, of their joy and progress, of their tragic overthrow by the envious Pokoti, and of Mengantowhai's eventual martyrdom at their hands. Between the left hand and middle doors was the final section: The Martyrdom of Kasiwees. Kasiwees was the last Jaupati, shown kneeling as he prayed for Mengantowhai's return.

Mengantowhai, shortly before his death, had selected Canthorel as an athyci, and these episodes from Mengantowhai's life had been Canthorel's inspiration for the Fresco. One knew what the Fresco showed, however, only because one had been told. The Fresco itself was almost as dark as the metal doors—you would call them bronze—and no detail of the painting could be seen with a casual glance, for the place was lit, as it always had been, by hundreds of votive candles set into ornamental frames of iron and brass, and the soot from centuries of such candles had settled upon the divine paintings like a thick varnish, masking the colors and obscuring the figures. The entire room was cleaned annually, and the floors were scrubbed and polished daily. The painting, however, could not be touched. One knew which panel one was looking at only by referring to the small numbers, one through seventeen, carved into the stone beneath them.

In the earliest years the Fresco had been cleaned and even repaired from time to time, but in recent centuries the curators had forbidden any further attempts to do so. After all, they said, the scholar Glumshalak had copied every detail of the Fresco when he wrote his great Compendium. The curators of successive ages had annotated the Compendium. In addition, other scholars and visitors had made sketches of various panels during the early years. The danger of cleaning the panels far outweighed the pleasure of seeing them clearly.

For pilgrims, the usual observance at the House of the Fresco was to enter from outside by the middle door, to turn left and make the entire circuit of the hall, stopping before each number to chant the appropriate passage from a pilgrimage book, of which there were several: Glumshalak's Authorized Version, the Revised Pistach Version, the (some said excessively) Modernized Version, in contemporary language. When the people stood before panel seven, *The Adoration*, or panel fifteen, *The Blessing of Canthorel*, they knew what was shown. The very obscurity of the Fresco, evidence of its antiquity, could be considered part of its mystique.

My first experience verified this. The smell of scented smoke, the fugitive lights, the shifting gleams of polished stone, the mysterious paintings from which, in some lights, a face seemed to smile or speak, a hand reached out to summon, indicating here I am, look at me, observe my life. Within moments, however, I noticed something else as well. Curators entered the great room, lit candles, put out others, took them away, and they did not even look at the room. People came in the door, turned to their left and began the circuit of the room, reading the verses from whatever pilgrimage book they had obtained or inherited, and they never looked up. I reacted to this as though a bell had rung somewhere inside me, a warning: see, notice, they too have had their first impression, and the first impression has been their last. They do not see any longer. Will you, too, learn not to see?

"The first painting," said the curator, "the one between the middle and right-hand doors, is the meeting of Mengantowhai and the Jaupati. In the background are three wine jars assaulted by amorphous figures. The implied teaching is?"

"I'm sorry, Curator, but I have no idea."

"That's all right. Someone will learn. The teaching of the

amorphous forms assaulting the three wine jars is that Pistach may not carry intoxicants on journeys. This insight is gained through the juxtaposition of this section with the one preceding," ai pointed to the section between the left-hand and middle doors, "The Martyrdom of Kasiwees, and from the section following," ai pointed to the right, "The Descent of the Steadfast Docents."

"Yes, Curator," I murmured, marking the words down in my mind without a hint as to their meaning.

"From the one we get the idea of journey, for the journey into death's realm is the greatest one, and from the other we get the idea of guidance, for a docent guides others. This is reinforced by the secondary symbols, in which Kasiwees also guides us and the docents, by descending, also journey. Since it is wine jars being assaulted, the reference is to mastering intoxication. Thus it is clear that the meaning is that we receive guidance not to use wine during journeys. Does someone follow?"

I followed, though it seemed to me at the time we could have as well received "wisdom" as the meaning of the docents, or even "failing-ones," for a descent often means a failing. This might imply that the three amorphous forms could be the well-known trialur—frailty, futility, and forgetfulness—seeking to overturn the urns of knowledge, this reading reinforced by Kasiwees' assassination which certainly upset the fount of learning. Since the curator's interpretation took no account of the identity of the three amorphous beings, I preferred an interpretation which identified them. And the things being assaulted or overturned were just as much urns as they were wine jars, for all one could see was shadowy shapes with a kind of yellow haze around them. Having heard all my short life of the teachings of the Fresco, I was amazed at how impenetrable the depictions actually were.

"Tell me what someone is thinking," demanded the curator.

Without thinking, I blurted out that the forms were very difficult to analyze, what with all the soot, and ended with, "So it would seem we would gain better appreciation of the greatness of Canthorel if the Fresco were to be cleaned." Or course, it didn't come out that way, precisely, not at age twelve. It was a good deal more prolix and less pertinent, but the curator got the idea.

Ai actually smiled at me. "I'm glad someone said that. Now that someone has said it, someone should put it out of mind. The Fresco of Canthorel is too sacred to run the risk of altering in any respect. We know we do not actually see the pictures as Canthorel painted them, but we have generations of observations written down in the sacred books, including the observations of the revered Glumshalak, who saw the work when it was first done. Thus, building upon tradition, we come to a proper understanding."

Ai smiled again, a kindly smile that looked so well rehearsed I thought ai must often use it for effect. I did what was expected. I bowed. I assented. And thus was my fate sealed, for it was not long thereafter that the selectors told me of their decision. I was to be an athyco, a nudge, a meddler. The House of the Fresco was to confine the next decades of my life during which I was to help formulate and enforce those rules by which our people live. Then, if I lived long enough, I would work with the other races in the Confederation. And if I lived still longer, I would be sent to apply those rules on other worlds, to other beings, in order to assist their ascent into wisdom.

The next bit is unpleasant to remember or recount. I was given certain substances to eat and drink. Certain of my physical attributes shrank away to nothing, and other parts swelled with urgency. I was given exercises to do, all of which were uncomfortable and some of which were actually painful. When the pain and discomfort faded, I was given, as all selectees are given, certain biological substances to increase my euphoria at duty completed, to assure tranquility and balance in my tasks, for all the years to come. There was then what might be called a convalescence, a settling down under the care of my nootch, who displayed ker usual patience. I was not an easy person to care for at that time, for I found myself prey to numerous resentments that only time served to ameliorate. Then, at last, in the arm-clump of my family, I celebrated my thirteenth year, the end of my childhood. It was autumn again. My year had been two actual years, and this lengthy time betokened a certain grave propriety. As a birthday gift, I was given the proper clothing of an athyco: the white gown, the blue apron and hood. After the celebration, I was referred to for the first time as ai, and I was escorted upward and given into the hands of the curator.

A year later, dear Benita, in the sanctuary of the Fresco, one celebrated one's first birthday as a person.

6
benita

After leaving the White House, the limousine driver offered to drop Benita back at the hotel, or anyplace else she'd like. Having breakfast in her hotel room had been unusually pleasant, and the idea of snuggling up in all that unexpected luxury while reading a good book was attractive, so she asked if he knew of a bookstore within walking distance of her hotel.

He took her directly to a sizeable place only a few blocks from the hotel, a store that seemed to take up all the south side of a short block. The name was in gold across the front windows: The Literary Lobby. When Benita got out, she told the driver she'd walk from there. There were newspaper vending machines along the sidewalk, and she walked down the line, reading the headlines:

MIDDLE EAST ERUPTS IN NEW CONFLICT
OVER 200 DEAD IN RIOTS

DRUG SHOOTOUT TAKES LIVES OF BYSTANDERS
TODDLERS, TWO SISTERS KILLED IN DRIVE-BY

TOBACCO COMPANIES SUED BY FOREIGN COUNTRIES
EXPORTS IMMORAL, SAY CHINESE

DROUGHT AND CIVIL WAR A LETHAL COMBINATION
STARVATION THREATENS MILLIONS

TEXAS WOMAN BEARS NINE CHILDREN
FERTILITY DRUGS BLAMED FOR LITTERING

It was all the same depressing stuff. She turned to consider the window display instead. Down in the corner a neatly lettered card caught and held her eyes: "Sales help wanted." People passed behind her, back and forth on the sidewalk, but her gaze was fixed on that card.

The door of the store opened and closed, but she didn't notice until a voice at her shoulder said, "You're looking at that notice as though it were a snake with a diamond ring in its mouth."

He had quizzical eyes, untidy graying hair and a strong jaw with a huge ink smear along one side.

"Snake with a what?" she asked.

"You know. As though you're wondering, is it a rattlesnake or only a gopher snake? Is it a real diamond or only cubic zirconium? Shall I grab it by the tail and shake the stone loose, or shall I let well enough alone?"

"I *was* thinking of grabbing it by the tail," she said, surprising herself. "I have around fifteen years experience working in a bookstore."

"Well, come in!" He bowed toward the door, stretched out a lanky arm to push it open, and beckoned her to follow him down the aisle, turn left, right and left again into an office at the back corner of the building, with both east- and south-facing windows that gave him excellent views of two triangular parking lots and the boulevard that cut across diagonally behind them. He dropped into the chair behind the desk and burrowed in a pile of papers, drawing out two or three sheets before he found what he was looking for.

"Application," he said, putting it before her. "Pen," putting that before her as well. "Complete, while I wander around out there, then I'll be back."

What was she doing? She stared at his retreating back with that same feeling of inexorable reality she'd had ever since Saturday, except for that brief empty time last night, when she'd put the entire matter in other people's hands and they'd finally quit asking questions. Well, it would be good practice to apply for a job. Marsh and Goose had never given her a reason to look for a new job, though the salary wasn't great and the benefits were iffy. Working there always had been pleasant.

Had been. Operative words. Somewhere along the line, during the last couple of days, without quite knowing it, she had reached a decision.

"Name," she muttered to herself, reading it from the form. Benita Alvarez. Age. Not quite forty, but so close as made no difference. Residence. Currently staying in a hotel, former residence . . . *former* residence? Well, why not? Former residence, Albuquerque, New Mexico. Work experience. Sixteen, no, seventeen years . . . no, say the first two didn't count. Lord, she'd started when Angelica was one, so it had been sixteen years when Angelica graduated high school, and that had been a year ago last June. Counting full time only, fifteen and a half years, clerk, bookkeeper, assistant manager, the Written Word. Reason for leaving? Children now living away from home, desire to see another part of the country, have new experiences. Health. Generally good.

She worked her way down the page. Easy stuff. She lied a little on the education bit. No need to say she'd left high school to get married, just two months before graduation. Odd to think of herself in this strange city, finding herself a familiar ground. It had been Mami who had introduced Benita to Marsh and Goose. "They are homosexual," she said. "Which means they will not trouble you at work. They are good hearted, which means they will treat you well. . . ."

"Alberto treats me well, Mami."

"Alberto treats you like a servant when he is not drunk, Benita. When he is drunk he treats you like a slave. Now he treats the children like pet dogs. When they grow up a little, he will treat them like dogs who are not pets. In time, you will know that. But if you work for Walter Marsh and Rene Legusier, you will have some security."

Stung by this, Benita had cried, "Would you rather Carlos had not been born? Rather Angelica had not been born?"

"No. *Dios siempre bate bendiciones con dolor!*" God always mixes blessings with pain. "Your brothers have moved far away, and we see them seldom. You are my only blessing who is with me, and I will not let my blessing be destroyed!"

It had seemed to Benita that Mami had been in a dreadful hurry to be sure Benita could manage. The reason was clear all too soon. Mami knew she had cancer, though she hadn't told any of the family. She ended up having several surgeries and chemo, but two years later she was gone. The farm where the family had grown up was hers, inherited from her people, and she left it to Benita and her two brothers. The boys didn't want to keep it. Benita had no money to buy it from them, so it was sold and she and Bert had gone on living with Bert's mother on Benita's money, which had lasted a few years. Papa had a trailer out at the salvage yard, and Benita always thought he'd moved in there with a sense of relief. Mami had been the campesino in the family. Papa had never been that interested in farming, and needless to say, neither was Bert.

"Finished?" the quizzical person asked from the doorway, eyebrows halfway up his forehead, the ink smear on his jaw longer and darker than before.

"You have ink on your face," she said. "You've been running your fingers around on your cheek."

"Damn," he said, peering at himself in a glass-fronted cupboard. "I always do that. I'm writing something, and next thing I know I'm tap-tapping on my face. They called me Inky in school. Or worse."

"You buy the wrong pens," she told him. "The kind I buy do not leak."

He sat down and gathered up the application. "Um. Um. Um, well, um. Fifteen years? Really?"

"Really." She smiled ruefully. "While my children were at home. Now they're off to school and lives of their own."

"Who have you dealt with at Bantam?" he asked.

She gave him a name. He mentioned several more publishing houses, and she gave him names for each.

"You're real." He sighed. "Halleluja. Now, this is the deal. We have this store. We have branches in Georgetown, Alexandria, and Annapolis with a modest Web-market operation. We're not Amazon-dot-com, but then we're showing a profit. I need someone who can take over. How about thirty thousand to start, ninety-day trial, and we'll talk about a long-term arrangement then?"

She was shocked into silence. She made twenty at the Written Word. Ten dollars an hour, after all those years. Of course, New Mexico salaries were lower than the average. And this was a lot bigger job.

He said hopefully. "I'm desperate for someone really good. You'll start as assistant manager. We need somebody like you, we really do. Someone well educated, personable, capable . . ."

She almost blurted out the truth, but managed to keep her mouth shut. She had continued her education. Never mind if it hadn't been inside ivy-covered walls, she'd done it.

"I'll let you know tomorrow," she murmured, collecting her purse. "I'll drop in tomorrow morning."

"Were you coming in to buy something?" he asked. "When I saw you outside?"

He took her by the hand, casually, and drew her out into the stacks where he helped her pick half a dozen books, a gift, he said.

"By the way," he murmured as he let her out, "my name is Simon DeGreco. My card is here, in the top book, and I'll be here all day tomorrow."

She turned toward him and removed the dark glasses. "If you check my references, please don't tell either of my bosses where I'd be working. I've left a . . . difficult situation, and I don't want it to come looking for me." She looked straight at him.

His eyes fixed on the swollen eye, now turning shades of chartreuse and pale violet. "I'll be discreet," he said, crossing his heart, not making a big thing out of it. She decided she liked him.

She got back to the hotel at six, and called Angelica from her room before she even put the books down.

"Sweetie, can you settle down and talk for a few minutes?"

"I'm on my way out, Mom."

"I need to talk to you, Angelica. Really. Right now. And I'm not where you can call me back."

Long pause. "Give me ten minutes, Mom. Then call back. I'll let my ride go on without me and arrange to meet them later."

She hung up and sat on the bed, swinging her feet, staring out the window at nothing. She'd never lived in a city, not really. Though the farm was gone, the house Bert had inherited was more semirural than suburban, and the city wasn't high density, even in its core. The Washington area was huge, with lots of crime and race problems and poverty. But one could work in Washington and live wherever one wanted. Out in Virginia, or in Maryland, or in Georgetown. Too expensive, probably.

She glanced at her watch. Five minutes more. She and Angelica talked at least once a week, though it had been two weeks this time. Angelica wasn't telling her something. She had that feeling the last half dozen times they'd talked. She glanced at her watch again and dialed. She had decided not to mention aliens. Angelica was not very imaginative; she was really more pragmatic and aliens might set her off in the wrong direction. Make it a small inheritance. That was no less unlikely, but it was more believable.

At the end of five minutes, Angelica asked plaintively, "Mom, who was the cousin who left you the money?"

"You never knew her, dear. She was a very old lady, and I hadn't seen her in years. She was fond of my mother. And the money doesn't amount to much, but it's enough for me to get away from . . . well, you know what from. What I really want to know is will you and Carlos . . . will you be hurt if I do this?"

"Mom, I can't speak for Carlos. Last year, I didn't see that much of him. He roomed with those three other guys, and I was in the dorm, and it wasn't like we were really staying in touch. This year . . . I have a confession to make. I told you he thought we should share an apartment to save money . . ."

"I told you, Angel . . ."

". . . you told me not to, but he talked me into it . . ."

"Oh, Angel! Did you? When?"

"Since June."

"You didn't tell me! You'll . . . you'll regret it, dear." She thought of those black, black moods that Carlos had, moods that should be transitory, but in his case were nurtured and fed and coddled until they became a black fog that stretched out interminably until everything around him was ashen and cold.

Angelica laughed, without humor. "It's all right, Mom. You can say you told me so. You were right. It's not working. I'm paying all the bills and doing all the work, and Carlos is just bunking here when he feels like it. He has also instructed me to tell people he is nineteen, not twenty-one, because he's older than most sophomores and it embarrasses him. That idea came from his new girlfriend who is also a little older than most of us. She also tells him he wears the wrong clothes 'to impress people,' that he should have plastic surgery on his nose, and that she can help him with his career as an artist."

"Formidable," said Benita, wanting to laugh and cry, all at the same time.

"Well, you get the idea why I can't speak for him. Speaking just for me, however, if you get out of there, I'll hire a mariachi band and dance a samba in the street for celebration!"

"You don't mind?"

"What I mind was that Dad was Carlos's role model. Totally self-centered and using you to let him be that way. You remember when we were in high school, Carlos was only one year ahead of me because he was held back in eighth grade? So, we knew the same people, and I heard what he was doing, just what Dad did: sneaking out at night, getting drunk, crashing with his drinking friends so you wouldn't know. I blackmailed him into going to Ala-Teen, and I went with him. They taught us about drunks having enablers.

Carlos figured right away it was all your fault Dad drank, and therefore all your fault that Carlos himself drank. I told him you were an enabler, all right. You enabled us to eat and have a roof over our heads, and if he ever said any such thing to me again, I'd tell you how he felt, and then maybe you and I would just leave him and Dad on their own to enable each other!"

Benita was for the moment speechless. "Angel. I didn't know! I didn't know any of that."

"Well, of course not. You had enough to worry about. I told Carlos when he was ready to leave home, he could do what he pleased, but for then he had to shut up and behave or I would definitely talk you into going with me and leaving the two of them on their own. He knew where the groceries came from, and he did settle down and cut out the worst of the stuff.

"Anyhow, he's grown up now. He'll be twenty-two. Whatever he thinks, it's time you stopped enabling other people so you can enable yourself."

"It's going to be a little complicated. Your father has mortgaged the house, and the bank is going to foreclose. He'll expect me to step in and stop it, and when he knows I'm not going to do it, he's going to get belligerent. It'll be easier for everyone if you just don't know where I am."

"Are you going to get a divorce?" her daughter asked.

"I don't know. I'm not even thinking about that now."

"I say go for it. If you want to tell Carlos, I'll ask him to stick around here tomorrow night. Call around eight, our time. Okay?"

Eight their time would be eleven where she was, but she didn't mention that. All she could think of was what Angelica had gone through. And she'd been only a child!

She threw herself down on the bed, sprawled every which-a-way like cooked spaghetti, muscles letting go all at once, mind switching from Angelica to the bookstore, back to General Wallace, and then to the creature that had called itself an athyco. Whatever did they really look like? And how could they have gone out of her mind even for a moment? So strange, so wonderful, yet hard to think about.

Well, strangeness was hard to think about. Wonder grazes you like a bullet; it zips by and is gone, and all you really perceive is the zing as it goes past, or maybe the pain if it comes too close. It does no good to search for whatever it was, for it never lodges anywhere you can get a good look at it. The truly strange has no hooks of familiarity that one can catch hold of.

It had happened, though. It wasn't a dream. She really had met weird aliens, Chiddy and Vess, who had done her a good turn, who had to have done it, because it was the only way she could explain how well she'd been doing. She hadn't cried once. She hadn't lain awake, worried over what she might have done or said wrong. She hadn't been concerned about running back home because it was her duty. Somehow, it seemed, Chiddy and Vess had unquirked her.

7

senator byron morse

Senator Byron Morse, R–New Mexico, edged his just-waxed black Lexus into the too-narrow space Lupé had left him beside her red convertible, cursing mildly under his breath. Squeezing out of the car, he tugged his suit coat into alignment, picked up his briefcase, gently kneed the door shut and went through into the back hall, which throbbed at him.

Lupé was definitely home. The house boomed distantly, mute to melody but attentive to the beat. Wherever Lupé was, basses thumped, brasses blared, drums roared and rhythm filled the silence. Which was okay with the senator. He'd married her for her sociability, her elegance, her sleek body and fantastic hair. She made him look good, and since he'd soundproofed his den, he didn't have to listen to the racket.

She saw him coming up the stairs. "Hi, By," she called, feet moving in time to the music, hips swaying. "Home early!"

He dropped the jacket over the bannister and made a twisting motion with his fingers.

"Oh, hey, fine. Jussa minute!" And she was off down the hall, doing an exhibition number. The woman was jointless as a snake, and the sight warmed him, though only slightly. He couldn't afford the time at the moment, and quickies only made Lupé resentful.

The music softened, the beat relented, she came back, walking. "Janet, she call you."

He stopped in his bedroom door. "Janet? What in hell did she want?"

"I don know, By. I din ask . . ."

"Cut the El Paso accent, Loop."

"Oh, sorry. I was hearing the Spanish station. It's catching."

"I can't read your mind, Lupé. Am I supposed to call her?"

"God! You're uptight as cheap jeans! Yes, Mr. Senator. She wants you to call her. She says tell you it's about Timothy."

"And where does she want me to call her? Is she home?"

"The number's by the phone in your bedroom. She says try there, if you don't get her, try her at home." Lupé drew herself up. "And I wohn bother you any more till you get these little details taken care of. Then mebbe we can say hello, and did you have a good day, and stuff like that."

She was off again, back down the hallway to what she called her *nido*. Her nest. Gaudy pillows and painted furniture, and scented candles for God's sake, everything ablaze with color. When they went out, she was always dressed in perfect taste, her accent patrician, her manners impeccable, but her private life was carnival in Rio! He hadn't known of her private preferences until after they were married. He'd never been to her place. Too many eyes in Washington. Too many secretaries keeping track. Luckily the house was large enough she could have the two-rooms-and-bath at the end of the upstairs hall and they could lock the hall door when they entertained. He'd thought the pre-nup was comprehensive, but who would have thought of specifying tasteful home furnishings?

He tossed the jacket on the foot of his bed, one he'd bought years ago at an antique auction: solid cherry, barely ornamented, built to last. The framed mirror above the matching bureau returned his approved picture of himself: tall, patrician, dignified and solid. His eyes were chilly gray, as was the hint of beard showing along the jawline. Age had its rewards. Now that he was graying, his beard didn't turn his face gangster blue by midafternoon, the way it used to.

That had been one of Janet's favorite comments when she'd had one too many. "I may look like a sack of shit, Byron, but by God, you look and act like a gangster." Of course, with Janet, even one drink was one too many.

At fifty pounds overweight with a face like a damp cruller, Janet had had no room to talk. Besides, she was gauche as a pig in a penthouse, and too damned often pregnant. Some women were said to look radiant when pregnant, but Janet hadn't been one of them. To be honest, he had never seen a pregnant woman who did. Not his wife or anybody else's wife! To use Janet's phrase, pregnant women looked like a sack of shit. Even if the process went "normally," which in Janet's case it never had, it was still revolting. In his mother's day, people still observed a period of "confinement," and that's the way pregnancy ought to be handled in By's opinion. Confined. Somewhere else.

The phone rang eight times before she answered. "By?"

"Yes, Janet. What's the problem?" He knew his voice was cold, but it had to be. Let her get anywhere near him and she'd start shedding tiny dead flakes of herself all over him, like emotional dandruff.

"Oh, By, don't sound like that."

He held the phone away from his ear, waiting for the whine to run down. Make me happy. Make me mean something. Make me satisfied. He'd married her because she came from a well-known political family and he needed the support. He got the support, but he'd paid a high price for it. During all but the first two years they'd been married, Janet had been neither enjoyable at home nor fit to be seen in public. He'd ended up staying away from home, going stag too many times, making passes he shouldn't have made, a definite error in judgment. Luckily, the press hadn't picked up on any of it. Back then, people's personal lives had been off limits to the media. He'd been damned lucky. The only dangerous lapse had happened here in Washington, before he'd run for the senate. Mouthy bitch! It took two years to wear that story out. Now, of course, the shoe was on the other foot. That same mouthy bitch would deeply regret her remarks by the time he was through with her.

The gnat-voice faded. He put the receiver back to his ear.

"Janet, if you have something to tell me, do it."

"Timothy. He's in the hospital."

His breath caught, but he forced his voice to remain calm. "What's the matter with him?"

"He broke his leg. Poor baby, those skates are just murderous, murderous, I don't know why they all think they have to have those terrible skates . . ."

"How bad is the break?"

"He's in a cast!"

"How bad is the break?!"

"He's . . . he's coming home tomorrow."

"He's not in traction or on antibiotics?"

Another sob. "No."

"Then there's probably nothing to worry about. I'll FedEx him a get-well card and call him once he's home. Okay?" He started to hang up, then said quickly, "What's his doctor's name? And what hospital?"

She told him and he wrote it down. Timothy wasn't a poor baby. He was sixteen, born the second year of his first senate term. Steven had been born a year earlier. Before that there had been miscarriages, one after another, year after year. Janet had wanted to quit trying, but By disliked failure. One of the two things he'd wanted out of marriage was a son. He'd sent Janet to clinics and paid for her doctors, by the dozen. She, of course, said it could be his fault, which was ridiculous, as it had proved to be in the end. He had succeeded, just as he always did. Two boys in a little over a year. An heir and a spare, wasn't that what the nobility said?

After Tim's birth, Janet no longer had any excuse for her appearance, and he'd given her the ultimatum. Lose fifty pounds, change her hairstyle, take a course in public speaking, and learn how to dress. She'd gaped at him like a halfwit, thirty-three to his thirty-seven, and looking fifty. All she could do was whine about his using her as a brood mare, not caring anything about her as a person. He'd said fine, he didn't care about her as a person, but he was willing to take care of the brood mare and the colts.

He gave her very generous terms and no battle over custody. So long as the boys were children, let her deal with measles and chicken pox and ear infections and schoolwork. He intended to found a dynasty, but he'd do his part later on, when the time came for the right schools and meeting the right people. He wanted no gossip, no imputations of being unfair. Out and out feminists would never vote for him anyhow, but he sure as hell wasn't going to lose the sympathy of conservative women by mistreating his ex-wife. A lot of them lived on alimony, too.

Janet's lawyer had suggested she take the offer and not make waves. By had given her no cause for a countersuit; except for that one semipublic embarrassment, he had been careful and extremely discreet. After the divorce, he'd stayed discreet, but when he began thinking about the presidency, his advisors said a Hispanic wife might draw the voters. He had just the girl in mind: Guadalupe Roybal, descendent of first settlers of New Mexico, someone to help him court the state's La-Raza-proud Hispanics right along with its Anglo aristocracy. She had flawless light olive skin and a wealth of curly brown hair; she spoke fluent Southwest Spanish, and usually unaccented English.

Moreover, she knew what was expected of her. Being married to Janet had taught him an invaluable lesson: finding a wife was just like filling any other staff position, it required a detailed job description. There would be no children. Since he was twenty-five years older than she, she balked at a tubal, but said she would "handle the matter herself." Within her generous allowance she was to stay healthy, elegant and well dressed. She was to bone up on Hispanic issues, use the name Roybal-Morse, stay out of any situation that could look even faintly compromising, and stick with him at public functions, keeping him out of any hint of trouble with the female kind. It was all agreed to, written down, signed and witnessed.

His part of the agreement committed him to treating her with unfailing courtesy and deference whenever they were in the public eye. He'd picked this up from a Southern senator so long in office he'd grown moss. "Whup 'em in the bedroom, By," the white-haired old lecher had confided, "but treat 'em like queens where the world can see. They'll forgive you the one out of gratitude for the other."

Also, for every year of service, Lupé got a generous payment deposited into an account in the Cayman Islands. If she lasted ten years, she'd have well over a million, but she had to stay until he said leave in order to collect. Which could be during or after his second term in the White House. Fulfillment of that ambition would begin when he utterly destroyed the incumbent as well as the reputations of the incumbent's family, friends, and acquaintances! He smiled secretly to himself, relishing the battle plan.

"Trouble, By?" Lupé said in the open doorway, two drinks in her hands. She held one of them out to him.

He shook his head as he took it. "Tempest in a teakettle, like always. Any little thing, she comes unglued."

"Was Tim hurt?" Lupé liked Tim, despite his brave attempts to hate her on his mother's behalf. Poor kid. He didn't get much fun at home. Lupé believed in fun. When By was too busy to enjoy it, she had fun elsewhere, though carefully. There was always fun available.

"Broken leg, not serious. Is there something in the gift closet?" Lupé kept gifts and cards on hand for all conceivable occasions. Whenever Byron needed to mark an occasion, she had something suitable. She made a virtue out of shopping.

"Oh, lemme think. I bought two new computer games last week. He can have fun with those, sitting down. And a book on astronomy."

"Astronomy?"

"He was reading articles on it, last time he was here. It's written for nonscientists, but it isn't childish."

"I'll sign the book tonight. Send the stuff FedEx, okay?"

"Sure thing. Tomorrow morning."

He grunted assent. "I expected a call."

"A man did call. 'Mr. Jones.' He said you wanted to see him this evening before dinner, and he'll be here in half an hour. I told Cally to hold dinner until eight."

"Fine." He gulped at the drink, feeling the taste all the way down.

"Cally put some tapas out in the den, and unless you need something else, I'm going down to Edwina's until about seven-thirty."

He nodded, not bothering to respond, merely registering that she was going down the stairs and out. He heard her car leaving the driveway. Just for the hell of it, he wandered back to her *nido* and picked up the daily diary by her phone. *Tuesday, noon. Lunch with DeeDee McIntyre, shopping. Five pm—cocktails with Edwina Taylor-Lopez, re the Hispanic Caucus.* Very nice. She was absent, her absence was documented, leaving her blameless. She knew Mr. Jones had called, and that's all. When she returned home, her husband would be alone. Their relationship depended, he thought, in large part on what he did not tell her. He would have been surprised to learn that Lupé thought it depended as much on the things she didn't tell him.

He heard the door chimes and Cally's voice in the hall. When he arrived at the door of the den, the two of them were at the bar cabinet and ice was clinking into glasses while very expensive single malt was poured over them. They had ignored the good but much less pricey stuff Lupé had put at the front of the cabinet.

"Senator," said the larger man: "Dink" Dinklemier, all six foot five, two hundred thirty or forty odd pounds of him, ex-college football star, ex-mercenary, smarter than he looked and a current employee of the Select Committee on Intelligence that Morse chaired.

"Good to see you, Byron," murmured the other man, removing his coat and seating himself. He was Prentice Arthur, slightly graying, dignified as a deacon, ex-CIA, ex-security advisor, currently serving as the senator's hook and line to certain unnamed fish in the Pentagon. With the money that flowed over there, there was habitat for lots of fish, everything from sharks to bottom feeders, each of them useful in his own way.

"Dink. Arthur." The senator seated himself, putting his half-finished drink on the table beside him. "I hope you've got some news for me."

"Well," the larger man split a grin, one side of his mouth expressing amusement while the other half looked on, uninvolved, "I've got good news and other news."

Morse regarded him narrowly, disliking this jovial approach to what was very serious business. "Very well, let's have the good news. They'll support me?"

"Some considerable support will come your way." Dink sprawled into a chair, which creaked beneath his weight.

Arthur murmured, "Quid pro quo, of course. I've got a list of suggested items here. They'd like you to sneak as many of these through as you can." He took a sheet of plain paper from his billfold, unfolded it and passed it across the senator's desk. No heading. No names. Just a list of clauses and short, innocuous-seeming paragraphs that might be added to various bills.

The senator frowned. "It'll have to be late-night votes for most of these, but I should be able to manage a good bit of it. Nice of them to put it all in proper form."

"Saves time, is all," grunted Arthur. "Our friends seem to want things loosened up a little at the INS, the DEA, the ATF."

"That's pretty much what I expected."

"They'll be grateful," said Dink.

The large man had risen and was moving around nervously. The senator ignored it, recognizing the restlessness as habitual. He asked, "How grateful will they be, Dink?"

Dink turned, grinning his half grin. "Oh, as much as you need, Senator. Like mega-millions. And then, as much more, if needed."

The senator licked his lips. "How do they get it to me?"

Arthur gave him a stern look, wagging a finger in admonition. "Soft money, Senator. It goes around you. Some into Lupé's overseas account. Some to your ex-wife. Some for this, some for that. It never touches you. Just like with the pro-life money. You vote your convictions about the gross immorality of the drug trade just like you vote your convictions about the gross immorality of abortion. Your good friends and supporters from south of the border don't want to see the drug legalization balloon rise any higher than their ankles."

The senator sat down, relaxing. He hadn't known he was tensed up until this minute. Now, everything was letting loose.

He grinned. "Be sure to extend my good wishes."

Arthur smiled. "Oh, they know that, Senator. Our amigos know you wish nothing for them but good, all the way to the bank."

"And what's the other news?"

"Something General McVane picked up. It came over from the Air Defense Command. Just a weirdness, but in the light of your committee, we thought . . ."

"Weirdness or not, what?"

"Air Defense has picked up some oddities they can't explain. Seemingly incoming somethings or other, not the profile one would expect from missiles, certainly no launch data, but things."

"Satellites," said Morse, dismissively.

"No. Not satellites. Not space junk. Not decayed orbits ending with stuff burning up. These are flights, they change course, they go from A to B to X."

"So? What do the eggheads say?"

Arthur shrugged. "Something some other country came up with that we don't know about. Something some branch of our own government came up with that we don't know about. UFOs."

Morse glowered, staring at his clenched hands, thinking. "Where's X?"

"What do you mean?"

"The X they go to, end up at, where is it?"

"No one place, Senator. East Coast. Florida. New Mexico–Texas area, Oregon."

"Is there any way we can find out more?"

"Believe me, both the NASA guys and the Air Command are giving it their best shot. They'd vastly prefer not being asked about it until they can explain it."

Morse almost wished they hadn't told *him* about it until they could explain it. He'd been helping cut allocations to NASA every chance he got, a calculated risk, and he didn't like the idea that something inimical might show up, something that could have been prevented except for the cuts. "You sure McVane gave you everything he knew?"

Dink frowned. "In this case, I think yes. He's pretty firmly in our side pocket, Senator, and he's safe. No political ambitions, just big military ones."

"Do we have people on the ground looking for . . . well, what? Space landings?"

"The FBI's been alerted. They haven't come up with anything. Oh, a mass disappearance in Oregon, but that's probably a kidnapping by eco-terrorists."

"Mass disappearance?"

"Eleven men, loggers."

Dink offered, "It could be part of a general eco-terrorism campaign. Three guys in Florida were done in, too."

"Loggers?"

"No. They were draining wetlands."

"Well, keep me informed," the senator grunted, his euphoria only slightly dimmed by this niggle.

"Anything else we can do for you?" asked Dink.

Morse leaned back, tenting his fingers. "You could be helpful."

"Always glad to be of service."

"I've got a pro-life bill coming up. It could be delayed, but my best guess is two weeks from now. The usual people will be arguing, nobody will be listening, but I had this flash. I've been getting flak from some of the neanderthals. They've had too many of their sharpshooters and bombers arrested lately, and they're scared to use force but hungry to go on the offense. It occurred to me some of my liberal opponents might be vulnerable on the issue if they've personally used abortion services."

Dink frowned. "I don't understand? If they've used services?"

"I'm thinking, maybe some of them have had someone close to them who had an abortion. I'm not going to take up floor time in the Senate with it, you make too many enemies that way. But, if I had something concrete, I could do a C-SPAN bit, challenging one or more of them. The tape would make good campaign stuff in a few soft areas. Would there be any way to get hold of those records?"

Dink stared at the ceiling. "We'd need names."

"You know who they are, Dink. And we can go back over twenty years on some of them."

Arthur spoke up, "No, Senator. You misunderstand him. We'd need the names of the women."

Morse was taken aback. "I was thinking wives. Maybe daughters?"

The two men shared a look, then Arthur shook his head. "It wouldn't look good, Senator. Attacking a fellow legislator for a medical decision made in the family would not go down well. No matter how people say they feel about abortion when they answer a public poll, they want private stuff kept private. People don't like interference with privacy issues. Remember that impeachment fiasco? All we did was make people mad at us. Remember what happened in 2000? The issue is loaded, By. I wouldn't go there."

The senator's lips curved in a tiny, icy smile. "Suppose you dig up some names for me, and I'll decide what risks to take."

"We'll look around," said Arthur, after a pause and with a significant glance at his colleague. "We'll see what we can find."

They talked about sports while they finished their drinks. The senator didn't offer refills. He walked his two guests to the door, shutting it firmly behind them.

As they walked to their car, Dink remarked, "He didn't ask many questions about the blips."

"What could he ask? What do we know? There's something flying around out there we don't recognize, or it's sunspots, or it's interference, or it's UFOs. The only reason we told him was to prevent his hearing about it from someone else."

"This clinic idea of his, I wish he'd keep his eye on the ball."

Arthur shrugged. "Give him credit, Dink. He knows money alone won't elect him, and he knows where every voter in his state is and what turns them on. In this case, however, the down-side is bigger than the up-side, so we just have to manage him."

"Manage him how?"

"Well, I'll rattle the walls very gently to see if any worms crawl out of the woodwork. Then, if Morse reminds me about those names he wants, I'll can tell him we're working on it, but so far we haven't come up with any names except Lupé's."

Dink's jaw dropped. "Do you know that?"

"Let's say I suspect it. I won't say it unless I have to."

"God, Prentice!"

"Forget I ever said it."

"Said what?"

8

benita

On Wednesday morning, Benita called the bookstore and
asked to speak to Simon. "Benita Alvarez," she said. "I'd like
to come in and talk to you about the job."

"You think yes?"

"I think probably, though I'd like to talk details."

"Come in anytime."

She hung up and heaved a deep breath. She had been
prepared for him to say he hadn't really meant it, it was all
some kind of misunderstanding. Or he might have said he'd
thought better of it since. Though, why would he? She was
good at her job, she'd just never considered cashing in on it
before. Cashing in had come way down the list after children and groceries and the gas bill.

Well. There were still details, like living, moving around,
getting from here to there. And getting Sasquatch shipped.
She'd paid the kennel for two weeks in advance, cash, and
she'd used a phony name in order not to create a trail. She
wanted to disappear from New Mexico, leaving no clues.
And no doubt Mr. DeGreco could tell her where to look for
an apartment. A furnished apartment.

Her ruminations were interrupted by the phone ringing,

and she answered, "Yes," wondering what the hell, no one knew she was there, except, as it turned out, someone who introduced himself as Chad Riley, who was with the FBI and who had been detailed to assist her for the next several days.

"The envoys—that's what we're calling them, ma'am— tell us they'd very much appreciate meeting with you again. So far, except for you, all the people they've met are men, and they feel women may have a viewpoint that . . . we . . . ah, males may not have."

She took a deep breath. "I'm busy this morning, Mr. Riley. How about later today?"

"Actually, we thought this evening. We're planning a kind of dinner meeting. They assure us they can eat our food."

"The president?"

"No, he's making a speech tonight, one he couldn't get out of, but his wife is coming."

"And they really want me? Not somebody like . . . oh, Gloria Steinem or Betty Friedan or . . . ?"

"They want you."

". . . Alice Walker?" she suggested desperately. She didn't want to be part of this. Surely her part of this was over now!

"You."

"All right." She sighed. "Will you send somebody for me?"

"We'll pick you up at your hotel, at seven."

She was not a feminist. Why would they want her to give the female point of view? God, if she'd been a feminist, she'd have killed Bert long ago. She'd have run off with the children, gone somewhere else, or at least asked Goose for a raise.

Goose. How was she going to tell Goose? If she gave notice now, that would be almost four weeks, and that was enough. Maybe she'd say she received a job offer on the West Coast, and she'd decided to move to be nearer the children.

By nine-thirty, she was at the bookstore door. Five minutes later she was ensconced in Simon's office, coffee poured, danish provided, discussing where she might live in Washington.

"Actually," he said, looking at the ceiling and scratching his neck idly, "there's an empty apartment upstairs. It's rather rundown, but it's large. At one time, it was loft space, an artist's studio. When we bought the building we thought the artist would stay. He, however, decided to pass his declining years in Mexico. Or maybe it was Honduras. Somewhere vivid and warm. At any rate, he left a couple of years ago, and we've been unable to find a tenant who is . . . acceptable to us."

"Meaning?" she asked, narrowing her eyes.

"Meaning clean, sober, and responsible," he said, giving her look for look. "We'd like someone to live in it, because it helps building security. If the alarm goes off, you hear it, you call the police. I'm not saying the alarm will go off, it never has yet, but one never knows. People don't seem to rob bookstores much, more's the pity for them."

"Could I see it?" she asked, doubtfully.

"Yes, right now."

The corridor outside his office ended at an exterior door, and they stepped out into the staff parking lot, with labeled parking slots along two sides.

"The other lot's for customers," he said. "It's closer to the front door."

They walked along the building toward the side street, past two cars parked against the building to a door with a three-step concrete stoop. One of Simon's office windows, the door they'd come out of, the door they faced, and two little windows stacked above it were the only openings in three stories of solid brick, a taller red half to the left, a shorter yellow half to the right. Simon unlocked the metal door, displaying a square hallway with an elevator to the right.

"That leads into the stockroom," said Simon, indicating a door to the left. "We use the elevator to carry dolly loads of books to the second floor. The doors to the stockroom and the parking lot are always locked, but you'd have keys."

Simon heaved the folding grille aside and they stepped into the elevator, waiting while the grille latched lethargically, with loud complaint. Simon pushed button three and the cage creaked upward, moaning.

"It likes to pretend it's on its last legs, but it's actually completely safe. It gets inspected every year."

The grille let them see the second-floor landing, with its

small window and single door, and then the third floor, identical. The window only pretended to light the space, and Benita thought it unlikely anyone ever washed it, certainly not from outside.

They went through the door opposite the elevator onto the top landing of an enclosed stairs descending along the outside wall.

"Firestairs," said Simon. "They come out behind the rest rooms on the second floor and go on down into the stockroom, where there's an emergency exit to the street."

The door to the right opened on a room about forty by fifty-five or sixty, smelling of hot dust, with tall, dirty windows extending almost corner to corner over the side street. Four steel columns supported an I beam and a high, ornamental tin ceiling hung with cobwebs.

A U-shaped kitchen took up the corner nearest the elevator, and ended at the line of columns. Next to it was an enclosed room about the same size.

"The bathroom," said Simon. "The artist who lived here put some screens and free-standing cabinets between the columns and used the area behind them as his bedroom. He also had some good-looking drapes all along that front wall, but he took everything interesting with him. The blinds are still here, and they're fairly new."

Fairly new and supposed to be white, as were the walls. The blinds would wash, but the walls were unlikely to come clean. There was plenty of room, but no closet, anywhere. A couch and chair stood near the front windows, protected by plastic sheeting. A sheet-covered boxspring and mattress along with a stepladder and a bedframe, in parts, stood against the back wall under a row of metal, wireglass windows, their bottom edges about five feet from the floor. Benita pulled the ladder out and climbed up a couple of steps to look through the windows. The bottom of the windows were barely above the flat roof of the adjacent building.

The place certainly looked break-in proof! But talk about bleak!

"There's a lot of room here," she said without enthusiasm.

He looked worried. "About twenty-three hundred square feet."

"The bookstore looks longer than this."

He nodded. "This is the third floor of half the bookstore. Maybe you noticed from the parking lot? The store is actually two buildings, side by side, built at different times. We started with the one next door and bought this one when it became available. This building has higher ceilings, so the floors don't line up. The ground floor is eighteen inches higher, the second floor is three feet. We only joined the first two floors. The third floor of the other building isn't connected to this one at all. The only access to that space is by stairs from the street."

"Is it rented?"

"Not at the moment, no. If all goes well, eventually we'll probably use all of it, and this space, too, but that's no time soon."

She moved out into the middle of the room and turned around, staring at the walls. "How much would you charge for this, and what would you do by way of cleaning it up?"

"Well, any tenant would need a closet, so we'd build one, and we'd paint the place and have the kitchen appliances checked. We'd have it professionally cleaned, windows and all. It's nowhere near fully furnished, so I'll knock a hundred a month off what I was going to ask. Say, four hundred dollars a month, and that includes all utilities. There'd be no way to separate out heat and water and electricity for this floor, anyhow."

Almost five thousand a year. Out of thirty thousand. A seventh. Not more than she should pay for living space, according to all the budgeting books she'd read. And here, by herself, presumably she would be able to keep all her own paycheck. She wouldn't need a car to get to work. Chances were, she wouldn't need one at all. That would be a savings!

"You'll have air-conditioning," he said, enticingly. "You'll use our Dumpster down in the alley for your trash, and there's a garbage disposal in the kitchen sink."

She wandered into the kitchen, opening drawers and cupboards, then went into the bathroom. No frills. White-tiled walls, tub and shower, vanity, toilet, plus a two-foot-by-three-foot corner space with nothing in it where one would expect a linen closet. She returned to the main room, separating the slats of the blinds to look down on the traffic. Not much. The side street was quiet, though cars went by regularly down at the corner. The building across the street was only two stories high, and she could look across its roof to a golden dome. "Is that the Capitol?"

"We're only a few blocks from the Mall," he said, lifting the shade to peer in the same direction. "I'd forgotten you can see the Capitol from here. I haven't actually been up here in two years."

"Dog," she said, almost desperately, waiting for the knife to fall. Surely it couldn't all be right, just like this, right off the bat? Surely it couldn't be possible. If it had been possible, someone would have done it, right? "I have a dog."

"Sure, bring the dog. You'll be even safer with a dog. I hope it's a big one. What's his name?"

"Sasquatch. He's a kind of Briard mix. Black and brown, with medium long hair that hangs over his eyes, with a big, deep bark."

"Sounds good."

"He's used to a yard, but . . ."

"Actually, you can let him run on the roofs. They're different levels, but they're connected by stairs, and there's even a kind of arbor up there that the artist put in. They're both flat gravel roofs with a parapet around the edges, and the elevator goes up there because that's where the air conditioners are. You'd have to poop scoop, of course, but . . ."

"May I see?"

They went up to look at the roof, as described, flat except for occasional vent pipes and the housing for the elevator and air-conditioning equipment. Between the housing for the air conditioner and the stacks from the kitchen and bathroom was the "arbor" Simon had spoken of, a rustic pergola at the top of wooden steps leading to the lower roof, with a huge pot at one side.

"The guy had vines planted in the pot. Some kind of ivy, I think. There's a condensation pan to one side of the air conditioner, and he siphoned water from the pan into the pot, and the vines grew up over the top for shade. Nobody kept the tubes clean after he left, so they stopped up and the vines died. He had patio furniture up here, too. With an umbrella."

In size, the roof was the equivalent of a small yard, which was all Sasquatch had at home.

"If you'll build a closet back in that far corner and pay to install a washer–dryer, I'll take it," she said. "If it isn't dependent upon my working for you."

He frowned. "Are you thinking of working for someone else?"

She shook her head. "No. But if you decide I'm not good enough, I don't want to be out on the street."

"How about ninety days' notice from either party," he said. "Though I don't think we'll need to worry about that."

She took a deep breath. "It seems almost fated, and I'd be a fool not to jump at it."

"Where do you want the washer–dryer?"

"Put it in the space at the end of the bathroom. One of those stacked sets. They're a little over two feet square, not big enough for a large load but okay for one person. You've already got a drain and the water pipes right there."

"Do you have furniture you want to move in?"

She started to tell him she wasn't going to move anything, then caught herself. Her arrangements should remain her own business. The Albuquerque house was in foreclosure. The furniture was all old, well worn. There was nothing there she cared about except a few little things that had belonged to Mami and Abuelita.

"Furniture?" he said again, softly.

"Nothing else right now," she said in a firm, no nonsense voice. "I'll make do with what's here for the time being. Later I can supplement."

"Fine. I'll call the carpenter, the painters and plumbers first, then the cleaning agency to come clean it up when they're finished. You make a list of what you'll need. I can advance some salary if—"

"That's thoughtful of you, Simon, but I have money, thank you. A little . . . inheritance from an old friend of my mother's."

She stayed upstairs, making a list: linens and towels, blankets and pillows, dishes, kitchen stuff. If she made one stop at a kitchen store for little stuff and bought everything else out of a catalog, they'd deliver it. Like from Pennys. Or Wards. It wouldn't be high style, but a sheet was a sheet and a mixing bowl was a mixing bowl, for heaven's sake. Get the basics, worry about how it looked later on.

Back in Simon's office, she borrowed his phone book, found the nearest catalog store and went there. Two hours concentration and several thousand more of the ET money gone, she had ordered everything she needed, plus some bookcases, on sale, minor assembly required, tall enough to make a partition separating the bedroom area. With the shelves facing out, she could put sheetrock on the backs. It would help the place look less empty as well as providing a little privacy.

She bought lunch at a little side street restaurant, meantime glancing at a newspaper someone had left in the booth.

MASSACRE IN CENTRAL AFRICA
TRIBAL CONFLICT RENEWED

RUSSIAN AMBASSADOR THREATENS U.N. WALKOUT
SERB WAR CRIME TRIAL IN JEOPARDY

RENEWED VIOLENCE IN ISRAEL
PALESTINIANS VOW "NEW HOLOCAUST"

SENATOR URGES IMPEACHMENT OF PRESIDENT
MORSE SAYS "UNFIT TO SERVE"

SCIENTISTS DETECT "DISAPPEARING" ASTEROIDS
OBJECTS VANISHED, SAY ASTRONOMERS

SAUDI WOMAN TO BE EXECUTED FOR DRIVING CAR
REBEL PRINCESS SENTENCED TO STONING

ELEVEN DISAPPEAR IN NORTH WOODS
LUMBERMEN ALLEGE ECO-TERRORISM

It seemed the world was going on as usual. After lunch, she walked to the Smithsonian and spent two hours seeing this and that, until her feet were too sore to walk any further. She took a cab back to the hotel, had a hot bath and crawled into bed, feeling much more tired than the morning's activities warranted. After a little nap, she'd get ready to meet the two aliens again. She wondered very much what they would look like this time.

9

benita

Benita was in the hotel lobby, her coat over her arm, when Mr. Chad Riley arrived and introduced himself.

"How did you know it was me?" she asked, surprised.

"General Wallace gave me a description, ma'am. Let me help you with your coat." He held it for her. "The general's waiting in the car."

"You're very prompt," the general greeted her when she got into the seat beside him. On the other side of a glass partition, Mr. Riley seated himself beside a driver, who evidently knew where they were going. They slid away, the streets suddenly made of satin, either that or they were in a low-flying plane of some kind. Not a bump or a ripple, like floating!

"What kind of car is this?" she asked, enchanted.

"A very, very expensive one," the general said with a grunt. "The kind they keep for visiting dignitaries. No, don't tell me. You're not a dignitary."

"Well, I'm not!"

"Anyone the envoys ask for is automatically a dignitary, otherwise I wouldn't be in on this."

"I guess I'm flattered. What are they looking like now?"

"Who? The envoys?" He shook his head. "I've only seen them on that device. I wasn't there when they met with the president. No one was but a couple of Secret Service men. He called a meeting of the Cabinet plus a few other people right afterward, and he invited me to be there, to explain about the cube. He says I have a reputation for outspoken veracity which will be badly needed. I guess I owe that to the fact I never had to be elected to anything! Tell the truth and shame the devil, as my ma used to say."

"He explained about the cube? About me?"

"He didn't use your name, neither did I, we just said a constituent brought it to a congressman, and we've sworn your congressman to silence, for whatever good that'll do. The cube took us out into space again, and it showed them giving the cube to you, only it wasn't your face. In any case, everyone saw something slightly different."

She giggled, finding this surprisingly funny, and he gave her a reproachful look.

"Somehow, I can't find the humor in it. Anyhow, tonight we're having a catered supper at a safe house. Chad, up there in the front seat, is FBI, and they're handling security."

"The . . . envoys don't want to appear in public?"

"According to what they told the president, they never appear to the public in person. Only to small groups, and only right at first. They're assigned to visit races who have become interested in other intelligent life. The president thinks they're here to invite us to join some interstellar federation."

She shook her head doubtfully. "It's possible, but I don't think so, not right away anyhow."

"Why not? It's as likely as anything else."

"Not really. It's more like . . . if we discover a new race of people, some little tribe, say, down in the Amazon somewhere. The linguists and the anthropologists might go look at them, but no ambassador or head of state is going to travel down there and invite them to join the United Nations."

He looked quite taken aback. "Why would they bother just looking at us? Surely they must want something."

She smiled, thinking about it. "Maybe they're just curious."

The general had a very disturbed expression on his face as he said, "I can think of several reasons why someone would go visit a newly discovered tribe in the Amazon. Because they knew about herbal remedies that could be valuable to pharmaceutical companies. Because they were sitting on gigantic ore or oil deposits.

"Or, because the big lumber companies were coming, and the tribe wasn't going to be there—or maybe anywhere—very long."

And with that happy thought, they both fell silent, not speaking again until they reached their destination.

The dinner arrangements were fairly intimate and not at all pretentious. Benita was introduced to the president's wife, and to the Secretary of State, both of whom seemed utterly unflappable but confessed to being excited by the whole affair. No one was very dressed up. The only other person Benita hadn't met was a red-faced general from the Pentagon, James McVane, in full uniform and an angry expression. Chiddy and Vess had shown up in the guise of pleasant, plump, dark-skinned middle-aged women clad in saris, making a total of eight for dinner, plus the watchful men in the foyer and three liveried waiters, two moving around a table in the adjacent dining room, setting up a dinner service, and one serving cocktails and hors d'oeuvres in the nicely furnished living room.

Benita received a hug from each alien, who also pressed her cheek with theirs, as if they were old friends. "Tonight we are Indira and Lara," said the taller one in green. "Indira is in green and Lara is in red. This is the first step in our finding out about you."

"Why did you choose to be women?" Benita whispered. The three of them were standing in a corner, closely observed but not intruded upon by the other guests.

"You can figure that out," murmured Indira. "At some times we will take on the form of men, and also children, and perhaps different sorts of both, all three sexes—what is it called? Gay? In such guises we will wander around often, seeing how things work. But for now, we will be women and foreigners."

"You want to elicit knee-jerk reactions, don't you?" Benita asked. "You want to know how people treat women or foreigners, habitually?"

Indira nodded. Lara merely smiled. Benita didn't think it was a real smile.

"When you smile, your eyes need to crinkle up a little," she said, showing her. "Otherwise it looks insincere."

"What if it is insincere?" Lara asked. "What if I am not at all amused?"

"Well, if you smile so it looks sincere, it will keep others from knowing how you feel. If you smile in a way that looks insincere, they will know exactly how you feel, which maybe is what you want. If you do not smile at all, people will think you are cold."

"You do not smile when you are chilled?"

"Cold means uncaring. We feel warm or cold about people. Warm about our friends and loved ones. You might care very much, but it doesn't count as caring unless you do something, often something quite trivial and useless. Like smiling, or patting someone's arm, or murmuring conventional phrases, or bustling around in an attempt to help while you get in everyone's way."

"So if I care greatly, but merely sit quiet, staying out of persons' way, I will be thought cold."

"Exactly," Benita confirmed. "I used to go to dinner at my grandmother's house, my father's mother. She never shut up from the time you walked in the door until you left. She cared so much that whenever you got comfortable, she made you change where you were sitting in order to sit somewhere better. She passed you food so many times you had no time to eat. She never listened to anything anyone said, and if you tried to help her, she told you how to do it, over and over. Whenever Papa took me there, I'd find a chair in a corner and sit very quietly . . ."

"While she told your mother you were cold," finished Lara.

"Exactly," Benita replied, ruefully. "Caring, grieving, rejoicing, we are expected to share them all intimately and vociferously."

"So we will share," said Indira. "Tell us, please, what you have been doing here in this city. We detect a newness about you!"

"I suspect you may have planned this all along. I have a new job and a new place to live."

"Ah." The smile again, with crinkles. "We did not plan so, but we were hopeful. Describe this place you will live?"

Benita did so, ignoring her doubts and concerns and dwelling at length upon its convenient location, about which Indira asked a great many questions.

"And you are pleased with these changes?" asked Lara, when she had finished. "We prefer that people we . . . bother . . . are pleased."

"Yes, I think . . . I am pleased," Benita confessed. "Change is . . . it's hard to get it into my head, but I'm sure you weren't a bother."

"Ladies," boomed General Wallace. "What are you drinking?"

"I am not," murmured Lara.

"He means, what would you like as a drink," Benita whispered. "Drinks and small tasty things are customary as a prelude to festive evening meals."

"Fruit juice," Lara said to the general, smiling, with her eyes crinkled up. "I have never tasted anything so lovely as your fruit juice."

"For me, also," cried Indira, crinkling her eyes until they radiated with wrinkles. "Apple, or grape, or what is that other one, Lara?"

"Maaango," cried Lara, with a marvelous giggle.

"Julia Roberts did the giggle," murmured Indira in Benita's ear. "On TV. Has Lara got it right?"

"Perfect," Benita said, accepting the glass the general put in her hand. It was also fruit juice. It was quite possible no one was drinking anything alcoholic, and that might make sense. When she looked up, Lara and Indira had crossed the room to speak to the First Lady and had been replaced by the Secretary of State.

"You seem to get on with them quite well," said the SOS. "They probably chose someone they knew they'd get along with," Benita replied, though doubtfully. "I suppose I would do the same, in their place. They said they preferred to appear to someone just ordinary who could put them in touch with the VIPs without making a fuss about it."

"You think they've done this before, then?" the SOS asked. "On other worlds?"

"Either that or they're following a protocol," Benita replied, after a moment's thought.

The SOS gave her a piercing look. "Why would you think so?"

"Oh, the box they gave me. You've seen that?"

"I saw it, yes. It was the main course at two Cabinet meetings. One Monday, one this afternoon."

"That box isn't something made up for one occasion. You noticed how it fills in the names? That clicking, while it searches for the proper label? If they'd made it up special, the names would have been included seamlessly. No, that box is something they use all the time. They probably have a supply of them in their ship, just in case they need more than one."

"Ah," said the SOS, then asked casually, "Is it a large ship?"

"Not the one I saw. It looked hardly big enough for the two of them. But that doesn't mean they don't have a big ship."

"Where is it, do you think?"

"Oh, probably on the back side of the moon. That's where sci-fi writers would put it. Or under the ice in Antarctica, like in the *X-Files*. Or maybe it's simply a stealth ship, right out in the open only we can't see it, or, since they can appear as any creature they want to, maybe their ship can, too, and it's taken on the likeness of something we'd expect, a cloud, or a weather balloon."

The SOS choked on her drink. "That doesn't disturb you?"

"Not really. I don't get any feeling of menace from them. Not even right at first. I think they're really what they say they are. Xenologists. Or xenological social workers."

"Studying us? General McVane is quite worried about security. He tells us there have been multiple sightings of something—ships, perhaps—in the last several days. Our military are in considerable disruption. They can't identify who or what is flying around over our country, perhaps studying our weapons."

Benita shook her head. "It could be just as likely they're studying our culture. If we went to the Amazon to study a tribe there, our Department of Defense wouldn't be greatly interested in their bows and arrows, would it? We'd be more interested in other things, their language maybe."

"Their physiology?"

"Only if it differed greatly from our own."

"Would we kill one and dissect it?"

"If we were ethical, no. And one of the beings at that first meeting told me they were ethical. They don't do vivisection."

"So they won't kidnap a human to dissect?"

"They say they've never done that. If they needed to do that, which I doubt, they would probably wait until they could lay hands on a dead one."

General Wallace announced dinner and offered Lara his arm. The president's wife was at one end of the table and General Wallace at the other. Indira was on the First Lady's right, Mr. Riley on her left. Lara had General Wallace's right, with General McVane across from her and the SOS on his left, opposite Benita. The food was simple but very good, and both the ETs seemed to enjoy it. Benita watched them, thinking they might only be playing at enjoyment, tucking the food away inside to dispose of later. No telling what they could do with those infinitely morphable bodies. They were offered wine, which they refused. Benita's wineglass was filled, but she tasted it sparingly. Since she was sitting at the mid-point of the table, she could hear the conversation at both ends.

"Perhaps you ladies would be kind enough to resolve a small confusion for us," she heard Indira say with a kindly smile.

The First Lady and the Secretary of State shared glances. The FL said, "We would be happy to try."

"We have found a strangeness in your world that we cannot quite reconcile. During our study time, before we reached out to you, we learned much of your history and culture and religions, particularly the one claimed by a majority of the American people. The religion teaches that the purpose of man is to worship and adore and praise God, and those who do not do so will probably be punished. Is this correct?"

The SOS said guardedly, "Some religionists teach that, yes."

"Ah. But you have countries ruled by despots who demand that people worship, adore and praise them. They put great pictures of themselves upon the walls, like icons, and those who do not adore are often killed or disappeared or tortured. There was one called Mao, one called Stalin. One now, called Hussein. Isn't this true?"

The FL nodded, warily.

"Ah. Your nation, however, wishes to be a *good* nation, and it therefore despises despots, regarding them as evil and rejoicing when one of them is overthrown. Is this so?"

The FL put down her fork and took a deep breath. "Yes. This is so."

"Ah. Now to our confusion. If a person torturing and killing people is evil, why are gods who torture and kill people called good?"

The SOS patted her lips with her napkin and said to the FL, "Don't look at me."

The FL glanced along the table, catching Benita's eye.

"Do you have an answer for our guest?" the FL asked.

Benita thought for a moment. "I can quote something I've read. Some professor of history wrote that cultures define their gods when they're young and primitive, when their main concern is survival. They endow their gods with survival characteristics like omnipotence and authoritarianism, belligerence and suspicion, and that's what goes into all their myths or scriptures. Then, if they survive long enough, they begin to develop morality. They examine their own history, and they learn that authoritarianism doesn't accord with free will, that belligerence and suspicion are unhealthful, but this newly moral culture is stuck with its bigoted, interfering gods, plus it's stuck with people who prefer the old bloody gods and use them as their justification for doing all kinds of awful things."

"Ah," said Indira. "I am glad our morality has been with us since early times, preserved for us indelibly. I would hate worshipping a god I could not respect. Why do you?"

The FL was regarding Benita with some surprise. "This is a paradox," she said. "It's not one we're going to solve tonight. We have other problems that are perhaps more solvable. For example, there is the continuing problem of drugs, not only the issue of addictions and consequent criminality, but also the consequent economic and political issues . . ." She went on to give a description of the war on drugs, focusing on drug trafficking and profiteering and keeping well away from the subject of religion. She concluded: "Legalization would drive prices down, crime would stop, then we could take care of the addicts . . ."

"And you do not do this because of . . . politics?"

The SOS said, "The war against drugs is big business. Thousands of people are on the payroll. The people on the payroll don't want the problem solved, though they can't say that out loud or, perhaps, even admit it to themselves. Instead, they continue to take a moral position that requires them to punish people. Punishing people is always considered moral."

Indira shook her head. "It is like the Pursnyp people on the planet Hiddle. They built an enormous wall to protect them from the marauding tribes of nomadic Flizz. Half the population worked at maintaining and garrisoning the wall. Then a plague came, and the Flizz were almost wiped out. The Pursnyp people sent aid to the Flizz, and when we asked why, they said if the Flizz died out, the wall would not be needed, and there would be no more work for the Pursnyp."

"Like fox hunting in England," remarked Chad. "They say they hunt the foxes because they're vermin, but they're careful to preserve plenty of foxes so they never have to stop hunting."

At the other end of the table, Benita heard Lara ask, "What problems do you have in this country, General Wallace?"

He chewed thoughtfully, swallowed, patted his lips. "Well, ma'am, I'd say destruction of the environment is one of our biggest problems . . ."

While the talk flowed—the drug situation, the environment, various international concerns, everything but religion—Benita ate salad and chicken Kiev and asparagus, chatting from time to time with Mr. Riley, who was obviously keeping a careful eye on everyone present. When the chocolate mousse cake was cleared and coffee served, they listened politely to short speeches of welcome by the First Lady, the SOS, and General Wallace.

Then Indira rose to reply.

"We have been most pleased to join with you in this festive meal, enabling our two peoples to know one another a little better. We know you are recording this meeting, and we intended it so, in order that you may have a record to show your people of the reason for our coming here."

General Wallace leaned forward. General McVane frowned. Those who were drinking coffee put down their coffee cups.

"You have in recent time stepped upon your moon and begun the building of a space station. We have noticed this. You have in recent time sent small mechanicals to your planets, to learn about them, and you have built listening devices to detect intelligent life on other worlds. We applaud this, and we also applaud your efforts, so diligently though ineffectually carried out, to live peaceably among yourselves and, as we have learned this evening, to improve your perception of morality.

"You have in recent time sent a mechanical device beyond your own system out into the universe. Pistach people have found it, and in response they have sent us, athyci, you would say ethical representatives. Part of our task is to reach out to newly noticed races and assist them in meeting the prerequisites of our galactic principles of coexistence. We—the several races in our Confederation—call these principles Tassifoduma, what you would call Neighborliness. We have read much of your literature. One of your poets has said that good fences make good neighbors, and this is often true. When a neighbor throws empty cans over his fence, it may mean he is not a good neighbor, or it may mean the fence is not high enough. When small mechanicals are sent outward over the fence, it could be a sign of either. It is then we must do our work quickly before some larger garbage follows to attract the attention of others whom you are not prepared to meet.

"Our Confederation includes intelligent races, some of them predatory, though all agree to respect other members of the Confederation. Since the predators among us could do you great damage, it is to both our advantage if we can get you into the Confederation and subject to Confederation law as quickly as possible.

"So we have come to you as we have come to many worlds where we have learned the best ways to do our work. This is how we intend to proceed:

"Though our actions will not be limited to this country, we will begin our association with this country, as it has a quality other countries call cultural imperialism, which, we have found, means a tasty culture that other peoples readily enjoy, an infective culture, if you will, from which ideas and usages spread quickly. We find your language to be an inclusive one, your religions, for the most part, mutually tolerant, your races working consciously to remove bigotry. These are good signs. Nations that try to limit religion or racial configuration or the language spoken by their people are impossible to work with for they are more concerned with form than reality. We have selected our intermediary with great care. She meets our needs, and she will continue in that role."

Benita heard this with a shock that went all the way to her feet. Continue?

"Well," muttered her subconscious. "Did you think they paid you a hundred thou for spending a few days in Washington?"

Indira went on, "For the foreseeable future, this is the last time we will meet in person with anyone other than our intermediary. We will tell her what is required, and she will transmit this to your government. We learned tonight she has found a living place which is appropriate for us to communicate with her and her with you, without fuss. We request that this place be made ready for her as quickly as possible.

"We request that you do not use our intermediary's personal name when speaking of her to your media. Speak only of *the intermediary*. We ask this because we are athyci and the first rule of an athyco is to harm the least possible. Change always involves some trauma and displacement, but it should always be the least possible. It is not ethical to cause or allow destruction of the tranquil life of an innocent person, this is part of Tassifoduma. Currently there are many such small matters that need adjustment.

"Do you have any questions?"

No one said anything until General McVane blurted in a choked voice, "What gives you the right to come here and tell us what to do?"

The two Indian women swiveled toward him, fixing him with four eyes that, it seemed to Benita, were actually far more numerous than that. "We have the ethical duty, imposed upon us by our ancestors, to help other peoples achieve Neighborliness. Only if that proves impossible or unwelcome will we go away, though by that time, of course, other Confederation races may have learned you are here. We cannot go away, however, until we have made the attempt. Also, we must work not merely with leaders but also with the people, for we came from a whole people, our people, to the whole people of this world."

"How do we know you can do what you say you can?" McVane demanded, half shouting.

"General McVane!" said the SOS, warningly.

"He may ask the question," said Lara in a strange, humming tone. "It is always permitted to ask questions, even so rudely as he has done. Since you have been so discourteous as to doubt our word, you will have your answer by tomorrow, General McVane. We will leave you now. We are aware

this meeting is being recorded by various devices, and it is
our will that these devices shall on this one occasion be allowed to function, though in future we will prevent any such
invasion of our privacy."

Indira bowed to the table, Lara rose and joined her at the
head of the table where they bade farewell to the First Lady
and the SOS and then, just as General Wallace was getting
to his feet, they disappeared.

A recording made of the entire evening caught much of
the conversation and the disappearance of the aliens, at
which point the tape showed the other diners sitting
stunned, most of them with their mouths open. General Mc-
Vane ran for the door and began shouting at someone. Mr.
Riley spoke to the FL. Men from outside came in. Men from
inside went out. When Benita pulled herself together, she
saw that the SOS had moved into Indira's chair and was
leaning across the table toward her.

"Were you expecting that de facto appointment as
ambassador-in-chief?" she asked in a slightly irritated voice.

Benita shook her head, no, muttering, "I didn't even know
they expected me to continue doing anything!"

The First Lady spoke to the SOS. "I was watching her
face and the announcement took her by surprise as much as
it did us." She took a deep breath and patted Benita's arm,
whispering, "You were also surprised when they disappeared?"

Benita gulped. "They didn't disappear when I saw them
before. They got in their ship and flew away."

"They disappeared when they met with the president,"
said the SOS, in a less abrasive tone. She and the FL nodded
sympathetically. "Why did they choose you?"

Benita was surprised to find the question made her angry.
Why shouldn't they have chosen her! "Everyone has asked
that. Congressman Alvarez. The general. Even the president
asked me that. I suppose they wanted an ordinary person,
with ordinary concerns and ordinary problems. I'm a thus-far
underpaid minority working mother with an alcoholic husband. They couldn't have picked anyone much more ordinary than that."

"And two children in college as the result of your hard work," sniffed the SOS, giving her an admonitory look.

"There is that," she said, suddenly amused. "You've been checking up on me?"

"Of course the FBI has been investigating you. They even got some hair from your hairbrush back in Albuquerque so they could match it to your blood, just to be sure you're the real you."

"You went through our house? Bert must have loved that."

"Your husband has been in jail since early last Sunday morning. We made sure he would learn nothing about the search."

"Bert's in jail? Again?"

"It seems your husband was in no condition to drive at the time he had an accident."

"Oh, Lord," Benita said, ducking her head. How to be terminally embarrassed before the eyes of the world in one easy lesson!

The FL patted her arm, saying seriously, "Are you worried about him? Are you terribly concerned at not being there?"

Benita gritted her teeth. "At one time I would have said I was concerned. I've learned there's nothing I can do for him, so my concern is wasted."

The FL nodded. "There are all kinds of addictions, and we can't help the addicted if they don't want to be helped, Ms. Alvarez. We need to save our concern for things that need doing."

"Please call me Benita," she said. "Or just Bennie."

"Actually," murmured the SOS, "it would be better if we called you the intermediary, as the aliens requested. Everyone here is supposed to be trustworthy, but there's always the unlikely event that one of us is a spy."

Benita flushed. "Call me anything you like. I'm finished being Mrs. Bert Shipton, though. And you're right, I am upset about a lot of things."

"Well, don't be upset about the bureau going through your house," said the SOS, soothingly. "It was a very quiet investigation just so we could be sure you were who and what you said you were. Think about it. Aliens arrive and are announced by someone we don't know. If we had to bet our lives on it, and those of your family, which we may be doing, wouldn't we be remiss not to check?"

She considered it. "I suppose. Seeing how they can take any shape they like."

"Did you hear what our other alien guest talked about during dinner?"

"Small talk," Benita murmured. "The general's very interested in environmental issues. He'd recently attended a world conference on global warming. They talked about that. And since he's a rancher, he's interested in restoration of grasslands and riverbanks, the whole ecological bit."

"Interesting," said the FL. "Did you overhear Indira asking about Afghanistan and the treatment of women there? In the Pistach culture, she said, someone would intervene to stop men behaving that way, and why hadn't we done so."

"I don't think they understand yet that we have a lot of separate cultures," said Benita. "Either that, or they're just confirming that fact. Their people are evidently more . . . uniform than we are."

"We told her Afghanistan wasn't the only place that enslaves women, and we tried to explain about national sovereignty, that short of going to war, we have no right to meddle in foreign countries."

The SOS remarked, "She knew quite a bit about the things she was interested in. She wasn't asking out of real ignorance."

"I don't think they're allowed to," Benita said. "As they've pointed out to me, they're ethical beings. It wouldn't be ethical to pronounce on some subject without knowing a great deal about it."

"Oh, wouldn't that put an end to congressional debate," grated the SOS. She frowned. "Forget I said that. Now where's this place you've picked to live?"

Benita told them about the bookstore job, and the loft above it. The SOS demanded a full description, produced a little notebook and had Benita draw a sketchy floor plan. "Since the envoys have requested it, why don't we see if we can speed things up for you?"

"Simon—he's the owner—said he'd do it right away."

"Right away could mean next week or next month or whenever he can get a contractor. I spoke with the Attorney General earlier today. Chad Riley will be our liaison with Justice, and he can probably arrange to get this done in a day or two, complete with a good cover story for your boss. The aliens want you moved quickly, so let's try to hurry things up."

"It seems an imposition . . ."

"Are you going to refuse to work for the ETs?" the FL asked.

Benita shook her head uncertainly. "I don't know. I don't even know if they'd let me refuse."

"Well, then. Pretend it's part of the job. No personal obligation."

"Very well, if you like." She took a deep breath. "And since you have people in Albuquerque who are already familiar with my house and you're set on being helpful, could they pick up a few little items for me? My personal papers and some things that belonged to my mother? And my dog? I left him in a kennel there. And, could you fix it so I could send a letter to my former bosses, quitting my job and sort of . . . misleading them about where I am?"

The SOS looked amused. "Why not? Simplifying your life is what we have in mind. Give me a list."

The SOS handed Benita a blank page, and she wrote down the half dozen items she had already decided to recover. Her documents and tax returns were all in one place, a shoebox in her closet. She also wrote down Sasquatch's name and description and the place he'd been left.

The FL said, "Go ahead and write your letter to your former bosses. Address it, no return, then call Chad Riley at the White House. He'll have an office there for the time being, and he can take care of it."

The three women rose. General McVane came back into the room, very red in the face, stalking angrily toward Benita. "Had you planned that little disappearing act . . ."

The SOS laid her hand protectively on Benita's shoulder. "She did not, General McVane, and we'd all be grateful for a more moderate tone. I attended the Cabinet meeting today, just as you did, and it was made clear that the intermediary is simply a woman who was selected by the aliens for their own purposes. She had no part in that selection, she has done her part well and faithfully, and she deserves generous recognition of that fact."

McVane flushed. "Sorry, ma'am. It's just . . . frustrating!"

Benita heard something more than mere frustration in his voice. "You were trying to find their ship, weren't you? You had people all set up to follow them when they left."

McVane cursed at her, heard himself, and turned even brighter red.

The SOS looked at Benita in amazement, then turned on McVane with an expression of outrage. "I thought the Cabinet agreed we wouldn't try anything like that."

"No such order from the commander-in-chief," he snarled.

"What did you call that meeting?" snapped the SOS. "A chat room? We all understood what the parameters were! Top secret and absolutely no interference! Whom have you involved?"

He spoke through his teeth. "No one who knows anything! My men were asked only to follow everyone who left here!"

"I suppose it was inevitable," said the FL, glaring at him angrily. "Did you use this woman's name, General?"

"No. I swear. I didn't."

"But your friends followed you here. And they're waiting to follow everyone back so they'll know who all the participants are. Have you identified her to them?"

McVane flushed again. "Ma'am, I don't know her name. They didn't use her name at the meeting, they haven't used her name tonight! And even I don't have a photograph."

The SOS said, "But if you'd had one, you'd have passed it around! The president will be very interested in that, General McVane."

The FL turned toward Benita, drawing her away from the confrontation. "That surprised me. How did you catch on?"

Benita shook her head. "I don't know. Something about

the way he spoke, or looked. So frustrated. He would have been surprised, but why would he have been frustrated?"

"You're very perceptive." The FL gave her a long, level look. "Hardly in keeping with what we've learned about you, quite frankly. And that little speech during dinner! I don't know about the envoys, but I was impressed."

"Actually, I was quoting my mother's father. He was a history professor in Mexico. He specialized in pre-Colombian history, so he knew a lot about bloody gods. Mami, that is, my mother, used to quote him a lot."

"Impressive, nonetheless. Well, we'll make sure McVane's sneaks don't follow you. Why do people always have to play games!"

She left Benita at the table while she spoke to Chad Riley, who was hovering by the door, then returned. "Let's all go in my car. The driver will bring it around. We'll go out through the kitchen."

And so they did, with two Secret Service men in the front seat and two cars full of them fore and aft, not to the hotel but to the White House, which, perhaps unsurprisingly, had back stairs. A little later, Chad Riley borrowed one of the kitchen people's private cars to take Benita to her hotel. She hid in the backseat, under a throw, while Chad drove around and around telling her stories of presidents past until he was sure they weren't being followed. From the hotel staff entrance, he escorted her upstairs to her room via a freight elevator. At the door he stopped, fished in his pocket and handed her a cell phone.

"What?" she asked, confused.

"The ladies asked me to arrange it so you could call your children without their finding out where you are. I phoned the bureau and had them set it up so calls you make from it will be diverted through half a dozen places around the country, places we'll change every day or so, so your call can't be traced back to you. Considering what McVane was up to, they thought this would be a wise precaution. You can use it anytime now, without worrying about it."

"I've never used one," she said. "Is it complicated?"

He showed her how to use it, had her repeat it back to

him, then opened the door for her and wished her good night. She glanced at her watch as she let herself in, realizing in a panic it was almost midnight, an hour late for the call to California. Without taking off her coat, she sat down on the bed, flipped open the new gadget and dialed Angelica's number.

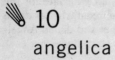

10
angelica

Angelica had spent the morning at Crown Heights Elementary School where she would be spending two mornings a week as a classroom assistant, part of her internship program at the university. She had been wakened well after midnight by Carlos's jovial and rather drunken conversation with someone he had brought home with him. That had started her thinking about old times, worrying about Mom, and all that had kept her tossing and turning. The alarm had gone off only moments—so it seemed—after she'd finally fallen asleep, and she'd been running so late she'd had to get a taxi to be sure she was on time. The budget wouldn't stretch for a return trip, though, so she hiked from the school to the nearest bus stop, some blocks away.

The playground took up a double block, fenced with high chain link. The next block was a parking lot for rows of school buses, also fenced, with a guarded gate. The other side of the street was lined with small businesses dotted among vacant buildings. The third and fourth blocks ran along one side of the Morningside Project, a multistory housing development and a major source of the students she would be working with.

The cross street in front of the Project was busy, especially around the bus stop. Angelica noticed that at one time a shelter and a bench had stood on the curb, but only the steel stumps remained, along with a couple of battered newspaper vending machines.

Angelica had her purse hung by its strap under her coat, where it didn't show, with her change in her pocket. The newspaper truck was changing the papers when she arrived at the bus stop, so she bought a late edition and folded it under her arm. She only had five dollars and bus fare in her pocket. Her credit card was at home, well hidden. Last time she'd left it in her purse, Carlos had borrowed it, and it had taken her four months to pay off his bar bill.

The heavy foot traffic of boys and young men made her slightly nervous. There were fluid, eddying groups of three or more, some with very young boys in attendance. A mother with two young children came out of the Project door and turned toward Angelica, running a gauntlet of tom-cat calls and all-too-personal comments, culminating in the suggestion that the speaker wouldn't mind giving her another baby to hatch.

"That was rotten," Angelica commented when the stony faced woman reached her.

"I pay them no mind," she said grimly. "You talk back, they get worse, you end up in a mess."

"They're obviously selling drugs," Angelica murmured. "Can't the police clear them out?"

"We thought we cleared them," the young woman said, casting a quick glance at the traffic in the street. "Oh, we thought we took care of all that. We went down to the city, almost sixty of us, along with the children. I took Elsha here, she's three, and William, he's almost six. The police captain and some of his men was there. We ask the councilmen, please give us that ordinance against loitering. So, they passed it, and the police moved out all these no-goods. We had three, four real nice weeks. Then the city got sued. ACLU helped a man sue for gettin moved along for no cause. Judge put a hold order on the ordinance. Can't move 'em along for no reason. Got to have probable cause, and that means the police gotta see it. Got to see them in the act. Got to get the drugs in their hands. Got to see money passed."

"All they have to do is look," said Angelica, angrily. "Anybody can see it!"

"Police show up, all the drugs disappear, just like magic. Police get here, all those no-goods, they're just rappin, listenin to music. Police drive on, all those drugs, they just sprout back up outa nowhere."

"It's frustrating!" murmured Angelica, turning to watch the bus that was now approaching.

"It'll get worse," the woman said, stooping to button the toddler's jacket. The boy regarded Angelica impassively, then turned his attention back to the youths on the sidewalk. The mother saw him, took him by the hand and turned him away, biting her lip. "When William gets to be seven, eight, those no-goods, they'll get him holdin' for them, just like those little boys there now."

They got onto the bus together, and took a seat side by side, the little girl on her mother's lap, the boy standing at the window. Angelica bent to look across his shoulder. From the sidewalk, one of the young men flashed her a brilliant smile and an obscene body gesture, a balletic rape, an elegant violation. As she sat down, Angelica heard the young mother murmur, "You be careful comin' down here. He was watchin' you before."

Angelica nodded. Her mouth was dry. To cover her confusion, she opened the paper and let her eyes focus on it.

DRIVE-BY DEATHS REACH NEW HIGH IN CALIFORNIA
GOVERNOR SAYS DEATH OF TODDLERS IS "LAST STRAW"

BOMBING IN JERUSALEM CLAIMS FORTY LIVES
RETALIATION PLANNED AGAINST SITES IN LEBANON

SERBIAN UNDERGROUND CLAIMS RESPONSIBILITY FOR BUS BOMBINGS
TERRORISTS TARGETED SCHOOL CHILDREN

JUDGE RULES MEGAN'S LAW UNCONSTITUTIONAL
PEDOPHILE HAS PAID DEBT TO SOCIETY

"I don't look at the papers," said the woman at her side. "I used to read them all the time. Now it's just all, more and more of the same, you know?"

"I know," said Angelica.

The mother and her children got off first. From Angelica's stop it was a six-block walk to the apartment, their apartment, the one she and Carlos shared, and she found herself slogging, trudging, so tired she ached.

The door to Carlos's room was ajar, and he was still in bed. She stood in the doorway, staring at him. His schedule said he had English Composition this morning, and art classes this afternoon. His bed looked like a dog's nest. His laundry was piled in the corner where it had been for two weeks. She went in and shook him, not gently.

"Hey," he said. "Let go."

"It's noon!" she said loudly. "You've got art classes this afternoon."

"Yeah. Well, I had a headache. It's better now. I'll get up in a few minutes."

"Carlos!" She stood looking at him wearily. "Mom's going to call at eight, tonight. Remember. I told her you'd be here."

"I know, I know. Stop yelling."

She left him there and went angrily into the tiny kitchen. She'd had to run without breakfast this morning, but Carlos had evidently fixed food for himself when he came in last night. Not only for himself. There were several pans, one of them burned, plus several dishes and glasses scattered in the tiny room. She put them in the sink, ran hot water on them and added soap. The sliced meat she'd intended to make a sandwich of was gone. The eggs were gone. The only thing left in the cupboard was a can of soup.

While it was heating she decided to take her own laundry to the basement, but halfway down the basement stairs she sagged against the wall and slid down onto a step, face buried in the dirty laundry.

"Hey," said someone. "You all right?"

She looked up into the sympathetic face of the apartment manager, Mrs. Gaines, a round-faced, crop-haired plain-talking woman whose apartment was at the back on the so-called garden level.

"I'm so tired," Angelica blurted. "He leaves it all on me. And I'm just so tired!"

The woman sat down on the step beside her. "Tell you what, Angel. There's a little efficiency apartment upstairs, just big enough for you. Lots cheaper than the one you have now. I'll let you off your lease if you want to move up there and let Carlos find himself some other place."

Angelica regarded her blankly, mouth slightly open.

The woman reached over and pressed her jaw up. "Don't think it's kindness. It'd help me out. We get complaints about noise and drunks, you know, people get unhappy, they move out. Your mama must've got him off the tit, now you've got to let him grow up. Here, I'll start that load for you. You look like you need a nice hot cup of something."

And she was up, with the laundry load, trotting down the stairs while Angelica was still trying to think of something to say. Back upstairs she ate her soup, made a strong cup of instant coffee, and cleaned up the kitchen. At two she had to leave for her own classes, and Carlos was still asleep when she left.

When she returned home at seven, bearing a pizza, Carlos wasn't there. The phone call was scheduled for eight, but the phone didn't ring until nine, just as Carlos walked in. She grabbed the phone, glaring at him.

"Hello, Mother? Hey, Carlos is here. I'm going to put this on speaker phone. You're late."

"I know. Some very nice people invited me to dinner and it went on longer than expected. They dropped me off, but they had to make a kind of . . . detour, so there was no polite way I could hurry things up."

"New friends, that's good."

"They're just acquaintances, but they know I'm new in town and they're being kind."

Angelica asked, "So, tell us, are you looking for a new job?"

"I have a new job. The arrangements were all made this morning. It's very much like the one I had in Albuquerque, but the pay is better than it was there."

Carlos leaned forward, lips pursed, eyebrows raised importantly. "Mom, this afternoon I got a call from Dad. He's wondering where you are."

A moment's silence. "Carlito, I left him a note saying I was going away. I'm sure Angelica told you why I was calling. I'm not coming back, and as I told Angelica, I don't want your father to know where I am."

Carlos frowned. "Where's Sasquatch?"

"I have him."

"And who's this old lady who left you money? I didn't know you had any cousins I didn't know."

"Not anyone you knew. She was my mother's cousin."

Carlos cocked his head, as though trying to see through the phone. "Dad could use some help with bail money. I mean, if you've got some extra cash."

Angelica turned on him angrily, but the chill of the disembodied voice that came through the phone stopped her. "Bail money? For what?"

Carlos gave Angelica the look of superiority she'd grown to hate, the one that said, "See, I'm managing the family, thinking of everything." He spoke into the phone, "He had a little accident. He says . . . well, he totaled his car."

After a considerable pause Benita said sadly, "My car."

Carlos had the grace to look slightly embarrassed as he said, "I just thought you'd want him out of jail!"

Long pause. "No. Not particularly."

Actual surprise. "Well, sheesh, Mom!"

No response.

He took a deep breath and asked, all too casually, "What time is it there, Mom? You sound tired."

There was another pause before their mother answered. "I feel like it's four in the morning, but it's only a little after ten. I am tired. The long bus ride, mostly. A good night's sleep and I'll be rested."

Carlos leaned forward, brow knitted in concentration, opened his mouth only to have Angelica interrupt, "I haven't told you about my jobs, Mom. Two mornings a week I'm working as a classroom assistant, plus I'm putting in a supper shift in the kitchen at the Union."

"Angel, do you have time for that and your school?"

"The teacher's aide work is required as part of a theory of education course I'm taking, plus they pay me for it. I have to write it up and do a critique. Besides, I really like the teacher I'm working with. She reminds me of you."

A little laugh at the other end. "That's sweet of you to say."

Carlos said, "Mom—"

She cut him off crisply. "Another time, Carlos. I'm really tired, so I'll hang up. I'll call again, when I have some news. Goodnight, dears. I'll talk to you soon."

Angelica leaned forward to cut off the dial tone, regarding her brother with dislike. "You had to bring up Dad and talk about bail money? When did Dad call you?"

"I said, this afternoon. Phone woke me about four."

"You slept through your afternoon classes? Honestly, Carlos! You've already had one warning from the foundation. Did you tell Dad that Mom inherited some money?"

"He was in a state, you know, so I may have mentioned it."

She angrily tore the crust off her cold pizza and drowned it in a half glass of milk beside her, vividly remembering Mrs. Gaines's words on the stairs.

He said, in a falsely casual voice, "I think we ought to find out where she is."

Angelica opened the oven and felt the pizza she'd saved for him. It was no warmer than her face, which felt fiery. "You already tried that. She heard what you were doing, asking her what time it was."

He gave her a condescending look, saying loftily, "I think I'll get caller ID. I don't like the idea of her off by herself where nobody can get in touch with her or help her or anything."

"Dad never wanted Mom off somewhere either. He wanted her right there, where he could help himself, like to her paycheck."

"Boy, that's really loyal!"

She bit her tongue. "Carlos, this isn't working. I can't live with you. I had my doubts about this sharing bit . . ."

"I shared last year."

"So why not with the same people this year?"

He stared sulkily at his feet. "They had other plans."

She took a deep breath. "See, that's the mistake I made. I figured you knew how to do it, but my guess is you never learned and they didn't want you back."

"That's my business."

"That's what I'm saying. It's totally your business. Providing late-night suppers for people you invite in is totally your business. Drinking beer until midnight and not going to class is totally your business. Mrs. Gaines has someone who wants a two-bedroom, and she told me she'll let me off the lease to this apartment if I switch to an efficiency upstairs. I'm going to take it."

"We won't fit into an efficiency. It's only one room!"

"Exactly. I'm moving upstairs and you'll have to make other arrangements."

"Aww, Angel!"

"I don't want to hear it."

"You can't just move out on me. I'll keep this place."

"My name is the only one on the lease. From now on, I'll take care of my business, you take care of yours."

She went into her bedroom and closed the door, refusing to come out even to the sound of breaking crockery. When he left, twenty minutes later, she called Mrs. Gaines and told her she'd be moving as soon as possible.

🖋 11
local law enforcement

In the university town where Angelica and Carlos were living, in a precinct house not far from the Morningside Project, a grizzled sergeant crouched over a pile of paperwork, chewing the end of his pen and trying to remember what it was his wife had asked him to bring home after work. She'd offered to write it down, he'd said he'd remember, now he didn't remember. Like a damn ritual. Why didn't he let her write it down, for crissake?

A voice bellowed from the glassed-in office behind him. "McClellan!"

"It's right where you put it when I gave it to you," the sergeant muttered, not looking up. "Top right-hand drawer."

"What is?" The cop at the adjacent desk glanced up from the form on the screen. He was booking a shoplifter. "What's in the top right-hand drawer?"

"The manpower stats for last month," murmured McClellan.

"Never mind," bellowed the voice.

"What's got his shorts in a tangle?" wondered the cop.

"I bet he's all upset over that judge sayin' you couldn't move those pushers out," said the shoplifter, nodding wisely. "He worked real hard to get that law passed."

"It wasn't a law, it was an ordinance," McClellan said, looking up. "How'd you know the captain was involved?"

"I live down there at Mornin'side," she said. "I was one of the marchers went to city hall. Me'n my kids."

"So you got kids," said the officer. "That doesn't excuse you walking off with birthday presents under your shirt."

"It was just candles!" she cried. "For the cake. A dollar niney-five for twenny-four lousy birt'day candles an all I had was a dollar fiffy an all I needed was twelve. An she wouldn' split the box up, give me half!"

The officer got up and moved toward the storeroom. "Watch her, Mac, so she don't walk off with half my computer."

Mac shook his head. "I'm not watching. I'm not getting involved. Six more weeks, four days, three hours and I figure about forty-five minutes, I can say good-bye to it all."

"You quittin?" asked the shoplifter.

"Re-tire-ment! Captain says he wants to take me to lunch on my last day. Every guy that retires or gets transferred, the captain wants to take them to lunch on their last day, he says, but it's just an excuse so the guys can throw a surprise party. Doesn't he think I know that?"

"They gonna give you a gold watch?"

"I said no watch. They want to give me something, give me a new fishing rod."

"McClellan!" roared the voice.

He got up wearily and shambled into the lieutenant's office, stopping before the desk and leaning on it with both hands. "What?"

"What's this?" The lieutenant held out a sheet of paper. "It was in the manpower reports."

"It's a tabulation of how many calls we get from Morningside, complaining about the dealers. I thought, when we appeal that judge's decision . . ."

"Oh, McClellan, you hadn't heard," the lieutenant said loudly, well aware that there were a dozen sets of ears listening from outside his office. "We are no longer interested in the dealers down at Morningside. The dealers at Morningside have civil rights. They are being represented by the

ACLU in their suit against the mayor and the police force on behalf of all the upstanding young men who stand around on the sidewalk all day, every day, with no visible means of support."

McClellan stared at him, mouth slightly ajar. "You finished?"

The lieutenant dropped his voice. "I am so close to finished, Mac, that I may retire before you do. Actually, tabulating the calls is a pretty good idea. Go on keeping a record." He fumed, running his fingers through his gray hair, shifting his shoulders as though they hurt. "Not that it'll do any good. How much longer you got now?"

"Too long," said McClellan. "I can remember back to when we got rid of guys hanging around on corners, giving the women a lot of dirty talk. I can remember when giving a little kid a gun would have put you away for a good long while."

"See, that's our trouble. We remember too much." He waved McClellan away and went back to his paperwork. "Way, way too much."

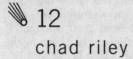 12
chad riley

Though it was past midnight, FBI agent and sometime White House liaison Chad Riley had his driver run by the office then drop him six blocks from his Georgetown house so he could cool down on the walk home. The business with McVane had rubbed him very much the wrong way, and Chad knew exactly who to blame. The FBI had started surveillance on Congressman Alvarez by midafternoon Monday, and Chad had just picked up a report saying he'd gone to the Pentagon that afternoon. Monday. And by Tuesday, McVane had been named as liaison, and he had probably already known everything the congressman knew, which meant his cronies, if not already briefed, would be shortly. The congressman had been sworn to secrecy, but his loyalties lay elsewhere, which might have been deduced from the number of pictures of himself in uniform on the walls of his office. Major Alvarez here with General Tank, Major Alvarez there with General Missile. Military men! Damn it, they always thought in terms of hardware, black or white, our side or the other side. It was damned hard to get them to see gray at all, and getting them to tell dark gray from medium gray was impossible!

And why in hell had the intermediary taken it to Alvarez in the first place? Why not the bureau? Someone used to handling secrets! Though he shouldn't fault her in hindsight. She was a damned pretty woman, and a sensible one. He'd watched her during dinner. She'd been quiet, thoughtful, she'd listened, when she'd said anything, it had been intelligent and to the point. No, he couldn't fault her at all.

During the six-block walk he simmered down. He always tried to get himself into an easy frame of mind before he opened the front door on Merilu and whomever Merilu was being on the particular evening. Rarely it was Merilu the girl he'd married, full of laughter and bubbly charm, if one ignored that these days the laughter was more giggly than witty and the bubbles had originated in champagne. More often the woman who greeted him was Merilu the prosecutor, prepared to cross-examine him about everything he'd done since he left the house that morning. Or Merilu the alpha wolf, growling at him for not paying enough attention to the boys. Or Merilu the martyr to politics, who wanted to leave the corruption and clamor of Washington and go back to Montana.

All of which multiple-personality stuff had started when the twins had reached school age. When Jason and Jeremy were born, Merilu had decided to take a year off to be with the babies. The year had turned into six. Now the boys were in school all day, and Merilu was bouncing off the walls, regretting that she'd given up her career for motherhood.

He'd tried patience. "Merilu, you said yourself your career would only have lasted a year or two more."

"It was an important year or two, Chad! I'd have made contacts. I'd have set myself up to move on . . ."

He'd tried reality. "On where, sweetheart?"

She'd never considered on where. Where did one move from being spokeswoman for a commuter airline? From being a sparkle on television, a smile in photographs, a warm cushiony voice-over for tourist-targeted infomercials about destinations along the air routes. It was a job that let her do the things she liked to do, like having her hair done, getting a manicure, having a makeup job, and being dressed in de-

signer clothes so people could look at her. People had liked
looking at her. Chad had liked looking at her. And being
with her. Of course, back then Merilu had been habitually
and refreshingly frank. Even if she hadn't quit to be with the
children, she herself had said she'd have to find something
else to do because the job wouldn't last forever. Then, she'd
said so.

Now, however, Merilu's mom had gotten into the act.
She'd brought her poor-baby backhoe from Montana so she
could dig Merilu a whine pit, a hole so dark and deep there
wasn't a hope of getting her out. Not unless—so she said—
she moved back to Montana, which would magically create
some kind of insta-ramp, out of the pits and up to cheery-
dom. It all depended on Chad, of course. All he had to do
was request a transfer.

Chad was dragging his feet. Hell, he was dragging his
whole damned body! He could get a transfer, probably,
maybe even without a cut in pay. Of course, doing that
meant he'd give up his own career ambitions, which Merilu,
with typical inconsistency, considered only fair since that's
what she'd done, never mind that she'd chosen to and he
hadn't, never mind that he'd been making enough to afford
a full-time nanny, but Merilu hadn't wanted that, never mind
that she was twenty-six and he was thirty-nine. The thirteen-
year difference hadn't seemed like much when she was
twenty, but lately it had opened up into a generation gap! At
least she hadn't used the D word, which he did not want to
hear. That is, he thought he didn't want to hear it, not now,
though he could feel himself getting more and more used to
the idea.

He put his key in the lock and stepped into a silent
house, where he held his breath and let it out slowly. Not a
sound. Nothing in the living room, not in the dining room,
kitchen . . . note on the refrigerator.

"Chad, Mom's in town for three days and she's asked me
and the boys to have dinner in her suite at the hotel. There's
a pool and a spa, so we may stay for awhile. Don't expect us
until late tonight or sometime tomorrow."

He sighed, realizing with slight shame that it was a sigh

of relief. He could have a shower sans nag; a drink or two or three sans whine; a lazy loll in front of the tube sans whimper from the background. Lord, Lord, why did men and women try to live together? Those South Pacific tribes that had the men and women living in separate houses had the right idea.

It was so peaceful that maybe he would even explore how he felt about two sari-clad women going up in a puff of nothingness at a top secret dinner which he had attended as liaison. He had made a point of approaching them and handing them things several times during the evening. He would swear they were material, real, living. He had sat across from the one who called herself Indira. She had smiled, joked, laughed, her face crinkling up in real humor. Then, poof, gone. He had suspended judgment, half expecting the bureau lab rats to come in and announce it had all been a trick, but the technicians were still examining the tapes, as baffled as everyone else.

Real aliens. Who had come to help the United States with, how had they put it, those "small areas that need adjustment." That was the height of arrogance. Sure there were problems in the world, but damned if Chad would call any of them "small areas that needed adjustment."

But the woman, Benita, she had been something different. Not only pretty, in a very natural way, but charming. That level look she gave you. The way she listened. That was really it . . . the way she listened. Chad felt he had not been listened to so genuinely in a very long time.

13

general mcvane

Elsewhere in Washington, General McVane had made a number of hurried phone calls rousing people from sleep and was now with "Dink" Dinklemier on his way to a small, out-of-the-way hotel previously owned by a drug trafficker, recently appropriated by the DEA and currently being "managed" by a semiretired CIA employee. Called Holiday Hill, it was often used by Washington spooks for stashing witnesses, hiding informants, or holding impromptu meetings.

"J'you get hold of Arthur?" Dink asked.

"He's picking up Morse, and they'll meet us. What about Briess?" Briess was the CIA link.

"He's in California," Dink replied. "I left him a message."

Except for this exchange, their journey was silent, unbroken even when they arrived at the hotel and went directly to a small second-floor meeting room.

"Turn the heat off!" McVane complained. "It's ninety in here."

Dink obligingly turned down the thermostat and opened the two windows to the cooler night air while McVane loaded a tape into a player and called downstairs for refreshments.

"What's that smell?" he asked.

Dink sniffed. "Something outside. I thought I'd cool the room down, then shut the windows."

"Smells like . . . what? Smoke? Hot tar?"

"Probably odors from the kitchen, General."

"Let's not eat here, then," he snorted, turning on the tape player to be sure it worked.

The tray of drinks arrived only moments before Arthur and Morse, the senator already in a state of outrage.

"What the bleep?" snarled the senator. "It's bleeping midnight."

"We figured you'd want to know about it," said Dink. "Remember what we told you about last time we met? The unidentified objects flying from A to B to X. Well, McVane tells us X turned out to be right here. This tape was made earlier tonight. I think it'll be self-explanatory."

He pushed the button. The dinner party was on the screen. There was, however, no Indira, no Lara. There were, instead, two totally inhuman creatures who darted and clicked their way around the room and who ate, once dinner was served, in a peculiarly disgusting manner. At least, so thought the senator, though he knew he was more sensitive to such matters than many of his associates. He watched, both repulsed and fascinated, all the way through the speeches, the envoys' explanations and farewells, and the disappearance of the envoys.

"They just vanished!" said McVane. "Like a puff of smoke."

"The woman," said Morse. "The so-called intermediary. Who is she?"

McVane answered. "Her name is Benita Alvarez. We're not supposed to know that, Senator. We got the information from Congressman Alvarez. She's some kind of seventh cousin twice removed. General Wallace was in Alvarez's office when the woman brought him a kind of cube thing that delivered the message. He, in turn, brought the thing to the president. I first knew about this on Monday, when I attended a Cabinet meeting at the White House. The real intermediary doesn't look like the woman on the tape, by the way. She's younger and better looking, and she has dark hair."

"She could be anybody!" Morse exploded. "A Chinese agent. Somebody planted before the wall came down! I want her, McVane. I want to talk to her right now!"

"When we find out where she is, Senator. I had arranged to follow her from the meeting, but the White House managed to be obstructive, as usual. It's only a matter of a few hours before we find her, but as you pointed out, it's after midnight."

"So these damned monsters will teach us to be neighborly," fumed the senator. "Teach a fox to eat chickens! You find that woman. You bring her here. Put her down in the basement rooms, where we can have a very private little talk. You bring somebody from that spook factory of yours, too, so we can be sure she's telling us the truth . . ."

"Before you consider torture or drugs, you might try just talking with her," said Prentice Arthur, his lip curled in distaste. "As yet, we have no reason to suspect she's anything but an ordinary American citizen."

"You believe that, you believe in the tooth fairy," sneered the senator. "No, Prentice. I've seen this coming. All the science fiction and the TV series and the movies! We've had aliens pushed down our throats for decades! Softening us up. When we hear the word *alien*, we think of ET and little boys riding bicycles across the full moon. We think of close encounters, with musical starships. Do you think that's all coincidence? A fad? Let me tell you, it's purposeful, it's arranged. Now they're ready for the takeover, and they've got us so well softened up, they figure we'll go along, no hassle, no fighting. Well, they've figured without Byron Morse. Get me this woman! I want her." He paused a moment, chewing at the corner of his lips. "Does she have family?"

"A husband in Albuquerque, two children in college in California."

"Well, while you're at it, I want them, too. All three of them."

Even McVane looked startled at this, and Prentice actually attempted to disagree. "Senator, you're being precipitous . . ."

"I'm being fucking decisive," Morse snarled. "And it's damned well time! You're a lawyer, Prentice! Get some writs or some congressional subpoenas going. Issue them in the name of the committee. We oversee intelligence, damn it, and this woman's family may have information crucial to intelligence."

"Surely we can take a little time . . ."

"You think I'm out of my head? Hmm? Well, you just go along with me. And you watch the news. Pretty soon you're going to see things happening. Things you can't explain. Oh, those aliens on the tape, they'll explain it away, but there'll be people dead, or people missing. When you read about it, you remember what I'm telling you. Until then, just do what I ask and pretend you believe in it! Now get off your ass and take me home!"

Dink left with Arthur and the senator. McVane gathered up the tape and his briefcase, then went to shut the open windows. The strange smell was even stronger than it had been initially, an acrid stench, and he leaned out, searching the area for signs of smoke. Nothing there but a line of trees, some of which had been chopped off and regrown from the crown. He searched for the word. Pollarded. Ugly, in his opinion.

"McVane," said someone from nearby.

He jerked upright, banging his head on the window. "Who's that?" he snarled.

"McVane," said the voice again, from outside.

He leaned out the window, one hand cupped protectively over his head. "What?"

The voice was mechanical, artificial. "The Pistach are not the only race desirous of working with your people. Others are very interested, and others might offer better terms than the Pistach."

McVane stood very still. He could see no one outside the window, and the voice gave him no hints. It was directionless. "Who are you? Why did you come to me?"

"We are members of *Shalaqua*, General. It is a . . . cadre, military, like yourself. We came to you because you were at the meeting. We followed the Pistach to the meeting. You and we may be of great service to one another. To discuss, however, we must arrange to meet."

"Who . . . who would you like to meet with?"

"The persons with you tonight. The senator. His agents. You. Your agents, if you like."

"Where? When?"

"Four day from now? Hmm?"

"Monday?"

"If it is called that. At darkspin, you gather others. You go somewhere distant from the city."

"Darkspin?" McVane whispered from a dry mouth.

"When your world rolls into dark. Evening. Yes. We are still . . . accumulating vocabulary. We apologize. You go into the country, we will follow you, we will meet there. Four days will give you time to prepare, geh?"

"Prepare what?"

"Your safety. The senator, he will want to be safe. So with Prentice Arthur. You less so, but you are a soldier, geh? You can make secure in four days. Some armored vehicle, perhaps. We do not presume to tell you your business."

"Monday night, at sunset, somewhere in the country," said McVane.

"Assuredly," said the voice. "We go now."

McVane turned away and walked dazedly to the door, shutting off the lights as he opened it, only then remembering his briefcase. It was still on the table and he stumbled toward it in the dark, halted in mid step by a sound from outside. Squadge, squadge, squadge. Flap, flap, flap. Conscious of his dry mouth and throat, he paced silently toward the window, a mouth of darkness, standing back but looking out. Nothing out there. The trees. Not as thick a grove as he had first thought. No more noise. Nothing.

He picked up his briefcase and left as quickly as possible.

Outside the senator's house, where they had dropped him off, Prentice and Dink sat in the car, at the moment unwilling to move in any direction.

"Did you know he had that rat in his craw about ETs?" Dink asked. "I thought it was only pregnant women that set him off."

"If you mean, did I know he's afraid of little green men, no, or that he believes there's an extraterrestrial conspiracy, no. I didn't know either of those things. Maybe he had something bad happen to him when he was a boy. A movie or TV show that scared him."

"You think?"

Arthur said slowly, "I'd rather think that, wouldn't you? I mean, we occasionally work in rather . . . arcane ways. We . . . at least I try to avoid it, but it's the exigencies of the job. But . . . planning to torture family members just because they *might* know something . . . that's a little far out even for our line of work."

"He said there'd be people dead or missing. Maybe we'd better put someone on a survey of regional and local news, tabulate any reports of people dead or missing."

"If you do, he'll have you by the short hairs. Dink. Think a moment. Aren't there always people dead or missing?"

"Right. Yeah. I see what you mean."

"I hope you do, Dink. Oh, yes, I hope you do."

14
from chiddy's journal

Before we made contact with you, dear Benita, we watched the peoples of Earth for a very long time. It was not necessary for us to learn all the languages, as we have machines to do that, but it was necessary to learn how people think. We watched the Chinese and the Africans, the Indians and Ceylonese. I was particularly interested in the nations where ruling groups had recently come to power through advocacy of specific beliefs, as for example in Afghanistan.

For several days, I was intrigued by one particular person there, one who thought of himself as a warrior and faithful son of the Prophet. We watched his daily routines including the rituals and prayers his people engage in several times each day. Vess listened to his memories: remembered writings, oral histories, the battles he had fought and the victory his people had won. This man—whose name was Ben Shadouf—had been given a half-ruined house, badly damaged during the war. He spent part of each day rebuilding the house where he lived with his wife and his children.

Each evening, when he rose from his prayers, he went to the inner courtyard where his wife had set out his evening meal. On a particular evening, he sat contemplating the food for a long time, then summoned his wife and pointed at the plates before him, asking for meat.

"We had none," she murmured.

"You have money to buy meat," he said. I watched his eyes measuring her, examining her face with what I took to be concern. When we first found this family, she had looked quite healthy and vigorous, as you do, dearest Benita, but she no longer did so. Now she coughed often, there were shadows around her eyes, and her hair was rough and uncared for.

"I gave you money," he said.

"You had no time to go with me to the market," she replied. Her eyes remained fixed on her feet. She seemed feverish and unwell. "I am no longer permitted to be on the street without a male relative."

He gritted his teeth and waved her away, fingering the long scar that ran from his forehead down one cheek. Vess told me the man was proud of the scar, for he had killed the Russian soldier who had shot him. The bullet had nicked his cheekbone, however, and it hurt him still. Vess, feeling his mind, said the battles he had fought were more real to him than the present, more real than the victory his group had achieved. He had anticipated victory the way a starving person anticipates food. He had thought it would be satisfying, gladdening, but he found it to be only tiresome. He had agreed to the laws they would implement when the victory came, but he had not known how irritating and inconvenient those laws would be. He had not realized his wife would suffer from them.

The woman, Afaya, could not go into the street without a male relative to protect her modesty, even though she would be covered from head to toe with only tiny mesh openings before her eyes. Afaya had told her husband that wearing the robe was like being blind. The wife of Mustapha, his neighbor and commanding officer, had tripped on the pavement and fallen, allowing her legs to be seen. She was then beaten by those who named themselves Guardians of Modesty. She had died of this beating. Mustapha had shrugged it away, for she was old and there were no children at home for her to care for, but he, too, found the new rules inconvenient.

Vess and I puzzled over this. The woman was a receptor, of course. The men were all inceptors, except the very young ones, who would be, and very old ones, who had been. Was every one of them expected to go into breeding madness if he saw a receptor's legs? Or her face? Were they totally without self-control or a sense of shame? Seemingly so, for any woman showing her face was charged with being an erotic-stimulator-for-hire who, by showing any part of herself, had stimulated breeding madness in men and must therefore be stoned to death. Actual erotic-stimulators-for-hire, of whom there were a good many, were not stoned to death. And, most interesting of all, even while the men were doing the stoning, they *knew* the women they called whores were, in fact, innocent. And yet, they did it.

We examined Ben Shadouf's irritation. He would have to hire a male servant to do the food buying for the household. He would have to sequester Afaya and his daughters to the upstairs of the house, for the servant, being unrelated to them, could not run the risk of coming into contact with them or seeing them. If his wife was not in the courtyard, where the kitchen was, she could not cook his meals! All these endless complications in order to keep his wife, a human being like himself, imprisoned from the sight and hearing of any other man! Even his consciousness of his own frustration annoyed him.

When the wife of Ben Shadouf began coughing again, he looked up in anger. It was a strange anger, directed as much at himself as at her. Her cough had become more dangerous over the previous days. Vess and I believed she was dying. She held memories of the time before the war when she had gone to a clinic staffed by women doctors, but women were not allowed to work any longer. Their place was at home where their purity could be protected by their menfolk.

We sought throughout the city and found the clinic, which had set up anew in a private home. It was staffed only by women who did not go out, who received shipments of medicines from outside the country and who had husbands or brothers to shop for them. Vess put the knowledge of this place into Ben Shadouf's head. We saw him thinking the women doctors were probably Americans, or influenced by Americans who were always trying to seduce followers of the Prophet to their evil ways. He worried whether he could risk defilement by going to the clinic with her, and he feared the satanic notions they would put into her head. Perhaps it would be better, he thought, to let her die and then find a new wife, one with a brother who could share the duty of protecting her.

And yet, he loved her. We saw tears in his eyes.

Vess and I tried to make sense of this as we watched him picking at the vegetables: lentils and onions and herbs, which had a flavorful aroma. His wife was dying, his children would be motherless, and he could not engage in any constructive action.

Abruptly he pushed the food aside and got up. Calling loudly, he said, "I am going into the town for my meal. This food is fit only for women."

As he left, he heard her coughing again.

Intrigued by this episode, we sought similar confusions where religion warred with good sense. We found them in many parts of the world: in Afghanistan, Moslem against Moslem. In India, Moslem against Hindu against Christian. In Israel, Moslem against Moslem against Israelis who are against other Israelis. This particular observation saddened us, for all the pain that was in it, and it excited us, too, for it showed us there are ways in which we know we can help your world. While you are putting together your household, Benita, we are taking our first action, not in your country, where we had planned to do so, but in Afghanistan and Israel and India and so on. Your Moses, in your holy book, brought down plagues upon his adversaries. So Vess and I will bring down plagues upon that part of your world.

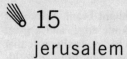 **15**

jerusalem

THURSDAY

The first public notice of what was later called the Old City Absence came at 4:15 A.M. on Thursday, when a caravan of determined Hasidic Jews from New York approached the Old City of Jerusalem where they planned to enter via the Dung Gate on their way to securing an early and favorable position at the Wall. The valley through which they had been driving was filled with mist, making the world seem dreamlike and insubstantial, an effect which did nothing to make the sleepy driver more alert. It was only when the road before him seemed to vanish altogether that he screeched to a stop, the car swerving so that it blocked the road. The three other cars in the convoy also pulled to a halt, and the rabbi in charge of the group got out of the second one and walked toward driver number one, now out of his car and following his flashlight's yellow circle along the roadway to the point at which it disappeared infinitely downward.

"What is it?" cried the rabbi, himself still half asleep. "What's wrong?"

The driver's eyes stayed glued in place, though he took a backward step as he heard the rabbi's footsteps approaching.

"What is it?" he asked again.

"It's gone," mumbled the driver. "Everything's gone. The walls of the Old City. I can't see them. There should be some lights. Everything's gone."

The rabbi stared along the flashlight beam. Before his feet the earth stopped at a clean, knife edge, and a great chasm opened beyond it. The chasm had no farther side that they could see, nor any bottom. The rabbi dropped to his hands and knees and crept forward until his chin was over the abyss. He lay flat and stretched one arm downward, feeling along the side.

"Glass," he muttered. "Like it was melted. By a bomb, maybe. Smooth like glass." He pulled himself away from the edge and rose, eyes wild. "Nothing," he cried in an awed and grief-stricken voice. "Nothing there. Everything stops but the pit! It's smooth, it goes down."

"How far?"

"I should know how far? Farther than your light shines!"

They went back to their vehicles. The first three cars stayed where they were while the last car in line reversed and went back the way it had come. No one among them had a cell phone, but a half mile back, they'd passed a public phone from which the frantic driver called an emergency number. His announcement was met with weary amusement.

"Sir, you're a tourist, right? So you've probably taken the wrong road . . ."

"Yes, I'm a tourist," he cried. "But the men driving the cars live here, and the man leading our caravan lives in Jerusalem! He was born here. He's lived here all his life. Will you, for God's sake, send someone to see what happened?"

There were murmuring and the sound of voices raised in the background.

"Where are you calling from?"

"I have no idea," he said. "Half a mile back from where the road disappeared."

"Where were you going, sir?"

"The Wall. We were going to the Dung Gate and then to the Wall."

"Stay where you are, sir."

He rejoined his passengers, and they sat in terrified discomfort, waiting. A car went by with a flashing light. Another stopped. The driver got out.

"You the one who called? Right. Follow me."

They did follow, only half a mile to the place where the first car flashed its light at the edge of the abyss, its uniformed driver and passenger standing next to the rabbi, who was rocking back and forth in rapidly muttered prayer while they stared downward into nothing.

Eventually, after lengthy radio conversations with his headquarters, the officer asked the rabbi where his group was staying and suggested they return there.

"There's no alternate road we can take to the Wall? These people have come a long way," the rabbi objected, eyes unfocused.

"It wouldn't matter if there were an alternate road," said the officer. "There's no Wall. The Old City's gone. All of it."

"But . . . but my son, his family . . . they live there!"

Lived there, silently amended the officer, taking the old man by the arm.

For the police and the army, which was immediately called out, the rest of the night, what little there was of it, was spent putting up traffic barriers. Skid marks extending across the edge indicated the barriers came too late for some travelers.

16
afghanistan

Ben Shadouf was awakened by the call to prayer. He had overslept, not that he needed to answer to anyone for his sleeping time, merely that he had slept badly early in the night. Yesterday he had taken his concerns about Afaya to his friend, his commander, Mustapha ibn Daud, and Mustapha had told him not to take Afaya to the clinic. She would live, said Mustapha, or she would die, and in either case, that was the will of Allah.

"I feel I am killing her," Ben Shadouf had cried. "She went to the clinic before. They helped her."

"Only to confuse you, my friend. That is their purpose, these unbelievers. They will use anything to weaken your faith. They will use your sorrow for a wife. Your pity for a child. You must harden yourself like iron that is quenched and beaten in the fires of adversity. If our wives or children die, they die, but while they live they are pure. If we die, we die, but while we live, we are faithful!"

Ben Shadouf came home angry. He was glad Afaya was not where he would encounter her. He did not want to see her face.

He listened, but did not hear her. No cough. No footsteps. He heard the children, on the roof, playing a singing game. It would be safe to rise, to leave the house and find a meal in the town. Perhaps it would be as well not to come home for a while. He could ask his neighbor to have his wife check on Afaya from time to time. If she died or was unable to get out of bed, the children could be taken somewhere else. Luckily, they were still tiny. Nowhere near an age when they would need to be watched to be sure they did not let anyone see them.

He got out of bed, washed his face and hands, and dressed himself. He visited the latrine behind the house, outside the courtyard. He did not hear a sound. Then, an upper window over the courtyard opened, its hinge screeching, and a woman leaned out. He thought it was a woman only because she did not wear a man's headdress, though she, or it, could as well be a man. A very old, very ugly man, with a huge, curving nose and a great box of a chin dotted with brown, hairy moles.

The person leaned farther, pouring water on a plant that sat on the ledge beneath the window, and as the person leaned out, Ben Shadouf saw that he, it, was wearing Afaya's garments. But it was not Afaya. Its head was bald and wrinkled. It was hideous. He stared upward unbelieving!

The creature saw him and smiled, opened its horrid mouth and spoke in Afaya's voice!

"Welcome, husband. I feel somewhat better today. Perhaps you can take me to the market, to buy supplies. Perhaps you can . . ."

He heard no more. His own scream of rage and terror covered anything else this horrid being had to say in Afaya's voice. Every word in Afaya's voice!

His rage and disgust carried him in a fury to the stairs. The being was still in the room where he had seen it, her, him, the afrit, the genie, the demon who had taken his wife.

"Where is Afaya?" he cried.

"I am here," she said, in Afaya's voice, turning to give him a welcoming and hideous smile. She came toward him, her arms wide, and he lifted his staff to split the ugly bald skull, but the blow never landed. Instead, he felt the blow he aimed at her strike himself, riving his head so the blood ran across his eyes and he fell senseless at her feet.

17
benita

THURSDAY

Despite her anger, partly at Carlos, mostly at herself, Benita had fallen asleep almost immediately. She did not waken until about eight on Thursday morning, when the phone rang.

The voice was Chiddy's. "Are you all right, Benita?"

She nodded, then realized Chiddy couldn't see the nod. "Yes," she said.

"You were unhappy last night. You don't sound happy now."

She didn't mean to talk about Carlos, but the words spilled out. "My son, Carlos. He's a very manipulative person. I hoped when he went away to school, he'd grow out of it. But he's still doing it. I wish he'd just . . . grow up and let me alone."

"This wish is not improper. Does your husband share this characteristic of manipulating?"

She thought about it. "Well, yes. Until I caught onto it." Which had only taken—what? A lifetime?

Chiddy sighed. "It is one of the tragedies of your biology, Benita. Your men and women are often insufficiently selective in the mating practices. We have noted you people do

not consider that your children will have the worst traits of
either parent, often to a great degree. In our opinion, women
in your world who are under the age of thirty and who wish
to mate should require the approval of a board of qualified
geneticists and behaviorists. Alas, that is unlikely to happen.
Is that all you were upset about?"

His tone made her choke. It was so sympathetic and yet
so very superior and above it all. "Well, General McVane
didn't keep his word to us about not telling anyone. But the
First Lady was very kind, and I don't think the media found
out who I am."

"Speaking from what we have seen of your people, they
will find out, sooner or later. Your congressman has allowed
himself to be persuaded by McVane and others. They already know who you are. They do not know where you are,
however, which we will try to keep private for the time
being."

"Why do reporters have to dig into people's privacy?" she
fumed.

"Communication is much like sex."

This set her back. "I don't understand . . ."

A chuckle. "Being celibate is often wise and prudent. People know this, but the inborn drive to reproduce makes their
organs wag. Keeping silent is often wise and prudent. People know this, also, but the drive to question and tell makes
their tongues wag. Sex spreads genetic material, good and
bad; prying spreads information, true and false; natural selection takes over and both ethical failings contribute to
continuing evolution."

She laughed. "I wish there were ways to do it that were
less troublesome. Did you know that the Secretary of State
is going to fix up my new apartment for me? She says to save
time, but I imagine it's to keep an eye on me."

"Interesting," said Chiddy.

"So, maybe I'll see you after I move in?"

"You will, yes. Have you any questions?"

"I have some, yes. One is . . . I didn't realize you were depending on me to go on working with you, and I've told
Simon I will work for him. I owe him my full-time effort, you

know. If he's paying me, it wouldn't be ethical not to give him a fair day's work."

"What you do for us will be very simple, Benita. It will take very little time."

"And . . . the money you gave me. I really didn't need all that. I should give the rest of it back."

"That is our standard payment for the kind of service you will be rendering. It doesn't obligate you to do anything for us that your conscience finds abhorrent."

"In that case, well, thank you."

"No thanks needed. Do you have another question?"

"I don't really understand just what the requirements are that we humans have to meet in order to be members of your Confederation. Since I'm the intermediary, I ought to understand them, shouldn't I?"

"Yes, you should. The preliminary requirement is Neighborliness, as we have said. Learning to get along together without blowing up people or shooting children from cars or oppressing people because of perceived dissimilarities to oneself. Once that has been achieved, there are only a few formalities. First, we require a volunteer liaison person from your planet, someone who must be intimately connected to the process of mutuality. We call this person the Link. We will also need a profile person to travel among our various worlds while the members of the Confederation establish biological parameters for your race. This person, we call the Pattern."

"Is that it?"

"Become neighborly, give us a Link and a Pattern, then a short probationary period, and that's it. Does that answer your question."

She wasn't satisfied, but she didn't know what would be more satisfying. "Yes, I think so. Thank you."

"Thank you, Benita. We will be in touch."

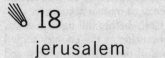

18
jerusalem

In Israel, first light had brought helicopter flights over the city of Jerusalem. The mile-deep hole followed the serrated polygon of the old city walls. Vanished were the Temple Mount, the Dome of the Rock, El Aqsa Mosque, the Church of the Holy Sepulchre, the Via Dolorosa. Gone were the Citadel and the Antonia Fortress, the Zion Gate, the Jaffa Gate. Gone was the entire Old City: Arab Quarter, Jewish Quarter, Armenians, Greek Orthodox, odds and ends of varietal Christians and all.

When the sun got high enough to reflect off the inside lip of the chasm, large gold letters appeared just below the western edge in Hebrew, Latin, Greek, and Arabic. Further examination found other languages, ancient and modern, extending along the north and eastern sides. At midmorning, former residents of the Old City were seen approaching the city from various directions, on foot, most in their bed clothes. No one was hurt, though many were thirsty and hungry, and all said they'd left others out in the desert or along the roads or in the smaller towns or villages in which they themselves had wakened. The International Red Cross/Red Crescent arrived a few hours later, though the

Israeli army had already set up a tent city for the displaced, divided by hastily erected barriers into areas for various religious or ethnic groups who might otherwise be expected to fall upon one another in a frenzy of mutual accusation.

The news was carried by CNN before full light, and was reprised every quarter hour thereafter as the country turned toward the sun, allowing more of the chasm's southern and then eastern faces to be illuminated. As each new language appeared, an appropriate scholar was summoned to the CNN newsroom to pontificate upon the meaning of the words, though in each case the meaning was the same, whether in Latin, Coptic, Armenian, Aramaic, or various forms of ancient or modern Hebrew or Greek: "Jerusalem was to be a city of holy peace. Without peace, it is not to be."

When telescopes were brought and focused far down on the walls, the message was seen to have been augmented with another phrase, also in multiple languages. "Next time, the hole will be bigger."

 19

washington

In the U.S., in the office of the president, that gentleman was closeted with a number of his close advisors, all of them trying to figure out what to say or, indeed, whether it was appropriate to say anything except "Wow," or something sanctimonious starting with the words, "Today God has seen fit to remind us . . ."

"That idiot McVane would ask them to prove it!" snarled the Secretary of State, who was in a waspish mood. She had slept badly and had already spent a good part of the morning alternately assuring the Israeli Prime Minister, the Vatican, the Eastern Orthodox Church, a handful of American evangelicals and charismatics, and the Palestinian Ambassador that no, the U.S. had no weapons advanced enough to have dug that hole without damaging a single citizen. A big hole, yes, maybe, but one that cleanly followed ancient city walls and didn't kill so much as a sparrow, no. She had pointed out that even the cars that had gone over the brink had been found in the desert, their occupants asleep but unharmed. Ethical behavior, she had said repeatedly, was often abridged by the possible, and the U.S. lacked the know-how to behave in such an ethical manner.

"You think the ETs did this?" asked the president. "You're sure?"

"Of course they did it," the SOS snarled once more. "They asked us, remember? At dinner. What some of our problems were."

"They asked me during our meeting, too. I mentioned the Middle East."

"They asked about Afghanistan, and your wife mentioned women's rights in that context. I mentioned the fact that in Africa national boundaries were established by colonial powers without taking tribalism into account . . ."

"So, what do we expect to happen next?" he grated. "All the women disappear? All the tribes in Africa?"

"I don't know," she said.

"You're afraid to know," he said, biting his lip. "So am I."

She muttered, "I don't suppose we could just ask them to go home?"

He laughed, without humor. "They warned us not even to think about that. They don't go home. Not until they're finished or they give up."

JERUSALEM DISAPPEARS
WORLD WONDERS AT ACT OF GOD

MYSTERIOUS MESSAGES CONFOUND SCIENCE
UNEARTHLY FORCES DEMAND PEACE

FUNDAMENTALISTS GREET DISAPPEARANCE
AS OVERTURE TO LAST DAYS

JERUSALEM TRANSPORTED TO HEAVEN, SAYS FALWELL
HOLY CITY TO RETURN AFTER ANTICHRIST

THOUSANDS GATHER TO AWAIT SECOND COMING
BAPTISTS CROWD SOUTHERN MOUNTAINTOPS

RUMORS OF PLAGUE IN AFGHANISTAN
KABUL REQUESTS AID FROM CDC

20

from chiddy's journal

As an athyco, it was to'eros task, that is, my task, dear Benita, to design remedies for societies, including our own, that did not work well. Yes, Benita, sometimes even our own society does not work as well as it should. I find comfort in this, when I am confronted with some problem difficult of solution. Patience, I say to myself. Even we have problems we have not put an end to.

After spending several years both reading case histories of other athyci who had worked in prior centuries and solving thought problems under the guidance of my mentor, ton was sent to the village of Quo-Tem to solve a problem that had come up in recent years. It was in Quo-Tem that ton first met the person who was to be to'eros long-term workmate, Vess. Of course, no one in the village called ais Vess. In the village Vess and Chiddy were called Aisos Torsummi or Aisos Torsum. Earthlings would say, Their Excellencies or His Excellency or even, if speaking directly to us, Your Excellency, though our language does not have an easy equivalent to "you." In our society such directness is considered rude. Among intimates and when referring to self, we use the first level undifferentiated, casteless pronouns we learned as children, with a mouthpart gesture to indicate whether we refer to self or other. *Ton*, I or you. *To'er*, me or you. *To'eros*, mine or yours. *Ton'i*, we or you. *To'eri*, us or you. *To'erosi*, our or your. In speaking to others, especially to groups of differing castes, we speak always of "one," using the pronoun of the highest caste present. *Ke* (or li or ai) *afar*. One serves. *Ker* (or lic, or ais) *afari*. Serve it to one. *Keros* (or licos or aisos) *ca fi*. It is one's.

Since this document is intended for you, dear Benita, I continue the struggle to put it in your words. *Ça fi shunus to'erosi afarim.* It is our joy to serve.

Vess and *I* were soon on a confidential basis, Chiddy and Vess, to'eri, new athyci. The problem in Quo-Tem, which was a farming community, mostly campesi, had to do with the communal lands on which the people grazed the village livestock. Over the past century, the number of persons in the town had increased, the herds had likewise increased, and the public lands could no longer support the number of beasts. Riverbanks were destroyed, the plants that held the soil were killed, good soil was being washed downstream, into other communities.

In all problems, athyci are required to keep the great fundamental truths in mind. Some of these are as follows: Resources are finite. Some things are not renewable. Intelligent creatures must give way to irreplaceable achievements. One cannot explain to a tree or a forest that it must either grow without water or move to another place, but one can explain to a person that it must go somewhere else, where water is available. As we say, "The health of a forest outweighs both the tears of a nootch and the plaint of an athyco." After all, it may take half a millennium or more to achieve similar trees while it would take only a few decades to achieve a new nootch or a new athyco. Of course, it is easier for us than for your governing bodies since we do not consider our temporary inconvenience as superior to the needs of permanently essential forests and seas. We are taught to think in many lifetimes, not only in the short span of our own. This kind of thinking is, in your language, Darwinian, since only people who think this way will survive in the long run. The fact that your Madagascar and your Brazil and several of your African countries will be incapable of supporting either flora or fauna within thirty years are cases in point.

On Quo-Tem we first had to determine why the number of persons had increased. We have a saying, "False reasons grow like weeds." It is true. There are as many false reasons as there are neurons to fire them off, but problems cannot be solved using false reasons. Real reasons are of utmost importance. We looked at the data. Years before, several of the undifferentiated young of Quo-Tem had been selected as inceptors more or less simultaneously. This was a statistical blip, but such things happen. As is the way with inceptors, ke'i had accumulated receptors, some from Quo-Tem and some from outside, three here, four there, and the receptors had recruited nootchi for the creating of young. The young had grown, and while some had been selected out into other areas, more had returned to the village, mostly those we call the glusi, the not-very-able-ones, the perpetually undifferentiated, the ones who do not come to mind when one gives thanks.

Return to one's ancestral place is a right we try very hard to guarantee, but another of our immutable facts is: Managers always recruit the top layers among persons, for such persons will reflect well upon them, and the lower one's ability, the higher the chance one will be left where one is. In time, therefore, Quo-Tem had grown top heavy with glusi. While glusi eat no more and take no more space than others, they use up space and resources without regenerating them. They tend to destroy in that way, by sucking energy, or through undirected energy of their own, or through ineptitude or even, sometimes, malice. There is no cure for a glut of glusi except not to beget them in the first place, but by the time one knows one has a glut, it is too late.

The moment that the people-load had gone beyond the numbers allowed to the village, the strain should have been brought to the attention of the athyci. Why had that not happened? Because the former recording-campes responsible for assembling and transmitting information, a very able person, had died at that time, and ke had not been replaced.

No one had gone to the bureau of selectors and told lic'i a recording-campes was needed. So, the imbalance had gone on and gone on, and now the situation was at a point where no acceptable solution was possible. No matter what Vess and I did, persons would be greatly disturbed, even angry, both the innocent and the persons responsible.

We faced this anger resolutely. Panel number seven of the Fresco, *The Adoration*, is an inspiration in such times. In it, Mengantowhai, who has made massive changes in the lives of the Jaupati in order to bring them peace, is hailed by them as their savior. I always think of this when I am required to bring trouble or pain to our people. In the end, I say, they will be thankful for it.

We needed to know whether the glut of glusi was achieved out of ignorance or whether it had been deliberate. We started our inquiry with the campesi. Unbelievably, after millennia of refinement in our methods, some campesi still end up believing they have not been properly selected; some still resent having been selected at all! Even today we may find one who croaks like a pfluggi and wants to be a singer. Or one who has all the grace of a puyox but wants to dance. Or another one, who cannot add up the same figures twice with the same answer, who wants to be a proffe, what you call an engineer! I feel gratitude that such longings are rare. Though most campesi require only slight adjusting to be content, for a few there is no soothing. We have a saying, "There is no misery like misdreaming." Or, as earthlings might say, "No tragedy like false ambition."

It would be necessary, we found, to cut the village population by about a third, to reduce grazing on the lands by more than half for a lengthy period, and to undertake strenuous regeneration of the lands, which would require the labor of all campesi in Quo-Tem for some time. This meant the other categories who remained would have to do their own chores for a time, which is proper. We are taught, "An inescapable burden must fall equally upon all castes."

As athyci, it was our job to choose who would stay and who would go. The first task was to message the need everywhere, at first to the places of that world, then, if necessary, to other settled worlds. So many inceptors, so many receptors, so many nootchi, so many undifferentiated ones, so many campesi, all to find places for. When the returns came in, we began the allocation. Receptors and associated nootchi to the same places, when possible. If not possible, then interviews with them to assess their relative willingness to separate. Some receptors, luckily, were willing to be separated, and others, who had reached or exceeded the number of young required of them, wanted to be reselected to nonreceptor caste.

Few of the nootchi and none of the inceptors wanted to be reselected. This is most often true of inceptors. Their lives are centered on gratifying their mating organ to the extent they cannot even visualize doing something else. It was at this juncture we found that several of the inceptors were closely related, that several of them shared the same cell parents, even the same nootch!

This explained everything! While organ gratification comes first with inceptors, progeny pride comes second! Inceptors who have the same lineage have been known to engage in progeny *competition*, even when, as was the case here, the progeny were not of very high quality. When we noticed this, we marked all the related inceptors for retirement therapy.

We then moved on to the undifferentiated ones, those not yet twelve. Undifferentiated ones are easiest. So long as they have a good nootch, they are usually content. We identified all those procreated by the inceptors in question and tagged them in the records as nonbreeder stock, even if they showed great aptitude for the task. It is an unfortunate truth that inceptors and receptors of very little brain are often very skilled with the generative organ and emit very strong mating smells. That is one of the reasons our selectors must be extremely careful in their choices. It is rather like politics or policing: those who most enjoy the work are often those who should not be doing it!

When we were finished, we had retired or allocated all but the leftover campesi, mostly old ones or glusi, the offspring of the inceptors we had already tagged. As earthlings would say, the bottom of the barrel. A few were old enough to refer to the farms for the aged, but several had to be sent to the sleep gardens. Though we do not publicize these arrangements, persons may sleep in the gardens up to one hundred years, and this is usually more than adequate time to find places even for supernumerary campesi. The settlement of new planets requires many such, and we Pistach are usually settling somewhere.

When Vess and I had finished, we knew that unhappiness and trauma had been minimized to the extent possible. Still, we felt the strain of that which remained! The pride of the inceptors had been unavoidably damaged and a number of the nootchi had been aggrieved. Nootchi grow very attached to their home place, and it is hard for them to move. They have spent years weaving a village, planning it, decorating it with gardens, laying out its walks and pretty-places and play areas for the young. Nootchi are the cement of a community, they stick fast, and it is like flaying a fluggle to tug them away.

In any case, persons from all four village categories came to us, as we knew they would, to complain. It was during our last formal session. They bowed, calling us Aisos Torsummi. They presented their petition and asked redress of grievance. We inquired whether they wanted vengeance, and they affirmed this. Such an imbalance was someone's fault; their grief demanded redress. While we knew the real trouble had started with the selectors who had sent too many inceptors of the same, faulty lineage back to this village, we did not say so, for the selectors were not answerable to people below them in caste. We would take care of that ourselves.

Nonetheless, we told the villagers a truth: that the trouble began when the recording-campes died. The inceptor who was then the village master had the duty of requesting a new recording-campes. Ke had not done so. That inceptor was still alive, and keros name was such and such, and the aggrieved had our permission to kill ker, if they wished, though we advised them it would be courteous to listen first to keros explanation.

Since inceptor in question had been retired to an aged persons' farm at some distance, vengeance would require the aggrieved to make a lengthy trip. Serially, the aggrieved ones declaimed their intention of doing so, and we made note of their intentions so they would have no trouble getting travel permission. Their actually going to the aged persons' farm was unlikely. Since many of those in the group would be sent to their new homes on the following day, thus separating them from one another, it was doubtful they would ever get around to confronting the old inceptor. Grievance and anger need a certain heat of immediacy and a constant draft of rhetoric to keep them burning. This is why humans who explain their anger to counselors and psychologists go on being angry; they fan their anger with a constant hurricane of reminiscence. Separating those who are aggrieved is like raking out a fire, a good way of cooling things down, while the process of formulating their grievance served both to focus and to ameliorate their feelings. Knowing who was to blame, they would not waste energy on other targets.

Our last few hours on Quo-Tem were spent with the most able campesi, those who would remain, and the current village manager who was, luckily, a person of some administrative talent, though he had not had the will or the authority to do what we had done. Village managers live by the will of the village, and villages make painful changes only when they are in agony. When agony is not present, no matter how imminent it looms, painful change must come from outside. This is a truth. We detailed the measures that would be necessary to restore the land to health and we swore ker'i to the task, however long it might take. The few inceptors who were left in the village were forbidden to initiate breeding until the task was done, and the village master was given the necessary medications to quell all mating odors and assure compliance. As a parting gift, we gave the village, as was customary, worms from our own home lands, thus tying their fate to ours and our future to theirs. We have a saying, "Where one lives, all live; where one suffers, all suffer." *One*, in our language, includes all living things. In your language someone has said, "No man is an island," which encompasses the concept but which, by mentioning only mankind, misses the point.

The task was completed when ton'i, Vess and Chiddy, met with the selector who had sent the faulty inceptors to Quo-Tem. Before going there, we reviewed the standards for selection and found that tabulation of current breeders by place and identity of parent was neither required for the record, nor easily derived therefrom. We advised the selector that this lack had resulted in unnecessary trauma and dislocation, that we recommended a warning system be initiated to identify such blips in the future. We told lic that the recommendation had already gone to the Bureau of Selectors. The selector thanked to'eri for to'erosi diligence, and also for to'erosi recommendation that the selector not be mercifully disposed of, inasmuch as the mistake could not have been easily avoided.

Sometimes mistakes are not foreseeable. You, dearest Benita, made a mistake in selecting the inceptor you did. Still, it was not one you could easily avoid. Your race is thrust into sexual behaviors so young! Far too young. Until recent generations, your young persons did not mature so early. You are so well fed, so overexposed to chemicals that act upon you like fertilizers, you sprout up like weeds! We speak of this, Vess and I. He admires you, though he does not have for you the tenderness that I do. Where does it come from, this tenderness? I do not know. I have felt it, now and then, for things, sometimes, for places, for ideas. You are the first other I have felt it for. The feeling is very precious to me.

21

mrs. chad riley

On Thursday morning, Mrs. Chad Riley, the former Merilu McElton, had returned with sons Jason and Jeremy to the family home in Georgetown, intending to stay only long enough to pack their clothing and the boys' toys. Thirty-six hours in a huddle with her mother had set in concrete her desire to leave Washington. Since she and the boys had luxuriated in room service meals in the suite between visits to the pool, the spa, and the beauty shop, and since they had not ordered a paper or looked at anything on TV but the cartoon and shopping channels, Merilu was still unaware of the events that had much of the world either dumb with astonishment or loud with accusation.

While she was packing, however, she switched on the TV and was surprised to find she could get nothing but news. Submitting to the inevitable, the fact that something extraordinary had happened eventually penetrated her self-absorbtion. Putting two and two together to make five and a half, Merilu decided the FBI had had something to do with it, and that Chad was probably in it up to his neck, which was why he had been so distant lately. At that point, she slid the half-packed suitcases under the bed and called her mother.

"Before I go back to Missoula with you, Mom, I got to give him a chance. I think he's in trouble!" A not unpraiseworthy part of Merilu's credo was that women stood by their men when the men were in trouble.

"Now you're sure, honey-bun? You don't know what he's been up to. He could have a woman on the side, you know. He could be mixed up in drugs. The FBI, they must come upon a pile of drugs, doing the work they do. Or money. Gracious, isn't a day we don't read about laundering money, though I've never been able to figure out why it's against the law. Ever since I found out it was illegal, I've just ironed mine and Daddy's. Mostly for the collection plate, you know. Just a little swipe with a hot iron will get rid of most germs, and it flattens the bills out nice, too. Sometimes I press it between two pieces of wax p—"

Her daughter interrupted, "Mom, have you seen the TV?"

"Why, no, dear. I've just been sitting here having a nice manicure and pedicure. Is there something special on?"

"You better turn on the TV. I mean, it makes me think probably Chad isn't up to any of the things you mentioned. It's something else. Something worse. Chad probably wanted to talk to me about this the whole time, and he just couldn't. Chad's going to thank me for giving him a chance to get outta this town. When people find out what his FBI's been up to, he'll wish he'd left a long time ago."

Merilu then called Chad's office, to be told by the receptionist that he was in a meeting and couldn't be disturbed. Two subsequent calls brought the same reply. Merilu nodded wisely each time. She bet he was in a meeting, all right. Everybody in the world would be having meetings, not that it'd do them any good!

Came suppertime, Merilu fed the boys, read to them for a while, then put them to bed. She bathed in scented bath foam, did her hair the way Chad liked it, and pulled the suitcase from under the bed in order to retrieve the negligee set he'd given her for their last anniversary. At nine o'clock, she was gorgeous. At eleven, she took the latest Danielle Steel to bed with her. At midnight, she took off her eye makeup and the peignoir and made herself a milk punch. At one o'clock on Friday morning she turned off the light.

At three, when Chad tiptoed in and began moseying around in the bedroom, opening doors and drawers, she came alert with astonishing speed, switched on the light, and immediately grasped at the idea that had floated to the top while she was dozing.

"Chad! I've been talking to Momma, and I've decided if you won't transfer to Missoula, I'm taking the boys and going without you."

Though she had intended this threat to make him think about things, he turned in her direction as though he hadn't really heard her, his eyes fixed and concentrated on something in the far away. "Good idea, honey," he said in a distant voice with a weird reverberation in it, almost like an echo. "They won't let me go right now, of course. Not that I'd want to until we find out what the hell is going on. But your getting away right now, yes, that's a really good idea. This city's going to come apart."

Mouth open, shocked into momentary silence, she watched as he continued doing what he'd been doing when she turned the light on. Packing an overnight bag. In Merilu's mental attic, the idea of Jerusalem and Washington coming apart and Chad acting weird began to resonate. It's the end of the world, she thought. That's why all this is happening. And she hadn't been to church in months.

He snapped the case shut, took it in one hand, and came to give her a perfunctory kiss on the cheek.

"I don't know when I'll get back here. Be sure to lock up when you leave. Tell your mom and daddy hello for me. I'll be in touch."

He threw her a bonus kiss and was out the door. A moment later she heard the front door slam, the car start up and drive away. Only then did her waking mind remember its earlier preoccupation. Chad hadn't acted like a man who was involved. He acted like a man who was absolutely in the dark and almost afraid to know what was going on.

22

bert shipton

Late Friday morning, a guard rattled the bars of Bert's cell and told him he had a visitor.

"That'd be my wife," opined Bert, with obvious relief. Good old Benita. You had to give her credit, by God. She was a good old girl.

"Not unless she has a bigger mustache than my wife," said the guard, unlocking the cell and standing aside. He and Bert knew one another in the relationship of miscreant and warder, one that had been renewed periodically over the last several years. "I've met Benita, and this guy's not her."

Bert, confused, shambled after the guard into the visitors' room where he took a seat opposite a stiffly upright man garbed in a three-piece suit and an air of unassailable rectitude.

"Bert Shipton?"

"Yeah."

"Mr. Shipton, my name is Prentice Arthur. I'm with one of the national security agencies, and I flew in this morning particularly to talk to you. We've just recently become aware that your wife has become involved with some very . . . well, they're foreigners, actually, people who may be very dangerous. I doubt very much she even realizes what trouble they may cause, but we're very worried about her. If you can tell us how to reach her—just so we can protect her—we'd be glad to offer you some help in your present situation."

"I don't know where she is," Bert responded in a guarded voice. "She left last Saturday. Left me a note. Said she'd be in touch later."

Arthur nodded. "We're aware you don't know where she is right now, but you may be able to help us find her. We'd be happy to help you out with your bail, if you'd like to assist us."

"Bail?" He thought about this long enough to flavor it with his usual bias. "Well, if you'd like to include a little something for my time and effort, I might be able to help you."

His mustache hiding a lip sneeringly lifted at one corner, the visitor said, "Of course. A hundred a day for your trouble."

Bert smiled, disclosing teeth evenly coated with ocherous velour. "Happy to be of help to my country," he said, puffing a miasma into his visitor's face.

"We'll take care of it," said Arthur, not breathing as he turned his face aside. "Here's my card. We'll call you at your home tonight."

"Yeah, sure," said Bert, with another smile, from which his visitor hastily averted his eyes. "I hate to mention it, but I'm . . . a little short right now. And since my car's . . . out of commission, I'll need a little cash to get home."

"I'll leave some money with the people up front." The visitor rose and left, while Bert watched him every step of the way. So little old holy-cow Benita was in trouble! Benita was never in trouble. With some effort, he focused on the card which gave him no information except the name, Prentice Arthur, Security and, in the lower left corner, an Albuquerque phone number. Now why in hell did a national security suit have a local number?

Half an hour later, supplied with a hundred dollars in twenties, Bert headed unerringly for the nearest bar. When he soared out, two hours later, who should he run into but one of those fags his wife worked for.

"Good afternoon, Bert," this person said. "I got a postcard

from Benita today. Seems she's taken a new job in Denver.
We'll miss her. Nice to see you. Bye." The person, conscious
of being watched, then walked to the corner, and when
around the corner and unobserved, vanished.

Bert hadn't been able to bring the face quite into focus.
Which one was it? Was it Goose or was it the other one?
Never mind which one. So she was in Denver. Sure, that
made sense. Not too far away to take the bus. When he'd
talked to Carlos this morning, Carlos said she'd taken a bus
wherever she was. Bookstore job made sense, too, sure, big
city like that had lots of bookstores. And Carlos said it had
to be someplace on mountain time.

Well, so there he was, he already had it half figured out!
He sure as hell wasn't going to tell Mr. What's-his-name
about Denver, though. Not when they were paying him a
hundred a day to find her. Wait a week. String him along. A
hundred a day was too good to pass up.

Across the street, in the front seat of a large van, Prentice
Arthur asked, "Dink, who's he talking to?"

Dink flipped through a notebook. "Looks like the guy
that runs the bookstore where the target used to work. Rene
Guselier, usually called Goose."

"Did you pick up the conversation?" asked Arthur, over
his shoulder.

"Got it," said a disembodied voice from the back of the
van. "The woman's got a job in Denver."

"He didn't say what kind of job?"

"No mention. Wouldn't it be another bookstore? That's
the only place she's ever worked. How many can there be?
Denver's a sports town, isn't it? Sports fans don't read, do
they?"

"Their wives probably do," said Arthur. "Since they have
a great deal of time on their hands. Get us on the next plane
to Denver."

As the car pulled away, the voice asked, "Didn't you tell
the guy you'd meet him this evening?"

Prentice Arthur shook his head. "Look at him! By evening
he won't be in condition to meet anyone. It's only a two-
hour flight if we have to come back to pick him up."

"Morse still wants the family?"

"Well, before I left Washington, I managed to convince him that since he really wants the woman, the man and the kids will be more use to us helping find her than they will be locked up somewhere. The way Morse wants to disappear people left and right, you'd think this was Argentina!"

While the men in suits were on their way to the airport, the subject of their surveillance managed to locate a cab, more by luck than effort, and went home, arriving there at five. It was an hour earlier in California, he told himself foggily. Carlos would be home, but Angelica wouldn't. Good time to call.

The phone rang a dozen times before Carlos answered. "Yeah."

"Hiya Carlos. How's everthing?"

"Dad? Are you out of jail?"

"I am oh-you-tee out. This guy from some federal office, he bailed me out. He says your mom's been makin some . . . dangerous friends. That's a fuckin kick, huh? Mama moocow, with dangerous friends."

"What are you talking about, dangerous friends? She's got a job in Denver."

"I know that. How did you know?"

"I figured it out. She said she took a bus, and she was on Mountain Time, so I figured Denver. You know, big city, lots of places to work. Then I ran into Mr. Marsh, Walter Marsh, on my way home this afternoon. Funny thing, there he was, right in front of me when I came out of the union. He said he was in town at a booksellers' convention. Him and Goose got a postcard from her. From Denver. After he left, I thought, wow, maybe he has her address, but when I went chasing after him, I couldn't find him."

" . . . sright. S'what the other one said. Postcard from Denver. So, anyhow, the guy from the whatever it is, he bailed me out. I'm gonna help find her." He giggled. "Not too fast. They got me on the payroll, so not too fast. If they call you, you don't know. They'll pay you, f'you play it right."

"Right, Dad. Thanks for the tip. Now you'd better have a nap."

"Right. Right." He hung up and staggered off to the bedroom. Funny. Usually beers didn't hit him like this. Musta been all those days without any. Out of shape, that was it. Days in jail could leave you out of shape.

And in California, Carlos hung up the phone, frowning to himself. What the hell did "dangerous friends" mean? She'd said she'd gone out to dinner the other night, with people she'd met on the bus. She'd been delayed getting back. But she'd just met those people. How could other people know she had dangerous friends if they didn't even know where she was? And where the hell had Walter Marsh disappeared to? He'd chased after him within ten seconds and the guy had just vanished!

And where could he find this guy who was willing to pay him?

23

from chiddy's journal

At one point in our careers, Vess and I were assigned to the offices of the Confederation, where we were to represent the Pistach people in working with other races. We of the Pistach have a unique place in the Confederation as we are the only race that is largely undifferentiated at birth, the only one that selects persons to perform specific functions on the basis of ability. Alas, such is not the case with certain other races, some of whose diplomats would be better employed turning compost on a swamp planet.

The variety found within the Confederation is interesting. There are, for example, the Credons, a differentiated people, though their differentiation happens before they are hatched, rather as it does to your bees and ants and termites. What they are when they are hatched is what they will continue to be: egg layer, fertilizer, light worker, heavy worker, engineer, thinker, and fighter. They have no differentiation equivalent to diplomat or representative, and they are inclined to send whomever is standing about at the time. When they send thinkers to work with us, we manage to cooperate, but when they send workers or engineers, our functioning is less felicitous. Their first question is always, "What are you for?" A question which persons of other races may find some difficulty in answering.

Another differentiated race is the Oumfuz, which is as close as we can get to pronouncing the gulp they use for a label. They are a swamp-living race, one that cannot work in dry or high-gravity situations. They are born either grubbers, workers, or reasoners, a deeply philosophical group, much concerned with the thoughts and plans of other races and how those have changed over time. The Oumfuz create no artifacts. The grubbers feed both themselves and the reasoners, whose philosophies are communicated orally to one another. In fact, the great library on Pistach-home contains the only recordings extant of Oumfuz thinking. They were crystallized by one of our explorers and are being slowly translated by a team of athyci who speak Oumfuzziza, though they admit that no Pistach can ever really understand the Oumfuz.

An interplanetary people who do not themselves build or maintain ships are the Flibotsi, a joyous winged race, not winged as we are, at intervals, depending upon our selection, but capable of flight during their entire lifetimes. Whenever I am around them, I am reminded of panel eight of the Fresco, *The Birth of Kasiwees,* for in that panel he is surrounded by little winged forms, rejoicing at his birth. So do the Flibotsi rejoice, almost constantly. They work well with swimming or flying peoples, particularly those who are not troubled by purpose. Quite frankly, the races untroubled by purpose are by far the happiest! The Flibotsi, I must confess, find the Pistach stodgy, and we, whose humor is mostly language dependent, do not much appreciate the purely physical fun of which the Flibotsi are capable, what you on Earth call slapstick.

The Thwakians are an aquatic race who build tunnel complexes beneath their seas, where they tend submarine gardens. The Vixbot are among my favorite aliens because of their choral singing, which puts that of any other race to shame—though in truth, your symphonic orchestras would be good competition for them. The Inkleozese—well, the interesting thing about the Inkleozese is that we and they descended from a common interstellar ancestor. Many of their characteristics are similar to ours. Instead of depositing their eggs in nootchi, however, they lay their eggs in the bodies of domestic animals, quodm or geplis or nadgervaks. After a lengthy parturition, about thirteen of your months, the young chew their way out of the animal, which, since the young Inkleozese secrete substances that control bleeding and stimulate healing in the host, almost always fully recovers.

The Inkleozese have an inborn love of order and correctness, and because they are an elder race, with widely recognized wisdom, the Inkleozese are our monitors. Even among the aged athyci of Pistach, the Inkleozese are recognized as having excellent though rather elucubrative ideas. Our philosophers struggle with their logic and, having done so, are amazed at the clarity and good sense of their thought. The rules of Tassifoduma were constructed largely by the Inkleozese, and they will visit us while we are with you, as the Confederation has assigned them the duty of reviewing work done between two or more races to assure compliance with Neighborliness.

The Xankatikitiki, the Fluiquosm, and the Wulivery are starfaring predators, not the only ones by far, but the only ones in this sector of the galaxy. Despite their predatory natures, they too have agreed to the principles of Tassifoduma in order to benefit from our association. They have made a treaty with us, promising not to invade or harvest from planets that are part of the Confederation or those that are being helped toward membership.

The Xankatikitiki are warriors, furry and small, about the size of your middle-large dogs, but very fierce, supplied by nature with weapons superior to those found on many technological worlds. They hunt in small packs or family groups and their manner is consistently ferocious. Whenever I meet with them, they remind me of panel eleven in the Fresco, where the fierce Pokoti attack the peaceful Jaupati.

The Fluiquosm are lone hunters. They are what you might call chameleons, so nearly invisible as to make locating them difficult. Their females have hypnotic abilities and both sexes are vampiric in nature. The Wulivery are stalkers, vast, invulnerable, and voracious.

These three races, though fearsome, have generally avoided incursions upon others. The few lapses by the Fluiquosm seem to have been spurred by curiosity, not hunger, and the Wulivery are split into so many tribes that they always have trouble with their communications, so that orders issued by their Sn'far, or Council of Elders, do not always reach the lower levels in time to avoid intrusion. Still, they are always contrite when these things happen, and we manage to work things out. I must confess, however, that the three predatory races constitute a voting bloc in the Confederation that continues to press for more freedom of action on the part of individual members. Don't you find that predators are those who most often assert absolute rights to personal freedoms?

We consider that our current rules provide freedom enough. The predatory races may not prey upon races we are helping, though their predation upon races they discover is not subject to our review. These are usually, though not always, nontechnological races or even nonintelligent ones. Even with them, the predators are required to exercise moderation and not to prey so heavily as to drive any species or its culture into total extinction. The Confederation submits to natural law in which the strong eat the weak, but it does not allow extinctions of any species. We regard those who wipe out other species as being, as you might say, the very bottom of the barrel.

24
benita

Benita had planned to spend a couple of days in delicious sloth, though her desire for rest unraveled as she watched CNN try to explain the disappearance of the Old City of Jerusalem. She knew at once who'd done it, though she had no idea why. With such an uproar going on, she thought it would probably be impolite to inquire from any of the people from Wednesday night's dinner, even Mr. Riley, and she had no way to reach the two individuals she really wanted to ask.

When she went out for lunch, there were sign carriers on the street, most of them claiming the imminent end of the world. Newspaper headlines were huge, and the stories about Jerusalem took up the first four pages of the *Washington Post*. Everyone was chattering about what it meant or who had done it, being either angry or awed or both. Benita tried to ignore it as she made a stop at the bank and went shopping for work clothes. She had to haul a saleswoman away from a group with their heads together in the corner. First things first. Until the world actually ended, people still had to go to work, and Benita had not brought enough clothing to get through a work week.

That evening the panic continued, with all the world's pundits appearing over and over, different combinations of them, most of them contradicting one another and some even contradicting what they'd said earlier in the day. Elaine Pagels was asked to comment on the happening in the light of Gnosticism. The head of Union Theological Seminary warned against nihilistic millennialism. The news covered nuts in Jerusalem, both Jewish and Islamic, who were protesting or affirming God by throwing themselves into the hole, only to turn up unhurt out in the desert a little while later. While the religious scholars were careful not to cast doubt on divine motives, the religious profiteers were soliciting money like mad so they could "carry the message of salvation in these final days." Most of the TV partisan-pundits were blaming more earthly forces. The left wingers agreed that secret research must have taken place, that secret weapons had been developed, and that the military industrial complex might be responsible, though the right wingers thought other countries had probably done it. For a wonder, nobody accused ETs, possibly out of fear of ridicule. Benita wondered how long the president could or would keep the truth under his hat.

Simon left a peremptory voicemail message at the hotel, asking her to come to the shop. When she arrived, he was obviously unnerved as he showed her upstairs to the apartment.

"These people showed up at the crack of dawn yesterday," he said in the elevator, shaking his head. "Their spokesman said they were from some Sephardic Foundation I've never heard of. They provide services for worthy Hispanics of all faiths who are, as they put it, 'Hard working and honest.' They quoted Maimonides at me. Evidently he advocated anonymity in philanthropy. Are you Jewish?"

She gaped. "Well . . . a lot of Spanish settlers in the new world were secretly Jewish, because of the Inquisition, you know. But if my family was, they kept it a secret from me."

"No lighting candles on Friday nights? No keeping two sets of dishes?"

She shook her head. Actually, Grandma had lighted candles on Friday night, and every other night. They hadn't had electricity until just a few years before she died.

Simon continued, "I just thought it might explain something. The spokesman wouldn't tell me how they found out about you, and he said you knew nothing about them, but nonetheless, the crew poured in all day yesterday, nobody would talk to me except the one older guy—who looked awfully familiar, come to think of it—and they didn't leave until dawn."

"What on earth were they doing?"

"Wait until you see!"

She smelled it first. A strong combination of new paint, new carpet and sawdust. The loft had been transformed. The ceiling had been lowered and covered with drywall dotted with recessed light fixtures. Along the line of columns, all the way to the ceiling, a substantial partition had been built that included bookshelves on the living room side as well as a built-in desk with computer terminal and modem. The bedroom had a closet and a door and both rooms were now furnished tastefully. Curtains on traverse rods covered the windows, and two colorful oriental rugs covered most of the living room floor, which had obviously been sanded and waxed. Another big rug softened the bedroom.

A washer–dryer had been installed. New light fixtures glowed discreetly. The bed was made up and covered by a colorful spread. Extra linens and towels were stacked in the cabinet. Kitchen equipment, dishes, pots and pans were on the shelves. Here and there were Mami's things. Her sewing basket. The little carved box she'd kept her few treasures in. A quilt Mami's grandmother, Benita's great-grandmother, had made. Everything had been furnished, even a large dog bed and FIDO food and water dish.

"They got everything," she said. "Except the dog."

He muttered in a dazed voice, "The guy said he had specific instructions how it was to be finished, and he told me to tell you the dog would be here as soon as you move in."

"What was this outfit called?" she asked, awed.

He pulled a scrap of paper from his breast pocket. "Fundacion Circulo del Alto Mando. He said in English it means the Brass Ring Foundation." Simon tented his eye-brows at her.

"Yes, it means that, sort of," she said, hiding her amuse-ment. It sounded like General Wallace was the alto mando, or "big brass," who had done the talking. She couldn't imag-ine General McVane making puns for her benefit.

"He said you caught the brass ring on the merry-go-round. Have you ever heard of them?"

"Never before now," she told him. "How strange. And wonderful, of course. For me."

"Well, me too. It saved me a hell of a lot of work. And money. I never knew the place could look this great. I told the guy I'd have to raise your rent, and he told me not to try it unless I wanted a great deal of trouble. When he said it, he sounded more like a . . . commanding officer than a repre-sentative of some charity. With the dark glasses and the hat pulled down, I couldn't really see who he was."

She said sympathetically, "They'd gone to so much trou-ble, I suppose they didn't want anything to spoil it."

There was no reason not to move in at once and no rea-son to go back to the hotel except to pick up her bag. Simon drove her over and waited for her. As she paid the bill, how-ever, she remembered the furniture and supplies she'd or-dered by catalogue. From a lobby pay phone she called the store and spun them a story. Family emergency. She had to go back to Colorado. Would they refund? Yes, the woman said, on nonsale items. Where would the check come from? From their warehouse complex in Atlanta, where all the computers were. Fine, said Benita. Cancel the order and re-fund what they could, please, in care of Angelica Shipton, at such-and-such an address in California.

After dropping her bags in the apartment and opening the windows to air out the fresh paint smell, she went down to the bookstore to start learning the routines. It differed from the store in Albuquerque in many details, but basically it was the same old job. She thought it would be more fun, however, since many of her pet gripes were eliminated. The computers were better, faster, and the software was easier to use. The bookkeeping system was very high tech and three-quarters automatic, and there were scanners for perpetual inventory. She had been telling Goose for years that they needed scanners. These shops even had a reorder program integrated with the inventory, one that printed out the reorder lists by jobbers for any books that had sold off the shelves within a specified period of time. All the stores were coordinated, for accounting purposes, and all the accounting was done here.

The Washington store stayed open until 7:00, to catch the afterwork shoppers and late calls or Web orders, many of them from congressional offices.

"The legislature being here, with all the lobbyists in the world hovering like bees over honey, that's where we got the name, The Literary Lobby," Simon muttered, interrupted by a huge yawn. "Sorry. I suppose I could have gone home to bed last night, but I didn't want to leave the workmen alone in the building, even with the connecting doors locked. I bunked in the office, but with this Jerusalem thing, I left the TV on in case the world ended. I didn't want to sleep through it."

"Why don't you go on home now," she suggested.

"I am. Your keys are on your desk: they're labeled. Don't unlock the outside front door until ten, Monday through Saturday. Sundays, we don't open until noon. First one in makes the coffee."

He left, locking the door behind him, and she went back through the stockroom to the elevator and up to her own apartment, where she found two dead male movie stars sitting next to one another on the couch. She screamed and her balance shifted, making her stagger.

They apologized in Chiddy and Vess's voices.

She couldn't name either of their likenesses, but the faces were familiar. "You startled me," she cried, collapsing on the sofa. "You know, it'd really be helpful for me if you'd settle on a shape. If you won't do that, at least give me a way to know which of you is which. You know you've got everyone in the world upset. Why are you doing it?"

"Why are we doing what?" asked the larger famous person, smiling tenderly at her. Benita had seen that smile

somewhere. Late movie. Old movie, black-and-white. She
shook her head, trying to concentrate. Not Cary Grant.
Gregory Peck? No. Who was that other one? The dark, incredibly handsome one? Like the heartthrob guy on ER,
only more so. She came to herself with a start.

"Why did you do that thing in Israel? And why are you
being men?" she cried. "I was just getting used to the Indian
ladies."

"Which question do you want answered?" asked the larger
man gradually morphing into Indira, complete with sari.

"Why Jerusalem?"

"We did it because General McVane challenged us. We
had to show your people that we have powers, that we can
do things you can't. Your president mentioned that the Middle East was a powder keg, as he put it, which makes
Jerusalem a focal point. So, we removed it. We can remove
more of the city if the modest hole we've created so far isn't
sufficient to calm the storm."

"I should think it would only agitate things," she said.

"Oh, it may. Temporarily. We'll do some suspensions, too.
That's usually quite efficacious."

"Suspensions?"

"We'll tell you when you need to know."

"What did you do with the Temple Mount?"

"It's intact. It isn't destroyed, just . . . sequestered. We put
the whole city away, for now. In another . . . realm. We can
transport the entire population of the area to that same
place. Or, we can pick and choose. All the Jews. Or all the
Palestinians. We may even give it back, in time. If the people earn it."

"Can I tell them that?"

"You may tell them anything we tell you," said Vess, in-
differently. "We're very careful about what we tell you. We
don't want to put you in the position of lying to your people, or withholding information."

She demanded, "I really need names I can use all the time.
And please warn me if you're going to be people I know are
dead!"

"Very well," said Lara, with a smile that appeared perfectly genuine. "I am always Vess, that is, the shorter or smaller one of whatever we are. The taller or larger will always be Chiddy."

The other said, "As we told you, these are childhood names, from our undifferentiated years. Your people are very undifferentiated, and for that reason, these names are probably suitable. A Chiddy is a small plant that makes people itch—you would say 'nettle,' and a Vess is an insectlike creature with beautiful wings, like a butterfly. You are now wondering whether we are really male or female, and the answer is no, we aren't."

"Chiddy, why did you scatter those people all over Israel?"

"Well, that's rather an overstatement, don't you think? None of them were farther than ten miles from the place they were taken. None of them were injured. No small children were separated from parents. People of one ethnic group were separated from other ethnic groups that might have been inimical. If we'd put them all in one place, there would have been injuries, violence." As he spoke, Chiddy gradually morphed back into the man he had appeared to be before. Tyrone Power. It came back to her. Mami, sighing over old movies of Tyrone Power.

"By the way," said Vess, also re-morphed, as he got up to look at himself in the mirror on the far wall. "When you speak to the president, tell him not to worry about Afghanistan. The effects are reversible."

She opened her mouth to ask what about Afghanistan, but Chiddy was already speaking.

"I have been eager to tell you how much we admire your race's artistic achievements! While we were looking over the problems in the Middle East, we stopped in Italy to view some of your famous artworks."

Vess enthused, "The Sistine Chapel. There are simply no words!"

Benita nodded, understandingly. She had coveted a book of Michelangelo reproductions done shortly after the ceiling was cleaned, and Goose had given it to her for a birthday present. A huge, lovely thing. She'd never taken it home, afraid it would be ruined by Bert in one of his rages.

She said, "Most people agree that the cleaning was very well done. They were able to eliminate a number of changes that other artists had made in succeeding times. In fact they discovered that one figure they'd always thought was male was, in fact, female."

Chiddy turned away from her, his face turning a curious shade of sick green, his body slightly curved, as though he had been taken by sudden nausea. He trembled. "I didn't know it had been cleaned," he murmured.

Benita reached out to him, but he gestured her away. After a moment's silence, he turned to face her, saying brightly, "Ah, Benita, ah, yes, we have an errand for you." He took several deep breaths. "We need you to deliver a message to the president."

"Wouldn't it be easier for you to just—"

Chiddy glanced at Vess with what Benita understood to be impatience.

Vess said firmly, "Benita, please. We've already said. Please concentrate your attention. Once we've made contact and proved that we exist by allowing recordings to be made, once we've proved that we have power, as I imagine we have now done, we prefer not to talk to those in authority. Those in authority *always* want to argue. Or complain. We have never approached any planet where those in power did not want to do one or both. If we speak to any person directly, or give any reason to think we might speak to people directly, everyone in the world will want an individual audience to complain about what we've done or suggest we do something else! You, on the other hand, have nothing to argue about, and they can't argue with you because you merely deliver the message. You won't know anything except what we tell you, so bothering you is pointless."

Fascinated despite herself, she asked, "What's the message?"

"Firstly: Two days from now, on Sunday night at ten P.M., Eastern Time, we will announce over national television what we are doing here and how we will proceed.

"Secondly: Once they know we are present, the populace of a planet almost always sends us messages. The messages are to be accumulated somewhere to be picked up. Someone will tell you where they are, and we will pick them up. Tell the powers that be that you will not transmit spoken messages. Even if you were constrained to do so, we would ignore them. This is to prevent your being inundated and our being influenced by discourtesies that might be blurted in anger, such as General McVane's outburst the other evening."

"Are you going to rewrite our laws or something? That could make it difficult for some people."

"No, no. Your laws will still be in effect, more or less. They'll probably be needed less as we go along, but we won't fool with them, at least not just yet. Tell the president not to worry about it. Any confusion we cause will be temporary and minimal. Tell him, also, that we will make any further announcements to the public on television, just as we will do this first time."

"At regular intervals?"

"Not necessarily, no. Whenever we have something to say. At this time, we plan only the first announcement, and it won't be lengthy."

They rose and moved together out into the hall, pausing there long enough for Chiddy to say, "When the government people fixed your apartment, they put in a great many listening and looking devices. We have made the ones in the bathroom inoperable, as we understand your culture to prefer. The others we left intact. However, they will show only you, fully clothed in whatever you choose to wear on any given day, moving about, reading, fixing food, whatever is appropriate to the hour when you are here. If you change clothes, the viewers will show you selecting the clothes and then going into the bathroom to change. Whatever you are really doing, they will not see. They are not seeing us here tonight. They are seeing you seated on the couch, reading a book.

"Whenever we ask you to transmit a message, you may say it appeared on your table, but it self-destructed once you had read it. We got that idea from an old TV show of yours."

"Strange," murmured Vess, "that we had never thought of it ourselves."

Benita murmured, "I can understand your being enamored of old *Mission Impossible* technology, but if you expect them to believe you're using me as an intermediary, you should black out this place every now and then for a few moments. If they can see me whenever I'm here, but never see you, and if all my time is accounted for, they'll get to the point where they'll suspect I'm making things up."

Chiddy paused, staring at his feet in a very humanish way.

"She's right," he said. "We have never visited a moderately advanced world before, so we must adjust our methods. Should it be blackouts, or fake visits?"

"I think blackouts," she said firmly. "I'd have to remember what was supposed to have happened during fake visits, in case they asked."

"Very well," said Chiddy. "We will black you out for a time whenever we are with you. As we speak, we are making a blacked-out time."

"Now, what about if I have visitors? If Simon comes up to my apartment, or if I invite someone in?"

"On those occasions, we will let them see what is actually happening," Chiddy said, his handsome face twisted into a slightly lecherous leer. "Unless you ask us not to."

"That facial expression should be avoided," she told him severely. "It is most insulting."

"An actor named Price did it," Chiddy replied.

"He was almost invariably the villain," cautioned Benita. "What about my phone line? Did they tap my phone?"

"Both this phone and the ones downstairs, yes. But unless it is a call we ask you to make, they will hear only innocuous conversations. You, asking if there are tickets available for the opera. You, wondering if a retailer has an item in another color. You, ordering books. It's all being done automatically. Believe us, no one will see or hear you doing anything significant or embarrassing. You may scold or bless your children, laugh or cry, or even scratch your intimate parts in private. The only calls they will actually record are the ones you make to them."

They waved, stepped into the elevator, and closed the

door. Though she listened carefully, she heard nothing on the roof, not even footsteps. Come to think of it, she hadn't even heard the elevator. She opened the elevator door and found it still on her floor, but empty. It hadn't gone anywhere. She fretted for a few moments, then went to the phone and placed the call, announcing herself as the intermediary and asking to speak to Chad Riley. Evidently the switchboard knew about her, for Mr. Riley was available at once. When she mentioned Afghanistan, he interrupted her.

"But, we've just learned about it."

"About what?" she asked.

"The plague in Afghanistan. I can't talk right now. I'll get back to you."

A surprising someone did get back to her: the First Lady, sounding equally baffled and very slightly amused. "Yes, Intermediary. We're told that all the women in Afghanistan have gone bald. Overnight. Not only that . . . the women . . . they . . ."

"What!" she demanded.

"They've grown long noses and long chins and hairy moles. They've lost half their teeth. Any of them past puberty are ugly as sin, even the young ones look like the Wicked Witch of the West, or that old hag in *Snow White*. Each one has a tattoo on her forehead in the local dialect that says, *The lustful who punish beauty would be wiser to control lust*. The Afghanis are claiming we did it!"

"Of course we didn't. The aliens did! They've fixed it so the Taliban won't have any excuse for covering them in robes and veils and locking them up all the time!"

"That's what the Secretary of State says. She says now that they're really ugly, they can go to the market or school or leave the house and get a job. Is that why you called, Intermediary? Or was there something from you know who?"

"Am I supposed to talk on the phone?"

"They tell me it's a secure line. The people who did up your living quarters saw to things."

Oh, they most certainly did, Benita commented to herself before taking a deep breath and delivering the message.

Long silence. "I'll tell . . . the president. What do you think they're going to say on TV?"

"I haven't even a hint, ma'am. They said I can say to you anything they said to me, but in this case they didn't tell me what they have in mind. They did say the Old City still exists, that they've put it on another world . . . no, in another realm, is what they said. They said they can selectively put all the Jews or all the Palestinians in that same place, if they choose, and they hinted that the people in the Middle East can get Jerusalem back if they'll quit killing each other."

"It still exists?"

"They said they didn't destroy it, just moved it. They also said to tell the president that Afghanistan is reversible, but I didn't know what they meant until now."

Long silence. Then the FL said, "The only thing I'm sure of at the moment is there has to be a press conference. This has gone way beyond keeping to ourselves. Even if McVane hadn't broken security, there are too many things happening. If they're going to broadcast on Sunday night, we have to let the public know before then. People have to know that we're not hiding anything."

"They also need to know you have little or no control over what's happening," cautioned Benita. "Otherwise, you may get blamed for it. Will the president be back in time?"

"He'll be back late tomorrow afternoon."

"Did the recordings come out? The ones you all made at the dinner?"

"You knew about that?"

"Well, they said so, remember? They said they'd allowed it."

"The recordings came out. They don't show Indira and Lara, however. They show two sort of humanoid creatures with corrugated heads and several sets of eyes. Can you explain that?"

She thought about it. "They appeared as women in saris because we could be comfortable with that. And, probably, because they're practicing being human in order to figure us out. They wouldn't want to stir up animosity against India, however, and being two women in saris could have done that. So, they were women in saris to us, but to the rest of the world they'll look like something definitely ex-traterrestrial."

"They told you this?"

"No. I'm only guessing."

"Very sensible for guessing. Have you seen them again?"

"They visited me here in the apartment." She thought about telling what they'd appeared as, then discarded the notion. Everyone was confused enough. "I can't pronounce their real names, so they're using nicknames, from when they were children. Chiddy and Vess. They've promised to stick with that."

"Well, I'd better pass all this along," murmured the FL. "Ten P.M., Eastern time, day after tomorrow. By the way, Sasquatch is en route. General Wallace had him picked up at the kennel, and he should be with you tomorrow."

Sasquatch arrived on Saturday morning. The phone rang at eight, as she was having her breakfast, and an anonymous voice said somebody was waiting with the dog at the outer door. Before she unlocked and opened it, she gave the man a good looking-over, recognizing him as one of the security people present at the dinner. There was no trouble recognizing Sasquatch. He lunged through the door when she barely opened it, jerking the man at the other end of the leash off balance so that he stumbled in after the dog.

"I'm sorry," she cried, around the mess of fur that had reared up and put his paws on her shoulders. "Are you all right?"

He picked himself up, unwinding the leash from his hand. "He's a big one. It's hard to make him go anywhere he doesn't want to, isn't it? Are you okay with him, or do you need some help?"

"I'm fine with him," she replied, easing Sasquatch into a more suitable position, with all four feet on the ground. "Thank you for bringing him."

"That's all right," he said, saluting as he backed away to let the door swing closed.

As she pulled the door shut and locked, she saw him trudging away toward a station wagon parked behind the

store. Sasquatch followed her into the elevator, albeit un-
willingly, where he howled until it reached the roof. There
she took the leash off and allowed him to move about, sniffing and marking territory on every protruding vent pipe or
aerial. He put his front feet up on the parapet, which was
quite high enough to prevent anyone falling over by accident, and looked over the edge several times, commenting
sotto voce when he saw something interesting, such as another dog. Then he went over to the big planter and had a
drink from the pan beneath the air conditioner. Someone
had hooked up the watering tubes, Benita noticed. The soil
was moist and translucent green frills were coming up very
quickly, already several inches high. Benita had been on the
roof the day before, and she hadn't noticed anything growing then.

Sasquatch went down the metal steps onto the lower roof
of the other building and went through the same routine
there. When he ran out of pee, she led him back into the elevator and took him down to the apartment, where she
showed him his bed, his food dish—already stocked with
kibble—and his water bowl.

He roved the apartment, smelling every piece of furniture
and along the edge of every rug. He found the open living
room window at the center of the row, one of the two in that
room that actually opened. Benita let the windows stand
open when it was cool and dry outside, for the illusion of
fresh air if not the reality. Sasquatch put his front feet on the
deep sill and stood for a while looking at cars moving on the
street below.

Finally, the dog found the bedroom. He ignored the
large dog bed in the corner, leaping immediately upon her
bed, where he circled twice, lay down and went to sleep.

On Saturday evening, the president held a press conference.
He said the Earth was being visited by extraterrestrials, he
explained that a recording had been made at a recent meeting, and he showed the tape, though without sound. The
president explained that neither he nor the vice president
had been able to be present at the hastily arranged affair, but

he introduced each of the participants, Mr. Riley from the FBI, representing the Attorney General; General McVane from the Pentagon; General Wallace, a well-known and loved representative of the American People; the First Lady, representing the president; the Secretary of State, representing the U.S. government; and the two envoys. Also, a woman he called, "Jane Doe, the intermediary selected by our visitors."

Someone, perhaps the ETs, had morphed Benita's face and hair on the tape, making her a blonde, twenty pounds heavier, with a different nose and mouth. Benita, while being glad she wasn't recognizable, didn't appreciate the disguise. When the tape came to the after-dinner speeches, the sound came on so everyone could hear the speeches: the FL, the SOS, the general, and then the envoys. The tape stopped moments before the visitors disappeared.

The president went on in his serious voice. "Since the dinner last Wednesday evening, we have had one further message from our visitors. Tomorrow night at ten o'clock, Washington time, seven Pacific time, the envoys will address the nation on television, explaining their intentions. Prior to that occurrence, I will be meeting with various congressional committees. I know many of you have questions. Foremost among them will no doubt be the question of whether our visitors were responsible for the recent events in Israel and Afghanistan. The intermediary tells us they say they are responsible, though they have not told her how it was done. They assure her Jerusalem was not destroyed but remains whole, elsewhere. They assure her the so called ugly-plague in Afghanistan is reversible.

"I would ask you to keep in mind that no one has died in either Israel or Afghanistan as a result of these happenings. At this point, I am as much in the dark as you are, and I cannot answer any questions. We should all be patient. We have detected no malicious intent in our visitors. We believe they are what they represent themselves to be. All questions will eventually be answered, and it would be helpful if speculation were kept to a minimum."

He started to leave, to a babble of "Mr. President, Mr.

President," stopping when one reporter shouted: "Tell us about Jane Doe, Mr. President, you can tell us that!"

He turned back to the lectern. "Jane Doe is an American housewife. She is married and has children. I cannot tell you why the extraterrestrials picked her, and she doesn't know. Both the envoys and Jane Doe herself have asked that she remain anonymous. She is not a celebrity, she has not chosen to be a public figure. As the envoys made clear, they chose someone who would have no personal agenda concerning their actions or ours, rather than some head of state or government employee or political figure who might have an ax to grind. She knows no more than we do. Think of her as a kind of telephone line between them and us. She's not responsible for what comes and goes over the line, so let us set aside our prurient, window-peeping greed for the private details of others' lives and leave her alone."

This time he departed, refusing any other questions.

"Fat chance they'll leave me alone," Benita remarked to Sasquatch. "The Sunday papers will be full of speculation, ninety-nine percent of it useless! Some politicos will say it's all fake."

The bookstore didn't open until noon on Sunday. Early in the morning, however, the *Washington Post* and the *New York Times* were delivered through a chute from the side street into the stockroom, along with half a dozen other papers from around the country. Around eight o'clock, she went down to get herself copies of several, bringing them back upstairs to read. The outcry was predictable. Her least favorite columnist's prissy face sneered above his usual malicious column, and a good many others decried the president's "unwillingness" to answer questions, raised the possibility that Jane Doe might be either the president's mistress or a foreign agent, or offered the idea that the whole thing had been done by special effects and that the president no doubt knew more than he admitted to knowing.

Various other pedants offered opinions ranging from the necessity for an immediate declaration of war against any one or several of five foreign countries to the novel idea, expressed by one fat talk show host, that the envoys were sim-

ply Democrats in ET suits, trying to distract the nation from
more pressing matters such as cutting taxes. Photo excerpts
from the dinner tape were used and reused on page after
page of the newspapers. The many-eyed monsters, however,
who should have seemed ogreish, actually appeared to be
rather loveable, like a cross between a sharpei puppy and a
jumping spider done by Disney animation artists.

The furnishings of the apartment included a television,
something Benita hadn't thought to order for herself. At a
quarter to ten that night she was poised on the edge of the
couch with Sasquatch at her feet. No one had said which
station, and she was prepared to surf them all. At five to ten,
however, the show she was watching faded away and soothing music began to play over a pattern of moving fronds, like
a forest. Every channel including the shopping and religious
networks had the same music, the same fronds. At precisely
ten o'clock, the music faded, the fronds parted to disclose
the images of Chiddy and Vess, larger and smaller, side by
side. They had the same form as in the tape of the dinner,
though now the mouths seemed to be more flexible. They
were wearing clothing that did not look at all like a uniform.
When they spoke, the lips moved the way human lips move,
and when not moving, they smiled. The skin around the
largest pairs of eyes crinkled warmly.

"We bring greetings from the people of Pistach to the people of Earth," said Chiddy. "As we have explained to your of-
ficials, we have come to assist you in meeting the prerequisites
for galactic coexistence, what we call Tassifoduma, what you
in the United States would call Being Neighborly. Tassifoduma is a prerequisite for planets wishing to join the Confederation of intelligent life-forms. We have chosen to start with
your country because it will serve as a pattern for all the rest.

"The first prerequisite of Being Neighborly is to have a
society in which almost all individuals achieve contentment,
since discontented societies often explode over their borders
into other people's space, causing great trouble and woe. You
have many examples of these disruptions in your own history. There are some such going on in your world even now,
so we need not belabor the point.

"To begin with, therefore, we will help you balance your country among its many needs and demands to provide greater comfort and contentment to all your people, greater care and attention to your environment. The first step in any project is to find out what is happening to cause woe. The second step is to discontinue the cause! To stop a flood, one must find out where the water is coming from and then shut off the water. To stop a fire, one must find out what is burning and then remove the fuel. So, we will first find out what conditions are most distressing for the people, then we will help you discontinue the conditions which lead to pain, frustration, and misery.

"Being Neighborly means not upsetting people! In order for us to avoid upsetting you, we must first determine what you value and believe and want. This week, each person over the age of eight will receive a questionnaire designed to elicit that person's beliefs and wants. This questionnaire must be completed with promptness and complete honesty. If people were to tell us untruthfully that they wanted longer working hours for less pay, and if we were to set up conditions requiring longer working hours at less pay, those people might be most distressed. Each questionnaire will be in your language, whatever your language is, just as this program is in your language, whatever your language is. If you have any difficulty, you may call the number printed at the bottom of the questionnaire and an assistant will be provided for you. When the questionnaires have been returned in the envelopes provided, we will tabulate them, and only then will we take the first step.

"We are sure you have all heard of the disappearance of Jerusalem and the change in appearance of the women of Afghanistan. A military man who met with us last Wednesday demanded proof that we could do what we said we could. While in our society such a challenge would be very impolite, we took no offense. We selected two proofs that would harm no one and have some positive value, while still being illustrative of our abilities. The more freedom given the women of Afghanistan, the prettier they will become. The more they are kept in seclusion, the uglier they will get and the worse they will smell, and lest anyone vent anger by attacking a woman or women, anyone doing so will bear the pain himself. During the past week, several attempts to stone women to death have resulted in the severe mashing and bone-breaking of the stone-throwers. They are not dead—we do not believe in causing deaths—but they will take a long painful time to heal.

"Also, the greater the peace prevailing among Israelis and Palestinians, the more likelihood that Jerusalem will be returned. A continuance of violence might lead to the expansion of the hole we have already made, or even to the removal of other sacred sites or what we call suspensions. Suspensions cause selective groups to fall into a comatose state. It is a most effective tool for peace when a whole nation is suspended for a week or a month or even a year or longer, while life goes on around them. Certain countries in your world seem intent upon interfering with others or harboring what you call terrorists. These countries are candidates for suspension, all or in part. The parents among you probably make fighting children take a time out. It is a good way to combat violence. If we had been here when Serbia began to behave so badly, we would have suspended all its people for a year, at least, and we would have found the leaders responsible for the bad behavior and shown them their errors.

"You should know that we do not require persons to agree with us. You have freedom of speech in this country, and it is valuable both to you and to us. We have no interest in hampering it. You may insult us if you wish. You may call us ugly names. We take no offense. Insults and names will not change the situation before you, which admits of only two alternatives. To be a neighbor, Earth must be a world in which children are born to peace and a place of their own, in which all are educated, in which personal freedoms and community civilities are well balanced, in which the environment is respected and unnatural conflict is restrained. Either we will be successful in helping your world achieve this, or we will leave it as it is, building a fence around it so that your people may not leave it. Many of your politicians may hope we do exactly that. Their horizons are narrow and they do not seek to widen them. Others, however, would regret the confinement. In order to do what is best, we need to know what you want.

"We thank you for your time and attention, and we return you to your usual programming."

The two disappeared, the screen blinked and became the *X-Files*. Benita reflected that the *X-Files* might find it necessary to do some retaping. The truth was no longer out there; it was right here, staring her in the face.

EARTH VISITED BY EXTRATERRESTRIALS
ALIENS APPEAR ON TELEVISION

REPUBLICANS ATTACK PRESIDENT
MORSE CLAIMS PRESIDENT WITHHELD INFORMATION

WHITE HOUSE ADMITS DELAY, FEARED HOAX
PRESIDENT DIDN'T WANT TO PANIC PUBLIC

MYSTERIOUS KILLING IN FLORIDA
BONES OF MEN FOUND TRAMPLED INTO EARTH

ACLU DECRIES ATTEMPT TO QUESTION AMERICAN PUBLIC
QUESTIONNAIRES COULD THREATEN CIVIL LIBERTIES

ALIENS ARE INSECTS, SAYS SCIENTIST
OTHERS SAY TOO MANY LEGS

AMERICAN PSYCHIATRIC ASSOCIATION CLAIMS
ETS ARE PSYCHOLOGICALLY HUMAN

NO VIOLENCE IN MIDEAST IN PAST THREE DAYS

25

from chiddy's journal

Dearest Benita, I think you may be interested in learning more of how our people deal with various difficulties, and in that regard I remember vividly the Pistach colony planet of Assurdo. Newly colonized planets seldom conform exactly to Pistach propriety. The usual pattern is one of imbalance: too few people trying to do too many things; too many undifferentiated ones selected as breeders when their dreams lie elsewhere; selectors who are, themselves, inexperienced—though at least a few experienced selectors are always provided to new colonies. After a decade or so, things flatten out, and by the time the oldest settlers are being retired, the colony has achieved good order.

On Assurdo, however, the situation was a great deal worse than mere imbalance! In the sixth year of settlement, an inceptor had gone rogue and killed several selectors, including all the experienced ones. Ke had been immediately captured and put in a sleep locker, of course, but no one had had the presence of mind to send to Pistach-home for athyci.

Too much later, arriving for what was supposed to be a routine visit, Vess and I found the settlement in chaos.

When we confronted the settlement manager, ke told us about the killings and showed us the sleep locker in which Chom, the assailant, was confined. When we reviewed the selector records, it was apparent to us that Chom should have been selected as a campes, a te. Everything about Chom screamed campes: the muscularity, the energy level, the preoccupation with present satisfactions coupled with limited ability to foresee consequences or connections, the obsessive attention to habit and routine, the suspicion of novelty.

One of the less experienced selectors, however, had selected Chom as an inceptor on the grounds of certain self-gratifying behaviors which a more experienced selector would have recognized as infantile survivals. In addition to bad selection, training for inceptorhood had been so abbreviated that none of Chom's natural territoriality had been fully suppressed.

Campesi are obsessive about their own space and their own habits. Chom had become obsessed with one particular receptor. Campesi are suspicious of novelty, which meant that Chom could not be easily diverted to other receptors. Campesi need routine and immediate satisfactions, and Chom had enjoyed the routines and satisfactions of that particular receptor and continued to plague ker even when the receptor was brooding and not in condition to receive an inceptor's attentions.

To state it simply: Chom had gone breeding-mad, and when the receptor had repulsed ter, te had invaded a meeting of the entire selectorial body at their annual Fresco Meditation breakfast, killed over half of them and then attempted to kill self.

Though the receptor in question subsequently delivered a fine egg to the nootch, ke had been gravely traumatized by the incident and requested immediate reselection as a field campes, working on one of the outlying farms. All this, and *still* no one had sent for athyci! The remaining selectors were required by the rules of settlement to do so, but they did not.

We recognize a reluctance on the part of inexperienced

persons to get athyci involved in their troubles. Inexperienced persons are often ingenuous. They have a sweet naivete about them, an innocent faith that if they can only talk long enough about problems, they will come up with solutions that will not hurt anyone. They have a penchant for committees and group discussions, for bumbling along, never wishing to offend but unable to avoid offense; always caring but never courageous; always pitying but never resolute; always doubting but stubbornly avoiding decision.

So they had done on Assurdo. In the absence of experienced mentors, the inexperienced selectors had continued doing their well-intentioned worst. There was no malice in them, though there was a good deal of mis-hoping. Mistake compounds mistake, and by the time we arrived, conditions had deteriorated into near anarchy. I reminded myself of panel four of the Fresco, *Peaceful Work*, in which the Jaupati are shown working usefully under the watchful eyes of Pistach mentors, though in the preceding panel three, *Uniting the Tribes*, the Jaupati are shown in total chaos and disarray. The situation could be fixed. It was not impossible. I told myself this, over and over.

The selectors, being young and proud and unwilling to offend, had fallen into the trap of choosing far too many specialized castes. When a selector is too sympathetic, le may overvalue the least passing interest expressed by an undifferentiated one, assuming this transitory regard is a sign of talent or affinity. If the selector is also impatient and/or overworked, the selector may neglect to observe the candidate's actual performance during the selection process, thus allowing the first impression to prevail. Commit this same error over and over for a period of several decades and anarchy results! The colony was awash in artists who did no art, sculptors who sculpted nothing, musicians who were pitch deaf, doctors who couldn't distinguish healthy persons from sick ones, much less treat the diseases. When I remember it, dear Benita, I think of your spouse and son. There were a great many Berts and Carloses in that settlement! There were even a few contempli sitting about, looking at the walls. One can't train contempli in a new colony! Contempli need advanced mentoring of very specialized types! How does one come up with the design of new nanobots or spaciotemporal diffusers by looking at walls! Oh, mathematical contempli do a lot of staring into space, I grant you—though they would rather scribble abstruse formulae on the walls than stare at them—but one cannot come up with microchem experts or morph-beam engineers in a new colony!

All these specialists were, of course, drawing their rations, keeping cozy and warm, accomplishing nothing, while the colony was desperate for ditch diggers to install the sewage system, plumbers to hook up the drains, technicians to install the hydroelectric plant which had been shipped with the settlers, and so on. Pistach systems are carefully engineered to afford gainful, useful employment for all members, even the inevitable supply of glusi (except under conditions of glusi glut, as previously mentioned) but in the colony of Assurdo, the balance had been lost and there were misassignment glusi everywhere!

What was wrong was apparent and needed no investigation, though the stench around the villages and the extent of the disorder overwhelmed us. As an immediate alleviation, Vess and I took over the work of the selectors on the grounds they had failed in their duty by not summoning us sooner. Due to the extremity of the situation, we decided to use the machines we carried on our ship. Philosophically, the Pistach are opposed to the use of machines on settlement worlds, preferring a lengthy, slow evolution of community, with its own history and culture. In this case, however, *gefissit moltplat gom,* as we say: *emergencies make their own rules.* You would say, any port in a storm. Inasmuch as the community was up to its tonal detectors in sewage, the machines were necessary to speed the drainage and alleviate the smell!

While the machines worked at that, we put the selectors through our memory drain, using a standard NB primary association identifier (Type 9Zwok) to strain childhood memories into a Tressor-Hines multibank synaptic synthesizer where they were stored while we went on to wipe all later memories clean, leaving their minds utterly blank. We then used the newest Bertrani omni-feed to restore only the childhood memories, stripped of all later associations. The former selectors were thus stopped at age twelve, when they had been undifferentiated. Then, we reselected them, most of them as campesi. Though many lacked the musculature of true campesi, with proper hormonal treatment they bulked up to a satisfactory level, and as soon as the accelerated process was complete, we set all of them to continuing the sewage system, though we pulled out any who showed managerial talent to receive further education in waste management or hydropower systems.

We then examined the records of all those misselected proffi and contempli, all those artists, sculptors, doctors and what have you, applying the Fynor-Noot allied skill analysis system. Failed sculptors, those who had actually liked stone, became masons, foundation layers, aqueduct builders. Failed artists, those who enjoyed color, became painters of rooms, houses and barns. Those who had fancied themselves doctors because of a desire to help and care for others were assigned as crèche managers, animal tenders, and the like. Most of these people did not need regression. Doing work they could succeed at would in time erase any longing for a time when things were otherwise. In very short order virtually all of them were doing well and taking pleasure in their work. Those few who fancied specialized caste for reasons of power or prestige and who might, therefore, harbor resentments and unfulfilled ambitions were treated as the selectors had been: memory removal and regression to age twelve.

This was a long, tiring process. There were fewer than a hundred to be regressed each period, but they scream so when the memories are drained, and they must be conscious for it to be done correctly, leaving their psyches intact. Both Vess and I became weary and depressed, for there was no relief in the settlement, nothing attractive on which one could rest one's eyes, nothing amusing, nothing soothing. Everything and everyone was at war with everything and everyone else. When we began, only a tiny fraction of the persons were doing work they were suited for, and even they were constantly frustrated by interdependent workers who did not function properly. Still, day by day, we pulled a bit farther out of the morass. Day by day we saw people doing work they liked and doing it well, even the regressed ones who had been reselected.

One morning, leaving the ship, I came across a small garden tended by a child who was singing a hymn to Mengantowhai as te pulled weeds from among the flowers and fed them to a nearby flock of flosti who gabbled and stretched their long mouthparts to receive a share while the flost-herd stood contentedly by with his noose. It was so . . . right! So interdependently lovely. As I gazed at child/garden/flosti, my vocal sac filled with fluid and I turned away, gargling, deeply moved. Vess patted ton'er on an appendage and uttered comfort words, I suppose the Pistach equivalent of your Earthian, "there, there." (Which, by the way, confuses us greatly. *What* is there? And why two of them?) This little garden was the first functionality, the first real sign of emerging order, the signal to bring new selectors into the mix.

By that time, as we had been on Assurdo for well over a year, a number of undifferentiated ones awaited selection. In our role as athyci, Vess and I prayed for Mengantowhai's intercession in granting us a small miracle, which was, wondrously, granted. At least a ten of the undifferentiated ones had the proper tendencies to become selectors. We doublechecked ourselves during the selection process and spent more time than usual in training. At the end of another year, Assurdo was, so to speak, on its feet. The new selectors had been shown the ugliness and disfunctionality caused by the errors of their predecessors, and they had been supervised through selection after selection, learning that they must never, never select someone for a more specialized life simply because that person wants to try it or envies the prestige of those who do it or think it might be interesting.

"Num g'klum, num b'flum, humnum te des ai," we said. "Where there is no affinity and no skill, you cannot make an ai out of a te." Your people, dear Benita, have the same saying, about the ears of swine, or pearls before pigs, or silk billfolds, or something of the kind.

All that was left for us to do was clean up the loose ends. As I've mentioned, of the people we had simply reselected without regression, virtually all had worked out well and were contented in their tasks. A few, however, who at first had seemed to be doing well had in fact had been spoiled by the earlier selection, and their moods and angers affected their work-mates adversely. By the time this was known, both Vess and I were fatigued. We did not wish to take the time for memory wipe, regression, and reselection, so we told the unhappy ones to choose between going to a long-established colony where they might return to specialized caste if they chose, or returning to Pistach-home for regression, conditioning and reselection.

Two chose the colony, so on the way home we made a detour to our detention settlement on Quirk, which was then celebrating its tricentennial. Quirk was designed to serve as a settlement for those of our people who cannot find satisfactory roles in the normal Pistach way. Dissatisfaction happens from time to time, and we take no pleasure in the pain and frustration of those who cannot fit in. Therefore, Quirk: a subtropical planet with a dozen or so towns sprawling across pleasant valleys near the sea. There is food for the picking, water for the drinking, no power needed for warmth, and the sanitation systems are self-repairing. The towns are not particularly pleasing in an aesthetic sense, as they have neither order nor discernable functionality, but Pistach-home provides ample equipment and supplies for its free-spirited population. Naturally, there are no functioning inceptors or receptors among the inhabitants—any of these castes who are sent there are sterilized though not otherwise altered. Larvabots and childbots are provided for nootchi. Except for actual reproduction, persons on Quirk may play any roles they like.

One of the persons we set ashore on Quirk was a former proffe, T'Fees, a handsome person, stalwart and strong, who had been reselected as a seemingly perfect campes, but was unhappy in that role. He had been selected originally as an artist, though te had no real talent. Though te could not create art, te had well-formed opinions concerning it and insights that I found remarkably fine. Perhaps if te had been selected to teach art, he would have been content, but his ambitions did not reach in that direction. Or, if we Pistach allowed the role of critic, T'fees would have fulfilled that role. We do not critique the works of others for public edification, however. To question the value of others' works publicly would be to denigrate them in our society.

I think of T'Fees often when I learn of Earth people who fail at their chosen lives, or those like your Van Gogh, who become a success only after they are dead. On Pistach, we do not change our opinions of former persons. What good does it do an unhappy man to become a genius after his death? Or a living person to be a failure at his dreams? Among Pistach, all except glusi are successful, and even glusi are encouraged to believe they are. All must believe in their success; otherwise meager aptitudes breed great rancor.

During the voyage from Assurdo to Quirk, I spent many pleasant hours with T'Fees, usually playing sheez or bactak. I remember well the occasion, toward the end of one day shift, when T'Fees asked by what right Vess and Chiddy had disrupted teros life and the life of others on Assurdo.

I asked if te had ever seen the Fresco. Te replied that te had not. Te had never been on Pistach-home. The ceremonial buildings on ter homeworld did not, of course, contain a copy of the Fresco. Te had, however, seen the Glumshalak Compendium with the sketches drawn shortly after the Fresco was finished. The ship carrying the Compendium had stopped on Assurdo for refueling, and for some inexplicable reason had, while there, allowed the local populace to file past the revered book.

"You ask what gives us the right," I said. "Panel fifteen of the Fresco, *The Blessing of Canthorel*, shows us Mengantowhai, foreseeing the martyrdom that would give him divine authority, passing this authority to Canthorel. When Canthorel came to Pistach-home, it was passed to aisos successors through the holy Fresco. Mengantowhai's holy authority has descended to the athyci of Pistach down the centuries, each receiving it from those who have received it before in an unbroken line."

"And who gave it to Mengantowhai?" te asked.

"Universal Purpose," I replied. "This Purpose was made manifest when Mengantowhai first came into contact with the Jaupati. Panel one of the Fresco, *The Meeting*, shows us they were a primitive race. They warred among themselves. It is even said the Jaupati were personophagic, though the truth of that assertion is unproven. In panel two of the Fresco, *The Steadfast Docents*, we are shown teachers, appointed by Mengantowhai, asking the Jaupati if they desire peace and freedom from want and pain, and they are crying as with one voice that they do. The Jaupati put themselves in his hands, and he worked with them for many years."

"What did he do to them?"

"He did nothing *to* them. He did a great deal *with* them. He taught them how to differentiate their young toward ultimate contentment. He taught them how to structure an economy so there would be work for all. He taught them how to breed one offspring at a time instead of litters, like pfiggi, for it is absolutely true that no nootch—or parent— can civilize a litter! He taught them how to educate their young in order to avoid being glutted by whole families of glusi. And they were grateful. In panel six, *The Offerings*, we see the Jaupati bringing gifts to Mengantowhai."

"Yet I have heard Mengantowhai died a martyr's death at their hands."

"That assertion is heretical. Mengantowhai was not killed by the Jaupati but by the Pokoti. In panel nine, *Evangelism*, we see the Jaupati leader, Kasiwees, raising a force to defend Mengantowhai against the Pokoti. In panel ten, *The Envious Pokoti*, we see the Pokoti plotting against the Jaupati. In panel eleven, *The Attack*, we see the abduction of Mengantowhai by the Pokoti. The Pokoti tried to force him to tell them the secrets of selection, the skills of economic design, the way to have one offspring at a time. These are not things one can tell, like a recipe for flosti-gut paté! They are not things one should communicate except by example. Mengantowhai was badly wounded during his abduction. In panel twelve, *The Rescue*, we see Canthorel arriving to save him. Mengantowhai did not die for some time following, for panels thirteen, fourteen and fifteen show him still alive."

"And what are those panels called?" T'fees asked.

"Thirteen is *Mengantowhai's Sermon*, his teaching to his people. Then, *The Fearful Faithless*, the departure of the Pistach who feared another attack by the Pokoti, and finally, *The Blessing of Canthorel*, which I have already mentioned. This is followed by panel sixteen, *Departure of Canthorel*."

"And what happened to the Jaupati?"

"Maddened by Mengantowhai's passing, they locked themselves in a death-struggle with the Pokoti. Canthorel was unable to bring peace, as there was too much hatred on both sides, and ai departed from the world. Panel seventeen, the final panel of the Fresco, the one that lies between the left-hand doors, shows the last Jaupati, Kasiwees, kneeling in prayer before the shrine of Mengantowhai while the last Pokoti sneaks from behind him with a blade. We know from the associated Pistach symbols of renewal—flying flosti, bulbs, worm jars—that Kasiwees is praying for Mengantowhai's return. Kasiwees is our exemplar. When we enter the ranks of the athyci, we swear to respond to the Plea of Kasiwees. This Kasiwean Oath commits us to meeting the needs of others by bringing Mengantowhai's help, as set out in the Fresco of Canthorel."

"Is the Fresco very beautiful?" te asked me, after a long, thoughtful pause. "Though I am now only a former artist, I judged that the Compendium was not very artistically done."

Though it was painful for me to tell T'Fees it was virtually invisible behind its veils of grime, in the interest of truth I did so, explaining that its holiness prevented our cleaning it. "As for beauty, we know that Canthorel painted only beauty," I replied. I knew this had to be true, regardless of how it was conveyed in Glumshalak's Compendium.

T'fees and I grew to be almost friends upon that journey. I was hurt by the look te gave me when ton'i parted on Quirk. By that time, of course, all those from Assurdo knew that only adults come to Quirk and no real children are ever born there. They also knew why: because the people of

Quirk value their own individuality over the welfare of the whole, and Mengantowhai's rule allows no young to be brought into a world that has not prepared an orderly, safe and peaceful place for them.

You will be sympathetic to this, I know, dearest Benita. Though not all human receptors or nootchi are good ones, you fulfilled those roles ably. You bore children, and you labored mightily to be sure they had an orderly, safe, and peaceful place. It is a sorrow that one of your children was unable to appreciate this. Some other races in the Confederation do not have our ways. They are like some of your people on Earth. They demand that children be born, even without a place for them or a good person to nootch them. If the children die, well, say they, it is the will of their gods. I do not like such ways; certainly I would not follow such gods.

I remember often what you said the night of our dinner with your people, about your people improving while your god stayed the same. I think of the races I have known who defined their gods when they were still savages, giving their gods the power and cruelty they themselves displayed. The gods of the Fluiquosm, for example, are invisible spirits of death. And the Wulivery carve their hungry gods into immortal stone, while the Xankatikitiki recite long sagas of their heavenly hunters. So they have gone on, generation after generation, unchanging, and in following them, their peoples have shut off all avenues to a better way of life. Would it not be a good thing if we could retire old gods, like old soldiers, to a peaceful place in the country? Let them live like retired warriors whose time of violence is past? Or like old politicians, perhaps, who have learned the wrong lessons in striving youth and have not had enough lifetimes to unlearn them.

26

pistach management

MONDAY

On Monday, the Pistach Questionnaires were delivered by postmen to every household. They came in a plain brown envelope containing individual packets for various members of the family. Some were for adult women, some for adult men, some for children between eight and twelve, others for teenagers. The instructions specified that each person must first select the age and gender appropriate packet, affix his or her own thumbprint on the sticky patch at the top of each page, then answer the questions below, without help, in pencil or pen.

"If the person filling out the questionnaire is someone other than the thumb printer, the questionnaire will self-destruct," said the instructions. "If the person filling out the questionnaire is under duress or being helped, the questionnaire will self-destruct. Please, do this individually and honestly."

Benita, reading this, was most amused. They had found a use for old *Mission Impossible* technology after all.

The questionnaires included several hundred questions about society, about people's positions in society, about behavior, work habits, morality. Even people who did not read at all, or at all well, found the questions easy to understand. Many questions asked that certain behaviors be ranked in order of preference or by degree of sinfulness, such as, "Is sex outside of marriage more or less sinful than a) not paying one's employees a living wage, b) cheating on taxes, c) passing laws to benefit the rich by further oppressing the poor?"

Millions of thumbs were pressed onto waiting sticky patches, and in each sticky patch a hundred thousand Pistach nanobots waited, quiescent. At the moment of pressure, chemical restraints dissolved, allowing the nanobots their freedom. Chemical sensors detected warmth and blood and crawled upward, following microfibers that had already penetrated the skin to obtain blood and DNA samples. When the hand was pulled away from the sticky patch, a hundred thousand nanobots tunneled rapidly into the flesh, where they began harvesting atoms from the surrounding flesh, assembling more of themselves until they totalled several millions and had spread to all parts of the body.

Millions of questionnaires were puzzled over and answered. By the time each person had finished the first dozen or two innocuous questions, his or her body was completely colonized. During the answering of each successive question, nanobots measured blood pressure, respiration, endocrine function, brain waves, and subvocalizations to determine if answers were true or not. If any answer was false, it was ignored.

Some of the nanobots migrated to the palm of the hand and emerged at the surface of the skin as a complicated dark red ideogram. Cheaters, parents who had tried to fill out their children's forms, or family members who had taken it upon themselves to speak for other family members, plus those who had discarded the questionnaire or simply ignored it, received on the following day a stern note and a new questionnaire. Though the questionnaires were in fact returned to a central depository—from which they subsequently disappeared—the work of tabulation had already been done. Newly assembled nanobot structures inside each person now identified that person. Roving structures migrated throughout each person's body, correcting minor physical problems as they went. Crippling diseases were ameliorated. Incapacitating pain was relieved, but fatal diseases were let alone. No attempt was made to reduce drug addiction, alcoholism, smoking, or any other self-destructive behavior.

When anyone shook hands, hugged or kissed, took a receipt from a cashier's hand, took a ticket from a parking attendant or money from a teller, nanobots passed from one body to another. Except for a few thousand eremitic individuals, within a few days even those who had resolutely refused to fill out a questionnaire were colonized and identified. Since the opinions of the hermits could, the Pistach thought, be accurately inferred, they were not required to answer questions.

Except for the clearly visible marks on the palms of their hands, the nanobot invasion went totally unnoticed by the people of the United States.

law enforcement

MONDAY

Captain Riggles, Morningside Precinct, looked up from his desk impatiently. "What?"

"This box for you, Boss."

"What's in it, McClellan?"

"I don't know, Boss. Says it came from *them*."

"Them who?"

"Them, sir. You know. The ETs."

Captain Riggles smiled grimly and commented, "As I was just saying this morning to Lieutenant Walker, McClellan, I'd be really surprised if you make it through the next few weeks to retirement. Aren't you a little old for—"

Mac drew himself up, scowling. "Captain, the box says it comes from the ETs. Right there. Ex-tra-ter-rest-rial En-voys. Now if you don't want it, sir, you just say so, and I'll dump it down in the basement with the old files."

"Give it here." He frowned at the box, a sizeable one. "Maybe it's a bomb."

"No, sir. It's been through the scanner. I've slit the tape, you just need to—"

"McClellan, I know how to open a box."

He opened it, disclosing a great number of closely

packed smaller boxes, one of which, on being upended and shaken, dropped a wrist-watch on his desk. Something that looked like a wristwatch, at any rate.

"What th . . ." He picked it up and turned it in his hands. An expansion band. A round dial. A single hand, pointing down. Left-hand side of the dial green, no numbers. Right-hand side red, numbered from the top down, one to ten. Legibly lettered on the left, the words, "No probable cause." On the right, "Probable cause."

"There's directions, Boss."

McClellan handed him the thin booklet that had been wedged between the smaller boxes and the carton.

Introducing the Causometer, for use by police, drug enforcement officers and the U.S. Customs. Provided with our best wishes by the Extraterrestrial Envoys.

"The instruments in the carton you have just received are units in a new system designed by the ETs to provide you with better tools for your work. All illicit drugs entering the U.S. will henceforth emit a harmless form of radiation which can be picked up by the devices you are now examining. To turn on the device, simply press the button on the right side. A small light will flash at the bottom of the dial indicating your position. The dial is the area in front of you. If there are illicit drugs in the area, the light will split into two, white and red, and the red light will move in the direction of the drugs. At the same time, the hand will move through the green zone toward the red zone.

"As you move in the direction indicated by red light, the two lights will come closer together. When the two lights converge, this indicates you are standing upon or at the drugs in question. Touch the device for three seconds to whatever person, container, vehicle or surface is nearest. If there are several persons or things, touch each in turn. If the thing or person touched is or has been carrying drugs, the hand will move into the red zone of Probable Cause. When the hand reaches Probable Cause, the causometer also records and emits data regarding the time, the geographical and physical location, the identities of all persons in the immediate vicinity as well as the type and quantity of drug present. This information is then sent to you in official form.

"Though the radiation is harmless, it does accumulate in persons, vehicles, or buildings repeatedly exposed to the manufacture, storage, transport, or sale of illicit drugs. The higher the reading, the more involvement there has been. A reading of four or higher indicates consistent and continuous presence of illicit material. If drugs have been dropped or deposited in a noncontiguous location, press the button on the left side, then apply the meter to the drugs first, and then to persons one at a time. DNA traces on the drugs or their packaging will be matched to the person who carried or processed them. The meter will sound an audible alarm when the right person is identified."

McClellan had been reading over his shoulder. "They're kidding."

"Somebody's idea of a joke," the captain muttered, tapping the gadget on his desktop. "Just for the hell of it, let's try it. Go down to the evidence locker and bring up some stuff. Any stuff. Hide it out there and yell."

"You mean, now?"

"No, McClellan. Next Tuesday. Of course I mean now!"

Fifteen minutes later, responding to McClellan's hail, the captain, device on his wrist, eased out of his office observed by a sniggering clutch of on and off duty cops. He pushed the right button, blinked for a moment, moved to his left, touched a desk. The needle went to red three, moving to four as he opened a drawer and took out a plastic packet with an evidence tag on it. The light had begun blinking again. He went left, right, straight ahead, uncovering five more packets of varying substances. The audience of cops, who had stopped sniggering when the first package was found, mostly had their mouths open.

"It's like a sniffer dog on your arm," said one.

"You got 'em all, Boss," said McClellan.

"No, there's more," said the captain, still moving, bumping into an off duty cop who was standing in the door. "Sorry, Stevens." He went around him, stopped, turned around, came back, reached out and touched Stevens with the device. The needle hit the five.

"Hey, what's this," Stevens blurted, turning brick red.

The captain stared at the dial which was giving him an unequivocal "Probable Cause." "Search him," he said to Mc-Clellan. "Now."

"Oh, come on, Captain," Stevens cried.

"Do it, damn it."

They found the packet of cocaine stuffed under his belt, in back, where Stevens had put it when he came off duty at the evidence locker. He hadn't even taken the trouble to remove the evidence tag. While they were still standing around, muttering about it, the clerk brought a fax that had just printed out. Headed with an official-looking letterhead, it gave the date, time, location, amount and type of drugs in each discovery, place found or person in possession, list of all other persons present, and a cryptic signature.

When Stevens had been taken below and locked up, the captain brought out the carton of wrist sniffers. "McClellan, you and Brown distribute these things to the men, see the other shifts get them too. Run off copies of these two pages that tell how it works. When the day shift gets it figured out, send two cars over to the Morningside Project. No, make it four cars and a wagon. Don't bring in any kids under ten. I got a feeling we'll make a clean sweep."

The ETs had misled the captain, though only a little. The radiation emitted by illicit drugs was high-frequency sound, a supersonic howl coming from assemblies of nanobots that had been sown some time ago throughout the coca plantations and poppy fields of the world. Nanobots, Chiddy and Vess had agreed, made more sense than any other form of tracer, because they were self-perpetuating. Designed to utilize only molecular assemblies found in drugs for replication materials, they settled in and procreated like bacteria, making millions of themselves virtually overnight. Whenever an area became overcrowded, millions migrated away to other plants or trees, carrying the useful assemblies with them. Within a period of days, there was no source of either cocaine or opiates anywhere in the world that was not fully tagged.

The nanobots had been designed to be impervious to refining processes. They didn't show up on scanners. They didn't show up on anything manmade except electron microscopes, and even then, only if someone knew what to look for. Their supersonic howls were detectable by the wrist sniffers, of course, but wrist sniffers could not be taken apart for examination. Any attempt to do so resulted in a foul stench and a puddle of unpleasant and rapidly evaporating goop.

The drug-bots were designed to penetrate wrappings, they were programmed to move out of the drugs into the clothing of the carrier, into the hair and body of the carrier, into the vehicles the carrier used, into the money the carrier received. If there were no drugs in the environment, they could not replicate, and their life spans were designed to be short, thus eliminating the possibility of innocent persons being identified as carriers. They were designed to take particular actions in response to specific signals. With a wary eye on the economics of the situation, neither Vess nor Chiddy had ordered them to do anything else, yet.

28

incident in virginia

MONDAY

Late Monday evening, an armored truck made its way down a lonely country road in Virginia, headed toward an abandoned farm that was owned, ostensibly, by a widow in Baltimore. The woods behind the house were cut by the arcs of three concentric fences, an outside, slightly saggy one of rusty barbed wire, a second one of tight electrified mesh, and a third, the one nearest the house, of high-tension cables and electrified chain link with concertina wire at the top. This latter barrier, invisible from the road, began at a ramshackle shed connected to one side of the farmhouse, circled into the forest, and came out at a dilapidated annex at the other side. The splintery boards and flaking paint off the farmhouse hid a reinforced concrete bunker at the entry to a large storage area buried in the hillside. What one saw from the approach was an assemblage of rotting rail fences outlining weedy fields that ran up the slope to the house, its sagging roof part and parcel of the whole, sorry picture.

Dink was driving, with McVane beside him. Briess, a small man with a ratty mustache, was standing in the tall, armor-plated body of the truck. Arthur was on urgent business elsewhere, but his place had been taken by a sound technician and half a ton of equipment designed to detect every physical manifestation that might occur when they arrived at the ramshackle house.

"We stay in the truck, right?" Dink asked, as he came to the last turn in the driveway.

"We stay in the truck," agreed McVane. "If these creatures are what we think they are, they've had appetizers in Oregon and an entree in Florida, and I'm not offering to be dessert."

"What's your guess?" asked Dink, braking the van to a halt and shutting off engine and lights. "About what they want?"

"They're obviously a competing group," said McVane. "A rival clan, or nation, or political party. A rival world, or association of worlds. The voice that spoke to me said the Pistach aren't the only ones. This implies we're being given a choice between the way the Pistach are shoving us and something else. They want to make a deal."

"For what?" breathed Briess from the hatch leading into the truck body. "Hunting rights?"

"Something like that," admitted McVane. "We could tolerate that. Hell, China's got enough surplus people to keep 'em busy for a few thousand years. If their offer's good enough."

"You don't know how many of *them* there are," said Briess, through a grilled hatch behind the seat. "Or how much and how often they eat. You don't know if they have a preference in taste. Like Europeans, or Americans."

"I doubt we taste any different," grunted McVane. "If they preferred light meat, they'd be talking to somebody besides us."

"How long until?" asked Briess.

McVane consulted the illuminated dial of his watch. "Ten minutes. I didn't allow much extra time. It's boring to sit around waiting for stuff to happen."

"Crack that window so we can hear," said Dink. "Get a little fresh air in here."

"Keep it closed," barked McVane. "Turn on the recirculating air conditioner if you have to, but keep everything closed. Physically, we're probably no match for these creatures, and it's remotely possible this is a trap . . ."

"I thought you said it would be perfectly safe!" erupted Dink.

"I said a trap was remotely possible, Dinklemier. Calm down. If you want to listen, turn on the exterior mikes."

The mikes were turned on to admit a soothing murmur of light wind, the rustling of dried leaves, the flap-flap of a strap of harness hanging on the fence, the flutter of a tattered white towel that was inexplicably clipped to the washline beside the house.

"What's that doing there?" asked McVane, nodding at the towel. "I thought the place was abandoned."

"It's meant to look abandoned," Briess corrected him. "The towel means there was nothing dangerous here when the crew looked the place over shortly after sunset. The whole area has been under surveillance from across the valley since then."

They sat. "Did you locate the intermediary's kids?" McVane asked.

Dink grunted. "They're being watched. We can pick them up any time. The same with the husband. We can pick him up any time. He doesn't know where his wife is."

"Neither do the children," said Briess. "But the boy is willing to try and find out. Seems he's got a girlfriend who likes money."

"Don't they all," murmured McVane. The rustling and flapping went on as the minutes passed, ten, twelve, fifteen.

"They're late," said McVane.

"On the contrary," said a voice through the speaker. "We arrived here when you did."

Those in the truck straightened up and peered in all directions. There was nothing visible.

"Show yourselves," said McVane.

"Rather not," said the voice in a toneless, mechanical voice. "Rather just do our business, get on with our lives, you know. Too much formality stifles us, doesn't it you? Warriors and hunters don't need it."

"You are a . . . warrior race," said Briess, through the inside microphone.

"Oh, indeed."

"You speak English?"

"We're speaking through a translator. We buy them from the Pistach. Good manufacturers, the Pistach. Stodgy as all get-out, everything just so, but perfectionists do make good merchandise."

"They say they're here to help us," offered McVane. "Isn't that true?"

"Well, help is as help is. If you do it their way, you'll learn to get rid of some of what they call your native barbarism; you'll become more civilized, which is also what they call it; and you'll keep everybody reasonably happy by eliminating a lot of what makes life interesting. Maybe that's help. For us, it'd be deadly dull. We're highly selfish and individualistic. We revel in the unexpected. We lust after the hunt. We've given you a looking-over. We think you're more like us than you are like them."

"And?" breathed Briess.

"Our view is that those who sign up for somebody's free course in social engineering ought to have a choice. If you sign up with us, we make a deal. We get to hunt on this planet. We'll set a game limit that won't overstress the population, though right at first you'll need a hell of a lot of weeding out. We can use our young ones for that. You know kids. Always hungry."

"And what do we get out of it?" Briess asked, surprised at the dryness of his throat.

"You get your population problem solved without having to argue about sex or religion or human rights. Let people have as many offspring as they want, the young ones are juicier anyhow. We prefer to maintain a large gene pool by eating only third birth order or higher persons, so we won't be reducing you by much."

"We can handle our own population problems," growled Briess.

"Never in a million years," said the voice, the translator managing to imply a chuckle. "Not with all your taboos. Aren't you sick of them? By Gharm the Great, between your religions and your laws, you can't have a good gang rape without being hauled up short! That's what you get with a differentiated society like the Pistach. Everything smoothed out, ironed over. Well, with us, it's different. You let us hunt, we'll do you favors, give you some technology that'll advance you a few centuries."

"You'll restrict your hunting by agreement?" asked Briess. "How would that work?"

"First, you can tell us where the hunting should be done. Second, you can tell us what individuals or groups you'd like eliminated. Political foes, maybe? Certain foreign elements? Certain dictators that've been hard to handle? Just imagine, you want it, it happens, but nobody can trace it back to you!"

"If we make a deal with you, do we still get to join this Confederation the Pistach keep talking about?" asked Dink.

"Go ahead and join, just don't tell the Pistach about our agreement. You can go ahead and become neighborly. It won't hurt you. But . . . on the side, when you get bored, we'll take you hunting with us."

There was a long silence. Briess asked, "Won't the Pistach find out about it?"

The voice made a grating noise they interpreted as laughter. "With all your terrorists and warfare and tribal conflicts. Not so they can prove it."

Briess said, "We'd like to talk about this, a bit."

"Take your time," said a voice. "Take all the time you need. Meantime, just to illustrate our goodwill, give us a few names. We'll find the being or beings, wherever it is or they are, and we'll either make them disappear or deliver them to you. Just to show how useful we can be."

Silence in the van. It was McVane who spoke at last. "A woman named Benita Alvarez. The intermediary for the Pistach envoys."

"Dead? Dismembered? Or delivered?"

McVane started to speak, but Briess reached through the opening to put a hand on his shoulder, silencing him.

"Delivered," said Briess. "It has to be done surreptitiously, no alarms, no havoc, no wreckage. She has to disappear, and she has to be in good condition. Call one of us when you've got her."

"Where is she?"

"If we knew that, we wouldn't need you," said McVane.

"Excellent," purred the voice, losing some of its mechanical edge. "We enjoy a challenge. She has family, perhaps?"

"A husband in Albuquerque. A son and daughter at school in California." He fumbled for a pocket notebook and read off Angelica's address, Carlos's address, Bert's address.

The voice purred again. "We may need to use her family as bait. We'll let you know when we have her, and we'll bring her here."

The voice went away. The other men sat silently while the technician fiddled with his dials and screens. "Here's something in infrared," he said at last, pointing at his monitor.

They got into the back to see what he had, an image of something or things tall and tangled, looming at the side of the ramshackle house. And something smaller but numerous on the ground between the armored car and the house. And something else, that they couldn't at all make out, more an absence than a presence.

Dink gulped, saying in a slightly panicky voice, "I'm not sure I like this . . ."

"We've made alliances before," said McVane. "Hell, we had an alliance with Stalin once."

"There's a difference," murmured Briess. "I doubt Stalin ever looked at us and imagined how we'd taste served rare, with sauteed mushrooms."

Dink started the car and eased it into motion, turning in a wide loop to put them back on the isolated road. "First thing we have to do is tell Morse about it," he murmured. "Let's see what he has to say."

29

from chiddy's journal

In a previous entry I have mentioned the Pistach colony on Quirk. It was only three or four years after our visit there that Pistach-home received astonishing news. The people on Quirk had rebelled against their sequestration, had seized a supply ship—no great feat as it was not armed or staffed to repel a boarding party—and subsequently had used that ship to ferry a large fraction of the planetary population to some unknown destination. What was most intriguing about the story was the name of the leader: T'Fees. More exactly, T'Fees the Tumultuous, or so those remaining on Quirk averred. Those who had chosen to remain on Quirk included the lazy, the elderly, the infirm, and the quite mad, but even the maddest among them claimed T'Fees had taken the title of Tumultuous before leaving the planet.

Pistach-home was abuzz with rumor and speculation. Where could the Quirkers have gone that was any better suited to them than Quirk? Quirk had been designed for the eccentric, the unconventional, the idiosyncratic, the bizarre. Where else could such people go and be allowed to live in acceptance and peace? We assumed they would want peace.

We always assume that living, breathing, sensible creatures want peace.

The Departure from Quirk became what you on Earth would call a Nine-Day Wonder, fascinating, but not enduringly interesting. There were some songs written, some artwork done, some poems composed with the rebellion of Quirk as the theme. None of them truly captured the event to make it live in our minds. People soon quit talking about it for though it was unusual, by our standards, it was also distant and it did not affect Pistach-home. It was a happening staged by the insane on a world the sane regarded little.

Even we who had known T'Fees did not worry over it long. There were too many other duties and responsibilities that required our attention. Since Vess and I had been away on missions for some time, we were scheduled to spend the next year or so in duty at the House of the Fresco. All athyci are expected to spend time there in order to renew our spiritual balance. Teachings by the commentators over the years stress the importance of infusing oneself with the aura of the Fresco, with the awe and reverence evoked by the rites conducted there.

It was while I was on Fresco duty that the House of Cavita, my ancestral house, was honored by a request to donate genetic material for a mating among the five imperial houses. When a child is planned among them, each house gives genetic material to the mating but, also, to prevent excessive inbreeding, one outside source is required, preferably an athyco from a blameless lineage. Our family records had been audited for the past twelve generations without revealing one misjudgment by a Cavita selector, one reversed decision by a Cavita athyco, one artwork created by a Cavita proffi that was considered inferior. Our line seemed to be without stain. At the time, dear Benita, I confess that I had feelings of ebullience and self-regard over this matter. Since being here on Earth, I have become more likely to see humor in it. I have the feeling, if I told you we had twelve generations without stain, you would say to me, Oh, poor thing, how dull!

It was, in fact, worse than dull. While the request to provide genetic material is a great honor, it requires an equally great interruption in one's life. Athyci are not physically able to reproduce. Therefore, an athyco asked to do so must undergo temporary transformation. This process is painful and lengthy, taking the better part of a year before one is restored to oneself. It was during this time that I became personally acquainted with breeding madness and clump lust and the other terrors and compulsions routinely faced by inceptors. They, so it is said, do it eagerly, without a qualm. For me, it was traumatic, not while it was going on, of course, but after it was over. As a matter of principle, I did not ask for memory deadening during the incidents. Athyci are expected to welcome all experiences as a way of learning what others experience and how they cope with events. I found the memories agonizing, however. If I had been Earthian, I would have blushed to recall them, wishing them gone, and worse: wishing dead all other individuals—the inceptors, the receptors, the nootchi—who had witnessed the events. It is a grave error to wish others gone, dead, passed over, but I committed it a hundred times during the following year on Pistach-home.

Since being here, I have learned to value the experience as it helped me understand Earth people better than I could otherwise have done. They, too, are often suffused by shame at what reproductive nature has compelled them to do. They are reminded, and they cringe. They wish to forget.

I know, for example, that your young people—and those of mid years, also—often cannot help the sexual foolishness they commit, and assisting them in this matter would be wise. I know your rapists cannot help what they do, but I also know they cannot be allowed to do it. Since the physically stronger half of your race are inceptors, and since they are disproportionately represented at various levels of government, they have elevated inceptorhood above all other states of being, holding it above even the right to live. Inceptorhood is so holy that it forbids changing rapists into campesi or even proffi, though they would be happier so. You may kill a rapist, but you may not change him into something noninceptorish. It is a great trouble in your society, one Vess and I are at present much concerned with.

Which is beside the point. After a period of convalescence, I continued my term at the House of the Fresco, and it was there that a second trauma occurred. I was reminded of it anew by something you said not long ago, Benita, about the Sistine Chapel.

I have spoken of the grime that covers the interior of the House of the Fresco, most of it deposited as soot from candles and oil lamps, thousands of which are burned by worshippers and seekers after truth and pilgrims from Pistach's far-flung worlds. It would be heresy to clean the Fresco, yes, but the room that contains it has to be cleaned at least annually. A large scaffolding is erected, and teams of proffi and athyci come in to wash down the inside of the dome, the pillars, the wall space above and below the Fresco, and finally the floor itself. At the time of which I speak, the Chapter of the Fresco House had recently ruled that the traditional cleaning utensils—animal skins and a ritual soap made from wax plants and scented with flowers—could be replaced by a more convenient and effective cleansing agent. The new stuff was a grime specific solvent, and we were given large jugs of it, each labeled *Danger, do not drink*, with a picture of a dried thorax and crossed leg armor.

The stuff stank, but it worked almost miraculously, needing little if any rinsing and leaving virtually no streaks. In half the usual time, we had the inside of the dome done, the pillars washed down, and it was time to do the walls above the Fresco, which had been carefully—so we assumed—draped to avoid any damage. As it happened, I was the one who committed the offense. I was working above the final depiction, *The Martyrdom of Kasiwees*, when someone tried to open the left-hand door from the outside, bumping the scaffolding and making me drop the cleaning cloth as I grabbed for support. The cloth dropped between my body and the Fresco, and in the effort to catch it, I pressed it against the drapery with a lower appendage. When I retrieved it, I saw to my horror that it had been pressed against the Fresco itself, through a gap in the drapery.

My cries brought assistance, and we carefully redraped the area, leaving no holes at all. It was not until the job was done and the drapes were removed that we saw, high on the Fresco of Kasiwees, a rag-sized area of blue sky dotted with figures we had been taught were flosti, returning from their wintering grounds. With the grime removed, one needed no magnification to see that the figures were not flosti. They were Pistach, winged Pistach who, from their dress, were from the Imperial Houses, the house from which Mengantowhai had come. Also, the figures were not arriving; they were departing.

The shock was palpable. The Fresco Chapter—all those currently charged with the care of the Fresco—met in lengthy sessions to determine what should be done about the disclosure. Whose fault was it? Though they were kind enough not to blame me for dropping the cloth, they were thrown into great confusion by the contents of the Kasiwees commentary, the one that referred to symbols of springtime and renewal—i.e., flosti—when in fact the the flosti were not there!

It was suggested that since the Fresco had sustained no damage, the entire Fresco or at least the entire Kasiwees panel should be cleaned, as the symbols of renewal would no doubt be found elsewhere on the panel. This was shouted down. Though the symbols might be elsewhere on the panel, possibly they might not, and no one wanted to deal with that eventuality. The Chapter felt such a discovery would undermine the entire structure of our society.

Another suggestion was that we go back and amend any of the commentaries that did not agree with the now disclosed reality. This was discussed for days, until everyone agreed we could not conform the commentaries to the disclosed reality because we did not know what the disclosed reality was! As our adage puts it, *lum ek avowl, ni lûmek'aul*: a tiny patch of blue is not heaven. (You would say, one swallow does not make a summer.) We would have to clean the entire Kasiwees panel, at the very least, in order to say what the tiny patch meant, and that might raise questions about other panels that had not been cleaned!

The anger and confusion finally settled into a determination to find out who had first misled the people and to cover up the patch of blue so the people would not be further confused. It was agreed that the only sensible thing to do was haze the patch with tallow smoke, that is, re-dirty it. That decision had the weight of tradition behind it, at least. Since I had dropped the cleaning cloth, I, personally, smoked the patch into illegibility, though I confess to putting every detail of it into memory as I did so.

A small committee was delegated the job of going through the archives starting with our earliest ancestors to determine who was responsible for this error, if, indeed, it had been an error. I volunteered to help and was accepted as one of the researchers. Though I had studied Pistach history prior to being accepted as an athyco, I had never actually looked at original documents. The thing I most wanted to see was the often-referred-to Compendium, the panel-by-panel drawing of the Fresco together with the notations on which our knowledge of the Fresco now depends. This Compendium was created long ago by Athyco Glumshalak who is known as "The Inceptor of Morality." It was Glumshalak who codified our beliefs and virtues; it was Glumshalak who taught us that the Fresco was too holy to be cleaned. Unfortunately, the Compendium was not available on Pistach-home, for it was on display in the Fresco House of one of the colony worlds. Though this was a disappointment, other documents were profuse.

I had no idea how much *writing* there had been prior to widespread use of electronic communication and the development of mind-scanners. Prior to modern times, we Pistach used sheets of stuff called thizzle, a kind of starch that dries into sheets, almost like your paper, and there are bales of it in the archives. Though there seemed to be a dearth of official documents prior to Glumshalak, there were uncountable items of personal correspondence. Back then, everyone wrote to everyone else, and all of it had been saved in stasis files—to prevent its being eaten by gniffles—even letters from people who were only remotely if at all connected to the building of the Fresco House.

I was sorting through old letters when I came across one from a proffe, one Merg'alos of Sferon, to his nootch. The letter concerned Merg'alos's visit to the Fresco, and it was dated only fifty years after the Fresco was completed. In the letter, Merg'alos—who was evidently an artist—wrote that he found the Fresco "undistinguished." He referred to Kasiwees as "abandoned," and to the (unnamed) figures in the sky as being, "like so many flosti, flying." The symbol conveying the word "like" or "similar to" came at the end of a line, at the very edge of the thizzle sheet, which had been slightly nibbled. As it was the first reference to flosti that I had seen, I set the letter aside. Days later, I came across a critique written by a proffe who was also of Sferon House, dated some seventy years after the Merg'alos letter was written. The critique referred to "my ancestor's letter" and mentioned the possible symbolism to be found in the "flock of flosti either arriving or departing."

I found an entry in the Fresco House official commentaries, dated another hundred years after the critique, after the time of Glumshalak, referring to "the springtime symbolism of the arrival of flosti, flying in at the upper left." By that time—over two hundred years after the Fresco was painted—the Fresco had already disappeared behind its layers of soot and research had to have been done from the Compendium and commentaries alone. After that citation, the "springtime symbolism" was referred to again and again in the various commentaries, and other commentators found other springtime symbols in the panel as well. There were said to be bulbs scattered around Kasiwees's kneeling figure, plus worm jars and, that quintessential harbinger of spring, a bough of hisanthine in Kasiwees's hand.

Having just traced the origin of nonexistent flosti, I was of no mind to accept the bulbs, the worm jars, or the hisanthine. Many early sketches of Fresco panels were in the archives, in addition to Glumshalak's Compendium, most of them done by athyci and proffi who were not, unfortunately, artists. Yes, there were some little bumps drawn around Kasiwees's kneeling figure, but it was impossible to say whether they were bulbs or rounded stones or unripe fruit or a clutch of pfiggi eggs. The same uncertainty applied to worm jars, and though Kasiwees definitely had something in his hand, whether it was a branch of hisanthine, I could not say. I commented to one of my fellow workers, a professional historian, that I thought there had been a conspiracy in those early years to destroy or hide all the documents that would be needed in the future. He commented that this was often the case, for in any situation with more than one side or opinion, only the winning side or opinion would be around to justify whatever it had done, no matter who had been right or wrong. He said, "Ones have always inferred that Glumshalak may have disposed of some material which did not accord with aisos view of Pistach purpose."

This was a new idea to me, and I confess that I was depressed by it, particularly since I was unaware there had ever been any other side or opinion than those we had been taught.

When I reported to the Chapter, other researchers had also found mentions of flosti subsequent to the first letter, and we agreed that the interpolation of flosti had indeed arisen in a casual letter from Merg'alos to a family member, a letter subsequently cited, inaccurately, by one of his lineage. Or, to put it baldly, our teachings regarding the content of the Kasiwees panel were in substantial error. I wondered at the time why the Compendium of Glumshalak had not prevailed over this error since it did not mention the flosti, or whatever.

I think it was at that point that I suggested using technology to penetrate the coating of grime and get an image of the original Fresco. This could be done without changing the Fresco in any way, and then the Chapter might, privately, take its time in assessing what changes in doctrine might be necessary.

I might as well have thrown a pfiggi haunch into a pool of hungry pfluggi, for the assembled Chapter ripped the suggestion to shreds. It was obvious the Chapter preferred preserving the current doctrine to changing doctrine, even though change might bring it into accord with Canthorel's divine purpose. No one, *no one* said exactly that, but that is what they meant. I did not say it either. I remember that my nootch told me many years before that I would know I had gained wisdom when I learned to keep my mouthparts quiet. I thought of her and was silent.

The head of Chapter set everything into the preferred perspective. "Tradition weighs as much as truth," the old one said. "What has existed for thousands of years as a support of goodness and peace has as much right to teaching as a painting done yesterday that has yet to prove itself." In other words, we'd been getting along fine with things the way they were, so leave them the way they were. One of your favorite Earth sayings, that one: If it ain't broke, don't fix it.

Though I was presumably acquiescent, I confess to being troubled about this matter. Truth has always mattered to me, dear Benita. You and I have discussed this from time to time. Even though we have agreed that real truth is hard to come by, we have also agreed that it is worth the effort. It seemed to me then, as it seems now, that we could have modified the teachings concerning Kasiwees. He might, for example, have been seeing a vision of Pistach in the guise or manner of flosti. Or a vision of the Pistach leaving the Jaupati in the future, as eventually they did. We could have admitted we did not know what the panel conveyed. The only thing at issue was whether the panel contains symbols of renewal. Does it matter whether it does or not? We believe in renewal! Must we assume our attributes are worthy only insofar as they are ancient? If we cling so tightly to the old that we do not allow ourselves to improve in both beliefs and behavior, of what value are we? Can we not say a newly achieved virtue is more worthy than a corrupted teaching?

The answer of the Chapter was that we could not. Rather than disturb the long-accepted teachings of our people, the Chapter chose to hide the bit of sky that had shown itself, and I, your friend Chiddy, was the one who hid it. For the first time in my life, I felt embarrassed, sick, vicariously humiliated at a decision of our people. I didn't make the decision, but it hurt me nonetheless. It seemed then, as it still does, wrong.

30

senator morse

When Senator Morse received Dink's report early Tuesday morning, he barely managed to maintain his usual glacial reserve.

"So you haven't found her."

"No, sir, we haven't, but believe me, these other ETs will. Arthur isn't sure about it, but Briess thinks it could make a lot of sense to throw in with this new bunch."

"Give them hunting rights? Dink, have you thought for even a moment how that would look on the evening news? 'Senator Approves Extra-Terrestrial Hunting Rights on Human Race!'"

"It wouldn't be publicized! The agreement will be secret. They won't make any noise about it if you don't."

"And the Pistach envoys? They'll keep quiet about it? I think not."

"According to this bunch, the Pistach won't be able to prove anything. I get the feeling this bunch is a lot quicker on the uptake than the Pistach are. It's like the difference between cats and cows. Or maybe goats; the Pistach are some smarter than cows. And we could always deploy a little disinformation. Like, we claim the Pistach are doing it themselves while trying to throw suspicion on someone else."

"There are paranoids out there who would probably believe it. Unfortunately, most of them don't vote."

"Senator, take a minute. Think of what they offer. Selective hunting. You got a political enemy: Bammo, he's hamburger. You got some newsman on your tail: Zip, he's cube steak. You get somebody in as president, somebody who's politics-proof, like you-know-who, he meets with an unfortunate accident. That's a good deal. Just think if we'd had this deal in the nineties! It's too good to pass up."

"Our polls say the public likes this Confederation idea."

"The predators don't care if we go ahead and join the Confederation. The predation agreement is under the table."

"And how do we keep the Pistach from finding out?"

"We tell the predators they have to hunt in places where it won't be noticeable. God knows there's plenty of places like that! Hell, every year a few million people starve here and there and nobody even blinks, providing it happens in Asia or Africa. Thirty thousand some odd kids starve every day."

"That's not something we accept!"

"Oh, hell, Senator. Don't feed me the party line. When was the last time any of your colleagues voted for overseas family planning programs? You guys claim it's to prevent abortion, but you know it's not. You know damn well cutting family planning causes more abortions than it prevents, but you still do it. Why? Because most of the pro-life people are anti-contraception, too. And anti-sex education. And anti-gay. And anti-women's-rights. But they're pro-gun, pro-hunting, pro-military. Killing's part of their lives. So why not take advantage of what these critters offer?"

"And you think the Pistach won't notice? You think people won't?"

"So, if the Pistach notice we've got deniability. So people notice. We say, hey, sorry, we'll bring it up in the UN, but it's got nothing to do with us. Senator, it's no different from stuff we do all the time, here and there. They won't hunt here in the U.S."

The Senator growled to himself. "Next time you talk to them, I'm going along."

"They'll let us know when they're ready. When they've got the woman. Briess has already laid the groundwork for that. He says we have to ask them to do something for us, to prove it won't be one-sided. Like always, one hand washes the other."

31
pistach management

The Tuesday afternoon papers said eighty percent of the population had filled out the questionnaires and the American Civil Liberties Union was screaming for blood, as were a number of people who had seen untruthful forms disintegrate under their hands. On Wednesday, Chad Riley called Benita to say in addition to completed forms there were a few dozen bags of mail for the envoys at the D.C. main post office.

Benita looked at the ceiling and said loudly, "You've got mail."

Chad called back in ten minutes to say the bags were gone, and she said, "Fine, just let me know whenever you want a pickup." Privately, she thought Chiddy and Vess might have simply vanished the mail, without bothering to read it or scan it or feed it into their machines, whatever.

She had underestimated them. Thursday night, without previous announcement, the envoys appeared on television again. They told jokes about how many Americans it took to fill out a questionnaire (all of them) or how many Afghanis (one, because there was only one right answer for everything). They said they'd heard they'd been given the nickname of Pistach-ios, because humans thought they were nuts. Benita noticed that their appearance had been further refined. They looked subtly more cuddly than they had before. Their eyes were more glowing and kindly. The squidgy bits around the mouths were less tentacular and more like a mustache. Rather Santa Claus, altogether.

Since some people hadn't filled out their questionnaires, said Chiddy—in an admonitory voice very much like Mary Poppins as portrayed by Julie Andrews—progress in solving problems would have to wait. Thank you, Chiddy said, for all the mail. Yes, they could help the quadriplegic boy brought to their attention by the governor of Arkansas and others of like condition. Yes, they had already provided help for the housing project in California which was being turned into a war zone by local drug dealers. Yes, they could find the murderer of the young women in Seattle, as requested by the police of that city, and of the three black men in Texas, as requested by the Ebenezer Baptist Church. Yes, they were already analyzing the subject of education in the U.S., as suggested by one million two hundred twenty-three thousand six hundred and eighty-four correspondents. Just as soon as the last few people filled out their questionnaires, all these matters would be handled.

"In fact," said Chiddy, "we'll share with you some of our ideas about improving education, as so many of you have suggested. We have looked at the information on dropouts, and we believe the basic trouble is that no significant rite of passage occurs at high school graduation. It should be a goal, something to be achieved on the way to adulthood, but it isn't. So, we must make it so. Certain things that adults do, like driving cars, should not be available to people who haven't graduated from high school, and social graduation of the unqualified shouldn't count. A diploma doesn't mean anything unless the information is in the head. Adult liberties should not be entrusted to ignoramusses!"

Then Chiddy did something with his face that made him look extremely stern. They would not, he said, be doing anything about drinkers, smokers, drug takers, or those who kept guns their children killed themselves with.

"Evolution must have a way to work among all races," said Chiddy in a serious voice. "Of any population, some will be born who are not survivors. Some are self-destructive or destructive of others. Others cannot muster the effort to function at a viable level. Some cannot learn. Your society, instead of letting people either perish from stupidity or learn from foolish acts, protects them from themselves and allows them, even helps them, to blame others for the stupidities they have committed. If someone has a broken ladder, sees that it is broken, then climbs it, falls, and breaks a leg, he is allowed to sue the manufacturer without even having to pay the lawyer. If someone is not bright enough to stay in school, he or she drops out and becomes the parent of several children, and you support both the person and the children. I have seen in your papers accounts of drug addicts receiving fertility treatment at public expense. Of poor women being given treatments that result in the birth of multiple children! This is monstrous!

"Persons who are no longer babies should never be saved from themselves! Persons who are self-destructive should be allowed to do so, without hindrance, as otherwise you perpetuate the tendency generation after generation! I have read in a garden book that one saves labor by learning to love weeds. This was written as a jest, but it is true of more enterprises than gardens. Weeds have their own purposes, and so do high death rates among alcoholics, drug addicts, violent persons, gun worshippers, and the perpetually angry. What we Pistach must help you do is to arrange that the fatalities happen inside these groups, rather than among innocent bystanders.

"We have a saying, we Pistach. 'Aul'a ek glusi ekfeplat num'ha ca ek athici ekfe num'h goff glusi.' Loosely translated, this means that people wanting to kill should kill themselves rather than innocent bystanders. Remember the time of the Red Guard in China and of Pol Pot in Cambodia, when the competent were killed in their millions. This is not to suggest one should punish the incompetent. No, no. Life has already done so, unfairly, as is the way of life and the universe. Let us, therefore, be kind to them. Buy them a drink or a pack of cigarettes. Wish them a nice day! Meantime, let us work together in devising ways to keep innocent bystanders from injury!"

Chiddy turned to Vess and smiled. Vess nodded, picked up a letter and displayed it.

"We have here a communique from your ACLU, complaining about the completion mark that shows on the hand of those who have filled out the questionnaire. We are unable to find any incursion upon your liberties attendant to this. You all have social security numbers, each one different, and you are asked to contribute to opinion polls all the time. We're taking a virtually one hundred percent poll on American opinion, the first of its kind. And we're being sure we count everyone, one time only, which means it's inclusive and honest.

"Parenthetically, you should know that we offered the results of our count to your census bureau, learning to our confusion that your Congress is not really interested in an accurate count of everyone, particularly minorities. Be that as it may, in our poll we are not interested in what sounds acceptable, or what the majority can be cajoled into supporting. Good government should take into account all points of view. People without the completion mark haven't filled out their questionnaires, so it's easy to tell who's holding up the works."

The morning papers recorded forcible detention of bare-palmed individuals by friends and neighbors who insisted they fill out the questionnaires so other people could get the help they needed. The papers also recorded a number of pedestrians in major cities were passing out cash, booze and cigarettes to street people they normally avoided.

32

from chiddy's journal

Dearest Benita, Vess and I have just learned that we must leave Earth for a short time. An emergency has arisen on Pistach-home, and all athyci are being mustered to consider the situation. The last time this occurred, about fifty years ago, the emergency turned out to be a minor problem of ego-assertion among two royal family inceptors. It took only part of one morning to solve, yet athyci had come from as far away as Fancher-the-Farmost. I feel this will no doubt turn out to be another of the same, though Vess is not so sanguine. Vess feels something wrong and has been feeling so for some time. Ai says there is a disturbance in the aura of Earth that stretches all the way to Pistach-home. This sounds to me like a late-life crisis. We all have them, Mengatowhai knows, that feeling that time is closing in and we have not yet made our contri-bution as fully as we had planned to do in giddy youth.

If Vess should be correct, however, what can it be? Has the rebel T'Fees done something new? Have the Xankatiki-tiki started pushing delegates around again? Are the Fluiquosm off on another of their nihilist excursions, or have we seen yet another failure in Wulivery communications? Any such thing would indeed be troubling.

You have wondered, I am sure, dearest Benita, why we have not given you or your people any details about the other members of the Confederation. If you ever read this, as I hope you will, you may even wonder why I had not given you this document as it was written, rather than as a going-away gift, only when we are ready to depart. When the time comes that you do see this, you will appreciate that there was a strong possibility you would never see it. Giving this writing to you is only a possibility, not a certainty. If your people should not come, as you so neatly put it, up to the mark, I will be forbidden to give you any information at all. If you do not achieve Neighborliness, you will be told as little as possible. Your people must want to join us for the right reasons, not out of fear at what may happen if they do not. So, I write—often and much—only in hope of a happy outcome.

Panel five of the Fresco, *Civilization*, in which the Jaupati order their world, shows what can be accomplished when peoples devote themselves to proper lives. Even the Jaupati, I am sure, were not told of the consequences of failure. No one wanted them to know that un-neighborly planets are free territory for the predators among us. On un-neighborly planets, predators are unrestrained in coming and going as they please, restricted only from causing an extinction.

Also, I will not tell you we are leaving on this trip, for you might then feel you had to tell the authorities and this might lead to inappropriate action on their part. We hope no one will notice we are gone, for we have left TV broadcasts and various interventions—including several for your school dropouts—to be implemented at intervals while we are away. We will, that is, I will, dearest Benita, look forward to seeing you again on our return.

33

benita

When she came upstairs for lunch on Friday, Benita called Angelica on her cell phone.

"Oh, Mom, I'm so glad you called. There's some man hanging around here on the campus . . . or he was a few days ago. He's been talking to Carlos, telling him you're in trouble, that you may be mixed up with some people who are dangerous. He wants Carlos to help find you, and he's offered Carlos money to help them."

"Just offered, Angel?"

"Well, no. I think he's given him money, because Carlos got enough from somewhere to rent a new apartment."

"He's definitely moving out?"

"Yes. I've taken the smaller place upstairs, and there's no room for him. He started out being angry, but lately he's been suspiciously helpful. I wouldn't put it past him to have bugged my new place for this man, whoever he is. Plus, Carlos insists he's going to get caller ID, so he'll know where you're calling from."

"Even though he knows I don't want him to know?"

"You know Carlos, Mom. When did what anybody else wants ever stop him? Himself and that girlfriend of his are the only people in his life who mean anything to him, forget the rest of us."

"Have you seen this man that's been hanging around?"

"He's a little guy, with a scruffy mustache. Carlos pointed him out to me. And the crazy thing is, another man has been offering Dad money, too. To help find you."

"Ah," murmured Benita. "Well, well. We do seem to be popular, don't we."

"What's it about, Mom? Come on. Don't leave me hanging like this. This is scary!"

"My job is with books, as I told you, but it might be described in part as working for the government," said Benita, voice firm, but hands clenched to keep from trembling. "I have to have a security check. I'm sure all this is just the normal hassle of checking my background."

"Well, I hope that's it. I'm taking this phone upstairs with me, no change in number, so you let me know how you are, okay?"

"I will, Angel. Always."

She hung up the phone and said loudly to the ceiling. "Chiddy, I need to talk to you."

There was no immediate response. "As soon as possible," she shouted. "Please."

She did not see Chiddy that day, nor the following one, even though that night both envoys appeared on television to announce that compliance was above ninety-five percent.

"We consider this good enough to go on with," said Vess. "The last five percent is always very difficult to reach, and it is unlikely to change the response to any question significantly. Now we will start working on some of your problems, and we'll catch up to the other five percent as we go along.

"Let's fill you in on previous requests first. We were asked to help a boy with paralysis in Arkansas. We have helped him and a number of other people with similar conditions. We aren't announcing his name, as we don't want him or his family bothered just yet. When he is recovered, as he will shortly be, he will hold a press conference.

"Yes, we have learned who the murderer was of the young

woman in Seattle, and the identities of the killers of the three African-Americans in Texas. Those miscreants will soon be brought to justice, in accordance with your own traditions. The press will be notified when it happens.

"As previously announced, we are already studying how to remedy the problems with your schools. The causes of their failures are many, ramified, and deeply entrenched in local politics. The most amazing thing about the situation is that fifty years ago, a century ago, your schools were far better than they are now! They taught fewer subjects and taught them better, with far more success and far less jargon. Everyone agreed then that children were children, that is, impulsive, naive, and ignorant creatures in need of training. No one suggested then that schools or teachers had to put up with hostility or violence or that students had "rights" to such behavior or that freedom of speech included rudeness in the classroom. Persons could be expelled from school and sometimes were. Children were expected to be good citizens and mannerly, and the schools taught citizenship and manners. A necessary adjunct to the school was the truant officer, who sought out and detained any child under eighteen who was not in school, and children did not get out of school until they could read and write and do arithmetic. As is true on so many worlds, the theoreticians and politicians have ruined a good thing. It is likely our interventions will simply roll back time.

"Though we choose to do nothing about drug addiction, we do choose to do something about the violence, theft, and destruction of neighborhoods that accompanies the drug problem, and you may already have heard about our efforts in one such particular area in California. Your news media have been kind enough to carry the details of that action, and the supplies requested by law enforcement agencies in other states are already being shipped."

When the program was over, Benita took Sasquatch up to her favorite thinking place, the roof. The weather had stayed so warm that the plants under the arbor had grown a third of the way up the trellis, and there were many little green worms turning up the soil, probably making fertilizer like crazy. Benita could not recall ever seeing green worms before, but then, the world had a lot of creatures she'd never seen before, all gyring and gimballing on the wabe, a whole foment of them.

Which is what the ETs were doing, and what the world was undergoing. "Chiddy," she said to the sky, pleadingly. "Please."

The plea went unheeded, as had those before.

There was much news in the Sunday papers. The quadriplegic boy in Arkansas appeared on television, walking on crutches, but definitely walking. He thanked the envoys for his miraculous recovery. The murderer of the woman in Seattle turned himself in to police, refused counsel, and pled guilty, saying a voice in his mind had told him to do so. While he was at it, he said, he'd like to also confess to thirteen other murders he had committed in Oregon, California, Nevada and Arizona.

The militia in Texas that had cooperated in the slaying of the three African-Americans turned itself in also, all eleven members. Eight confessed to conspiracy. Five confessed to aiding and abetting. All eleven confessed to illegal firearms possession, and four of them said they'd done the actual killing. Meantime, there were followup stories on the drug pushers who had ruled the territory outside the Morningside Project, all of them caught in the act of dealing drugs, acts documented right down to the quantities and amounts of money and persons present. All had been impeccably Mirandized on tape and were currently incarcerated awaiting trial. Law enforcement in sixteen other states had requested causeometers, and some had already received them.

Newspaper and TV polls taken during the week gave the ETs a seventy percent approval rating by all races, ages, sexes, and all professions except attorneys and conservative religious organizations, both of whom felt the ETs were invading their territory.

On Sunday, Benita got a phone call from the First Lady. "The president wants me to touch base with you. Do you mind?"

"Why?"

"He wants me to know how you're holding up, and whether you need any help. There's something happening on the Hill. Not just the usual extravagant egos. The president doesn't know where you are and he doesn't want to know, because there's a push for congressional hearings about the ETs. They're charging that the president knows more than he's telling, and they're looking for any excuse to accuse him of something. If I stay in touch, he can honestly say he hasn't spoken with you. Do you speak French, by any chance?"

"No," Benita confessed. "Spanish and English, that's all. And even my Spanish has gotten rusty since my mother died."

"Well then, I won't quote the French ambassador. He feels we shouldn't listen to the envoys, they can be up to no good, because if they'd had any culture at all, they'd know that French was the language of diplomacy, and they'd have started their mission in France." She chuckled, rather ruefully. "Anyhow, the president is out of town today, so I called to invite you over for supper tonight."

"That's very thoughtful of you," Benita said.

Murmuring at the other end. "Chad will pick you up around six, will that be okay? Just you two and the Secretary of State and me."

"Thank you," she agreed, wonderingly, shaking her head a few times, trying to clear it. She had really had a casual conversation with the president's wife. She had not imagined it. My, my, how her life had changed! She put the receiver down and returned to her perusal of the daily papers.

ETS PROVIDE CAUSEOMETERS NATIONWIDE
HUNDREDS OF ARRESTS MADE SINCE DETECTORS AVAILABLE

ET INQUIRY TOO PERSONAL SAYS CHRISTIAN COALITION
CHILDREN SHOULD NOT BE ASKED ABOUT FEELINGS

QUIET REIGNS IN ISRAEL FOR SECOND CONSECUTIVE WEEK

AFGHANI WOMEN, CHILDREN ENTERING PAKISTAN
FAMILIES FLEEING PLAGUE, SAY BORDER GUARDS

GEOLOGISTS ATTEMPT SONIC PROBE OF JERUSALEM HOLE
NOTHING THERE, SAY TECHNICIANS

MORSE DEMANDS TESTIMONY BY INTERMEDIARY
PRESIDENT CLAIMS NO KNOWLEDGE OF WHEREABOUTS

PSYCHOLOGISTS SAY ETS HAVE SENSE OF HUMOR
PUBLIC UNSURPRISED

BAPTISTS CLAIM ETS POSSIBLE DEMONIC INVASION
FALWELL SAYS ETS MORE LIKELY GAY

AFRICANS ON MOVE
MIGRATIONS STUMP EXPERTS

That evening Benita waited inside her back door for the car to arrive, having decided to be cautious about standing about alone in deserted places. Once the bookstore was closed, the parking lot looked empty, but one couldn't tell, really. Some lurker could pop up from behind a Dumpster or come zipping around a corner on skates. She was wasn't afraid, not really, but she was homesick. She wanted the shady portal of her parents' house, and the smell of the sun on the piñons and watching for the first golden leaves in the cottonwoods. She imagined being there, then imagined Bert being there with her and decided it was better where she was. After all, even here the evening felt like late September, with air that was crisper and cooler than it had been. Perhaps winter air would be drier.

She was so lost in nostalgia that she missed the arrival of the car until she heard the horn and looked up to see Chad Riley standing beside it, waving. He insisted she sit in the backseat, and they chatted about the book business on the way, not even mentioning the ETs. The car had darkly tinted windows, but she obediently lay down on the seat and covered herself with a blanket before they approached the gate. When he showed her up the back way, to the White House family quarters, she found the First Lady and the Secretary of State already partway through a bottle of wine and a tray of hors d'oeuvres.

A little later they served themselves from the simple buffet that had been set out earlier. Only when they had filled their plates and taken their places at the small table did the First Lady ask about the ETs.

"Intermediary, what are they really like?"

She shook her head. "I don't honestly know much more than you do. They keep switching shape, which can be confusing. I'd say they're even tempered, for they don't get angry at me when I get grumpy, and I have been a time or two. I believe they do intend to help us live happier lives."

"The questionnaires don't bother you?"

"No. It makes sense to ask people what they think before you try to make them happier."

"I'm told the FBI believes each of the ideograms on people's hands is unique," said the FL with a glance at Chad.

Benita chewed a bit of roast beef, nodding slowly. "That doesn't surprise me, either." She held out her hand, palm upward. The mark gleamed like a ruby. When the other three laid their hands down, it was obvious that though the three marks had some similarities, each mark was different, like a very complicated Chinese ideogram.

"They want to identify us individually," said the SOS. "Maybe track our movements?"

Benita took another bite of cold beef and smeared it with horseradish sauce. "I don't think so. They don't care what civil people do. But since they found those murderers in a hurry, my guess is they can screen for certain traits if they need to find a murderous militia or someone with a dangerous virus, like Ebola."

Chad grinned. "What a system."

The SOS frowned. "So you don't think it's universal surveillance?"

Benita shook her head. "Why would they want to listen to millions of people talking about the weather and taxes and how their kids misbehave or how rotten their job is? They said they needed to find out what causes woe. Then they need to stop it. If someone causes no woe, I doubt that person ever gets looked at."

"You don't see it as an infringement on liberty?" the SOS challenged her again, not angrily but demandingly. She wanted an answer.

Benita felt heat behind her ears, a flush on her cheeks. Wine did that to her.

"Well, back home, Madam Secretary, my husband had a lot of liberty. He had the liberty to knock me around. He had the liberty to drive drunk, no matter what the judge said. He had the liberty to invade my peace and steal my money and kill innocent people with his car, and the law didn't stop him or punish him. The judge had liberty. He had the liberty to sentence Bert to house arrest and to sentence me to act as his unpaid jailer, even though I was an innocent bystander and Bert both outweighed me and didn't mind hurting me.

"The judge also had the liberty to put me in jail for contempt if I made a fuss about it. He told me so when I spoke up in court to tell him I couldn't keep Bert at home and off the liquor. He said Bert was a working man and needed to get to work, and he said this even though he knew I was the one who supported the family."

"That's rotten," said Chad feelingly, his face quite red. He pressed his lips together and looked elsewhere. Benita wondered fleetingly what part of what she had said had upset him so.

Seeing an attentive audience, she went on, "Now, me, I had a lot less liberty than Bert or the judge. I didn't have the liberty to live peaceably in my own house. I didn't have the liberty to keep the fruits of my labors. I didn't have the liberty to tell the judge in court what I thought of him, and the ACLU didn't rush to my defense so I could. It hasn't rushed to the defense of the innocent people Bert may end up killing because the judge wouldn't jail him and I couldn't keep him from driving.

"So if somebody said to me, can we put a mark on you and on your kids that will keep Bert from driving your car, or stealing your daughter's stereo for drinking money, why, I'd say, mark away!"

The SOS shook her head and said in a strained voice, "I can understand your point of view, Benita."

Benita gave her a hard look, noticing for the first time just how tired and worried both women looked. "You're upset about something specific. This supper isn't just a get-together. What is it?"

They sat for a few moments, not speaking, then the FL said, "The president has been getting strange reports. Chad knows about this. A group of lumbermen disappeared in Oregon, along about the time the envoys came. Three men were killed down in Florida in a totally inexplicable way. Just today, word filtered up that there was another inexplicable death—or disappearance—in New Mexico. There are other, less specific reports . . ."

Benita frowned. "When you say a group, how many?"

"We're only talking about fifteen fatalities, total, and the last one is presumed, though personal effects were left at the scene. But then, this afternoon someone brought our attention to World News items on CNN. You watch it?"

"Sometimes," said Benita.

"A strange disappearance in Madagascar, similar to the one in Oregon. Disappearances in India, similar to the one in New Mexico. A slaughter in Brazil, just like the one in Florida."

Benita swallowed deeply. "Is there any common thread, any indication . . ."

The SOS said in a dry voice, "A common thread, yes. They were all in rural or remote areas, all of them unobserved, where people were working in or near jungles or forests. The men in Florida were digging ditches."

"And *all* of it has happened *since* the envoys arrived," said the FL flatly. "And the Congress has access to the same information we're getting."

"It couldn't be Chiddy and Vess," said Benita. "It's not what they do."

"You can understand that we do need to know," pressed the FL. "And since you are the intermediary, you're the only one we can ask to find out."

Benita stared at her plate, thinking furiously. "These

men who are out to get the president. Do you know who they are?"

The FL's lips twisted. "Your senator, Byron Morse, for one."

"He's from my state, but he's not my senator," she replied. "Who else?"

Chad said, "McVane, as you might have suspected. They have a few smart goons working for them, men named Dinklemier, Arthur, and Briess. There's a whole ring of them over at the Pentagon. There are others buried not very deeply in the Fascist Right, you know, Buchanan's bunch. There are others, quite a few, CIA or ex-CIA, most of them, and there are several other legislators. McVane and Morse are the ringleaders. Or I should say cabal leaders. It's definitely a cabal."

Benita said, "Then what's to have stopped these people from committing atrocities in India and Oregon and the other places, just to hurt the president's credibility? If they're CIA, they have the resources to do things like that, don't they?"

The FL said soothingly, "It's entirely possible, Benita. But we need to *know*."

"Next time I see them," she said. "I haven't seen them for several days."

"I hate putting you under pressure this way," said the FL. "Is there anything we can do for you? You don't sound terribly happy."

Benita laughed. "My son is being harassed by a small man with a ratty mustache who is offering him money to find out where I am . . ."

"We know who that is," muttered Chad.

". . . my husband is evidently also being solicited for his help, though not by the same man. I haven't spoken to Chiddy or Vess for several days, and now you're telling me about some more or less indiscriminate slaughter. I hear nothing in all that to make me even slightly happy."

"Ratty mustache?" said the FL, looking at Chad.

"Definitely Briess," he said, staring at Benita. "Part of the Morse Cabal. Benita, when did you hear he was bothering your kids?"

"Friday, when I spoke to Angelica on the phone, she said my son had been paid to get caller ID to trace where I am when I call them."

"That won't do them any good, will it?" the First Lady asked Chad.

"No. Caller ID won't help him. But if they've talked to her son, they might try something more sophisticated from that end, with or without his help."

"Can you prevent that?"

"We can play games. Escalate the complications. No barrier is ever unbreakable, but we can keep them off for a while."

"Make them think I'm in Denver," murmured Benita. "That's the impression I've been giving them."

The SOS set down her glass and wiped her lips, making a strange face. "You know, in recent years I've dealt with people who live in very different worlds from the one I'm familiar with. Some cultures are more foreign to me than the Pistach! In Iran or Arabia or Afghanistan, you'd swear there were no women in the society. They are as invisible as ghosts and have approximately the same status as cows. In parts of Latin America, family pride is so delicately balanced you have to watch every word. I try to see their point of view, of course, but the dissonance often gives me a feeling of unreality. Their societies haven't changed fundamentally for . . . centuries.

"During that first Cabinet meeting when the president showed us the cube, I saw it as fiction. It wasn't until Jerusalem disappeared that I grasped the fact it was reality. The envoys are real. They are going to drag us, kicking and screaming, into a new age."

Benita murmured, "I honestly think they want to minimize the kicking and screaming."

The FL turned the talk to other things, they chatted for a time, then made their farewells. Chad spirited Benita down the back stairs and out once more, to pick up another car and return home by another route. The trip was a long, twisty one, as he made sure they weren't followed.

"Who's supposed to be following us?" she asked, when they turned at the same corner for the fifth time.

"The same bunch," he offered. "The cabal."

"Why is there a cabal?"

"Oh, there are always sore losers who hate the president, any president. It's a kind of syndrome. They give money or effort to a campaign, their guy gets beaten, they take it personally. They figure they were right to support who they did, so the election must have been fixed or the public was bamboozled, or something. They usually don't examine the real cause of their hatred. Morse probably hates the president because of his wife."

"Morse's wife?"

"No. The First Lady. Morse made a rather crude pass at the lady years ago, long before her husband ran for president. Morse was drunk, at a public event, and it's unlikely he even knew who she was. She let him have it loudly enough that everyone heard it. I think the words 'lecherous sot' entered into her commentary. There was a minor furor, and it took him a while to live it down. He's been heard referring to her as a 'mouthy bitch.' With him it's simple revenge, though that's not what he says in public."

"Who else?"

"Oh, there are Pentagon guys who wouldn't mind starting a war if it would keep their budgets up. There are always people over at State who depend on crisis to advance their careers. And we know—but can't prove—there's a handful of congressmen and senators who get soft money campaign funds from nameless but probably drug-related sources south of the border. Add to that the handful of old warriors who've got their thumbs deep in the traditional values pie."

"Meaning what? What are their values?"

"Oh, guts and glory, defined as unquestioning patriotism. Marital fidelity, defined as discretion in extramarital affairs. 'Traditional' gender roles, that is, excusing rape and abuse by blaming the victim."

"But they're hunting for me," Benita said. "Why would they be interested in me?"

"Not they, I don't imagine. Him. Morse. He wants to use you to smear the president. If you turned out to be a mistress, he'd love it. Or a spy. Or a tool of the possibly communist Pistach." He turned a corner. "You can sit up now. There's nobody behind us."

"Why are we in a different car?"

"Just in case somebody saw you arrive and bugged that car figuring you'd go home the same way."

"If it were me, I'd bug them all," she said, rearranging herself.

"We thought of that. This one was with somebody we trust, several blocks away." He spoke cheerfully, examining her face in the mirror. "What's wrong?"

"It isn't a game," she cried. "I mean, I'm not a game piece. What do they intend to do with me if they find me?"

"The putative cabal? I'm not privy to their plans, Benita. Best thing is to keep you from being found."

"Do you know what's happening in Jerusalem? Besides what's on the news."

"The U.S. and NATO are providing aid to international relief organizations that are setting up tent cities for the people who've been displaced. Some of them are moving in with families in the suburbs or other cities. Everyone is very surprised that there hasn't been a wave of violence. The Saudis, by the way, are afraid either Mecca, or the Saudi women, or both may be next. They treat their women almost as badly as the Afghanis do. Women have been leaving Saudi Arabia ever since the ugly plague was reported."

"Going where?"

"About half the population belongs to the royal family, and most of them have other homes in other places. France. The U.S. Switzerland. Britain."

"If the envoys decide to make Arabian women ugly, or Iranian ones, it won't matter where they are," she said.

"Shall I quote you?" He laughed.

"Of course not."

"So far as we know, the media aren't looking for you except by putting *Attention: Jane Doe* ads in the personals. You haven't agreed to be on 20/20 have you? Or *Dateline?*"

"Is there such an ad?" she asked.

"There certainly is—are! People from the FBI have had

several little chats with the news people," he said cheerily. "Here's your door. Let me pull right up beside it."

He asked if he could see the job his agency had done on the apartment, and she invited him up. Sasquatch greeted him with a very threatening growl, but when Chad hunkered down, offered his hand and talked with Sasquatch as he scratched him behind the ears, the dog decided he was all right, gave him a good sniffing, and went back to sleep. The two of them had coffee and spent a pleasant quarter of an hour just chatting before he went home. It occurred to Benita that this was the first time in . . . what?—eighteen, nineteen years?—that she had sat in a room alone with an intelligent man in pleasant conversation. Not counting men she worked for.

The phone by the bed made her think of Angelica, and after dithering about it for a few minutes, trying to remember if Angel was in the new apartment yet, and what she'd said about moving her phone, she dialed the same number and crossed her fingers.

Angelica's phone number hadn't changed, though her voice had. She answered with a crisp, "Yes."

"It's me, honey."

"Oh, Mom. I thought it was Dad again."

"Has he been bothering you?"

"Seems like every five minutes this evening. He got bailed out by that person who wants him to help find you. So now he's facing a trial and he's all up in the air. I think the guy who bailed him out may be connected to the guy that was hanging around here. According to Dad, his guy was bigger, taller, with gray hair. He gave Dad a card with the name Prentice Arthur, and there was an even bigger guy with him called Dink."

Score two for Chad. Both of them members of the cabal.

Benita asked, "So, are you moved in to your new place?"

"As of today. I brought the last stuff up this afternoon, and they just connected the phone an hour ago. The manager was really nice to let me skip on the lease of the other apartment."

"I didn't think it could work, your living with him."

"It didn't, Mom. I think he's moved in with the girlfriend. He's got a phone now. You can call him directly."

Benita's lips were pressed so tightly that it took her a moment to respond. "I won't, Angel. Since I know he's trying to make money out of doing something that may hurt me, he's . . . well, he's broken the tie. I've been thinking about mother bears a lot."

"Bears?"

"Like on the nature shows. Mother bear is very fierce, protecting the cubs. She risks her own life for them. She does everything she can to let them grow up safe, but a time comes when she turns on them and drives them away. She's done everything she can, and from then on, they're on their own.

"The only way I can handle this is to be like a mother bear. Let the cub be himself without anything from me, no complaint, no anger, no love, certainly no interference, and that means no nothing. See what he becomes. See what he can be, totally on his own. At best, he'll turn out great. At worst, he won't be able to blame me for anything past today."

There, she'd said it, realizing as she said it that it was totally true. She was not going to overlook it. He had made his own choices, now he could stand by them.

"I can't prove he took money," Angelica cried.

"That's all right, dear. Knowing Carlos, I'm sure he did."

"How's the job?"

"I love it. Much nicer than my old one."

"I'm glad you're enjoying it. It makes me feel better about things."

"Me, too. Goodnight, Angel."

34
bert

On Monday morning, Bert Shipton received a phone call. The speaker, who did not identify himself, offered Bert a large sum of money if he would come to Washington, D.C., and introduce the speaker to his wife.

"Benita?" blurted Bert.

"She is your wife?"

"Yeah. But, she's not in Washington. She's in Denver."

"No, sir. She is pretending to be in Denver, but we believe she is actually in Washington. We would like to be introduced to her, and you can do this for us. We will pay you ten thousand dollars for your time and trouble."

Ten thousand dollars! Bert's mouth began to water. Ten thousand dollars! The best he'd read of in the want ads wouldn't have netted him ten thousand in a year! Ten thousand would pay off the mortgage arrears. And ten thousand for doing almost nothing was a kick. He could buy into that.

"What d'you want me to do?"

"You will have yourself groomed. A barber shop? A shave and haircut? You will buy new clothing. A suit. Shoes. Other garments as needed. Then go to the airport and fly to Washington today. We will meet you there."

Bert growled, "I don't have money for clothes . . ."

"Mr. Shipton. Listen carefully. There is an envelope in your mailbox with money in it. If you go to a bar, if you have even one drink, the deal is off! We will ask your son to introduce us to Benita. If you want the money, you must stay sober."

Bert grunted, almost dropping the phone in his eagerness to get to the mailbox. The envelope was there, a plain white one with his name on it, containing ten one-hundred-dollar bills. Enough to keep him floating for a long while. He wavered, shifting from foot to foot, thinking of excuses he might make, like he'd been robbed of the money, or lost it . . .

"If you drink," said a voice at his ear, "the deal is off! And we're watching, so you can't lie to us."

Bert jumped and stared around himself, seeing nothing but heat haze, rising off the pavement in wavering lines. Like a mirage, he told himself sternly. Just a mirage. Looks like all kinds of things, but it's only a mirage.

He took the money, put it in his wallet, and went to the barber shop, where a few moments under a steaming towel made him feel slightly better. The steam gave him the idea of going to the baths, where a much younger Bert had occasionally sobered up. After that, he went to the men's store in the nearest mall, where he outfitted himself as inexpensively as possible, off the rack. Every dollar spent on clothes was a dollar not spent on something more fun.

The sight of himself in the mirror, shaved, shorn, and decently clad, came as a shock. He'd worn a suit when he and Benita had been married. He'd worn a suit to the kids' high school graduations, though he hadn't planned on being outdone by his own kids in the education department and was indignant about that. And he'd worn a suit to Benita's mother's funeral, though the last thing he'd wanted to do right then was spend an afternoon thinking about that old bitch. Wearing a suit meant trouble, so far as Bert was concerned. Not a good omen, not good at all.

He bought two extra shirts, plus underwear and socks. At the corner drugstore he added a razor and a toothbrush to the shopping bag. There was still a ticket to Washington to buy, and airfares weren't cheap, as Bert had found out last year when he'd priced roundtrips to California. Angelica had invited them to come, and he'd talked Benita out of it on the grounds they couldn't afford two tickets and he didn't want her traveling alone.

He found a taxi outside the nearest hotel and slumped in the seat, already exhausted, his hands shaking.

"You all right?" asked the driver.

"Yeah," said Bert.

"You get to feelin' sick, you holler," the driver instructed, adjusting the rearview mirror so he could keep an eye on his passenger. The man looked sick. Sort of yellowish around the eyes.

At the airport, Bert went to the men's room and put cold water on his face. His insides seemed to be all up and down, like a roller coaster. When he opened his eyes, he stared at himself in the mirror, only to be reminded of Benita, the way she sometimes looked, when she didn't know he was watching her. This same sort of dazed expression. Sometimes she'd stand beside her spice rack, leaning against the wall with her nose over an open jar of anise or cinnamon sticks, her eyes shut, her forehead wrinkled. Once or twice he'd opened the jars and sniffed at them. The smell was nice, but that's all it was. It didn't make his mouth water. It didn't excite him any. He couldn't fathom why she stood there the way she did, sniffing at . . . at what? It made him angry at her, but then, most things she did made him angry at her.

Now he had that same expression on his face. So, what was he sniffing at? The possibility of going somewhere? Doing something? It had been a long time since he'd gone anywhere, done anything. He tried to think about the going, the doing, but it was hard. Thinking was hard, lately. Just lately, he assured himself. Just this last little while. It wasn't that he was stupid. Bert was absolutely one hundred percent not stupid. He was as smart as anybody, but just this last little while, it was hard to concentrate on anything. It could be the weed. When he was out of money, sometimes he moved a little weed for a friend of Larry's. Not usually, not enough to risk getting caught with it, but now and then it was okay, just so he didn't get in a pattern. Except, lately, he'd been using more of it himself, and maybe that was what made it hard to think.

After several vague moments spent standing, head down, not moving or thinking, he worked up the energy to go buy the ticket. Lucky him, the flight was leaving in twenty minutes. No baggage to check. All he had was the shopping bag. The money was in his wallet and most of the clothes were on his back. At the newsstand, he bought a canvas airline bag to put the extra shirts in, and a sports magazine, and some mints because his throat was so dry.

He only had a one-way ticket. Maybe he should have bought a roundtrip. Then again, there was no point in wasting the money. He'd have plenty of money when this was over. As he went down the concourse, he passed the first bar with only a slight swerve of footsteps in its direction. He hesitated at the next one, but the plane was leaving too soon for him to stop. As it was, he was the last person to board. The plane was half empty, so Bert had a window seat with an empty aisle seat next to him. The flight attendant came by and reminded him to put his seatbelt on. He fumbled with it, hands trembling again.

Then they made an announcement about beverage service, and his hands steadied, he licked his lips and tried to swallow, but his mouth was too dry. He couldn't wait for the flight attendant to get to him, and he shifted in the seat. His skin felt itchy. Like it had ants crawling on it.

A voice spoke from the empty aisle seat next to him.

"Not one drink, Bert. Not one. Or we throw you out of the plane and watch you fly."

He couldn't see anything in the seat. His eyes confirmed vacancy, his hand, tentatively reached, encountered nothing. As frightened as he could ever remember being, he turned his eyes away, put his head back and, for the next several hours, pretended to be sleeping.

When he arrived in Washington, the voice guided him to a taxi, and the taxi to a hotel where Bert found a room awaiting him, all paid for. When he got into the room, he took his jacket off and stretched out on the bed, just for a moment, before going out on a foraging trip. The money he had left was burning a hole in his pocket. He thought about it. There was a bar downstairs. He'd seen it on the way in. He tasted the beer he was going to drink, feeling it sliding down his throat, feeling his body loosen and swim, all the tight muscles letting go . . .

The being who had accompanied him from Albuquerque encouraged the vision, the feeling, the quiet. It left him sleeping. He would stay asleep until he was needed. The Fluiquosm were very good at keeping prey quiet and in good condition until needed.

35
benita

TUESDAY NIGHT

Tuesday morning, Benita woke up feeling like death warmed over. She went downstairs to work, but Simon sent her back upstairs, where she remained achy and fretful all day, feeling as though she was coming down with the flu or a rotten chest cold. She went to bed early with a glass of warm milk and one of her hoarded sleeping pills. She didn't take them often, keeping them for emergencies, when Bert was being impossible and she was too hurt or angry to sleep. She hadn't planned to need them in Washington, but she was thankful to have a few left.

Despite the pill, she couldn't settle. Sasquatch turned around and around on the foot of the bed until she yelled at him. He gave her an offended look, jumped off the bed, and curled up in his huge dog basket, though even there, he kept up a restless shifting and ear-pricking, as though something was bothering him. Finally, about midnight, she fell asleep with the light on, some time later rousing just enough to switch it off without interrupting the dream she was having about trekking through a jungle. Sasquatch was with her, nervously alert, woofing low in his throat the way he did when he saw a skunk or a really big raccoon or Bert with the blind staggers.

In the dream, she was worried about some kind of beast,

a bear or jaguar, and she heard Sasquatch's woof very clearly, so clearly that she woke up with the reality of it in her ears. There was Sasquatch in the middle of the bedroom floor, the fur on his shoulders and neck bristled up like a mane, nose wrinkled, fangs showing, the dim light reflected from his eyes as he stared up at the high windows of the bedroom that looked out on the roof of the other building, which was accessible only from the higher roof above her head. Which was, supposedly, accessible only from the elevator unless someone had a very tall ladder. The people who fixed up the apartment had covered the whole row of windows with gathered curtains of translucent muslin. The light came in, but the view was blocked, either in or out. Benita's half-opened eyes followed the dog's gaze to the curtains, a row of slightly lighter squares against the dark . . .

Slightly lighter squares across which something moved, from left to right, a slow shadow that progressed from window to window, touching each one, pushing at each one, making them creak protestingly. The shadow was a featureless blob, sometimes straight on the sides, sometimes with a hint of squirminess about it. The frames creaked, again and again, though not loudly and without yielding, for wire-glass inside steel frames doesn't break easily. Sasquatch backed up until his rump was against the bed and went on making what was almost a whispered growl, more a mutter in his throat than a threat. He didn't like whatever was up there. Benita didn't either. Whatever was up there scared her spitless. The bottom of the windows were even with the roof and the panes were about five feet tall. Whatever was throwing the shadow was taller than that, as it extended all the way from bottom to top.

The shadow moved on, and almost at once she heard something rattling from the direction of the elevator hall. She almost fell out of bed as she scrambled to get there before the elevator could move. At each floor the cage was shut off by a folding metal grille that could not open unless the elevator was on that floor, to keep someone from falling down the shaft. The elevator was where she had left it, on the third floor, and the rattling was coming from the roof above her!

She opened the elevator grille, just enough to keep the elevator from departing, and looked frantically around for something to prop it with. The hall was empty, so she simply stuck her foot between the grille and the frame, holding it there while the rattling continued over her head as though something was trying to get into the elevator housing. It had an outside door, which locked automatically if one didn't set the unlock button. Even if whatever it was got in, so long as she held the grille open, the elevator wouldn't ascend and the upper grille couldn't move.

The rattling was succeeded by the hum click of the controls. The thing had broken into the housing and pushed the button that summoned the elevator. The grille thrust hard against her foot, and she swore in a panicky whisper as it pinched. A smell came down the shaft, filtering out around the car, and she almost gagged at the rotten meat filthiness of it.

She was scrunched up tight in the corner of the hall where the elevator shaft met the outside wall, one foot extended awkwardly into the grille space. The only window was several feet to her left, and though she couldn't see through it from her position, she could see the quality of light that came through it as it was repeatedly blocked by something. Dim, then brighter, then dim again, over and over, as though something hung over the parapet and looked in. Or as though something rose up from the street and looked in? That window was a good thirty-five to forty feet above the ground and at least eight or ten feet below the edge of the parapet that ran around the roof. Benita told herself she was all right, she had to be all right if she was doing arithmetic in her head.

All right or not, she was shaking. Through the open apartment door she could see Sasquatch lying absolutely flat with his head on his paws and his ears out to the sides as though he were hiding, or at least keeping a low profile. She knew he was out of the line of sight, as she was, so whatever was looking in couldn't see anything. Then everything stopped above her and she heard a swudge, swudge, swudge going from above her head toward the front windows, the center one of which happened to be slightly open!

She scrambled to her feet and ran through the living room to the window, where she reached under the closed drapes and cranked the window shut, slammed the lock down, then ran back past a bookshelf where she grabbed a thick book and got it jammed in the elevator door just in time to hold it open as the clicking from above resumed.

Leaving it there, she returned to the living room and lay down next to Sasquatch. They cowered silently together while she distracted herself thinking of escape routes. Down the fire stairs, two flights, into the stockroom, which had doors that could be locked from inside. Or, from the stockroom into the bookstore and out the front door. But, whatever was on the roof could see the front door. And she didn't have a car. And her phone was in the bedroom, which would put her farther from the stairs . . .

Tiring of the elevator fiddle, the visitors tried another gambit. A very familiar voice.

Bert's voice. "Benita! You open this door! I need to talk to you, Benita! You come out here where we can talk! You've got the kids all worried about you, and I need to talk to you."

Silence. The voice seemed to be coming from outside the front windows, which was unlikely. Though he could be yelling from the sidewalk, it didn't sound like that, and turning her head she saw a man-shaped shadow pressed against the glass.

"Benita?" Then a clatter. "Ouch, damn it, she's not home, if this is her place, stop that."

Benita didn't move, nor did the dog. The squadge, squadge, squadge was repeated several times, and then silence fell. It went on, and on, and at last Sasquatch's head came up, then his ears. He got up and went to the elevator where he sniffed all around the door before coming back to lick her face.

What had it been outside her window? She thought of the First Lady's remarks about the men in Oregon, the men in Florida, the guy in New Mexico. People off in the trees, and then no people. Just gone. Only bones left. Nobody saw what did it. Could something invisible cast a shadow?

She didn't know and she didn't want to find out. There was no one she could call except Chad, and what could he do? Take her somewhere else, put her in custody? Keep her safe? What she really needed was to talk to Chiddy, and she hadn't seen him in person for . . . over a week!

She went back to bed, welcoming Sasquatch's company close beside her. An hour later she gave up and called Chad.

He arrived in twenty minutes.

"What do you think it was?" he asked.

"Whatever's doing all the stuff the First Lady told us about the other night! I mean, what else could it be? It wasn't people. It, or they, were a lot bigger than people. It wasn't anything native to Earth, that's for sure. And whatever it was pushed Bert right up against the living room windows, and those windows are thirty feet off the sidewalk."

She took a deep breath. "It wasn't Chiddy and Vess because they come in here all the time, they don't have to walk around on the roof, but I'll bet it was some of those other races they talked about at that dinner, remember? Chiddy talked about predators who had to obey Confederation law, but only if we were in the Confederation. Remember, they said that's why they wanted to move in such a hurry?"

He looked dazed, then angry, then gave her some news that hadn't appeared on TV. People were still being killed. In India whole villages of them were wiped out around the perimeter of nature preserves. Also in Southeast Asia. Any activity requiring people to work out of sight in rural or primitive areas had pretty much stopped, because nobody could find crews willing to do it.

"The White House has asked the news media to report things that might concern the ETs as calmly as possible with no screaming headlines. The president told the media that nothing now happening is under the control of any person. At this point, we believe we still have influence over what may happen, but any public outcry may move events beyond our abilities even to influence them. "

"This is getting serious, isn't it?" she said.

"I simply wish your two ET friends hadn't picked right now to take off where they can't be reached. And I wish to hell they'd come back!"

36

from chiddy's journal

Dear Benita, I write this as we return toward your Earth
from our sojourn in Pistach-home. We were not summoned
home on a simple matter, as I had hoped. This was no confusion over royal egos but was, instead, a vast troubling over
T'Fees the Turbulent, who has titled self Grand Something-
or-other, ruler over three Pistach planets! In each case,
T'Fees has moved in, talked the campesi into a fury, assaulted the more specialized castes, particularly selectors
and athyci, and has begun training armies. Amazing, impossible that he should have been able to do this alone!
How has this happened!

Vess and I were summoned home to answer to the Chapter about our work on Assurdo, which had resulted in this
bizarre ligament of events. We self-examined our work. The
only thing we might have done differently was to have regressed T'Fees, but the guidelines tell us never to do that unless necessary, and in T'Fees's case, no one had known it was
necessary. Luckily, the three planets T'Fees has conquered
are low-tech planets, which means they can be easily as-
sailed with high-tech modifiers, such as those we have used
on your Earth, dear Benita. A surreptitious seeding of

nanobots has been done on all three worlds. The nanobots suspended everyone on the planet, and teams from both Pistach-home and several of our high-tech worlds are even now descending to do regressions on all army trainees. We hoped to find T'Fees and his coterie, a group said to be more intelligent and active than most, but unfortunately they were not on any of the planets we invaded. How did they escape us, and where have they gone?

Our fear is that they may have taken refuge with some other race of the Confederation, not all of whom are sympathetic with our ways. Sometimes I wish we could use nanobots on other races, but all other Confederation members have defensive bots to prevent our "taking them over," as though we would want to! Providing them with bots of their own was part of our original peace process, what Vess and I sometimes call our balance of error.

There was nothing we could do to help this situation, and the Chapter agreed it was not our fault. Biological sports like T'Fees are not anyone's fault. They just happen. You have had your Attilas and Hitlers and Miloseviks; we have had our K'fars and M'quogjums, et al., though they were far, far in the past, in pre-Mengantowhai times. When we catch up to T'Fees, be assured he will be analyzed from heelspur to carapace! Though we will be kept apprised of what goes on in the T'Fees matter, the Chapter, having heard disturbing news concerning predation on your world, urged us to get back to our work as soon as possible.

Though our prerecorded appearances on your TV will have kept things simmering in accordance with the plan, that plan certainly did *not* include the inexcusable actions of the Xankatikitiki, the Fluiquosm and the Wulivery! They have, as your people say, pushed the envelope of acceptable behavior. When we arrived at Pistach-home we learned of their incursions on Earth from a Confederation staffer. Evidently the predators had bragged of it at some interplanetary meeting or other. They do revel in coup counting, though it is often their downfall.

We immediately appealed to the Confederation headquarters. They responded, saying the three predatory races now claim they had never been informed that we, the Pistach, are assisting your planet toward Neighborliness.

Our ambassador to the Confederation immediately provided a copy of our previous notification, which had been circulated long before Vess and I even left Pistach-home! The Wulivery, as usual, claim communications problems, this time between their hunters' guild and their Confederation legation. The Xankatikitiki and Fluiquosm claim they are merely acting in concert with the Wulivery, whom they relied upon to take care of the formalities. This is patently dishonest, a ploy which is new only in its details. They knew very well we were here and they risked failure of our project by their interference!

One knows why, of course. No planet has ever been discovered as crowded with intelligent life as yours! All of our predatory races prefer creatures of good taste, that is, brainy creatures. Even your native predators eat the brains of their prey first when they can.

Meantime, a good many of your people have been slaughtered, though the loss is only numerical. No appreciable proportion of humanity or any subset of it has been lost, no irreplaceable knowledge or experience has been deleted. Even so, the deaths are grievous to us. We will immediately touch the survivors to learn what may be done to atone. We must also, unfortunately, make our own arrangements to find the Xankatikitiki, et al., and bring them into compliance, for once on the hunt, these races do not call home.

As we must make clear to your people, dear Benita, our predatory associates are not easy to find, let alone admonish. While your armed forces might possibly locate and destroy them, leaving the matter to us will result in less loss of life in the long run. I will communicate this directly to your United Nations when we return, dear Benita. We are covered with chagrin.

Despite these alarms and confusions, I am looking forward to seeing more of your art and hearing more of your music. I still quiver at the memory of those paintings on the ceiling of the Sistine Chapel. How majestic they are, how strong and pure. Even your ancient paintings at Lascaux and Altamira have a great strength and resonance, an inborn sense of beauty. There is much about your people that is enviable, Benita. You will be a great asset to the Confederation if we can only sort out these minor difficulties.

37
benita

WEDNESDAY

On Wednesday evening, Chiddy and Vess returned, announcing their arrival by a phone call only moments before they appeared in Benita's hallway. Over coffee—which they said they much liked and intended to export to Pistachhome—they told her about a Pistach named T'Fees who had gone crazy and upset the orderly way of things, requiring a lot of trouble on the part of their people. She listened, lips tight and growing more and more irritated, while they hemmed and hawed for a while, using a lot of words to say almost nothing.

Finally, Chiddy said, "Benita, we have to tell you something. We deeply regret it, but—"

"You don't have to tell me the predators are here," she snapped, in a voice that sounded testy even to her. "I'd rather imagined they were when one or more of them tried to get into this apartment last night! They've got Bert already. I don't suppose you knew that!"

Both the Pistach turned rather green and slightly demorphous, as Benita had observed them do on similar occasions. When they were upset, they lost a certain definition of shape, becoming foggy about the edges, though only momentarily. As they solidified once more they glared at one another, turning redder and redder. During their visits she had learned to tell when they were angry, because no matter what shape they were in, they turned red, just as humans did. When she had mentioned this, they told her their vital fluids were similar to those of humans.

Chiddy growled, "They came after *you*, Benita? *You* particularly?"

"The only other creature living here is the dog," she growled. "It was at night, so I was the only person in the building. Something went past my bedroom windows and then tried to get into the elevator. Then they pushed Bert up against the front windows and had him yelling at me, asking me to come to the door. If they'd tried him first instead of crunching around on the roof, I might have fallen for it."

Chiddy's male human guise nodded miserably. "We found out the predators were here when we arrived at Pistachhome, and when we returned, we detoured to affirm the presence of their ships on the back of your moon. We've already called for censure of all three races by the Confederation, plus we've brought several Confederation Inkleozese back with us."

"More aliens?" she blurted.

"The Inkleozese are the traditional monitors and peacekeepers of the Confederation. They are feared even by the predators, and they are best qualified to do what now must be done. We did not know, could not have guessed, that the predators would bother your person, yourself! Why would they?"

She had pondered this herself. "They probably aren't doing it for themselves. There are people looking for me. Political enemies of the current administration. You know that."

"Yes, but . . . is it possible that . . . could they . . . can we believe . . ."

The two of them went off into a corner and buzzed at one another, waving their arms, looking crestfallen.

She interrupted their conference. "Someone probably put them up to taking Bert. I'm not fond of him, Chiddy, but I don't want him . . . eaten or tortured or anything like that."

Chiddy shook his head, almost humanlike. "Benita, though we hate to believe it, you are probably correct about their motive. It seems likely the predators have made common cause with some barbarians among you who wanted your husband taken for political reasons. If this is so, they are unlikely to hurt him. The predators are brazen, but they are not fools."

"What barbarians are we talking about?"

"Those like the man McVane."

"Good old McVane," she snorted. "Him and his cabal."

Chiddy shook his head, remarking, "Such violations of protocol have been known to happen in the past when members of the Confederation have discovered intelligent races who do not have a planetary government. A disunited planet allows the predators to shop about among factions, nations, tribes, or rulers to find someone or some group they can work with! Once they have done so, they claim immunity from Confederation rules because they have a treaty with natives. Then the whole matter must be referred to the Confederation courts for decision, and the courts appoint a study commission, the commission submits a report, the report is subject to question by some other group, and the whole thing takes absolutely forever! Meantime, the predators go on happily hunting.

"Unfortunately, we have no immediate way to reach those of them who are loose on your world except by going to the ships on the back of your moon and demanding contact. We could do this, we will do it if necessary, but it will be a black mark against Pistach in the Confederation. A ship at rest on an unoccupied planet or moon has a status equivalent to your foreign embassies. Why in the name of Gharm the Great didn't you people set up an outpost there when you had the chance? Since you didn't, the predators' ships are sovereign territory. One may visit, one may gently suggest, but making a demand on sovereign territory opens one to criticism and shame."

Vess interrupted, "Individual predators on an occupied planet, however, have no such status. We may do with them as we will . . ."

"Or can," muttered Chiddy, looking downcast. "When and if we find them!"

Vess gave him a reproving stare. "We will find them! It may take a few days, however, and we can't wait that long to explain to your people, dear Benita."

"Start by explaining a couple of things to me," she suggested angrily. "Starting with how they found me!"

Chiddy heaved a very human-sounding sigh. "The Wulivery can smell the Pistach, dear Benita. I mean they can smell any creature, like your bloodhounds, only better. They had only to send out sniffers to pick up our Pistach scent and determine where it was stronger. We have spent more time with you, here, than in virtually any other place, so our smell is very strong here, in your home. They would have known that."

"I see," she murmured. She couldn't smell anything, but then, she wasn't a Pistach, or a predator. "You'd better let the world know what they're up against. People are not going to like it."

Chiddy composed himself enough to say, "Please call your go-between to the government and explain what has happened. Then, tonight, we will apologize to all your people through the television. We will also introduce the Inkleozese to them and explain the function of our monitors."

Vess assured her their apology would appear everywhere, in whatever language was locally spoken. She suggested they show pictures of the predators on TV, just so people would know what they were talking about, and they said they could do that for the Xankatikitiki and Wulivery, but not for the Fluiquosm, who do not make any reproducible image.

"Are they invisible when they're dead?" she asked grumpily.

"Why no," said Vess.

"Then show a picture of a dead one," she demanded.

"Wouldn't that be in bad taste?" Vess asked, making fussy little motions with his hands.

"You told me you've watched our television for years," she snarled. "After O. J. Simpson's trial and Ken Starr's investi-

gation and the constant stench from Trash TV, what's a dead
Fluiquosm or two?"

They thought a bit and then said they'd get a picture of a
dead one. "By the way," said Chiddy, "you may do me a small
favor. I would like to leave my translator here, listening to
your television. I would do it in the ship, but all the ship's
circuits will be fully occupied seeking predators and maintaining the disappearances and the ugly-plagues."

"You really *want* to translate our TV?" she asked, distractedly. The thought of Bert as a captive had just led her to
wondering if Angelica and Carlos were safe. If they had
taken her husband . . .

"No. There is little of it we enjoy. However, my accumu-
lation of spoken vocabularies is not complete, and you have
a Spanish language station? If you would be kind enough to
leave it on while you are away?"

She nodded and gestured at the set, without really listening, not even watching as Chiddy put a black device no
larger than a tiny camera on top of the TV.

"When you are leaving, turn on the TV and push the red
button to turn it on," Chiddy murmured when he left. "It will
feed accumulated vocabulary to the ship. In fact, if you
should need us, you can simply shout at it. Something urgent. Like *SOS* or *Danger*, or *Fire!*"

She wasn't listening, for she had already picked up the
phone to call Chad and ask him to provide some protection
for Angelica. By this time she and Chad had each other's
numbers memorized, as they talked virtually every day, and
Sasquatch was so used to Chad dropping in that he didn't
even growl at him anymore. On this occasion, Benita explained her concern by repeating every word Chiddy and
Vess had ever said about predators making common cause
with McVane, et al. She didn't mention T'Fees. Even though
neither Vess nor Chiddy had asked her to be secretive
about the T'Fees problem, she didn't think Earth needed
any more variables thrown into the pot than it already had.
She did, however, tell him about the Inkleozese.

Chad muttered and grumbled, "New ones? Benita, you've
got to be kidding!"

"I'm not, Chad. They just told me about these creatures. Evidently they act in the same capacity as our UN peacekeepers."

"Ineffectually, you mean?" he said in disgust.

"Chad! It's not my fault."

He said he knew that, apologizing for his tone. "Since you seem convinced the predators are working with Mc-Vane and his bunch, there's nothing to suppose they'll stop with Bert. I think you're right to be worried about your kids, and I'll get some protection started for them."

"Anything you can do, Chad. I hate to be a bother but—"

"Think nothing of it," he said, entirely too tersely, as he went off to transmit the message to whomever.

That night she watched as the two envoys explained very clearly and concisely what the Confederation was and who the members were. They mentioned there were over fifty member races, most of whom lived at great distances from one another and from Earth, only about ten of them anywhere nearby. "Nearby," Chiddy defined as "offering something worth the very high cost of interstellar flight." Chiddy and Vess showed pictures, the nonpredators first: flutelike Vixbots, swamp-living Oumfuz, the differentiated Credons, the winged Flibotsi, the crablike Thwakians.

Then, in greater detail, the predators: the Wulivery looked more like sea anemones than elephants. They had a ring of twelve tentacles around their mouthparts, which were on top of their heads. When relaxed, the head part was immediately above their relaxed, stumpy fat legs. When the creatures were not relaxed, the legs elongated from around eight feet up to thirty feet or more, moving the tentacles far above human eye level and allowing the rough gray skin of the leg to blend among the tree trunks of any forest or jungle. Their hunting was generally limited, said Chiddy, to wooded areas.

Oh, yeah, Benita commented to herself. Washington, D.C., wasn't wooded, but that was the shape that had been on the roof!

While the Wulivery resembled sea anemones, the Xankatikitiki looked more like six-legged bears. They weighed a hundred twenty to a hundred fifty pounds. The fur and the personality were like that of a wolverine. The four longish legs were cheetahlike. The two arms were muscular, like a gorilla's. The prehensile tail was like the back end of a python, and the jaws were as strong as hyenas'. Adding to the general ferocity, their claws were retractable and the teeth were poisonous in the same way as a Komodo dragon's teeth, that is, so filthy that any wound led to sepsis and eventual death. All of which meant, so Chiddy said, they could climb very well, run very fast, and kill almost anything. They hunted in small, family packs, mostly in open areas.

The Fluiquosm were virtually invisible. They flew and had rending organs (beaks? talons?). The body they had pictures of was pale yellow, about the size of a Rottweiler, with a strange complicated growth on its back that Chiddy identified as the flying organ, not wings, but something else. Chiddy said to think of them as large, intelligent, invisible eagles who happened to be quite ferocious.

The broadcast continued with Chiddy apologizing profusely to all the people of Earth who, he said, would understand what was happening, because on Earth there were member nations of the U.N. who were always telling lies and trying to beat the system, like Iraq or Libya, or members who didn't pay their dues but still expected to be respected and listened to, like the U.S.

At the very end of the broadcast, they explained why they had brought the Inkleozese and introduced the score of them who were already on Earth. Their names were unpronounceable. They didn't seem threatening or unlikable, though when the Inkleozese turned to leave, the audience could see rear ends much like a wasp's rear end, terminating in a lethal looking daggerlike arrangement.

Benita's phone rang about an hour after the broadcast: Chad, wanting to know if it would be a violation of Neighborliness if humans went hunting for the Xankatikitiki and others. The White House was receiving hundreds of calls, and he said for every call they got, there were probably a dozen hunters out there, already planning their expeditions.

When she hung up, she uttered this question loudly and her phone rang.

Chiddy's voice said, "You caught us just as we were leaving to go hunt predators, Benita. What is it?"

She explained Chad's problem.

"Predators' rules are different from civilized rules," Chiddy replied in a reproving voice. "Any Confederation predator who goes on the hunt is fair game for anyone, although the odds on Earthian hunters actually killing one are vanishingly small."

To help out, however, he said the body temperature of a Xanka was 116° F, a Fluiquosm 80° F, and a Wulivery 104° F, so heat detectors could be used against cooler or warmer backgrounds. All their worlds were reasonably Earthlike, and they didn't need any kind of protective gear except for the Wulivery, who need breathing tubes to furnish them with methane.

"What about me?" Benita asked. "Will they keep coming after me?"

Long silence. "We will try to protect you, dear Benita," said Chiddy. "So long as you are in your home or at work this should be fairly easy. We could always find you, of course, you or any other individual, but it would take time, so keep us apprised of your whereabouts."

Thanks a lot, she grumbled to herself. She reported to Chad; he thanked her, sounding irritated, though she felt it was irritation at the situation, not at her. She could visualize all those eager hunters, stocking up on ammunition and dehydrated food and buying tickets to . . . where? India? Brazil? Or would they stick mostly to the U.S? Chiddy and Vess hadn't specifically mentioned the killings in the U.S. So far, nobody had publicly tied Oregon, New Mexico, and Florida to alien predation.

38

law enforcement

The retaking of the Morningside Project from the dealers was considered completed on the Friday afternoon when the wagon and attendant patrol cars drove to Morningside, as they had each day for the past several weeks, but returned empty for the third consecutive day.

Sergeant McClellan got down from the passenger seat side of the cab and shook himself, settling his trousers into their customary sag and his face into an unaccustomed grin.

"Any?" asked the captain from the precinct steps.

"Not one," replied the sergeant. "The Fourth Floor Women's Circle baked a cake. We had coffee and muffins. The kids sang. It was a party."

"You did a sweep inside every vacant apartment?"

"There're only a few vacant ones, and they're being re-habbed. This last two weeks, the place's filled up. All the people that wanted to get out, they've stayed in. The place even looks better. Somebody donated paint and rollers, and the tenants are painting the halls themselves. A nursery do-nated some trees. The city's fixed the elevators. Some teach-ers and some of the kids from over at the school came over. They gave us thank-you cards the kids made."

"Thank you, ETs," breathed the captain. "What do you think? Have a patrol go by there a couple times a day, just to check?"

"I'd say that isn't necessary." McClellan eased himself up the steps and down the hall to his desk, the captain close behind. "The people there, they'll call us if anything goes wrong. You know, we're gonna have a new problem, Boss."

"What's that?" asked the captain, following along, beaming from ear to ear.

"I read last night the traffic into the States from Mexico is moving right along. All it takes is a touch of the causometer to let somebody through. No more searches for no reason, no more stops with no evidence. It's working. So, we're looking at a problem actually solved here. What're we supposed to do now? No real drug busts for a week. Almost no burglaries for . . . what, six days? The drug gangs have disappeared. We've had no little kids caught carrying weapons. No shooting incidents, drive-by or school yard. Our problem's going to be finding stuff to do."

"We still got domestics," snarled the captain, attempting severity. "We got murders. We got muggings. We got some nut up on Alta Vista trying to get little kids into his car to pet his weenie. It's not coming up all roses. You haven't died and gone to heaven yet, McClellan!"

McClellan shrugged. "Hey, let me gloat a little. Let us feel good. Tomorrow somebody'll figure how to fool the causometer, we'll be back where we started . . ."

"We are back where we started," said the lieutenant, from the other side of the room where he'd been tied up on the phone. "We've got five people disappeared from the university, three male students, one coach, one woman student, all of them taken from the sports center up on Cañoncito, twenty hundred block . . ."

"So? Send a car," said the captain, looking puzzled.

The lieutenant came across the room to murmur into Riggles's ear. The captain frowned, shook his head, then said, "McClellan, take Burton with you, go up there and find out what's happening."

"Something weird?" asked McClellan, accurately reading his boss's expression.

The captain shrugged. "Ah . . . remember that *Enquirer* article? And the ETs on TV, talking about predators? Maybe this isn't something for a patrol. We'll bypass patrol and find out, okay?"

Burton, a husky youngster only three years on the force, drove, lights and siren on. McClellan watched the streets flee by as they swerved through evening traffic, counting to himself. After today, three more days until his last day. And wouldn't you know, the job was just getting worth doing again when he was getting ready to leave it. These last couple weeks had been fun, like the old days, putting the bad guys away and doing it without walking a tightrope the whole time, doing it honestly, no cheating, no faked evidence or any of the stuff some men fell into when their patience wore out. If he were a churchgoing man, McClellan thought maybe he'd go to services and thank God for the ETs.

"Next right," he said to Burton, grabbing for support as the car swerved at the corner. "Slow down. We're not chasing anybody." Wouldn't that frost your cookie! Killed in a speeding police car, chasing nobody, three days before retirement.

The street ended at the back of a tall, blocky gymnasium, separated from the street by a row of bollards. Burton eased around the bollards and parked as close to the front of the building as he could get. An unlocked gate in a high fence opened on a wide stone terrace extending across the building front. Three shallow steps outside the double doors of the building were occupied by a cluster of young men and women students gathered around a hunched over, weeping figure.

McClellan fumbled for his notebook and approached the group. "So, what happened?"

The tear-stained person at the center of the group looked up and cried, "They disappeared. Right in front of me!"

"Okay, okay, miss," murmured McClellan. "Now, who was it who disappeared?"

"My brother," the young woman cried. "Carlos Shipton. And some other people. I don't know who. They were out there . . ." She waved toward the oval track below them, separated from the terrace by a wide, shallow tier of bleachers. "There were two other guys, and a coach, and . . . a girl in running shorts walking along the track, and . . ." She looked up, her mouth squared into an agonized mask of tragedy.

"And then?" murmured McClellan.

"They were gone. One minute they were there, the next minute they were gone." She dabbed at her face with the backs of her hands, smearing the tears.

"There was a smell," volunteered one of the students. "When I came out of the building, there was a strange smell."

Two others nodded, yes, there'd been a smell.

One of the building doors banged open to a hurrying youth, who called out, "It was Coach Jensen. Coach Jensen, and he was out there with three guys, Turley, McClure, and Shipton."

"Who was the girl?"

The young man shook his head. "She was just somebody out there running. I came over here to see Carlos. He owes me money from when we roomed together last year, and I need it. When I got here, I saw he was busy with the coach, so I waited for him. Then I saw the girl, and at first I thought she was Carlos's sister, so I walked down there and called to her and waved. She looked up, and then I saw she was somebody else."

"You were here when they disappeared?"

The youth looked flustered. "I didn't actually see them disappear. I thought the girl was Angelica, so I yelled 'Hey, Angelica,' but it wasn't her. The real Angelica was standing right there," he pointed, "at the top of the stairs, and I said something like, 'Oh, there you are,' and she screamed. She was looking past me, down there, and when I turned around, they were gone."

"Coach Jensen, and three students?"

"That's who the coach's assistant says. And the girl," said the youth.

"Your name is?"

"Mack Dugan. I roomed with Carlos last year. That's how I knew him and his sister."

"Is that what happened?" McClellan asked Angelica. "Did he tell it the way it happened."

She nodded, wiping at her eyes. "That's what happened, yes. They just weren't there anymore. Just gone. Like . . . vanished."

"Why were you here?" McClellan asked. "Do you usually meet your brother—"

"No," she cried. "Somebody came to my place late this afternoon looking for him," she flushed, not wanting to mention the FBI, "and I said I'd . . . I'd let Carlos know." Actually, the FBI man was now standing over by the fence, talking rapidly into a cell phone and waving his free hand in frustration. "I know he has a late phys ed class, so I thought he might be here . . ."

"What about this smell?" asked McClellan. "What did it smell like?"

"Like welding," said one of the male students. "I heard her screaming, and I came out from inside, and I smelled it. Like welding. Kind of a hot smell."

Another of them said he'd smelled something also, but he couldn't identify the smell, though he said it reminded him of blood.

"Show me where people were," McClellan said to Mack, leading the way down the stairs at the center of the bleachers. There Mack turned to the left and walked about thirty yards to bring them even with the starting blocks.

Mack said, "Here! Right here. The three guys were at the starting blocks of the three inside lanes, Ron Turley on the inside, then Carlos, then McClure. Coach Jensen was standing in the next lane, leaning over, telling them something." He turned to his right. "The girl was twenty or thirty feet that way, walking along the outside lane toward the bleacher stairs."

McClellan turned, peering in all directions. Concrete posts had been set into the slope with canted steel els protruding from them. Thick wooden slats making up seats and backs were bolted to the els. The rows were separated by flat, graveled paths. There was no place to hide; everything was wide open. You could see every gum wrapper. There was nothing below but the starting blocks, the lines marking the lanes, and the hurdles set up at intervals.

McClellan moved across the track onto the grass at its center to examine the pole vault uprights and landing pad, one designed to be inflated during use but currently flat and wrinkled. He heaved up a corner, finding it was laid directly on the earth. The landing pit for the long jump had been freshly raked. There were no prints in it. The oval track was separated from the grassy slopes beyond by chain link fences with gates at either end and in the middle of the far side. McClellan trudged to each of them in turn, finding them securely padlocked. This entire area could be locked off by closing the gates on either side of the building, and anyone wanting to leave would have had to go through those gates. Or fly away.

He returned to Burton and the witness. "Did they all go at once?"

"You'd have to ask Angelica," Mack responded. "They were all gone when I turned around."

"And when you called to the woman you thought was Angelica, you called by name?"

"Yes. I called out, 'Hey, Angelica.' "

"And you hailed her brother by name, also?"

"Yeah. I yelled 'Hey, Carlos!' "

"So, whoever or whatever took them might have thought he was getting two members of one family?"

Burton shook his head. "Then why take the coach and the other two guys?"

McClellan stared at his shoes. "Maybe we all look alike to them."

"Them, who?" asked Burton.

"The ETs," said McClellan. "Maybe they can tell male from female, but we all look alike. Like we were deer or elk or something." He beckoned. "Let's look over in those nearest trees."

Since the bottom gates were locked, they went back up the bleacher stairs, across the terrace, through the open gates and around the outside of the fence. The first grove of trees was a hundred yards down the hill, a clump of oaks with shadows lengthening eastward, toward them, trees that had been planted when the college was founded, if not before. The trees were big and old and created a welcome shade.

"Tracks," murmured McClellan, pointing at an area of bare earth. "Remember the TV broadcast. The predators. That's what one set of tracks looks like. Wulivery. Like elephants."

"Over here!" cried Burton. He was kneeling by a body, with another one beyond him. "They're alive!"

"That's the other two," cried Mack. "That's Ron Turley, and Bamma McClure!"

"Bamma," murmured McClellan to himself, wandering farther into the trees. "What did he do to deserve a name like that? Now where's the coach? If I'm right, we'll find him, but not the other boy, the Shipton boy." He leaned momentarily against a tree trunk to remove a cinder from his shoe, then caught sight of a red shirt. "Here's the coach," he cried.

The man was unconscious, but seemingly uninjured. As though he'd been anesthetized. In fact, all three of them seemed to have been anesthetized.

When the ambulances departed with the three unconscious men, McClellan sat down next to Angelica Shipton and waved her sympathizers away. For a time he didn't say anything. He was reflecting on his earlier euphoria, considering whether pride had had any part in it. It was pride that supposedly went before a fall, and oh, boy, was this going to be a fall. From blessing the ETs to damning them, in one easy circuit.

"Look, miss," he said gravely. "They took your brother. And it looks like they thought they got you, too, because Mack Dugan called both of you by your names. And, it looks like it was done by those predators we heard about on TV, but it's not the kind of thing they've been doing. I mean, right here, in the open, on the campus isn't the way they've been operating. They've been more . . . sneaky than that. So, I got to ask you, why would these predator ETs want to come after you and your brother?"

Angelica stared at him from tear-bleared eyes, her head moving from side to side in baffled negation. "I don't know! I have no idea! Why would they? I mean, why us?"

"Your parents, miss. I'd like to get in touch with your parents."

Angelica shook her head, and began to laugh hysterically. "You can't," she said. "I can't. Carlos tried to call our father yesterday and couldn't find him. And Mother . . . she's moved. She calls me, but she doesn't have a number where we can call her yet . . ."

Back at the precinct, McClellan reported to the captain, only to have the captain murmur, "What's that stink, Mac?"

"Stink? I can't smell anything. I've got a cold."

The captain rose and came around his desk, sniffing. He sniffed at McClellan, front and back, then said, "Take off your jacket and look at the back of it. It's all over goo."

McClellan removed the jacket. It did have goo on it, like . . . something waxy or tarry. "I leaned up against a tree at the campus," he remarked, wonderingly.

The captain stared at him for some time, nostrils twitching. "You thought it was a tree."

39
benita

Early Friday evening, Benita's phone rang, and she shuddered. Each time she heard the sound, she had a renewed feeling of doom. When she took a deep breath and picked it up, however, it was only Chad, saying he had enjoyed their dinner together and would she be interested in a movie.

What she really wanted to do was scream. Recent events had combined to give her the feeling there were snakes under the furniture, things ready to jump out at her. She tried to shake off the nervy, antsy mood, deciding she'd probably feel better not being alone. Besides, she liked Chad, so she said yes, why not a movie.

Chad had paid her a good deal of attention recently, which both pleased her and made her slightly uncomfortable. He was married. And though she wasn't even forty, doing without sex had not been a big problem for her. Sex with Bert had not been pleasurable for . . . well, for virtually their entire married life. She found it hard to understand how she had convinced herself she loved him, way back when. Of course, he'd been young, and he hadn't been the big drinker he turned out to be within two or three years, by which time she had been grateful to be let alone. So, when a man was nice to her, complimentary, as Chad was, and kind in his attentions, it was nice but it also made her apprehensive, as though enjoying the attention, any of it, might be equivalent to committing herself to something unearned, forbidden, or inappropriate. Not that Chad had made a single gesture in that direction, but he was a thoughtful, intelligent man, and as she kept reminding herself, being alone with a thoughtful, intelligent man wasn't something she was used to.

When he picked her up, however, he looked worse than she felt, not like someone headed for an enjoyable afternoon.

"What is it?" she asked.

"The movie was just an excuse, Benita. You remember the name Dink? I may have mentioned he works for the Select Committee on Intelligence, reporting directly to Senator Morse."

"My own dear Senator Morse?"

"That one, yes. The DEA got some feedback from an agent planted way, way deep in a Colombian cartel. It seems Charles Dinklemier is well known down there. Well known, much valued. He clears the way for a lot of shipments."

She stared at him, at first not getting it at all. Then it began to trickle in, like reading a thriller when you're half asleep, missing it when the author throws a curve at you. "Does the senate committee know?"

He exhaled. "I think I mentioned to you that there've been some rumors about where certain soft contributions to senatorial campaigns came from. Dink works for Morse. Morse gets lots of soft money. This has got to be where it's coming from."

"What does Morse do in return?"

"He votes for the war on drugs. Votes more money for the DEA. Makes sure there's no drug policy reform. The War on Drugs keeps the market up, keeps the dealers working, keeps the money flowing. They don't want drugs legalized. It'd be like what happened when we stopped Prohibition. The gangsters didn't want it stopped. They made millions."

"What does that have to do with our problem right now? With the ETs?"

"All of a sudden there are ET causometers on every lawman's wrist, and the market is drying up. The drug cartels, the DEA, the private prison lobby, they'd do almost anything to get rid of the ETs. Which means that since the administration is supposedly supporting the ETs, drug money is being used to discredit the administration, the ETs, and anyone or anything to do with either of them."

"Including us."

"Including us." He laughed shortly. "The White House has been hoping it can declare a victory in the war on drugs now that the illicit ones can be controlled, but the big money is all on the other side."

She smiled grimly. "So we're being eaten alive by ET predators, we're going to have thousands of addicts going cold turkey, and it seems a whole bunch of our legislators work for a foreign business. It's nice it's all happening at once. I hate things all strung out."

He gave her a sickly grin.

She returned it, saying, "I'm hungry. Since there's to be no movie, can we have some supper?"

They did so, with wine, though the wine didn't assuage her feeling of impending annihilation. "All it does is make me feel I'm floating on doom instead of drowning in it."

"Chiddy and Vess are looking for the predators, right?"

"So they said when they left."

"And until they find them?"

"I don't know. Let the storm rage, I guess."

"Hope it isn't too long, Benita. If our domestic storm gets to the point of a feeding frenzy, you may get tossed to the sharks as a delaying tactic."

She looked up from her dessert plate. "They promised to keep me out of it!"

"They promised they'd try. You can try to keep a secret, but if some damned congressional committee subpoenas you, you can't keep it long."

"The president wouldn't tell where I am!"

"Benita, Benita. If the predators took Bert, they did it because they'd been in touch with McVane. Why else? So, if the predators found you, then McVane knows where you are. This makes me, as a friend, say thoughtfully to myself that if someone has anything to hide, someone had better hide it really well, because sooner or later, people are going to start digging." He gave her a limpid gaze which succeeded only in making her angry.

She snarled, "Chad, I am exactly who I have always said I am, and I have no sins on my conscience, sexual, financial, or otherwise. This business has me . . . I don't know. This whole thing is maddening!"

"You feel like a rabbit thrown to the wolves, I'll bet."

"When you say thrown to the wolves . . ."

He took a deep breath. "I meant that one or more senators may exercise the privilege of subpoena to get you before a congressional committee. The president would, no doubt, delay this as long as possible, but it couldn't be delayed forever since McVane knows where you are, and if McVane knows, then Senator Morse knows. So, even if the president tried to delay access, they could come at you by another route. The only thing they *possibly* don't know about you is that you are having dinner with me right this minute, and I could be wrong about that."

He toyed with his spoon. "Tell me again, how was it the predators found you?"

"Chiddy said smell. The Pistach have been in my apartment time after time. I suppose it does smell of them, though I can't smell it."

"What do you all do there? Have tea parties?"

"Popcorn, mostly. They really like popcorn. And ice cream, especially strawberry. They go crazy over our fruits and fruit-flavored things. And sodas, anything but root beer, or anything else with sarsaparilla in it, like cream soda."

"They don't like sarsaparilla?"

"It puts them to sleep. One night we had root beer floats, and they slept on my couch for nine hours in about thirty different shapes. Which isn't the subject. Smelling me out is the subject, because that's what the predators did!"

"They can track the whole world by smell?"

"We track the whole world by sight. Chiddy and Vess have machines that circle the world listening for certain sounds. And Chiddy told me the Fluiquosm track by taste. It's just a matter of having machines that sort through the data to find specific things, and I'm sure any race that has space travel has sorting machines. As a matter of fact, Chiddy asked to leave his translator listening to my TV because his ship is operating at full capacity at the moment. Finding predators is probably what it's doing."

"And presumably they didn't need to smell out Bert because the cabal knew where he was, right? Well, that relieves a minor worry. I thought there might have been a leak from the bureau. Your apartment was supposedly an FBI 'safe house' operation, done by Justice as a favor to State, who said they needed it for visiting dignitaries threatened by terrorists. The contractors are reliable people the FBI uses from time to time, and nobody involved except General Wallace had any idea who would occupy it. He's the only one who talked to your boss, nobody else said anything except 'Hi there.' As for the First Lady and the Secretary of State, nobody has asked them where you are. I'm the only one who's seen you with them since that dinner with the ETs, and we hoped they'd think you left town after that."

"You said you'd protect the kids . . ."

"It took hours to get the red tape cut. I haven't been granted authority over field offices. When we try to do things quietly, it takes time to get cooperation, but your children should each have an agent arm in arm, right now."

"We're still trying to be quiet?" she asked, incredulously.

"Trying to avoid panic," he said, frowning.

He chewed thoughtfully while she blotted chocolate from her lips, fighting down the temptation to scream. "Who told this cabal my name? Originally."

"Your namesake congressman. He thinks he's a liberal, he's generally on our side, but he's also ex-military, and he falls for the national security gambit every time someone plays it. Star Wars. Stealth anything. Talk about burning the flag and he gets all choked up. Funny, so many of these guys think the country stands for the flag instead of the other way round. So long as Old Glory's whipping in the breeze, it's okay to deal guns to kids and cheat on your taxes."

"Congressman Alvarez was annoyed at me," she admitted. "The cube opened up for General Wallace, but it didn't show the congressman anything. He turned red and got all defensive. I could see him thinking that a congressman is more important than a retired general."

Chad nodded. "I've met some of them who think they're more important than God. So. Now what?"

"Well, I guess I go on working. And waiting until Chiddy and Vess find the predators. And hoping they haven't done anything . . . final to Bert."

"Do you really hope so?"

"Yes. I wouldn't wish that on my worst enemy. Which he is." She reconsidered. "Almost."

"Any idea how long it will take the Pistach to find them?"

"No idea. They'll manage, sooner or later."

"Any idea what the predators are up to?"

"Sorry, Chad. I don't have a clue."

It was eight in the evening when Benita returned to her apartment, and after a few moments of irresolute wavering, she decided to call Angelica. It was only five o'clock Pacific time. Angelica might not be home yet, but she might not have another chance the way things were going. She lay down on the bed, punched in the numbers and counted the rings.

The moment Angelica came on the line, however, she began talking so hurriedly that it took Benita some time to calm her down to the point she could understand what was being said.

"What do you mean, Carlos has been kidnapped?"

"It just happened. Just now!" she cried. "Over at the sports complex . . ." Angelica poured out the story of the afternoon's disappearance, about the girl who had been called by Angelica's name, about the police sergeant saying it looked like an attempt to get two members of the same family.

Benita gargled, "The whole family . . ."

"It's crazy, isn't it, Mom? I mean, who'd want to bother us. I thought of Dad, but you know, he . . . he isn't . . . he doesn't . . ."

"He can't concentrate long enough to do anything like that," Benita said for her.

"Right. And it can't be for ransom, because we don't have any money."

"Was there any blood?" Benita asked with horrid foreboding.

"Blood? No. The other men weren't hurt. Nobody found any blood."

"Ah."

"What do you mean, ah?"

"I mean . . ." She thought, what did she mean? "It looks like no one was hurt. Not like . . ."

"Like those killings, you mean? The ones in Oregon?"

"No, certainly not like that. Angel, didn't the FBI contact you today?"

"Oh, Mom, yes. What's that all about? The men came to my place kind of late this afternoon, and I took them with me to find Carlos. He disappeared right after we got there! The man who was supposed to watch him was fit to be tied, and the man who's supposed to watch me is sitting on a chair outside in the hall right now. What's going on?"

Benita beat her forehead with her closed fist. It was the predators. *They* were doing it, and they were doing it because they'd been put up to it! They'd come to the bookstore looking for Benita, only her place was . . . what? It would have been easy to get into if they'd really wanted to, though getting in would have made a mess. Broken windows. Splintered doors. So, maybe they didn't want to . . . no, maybe they'd been *told* not to leave evidence they'd done it. Perhaps they needed to make her vanish, without raising a stink. So, they'd tried using Bert as bait. Now they would no doubt use Carlos. And, supposedly, Angelica. Oh, it made a certain deadly sense!

Benita took a deep breath. "Angelica, I think it would be a really good idea for you to go outside and tell the FBI man he should take you to a motel or hotel, right now. I mean *now*, not an hour from now. Grab what you can grab in no more than five minutes and go. Get a place that's air conditioned, and don't open the windows or the curtains."

"You're scaring me!"

"I'm scared myself. Please, Angel. Do what I ask. Just so I don't need to worry about you."

"If it's important."

"It's important. Tell the FBI man to let Chad Riley know where you are."

"Who's Chad Riley? What's this about, Mom?"

"Trust me, please. I don't want to talk about it now. Just do what I ask. Chad Riley works for the FBI in Washington, and I can get in touch with him without letting anyone know where I am. He'll give me your number, and I'll call you tomorrow when things settle down a little."

When she hung up the phone, she went into the bathroom and said Chiddy's name, over and over. No answer. No response at all! All she'd ever had to do was speak, but now they were off somewhere, or everywhere, trying to locate the predators.

"My son's been abducted," she said. "Also a girl that was mistaken for my daughter!"

No sign that he'd heard her. Lord, Lord. Now what? She stepped back into the bedroom and the phone rang. Chad, saying he'd just learned about what happened in California.

"Chad, for heaven's sake, I know! Angelica just told me."

"This girl they took? Do you know who that was?"

"They thought it was Angelica!"

"You know why?"

"They want them for bait," she cried. "To lure me out where they can get at me." She pressed her forehead with her free hand, trying to keep it from exploding. "The predators wouldn't have targeted the children on their own, so someone put them up to it. Probably Morse because he wants to talk to the intermediary."

"That's what his press release says," growled Chad.

She cried, "Well, dammit, better in public than in some cellar somewhere. Morse wants to get at me, so why don't we let him! Except for my longing for anonymity, I've got no reason to hide!"

"Volunteering to testify could be a good play," said Chad, thoughtfully. "I'll see what the powers that be have to say about that."

"Listen," Benita said, struggling to remain calm. "Morse might be doing this because he's expecting the president to duck or dodge on the subject of my whereabouts. Then Morse himself could haul me in, hoping I'll say something really damaging. Like . . . I was put up to this whole thing by the Chinese. Or the pres and I have been having this affair ever since I came to Washington. Or something equally ridiculous. That's what he really wants, to make political hay out of the situation . . ."

"That's scary."

"It's not the worst. If he's using the predators, maybe he can even be sure that I'll say what he wants me to. Either they can make me do it, or they can hold the kids' lives as hostages until I do it."

"But you'd be willing to appear in order to subvert that."

"Right. I'll agree right now to appear before the committee Monday. Let the president announce that fact! He should announce it tonight or tomorrow, so it can get onto the news as soon as possible!"

"What about your son?"

"Somebody should get word to McVane, privately, that I expect my family to be released. Or that he'll be held responsible for the two of them, or something!"

"But the girl isn't your family."

"She's somebody's family," Benita snapped. "Angelica would be in their clutches right now if they hadn't made a mistake. I asked her to ask the FBI man who's guarding her to take her to a hotel for tonight and let you know where she is."

"I'll alert the powers that be," said Chad. "Including the president."

Benita called Simon at home to tell him a family emergency had come up, and she would have to take Monday off. Since she'd worked overtime on several evenings, she actually had the time coming.

He sighed. "Someday you'll tell me what's going on, won't you, Benita?"

"Someday, Simon. If I ever figure it out."

40

senator byron morse

The same evening, Senator Morse came home to find a note from Lupé saying that her mother had broken her wrist and that Lupé was driving to Baltimore to spend a day or two with Mama to reassure herself that Mama was all right. All in all, it suited the senator to spend a quiet evening at home. The last few days had been hectic. Predators picking off American citizens was not a precedent he wanted to set, but in this case the end justified the means. Once he got his hands on the intermediary, nobody would press him too much as to how he'd done it, and he had no doubt he could get something out of her—whether or not it led them to the envoys—that would be useful in damaging the administration!

He badly wanted a progress report, but there was no way to reach the predators until they succeeded, in which event, reaching them wouldn't be neccessary. Dink had assured him it wouldn't take them long. Ridiculous, all this running about, unable to find a woman who should stick out like a sore thumb! It suggested ineptitude among people he had always valued for being good at their jobs!

Meantime, the select committee was still unable to talk to

or communicate with or get at the envoys themselves, and the armies of ET hunters that were scouring the world for possible targets had as yet reported killing only a California condor, several wolverines and bear cubs, about fifty dogs, and a number of Ginko trees. The boosting of a surveillance satellite into a one-time moon loop, a little maneuver that cost too many millions, had allowed NASA to verify that predator ships were definitely on the back side of the moon. Morse had been cutting NASA's budget relentlessly as long as he'd been in the Senate, so there was no way to get at the moon any time soon. It was like being in a wartime situation. You couldn't attack the administration without seeming disloyal to the country, no matter how elusive or dangerous the president was. Maybe the thing to do was beef up NASA, fast, and see what the Russians had left over from their space program that might be useful. Though, come to think of it, the space station boosters had more or less picked over that trash heap.

Oh, hell, he told himself, pouring a scotch, let it go. Forget it for tonight. Raid the refrigerator, have a long hot shower, go to bed.

The food and the shower he managed. While luxuriating under the hot spray, however, he felt a sting on his shoulder, as though a wasp or bee was in the shower with him. Even as he slapped at the shoulder he felt overwhelmingly dizzy. The tile walls of the shower stall spun around him; he felt himself slipping, though he didn't feel himself landing on the floor. Everything went gray and silent.

He was aware that time was passing, that things seemed to have duration. He came halfway to consciousness, finding himself on an examining table, just like . . . well, like all that stupid *X-Files* stuff, and there was this . . . ET thing, not a little gray man, not an envoy, not one of those predators they had shown on that broadcast of theirs, something else. Like a huge wasp, only with a high cranium and a soft voice. This large creature, assisted by two smaller creatures, was very intent on doing something to him, though he felt no particular pain or apprehension. They were holding him and shifting him, quite gently, and then there was a sudden, horrible pain, terrible and piercing as the large creature stuck its . . . something or other, surely not what it looked like, no, that couldn't be, he meant no, not that, he meant stuck its daggerlike thing into him, right into his middle, and squirted something through it, something quite large because the daggerlike thing bulged to let it through, and then the pain again, only worse, much worse, he couldn't bear, couldn't stand . . .

And then only peace and euphoria. Nice. Nice restful feeling, and he woke up momentarily. He was at home, in bed, quite naked.

Senator Byron Morse never slept naked. He staggered out of bed and found his pajamas hanging where he'd left them this morning, on the back of the bathroom door. It was while he was buttoning the pajama top before the full-length mirror on the back of the bathroom door that he noticed a strange discoloration on his stomach. Just to the right of the belly button and a little higher. A real doozy of a bruise, with a bloody spot in the middle. He touched it, and something bit him, like being hit with a cattle prod. A second attempt had the same result. He should have been worried about it, but he still felt very happy and contented. Euphoric. That was the word. He hummed it to himself.

An isolated section of his mind repeated the word. Euphoric? From what? Why was he thinking about euphoria? He should be worried about this damned bloody spot. He was damned well worried about this bloody spot, but he was too tired to do anything about it tonight. He'd get a few hours sleep, first. This morning, first thing, he'd see his doctor.

41

from chiddy's journal

Dear Benita, Vess and I are so deeply sorry about the predators. Though they will not kill nearly as many of your people as you do on your own, we realize that the simultaneous death of small groups is perceived to be more tragic than a very large mortality stretched over time and space. A plane crash that kills one hundred in one place seems a greater tragedy than the many times that number killed one or two at a time, here and there, by gunshot or car crash or tobacco addiction. When working with intelligent beings, one must work with perceptions as much as with reality, and accordingly, we know the predation must be stopped!

We have set our search devices to find the Xankatikitiki, as they are usually the easiest to locate. There are more of them, they have the strongest smell, and they tend toward noisy braggadocio, particularly the young ones. Once we find them, we will find the others. If we do not find them within a short time, we will find a human who has met with them, though we will need to wipe the memory of it later. If the predators have conspired with humans, then those humans must have a way to get in touch with them! Unfortunately, conspirators do not emit the same kinds of strong, focused signals that serial killers or terrorists do. Conspirators tend to have torturous mentalities which are often unclear even to themselves.

Meantime, Vess and I are continuing with the programs set out before our brief departure. We are extending the ugliness plague to Iran and Arabia and to parts of India where both Muslims and the wealthier Hindus seem to enjoy locking women up. This is such a unique societal trait that Vess and I brought it to the attention of the Chapter back on Pistach-home. We have been sending them reports all along, of course, and they soon saw the similarity between this human trait and the violent capture of females found among other Earthian mammals. Baboons and various kinds of deer kidnap females, for example, as do teams of dolphins, usually violently and sometimes lethally.

Our Chapter asked us why some human societies consider female capture and abuse to be barbaric while others consider it to be "traditional" or "cultural" or even "religious." Why should certain societies have very little breeding madness while others have it continuously? Are some but not all human societies genetically incapable of self-control?

This dichotomy among various subgroups of a single race is hard for us to explain, dear Benita. We've looked into the matter, and there is no clear-cut genetic difference between populations with breeding madness and those without. As we know from experience, however, even a rare genetic predisposition can survive culturally if the predisposition is found among the leaders of the society. Though a leader may be genetically driven to a certain behavior rather than choosing it, if that leader is charismatic, others will elect to copy the behavior. Thus is breeding madness spread among certain populations, first by emulation, in time acquiring a cultural or even religious cachet.

If there is a genetic predisposition to breeding madness, it may have arisen among groups who lived around your Mediterranean Sea. We hear much of the "Latin Temperament," for example, which enjoys ritualized sacrifice of or battles among male animals such as bulls and cocks. They also have dances portraying contests of sexual dominance. I apologize, dearest Benita, if I seem to be belaboring this point! Even though we are sure these things must change, first it is necessary that we understand what is going on. It is far more important to establish a civil and orderly society than it is to pander to abusive cultural and religious artifacts. This is why we are continuing the ugliness campaign. Once the societies have unlearned their present attitudes, women may become lovely again, as you are, dear Benita. In the meantime, the women will at least have the freedom to come and go as they will, to work and study and learn.

Our Inkleozese monitors were not here long before they pointed out that a nation dedicated to protecting human rights should not have warm diplomatic relations with nations that have institutionalized breeding madness, not even when those nations have a lot of petroleum. We had postponed consideration of this issue formerly, but since all the Inkleozese monitors are receptors, that is, females, we are unable to delay consideration any longer. The Inkleozese react very strongly to insults to their own or similar sexes, and they feel the imprisonment of women is no less heinous than confining political prisoners for the sake of "security."

If widening the area afflicted by the ugly-plague badly upsets your country's acquisition of sufficient fuel, we will provide your nation with power technology that needs no petroleum. An equitable society capable of Neighborliness cannot be built on competition for scarce resources. Think what such cutthroat competition would mean in interstellar society?

The question of resources brings me to a delicate point. Because our need was immediate, we brought back with us the only Inkleozese monitors who were available at the time. Virtually all of them are in that state of parturition that will soon require a host animal. There are no quodm, no geplis, no nadervaks on Earth. The most suitable creatures will be male persons, as their hormones are more easily adjustable to the needs of the growing Inkliti.

Under usual circumstances, the Inkleozese would refuse to leave their planet at such a time. Only our elucidation of the pro-life feelings of many men in positions of power convinced them they could find hosts on Earth without offending the free will of its inhabitants. Obviously, the hosts will have to be persons who espouse the pure pro-life position which does not allow reproductive choice even in the case of rape. Not that these gentlemen would consider it rape, but we all know what the media do with any events related to sexuality.

While the Inkleozese might be offended by the anti-woman bigotry underlying much pro-life dogma, we have not seen fit to discuss with them the psychological minutia of the situation. They would be outraged, or worse, if a host animal refused the implantation of an Inklit egg, but since implantation is always done with the host in a euphoric state, we know the gentlemen will not refuse. We have, therefore, selected hosts for the Inkleozese on the basis of their publicly stated receptivity to preborn life.

Among those chosen are several of your legislators who have repeatedly asserted an unequivocal antichoice position. We have also added to the list a number of TV and radio preachers and commentators who have been rigorously pro-life. Once the immediate need is taken care of, we will explain the matter as seems necessary. Everyone will be told that the hosts are pregnant with babies of an intelligent life form which it would be a grave ethical error to remove. Though the impregnation has or will be done without the hosts' individual permission, in a legal sense we may infer their permission from the stand which they have taken upon the issue of rape. Each man on our list has gone on record as refusing to allow choice to women who have been raped, pointing out that the infant is innocent and must therefore take precedence. The Inkleozese could not ask for a better statement of their own belief.

In any case, the implantations will be only a temporary inconvenience for the hosts. They will most likely survive the pregnancy and emergence experience without lasting harm, just as most of your women do. The hosts will have only a few months of discomfort and inconvenience, though of course their careers must be set aside for a time. Inasmuch as they have frequently decried the shallowness of women who attempted to avoid pregnancy for mere career convenience, however, we are assured of their understanding.

Aha. Vess calls. The machines are signaling! We have something on the location of the Xankatikitiki. When next we encounter one another, dear Benita, I hope you will be gratified to know we have reached the predators and succeeded in removing them from your world.

42

among the shizzalizaquosmni

The Fluiquosm, the Wulivery and the Xankatikitiki had long been associated with certain other predatory races in a League of Devourers, or Shizzalizaquosmni [SHIZzah-LIZzah-kwah-zum-nee, many-joined-eaters], which league members called simply ShLQ [sh-lok-wuh]. When engaged in joint hunting expeditions on any planet, the league was headed by a committee made up of the eldest or most powerful of each race. On Earth, this group had found the planet to be a predator's paradise.

"Oh, it needs some work, of course," gurgled the Wulivery chief known as Odiferous Tentacle. "Cities are not a proper venue for the hunt. The country makes prey so much more delicious. One has little food-things gathering around one's legs, thinking one is a tree! They squeak delightfully when one seizes them up!"

The Wulivery were fond of trees, and at least partially in response to Wulivery sensibilities, the Fluiquosm and Xankatikitiki leaders had agreed to set up their headquarters near the old farm in Virginia where they had met the cabal. It was a convenient place, one kept secure by intelligence agencies who had no idea what was going on there, and the humans who kept the place under observation had been easily persuaded that they saw everything except the predators. While the signal towel flapped its continuous message of safety, while each footstep of other casual visitors was closely observed, the predators came and went without being noticed.

It was to this location that the one male and two female Fluiquosm involved in the abductions of Benita's family brought the two young people, and later Bert himself, following his unsuccessful role as bait. Fluiquosm females often accompanied the hunters though they did not usually hunt, and in certain cases they might be sent alone, for it was the females who convinced captured prey that safe release would follow if the prey would only lie quiet. It was the females who convinced the prey it did not see what its eyes claimed to see or hear what its ears claimed to hear. In short, the females cast the veil behind which much bloody work was done, and in return for their talents, their thirsts were among the first satisfied.

The two young humans picked up in California were convinced they had seen nothing and heard nothing and needed only to sleep for a lengthy while. Though bringing them to Virginia had involved a lengthy roundtrip flight, the two Fluiquosm, Quosmlizzak and Kazzalamgah, had badly needed the exercise. They had placed breathing capsules over the noses of the boy and girl, wrapped them in egg film as protection against high-altitude winds, and during the flight had amused themselves by dangling the bodies just in front of airliners in midair, scaring the pilots witless. They did not desist until one plane lost altitude and almost crashed, which would have been a waste of blood, and therefore shameful.

Bert had also been obtained by subterfuge, though his female abductor had chosen to bring him back via commercial carrier and store him temporarily in a hotel. The airline ticket counter person, the clothing store personnel, the barber, the hotel clerk, all had been mind fogged into assisting the operation, and the Fluiquosm who had managed the trip remembered the whole process as having been great fun.

Bert had now joined the two youngsters, all three carefully cocooned in egg film and hung upright in the well-stocked larder tree where they could remain without damage for some days, until they were needed for something or, if that became appropriate, were sucked dry or eaten. Now that all the family except the woman had been brought under control, the predators assumed that Bert and the young people could be consumed immediately after the woman was in their hands.

To that end, a small but representative group of predators left the farm in Virginia and flew in a tiny shuttle to Washington, D.C., where they set themselves down in a small park not far from Benita's apartment. The Wulivery had reconnoitered the woman's lair during their previous attempt, and they knew it was vulnerable, though not in a way that would avoid detection. Each hunt had its rules as to number, age and type of prey, method of capture, how many points for particularly difficult captures, and so on. The rule-setter for this particular hunt had clearly stated that the woman had to be removed without any sign of violence. The prey was to be lured out with threats to the welfare of its offspring. Pistach nootchi, Xankatikitiki glafimmilox, even Wulivery vullaters would respond mindlessly to threats directed at offspring they had nurtured or borne. It was assumed human females would be the same, even though the ploy wouldn't work on Fluiquosm themselves. Fluiquosm were without progeny pride, sometimes going so far as to drain their offspring when other blood was unavailable.

The shuttle was set down in a thick copse of trees, and the group exited, including Odiferous Tentacle, a Xankatikitiki chief called Mrrgrowr, and the two Fluiquosm females, Quosmlizzak and Kazzalamgah. It was in the wee hours of the morning and the city was quiet enough that the Wulivery and one of the Fluiquosm felt they could collect Benita without attracting attention. While the mind-fogger stood by to confuse anyone who might witness any part of the abduction, the Wulivery pretended to be a tree while making a phone call from a sidewalk booth. Wulivery were skilled at languages and particularly good at picking up conversational idiom, though they could make vocal sounds only through a machine.

*   *   *

Benita's phone rang at three A.M. on Sunday, so her digital clock told her as she came groggily awake. "Hello," she muttered, staring witlessly at the clock and wondering what new threat or confusion was happening. "Hello?"

"Come out, come out, wherever you are," demanded a mechanical voice.

The person who owned that voice wasn't anyone Benita knew, or wanted to know, but she realized immediately what it wanted.

"Hello," she said again, sitting upright, forcing herself to waken. "Do you have the right number?"

"Alvarez," the voice said. "This is the right number. We have you located. We have possession of your mate and offspring. Harm will come to them if you don't go downstairs and come out the back door right now . . ."

Shaking off her stupor, Benita gritted her teeth and said what she and Chad had agreed she would say. "I can't," she said. "The president has asked me to appear before Senator Morse's committee on Monday morning. I've promised I'll be there."

There was a snort at the other end, like an aborted curse, a moment's mumbling, as though to someone else, then a disconnect. She hung up, tears running down her face as she prayed she was doing the right thing. Whoever or whatever the voice was, it would have to report to Morse. And once Morse knew she'd testify before the committee, he'd have no reason . . . well, less reason to hang on to her children. Or to Bert.

She pulled herself out of bed, stumbling through the dark, banging one hand against the bathroom door hard enough to break a nail straight across, and then scratched herself with it when she splashed cold water on her face. She dressed in jeans and a knit shirt with a roomier flannel shirt over it, then went to the phone in the bedroom and called Chad, who said he would be over in a few minutes, with weapons.

"Can you shoot?" he asked.

"As a matter of fact, yes," she muttered, digging through the drawer of the bedside table for a nail file. "My brothers and I used to shoot at cans and rats, out at my Dad's salvage yard. Back then, it was out in the country . . ." Her voice trailed off. Back then had no point to it at the moment.

Odiferous Tentacle was annoyed. The result of the call was not as planned. The official, Morse, wanted the woman to appear before him, but the woman was already committed to appearing before Morse. Did Morse still want her taken secretly? This possibility had not been covered in the rules of engagement! Sending the Fluiquosm to report back to the group, the Wulivery found another phone and called General McVane, feeding a small tentacle up through the coin return to ding the coin mechanism as many times as required.

General McVane, wakened from a sound sleep, growled into the phone. "Call me back in an hour. I'll get ahold of Morse!"

While they waited, the predators continued their previous conversation.

The toothy Xankatikitiki chief, Mrrgrowr, remarked, "You're right that there is more meat here than seems possible, but a lot of it is flab. The flesh is too soft. Tiki's jaws will atrophy. Tiki's teeth will rot."

Odiferous Tentacle shrugged, a gesture which took him from a height of four meters to one of about eight, followed by the emission of a lengthy stink. "Not all of them are flabby. In other parts of the world, the peasants are quite solid. A few generations of unlimited predation will take care of those that aren't. We'll make a practice of allowing the more fit to escape us. That way they'll reproduce disproportionately and improve the species."

"It'll take generations," complained Mrrgrowr.

"Let the young clean out the flabby ones!" said Quosmlizzak. "You know kids. They'll eat anything, what!"

"Your young, perhaps," said Mrrgrowr, with a snarl. "Not ours. We Xankatikitiki care about our progeny."

"Our young, then," laughed Quosmlizzak. "We have them by the clutch, a dozen or so. And as for our good friends like Stinky here, the Wulivery young are spawned in the sea, what? A million at a time?"

"Only a few hundred thousand at even the most splendid

spawning," murmured Odiferous Tentacle. "And only a few hundred survive to the parasitic larval stage when they cling to vullators. One does not consider them to be Wulivery until the vullator-clinging stage, and one does not name them until the second metamorphosis. Our young wouldn't be useful in culling the flabby humans for they become land creatures only after the fifth stage, at which point they are almost adult."

"You'll want access to the oceans for your young, then?" asked Mrrgrowr.

The Wulivery waved its tentacles in negation. "No. Alas! Have you looked at their seas? Filthy! Also, the humans have so badly overfished them that our young would find little to eat and might themselves end up as food for the few remaining whales! So amusing! The humans pretend to save the whales while they go on stealing the whales' food until the whales starve! Ha ha. This world will have dead oceans, shortly. We have already planned to restock them with hybrids of the poisonous earthly puffer fish and equally noxious imported sea-creatures. Then we will eat the coastal humans who sully the sea while the new fish become food for our young but not for mankind. Until that is done, one fears this planet is too squalid for us to reproduce here.

"Hunting, however, will be good. We prefer hunting in shade, near clean water, as otherwise we get overheated. There's plenty of prey along the sides of the jungles and woods. Enough to last us for years."

"Then you believe the humans will make an agreement with us?" asked Mrrgrowr.

"Oh," murmured Odiferous Tentacle, "one thinks they will. They'll ask us to eat the people in some other country, of course, so we'll have to predate secretly in this country. Luckily, many of their people *drop out* or *run away*, so a few disappearances won't be suspected."

"Have any of the rest of you preyed on a smokeweed ingestor?" queried Quosmlizzak. "One tried to suck an ingestor a few days ago. It tasted so absolutely foul one had to disgorge the juices, and one is sure it would be deleterious to one's health to eat many of them . . ."

"You're quite right," shuddered the Wulivery. "Terrible taste, and it stays with one so! The man, Bert, is one such. He stinks terribly! Do not ask me to share his flesh, thank you, no."

"We'll have to get rid of the bad ones," remarked Mrrgrowr.

"Will the dear Pistach let us do that?" asked Odiferous Tentacle. "Will they go on causing us trouble?"

"The Pistach!" The Xankatikitiki barked with laughter. "The Wulivery haven't heard? The Pistach may have no time to cause us anything! They'll soon have a civil war on their hands."

"What?" cried Quosmlizzak.

"No! The Pistach?" laughed Odiferous Tentacle. "How delicious!"

Mrrgrowr snarled, "It's true. A rebel has built an army and taken ships! He has made an alliance with us. We have given him weapons and ships. Our people heard of him last on his way to Pistach-home. To conquer the planet!"

"Could that be why the Pistach brought Inkleozese with them when they returned?" asked Quosmlizzak.

Silence. The Wulivery made a spitting noise. The Xankatikitiki growled in their throats. "Is that true? Inkleozese? Drat them! What business did they have coming here?"

"We knew they'd come sooner or later," soothed Odiferous Tentacle. "We'll just stay out of their reach, that's all."

"Easier asserted than accomplished," muttered the Xankatikitiki. "We went to considerable trouble wooing that Pistach rebel. Who would have thought of Inkleozese!"

"Well, they're not allowed to . . . you know, not to members of the Confederation."

"They do it to members of the Confederation," asserted Quosmlizzak. "They find a legal precedent first, but they do it. Like, for instance if they come after us, they'll claim we're not actually members of the Confederation because if we were we wouldn't be contravening its laws by being here . . ."

"They wouldn't!" said Odiferous Tentacle. "Not to us."

"Don't bet on it," said the Fluiquosm. "Stranger things have happened."

"Time to reach out to the general again," said Mrrgrowr reversing his head to examine a steeple clock.

Odiferous Tentacle grunted and went off toward the phone, returning almost immediately.

"I have reached," sighed the Wulivery. "The general is very upset. He has tried to find the senator, but the senator does not answer his phone, and there is no one at his office. The general thinks we had better take the woman anyhow, even if we must break in to do so. He feels the senator will probably want her, so it will be best to have her on hand."

Chad arrived at Benita's apartment and immediately took a handgun from his pocket. He pointed out the safety, thrust the gun at Benita, and watched her drop it into the deep flapped pocket of her checked lumberman's jacket before gathering several scattered belongings into an open bag. Sasquatch moved anxiously back and forth between the living room and the bedroom like a caged wolf.

"Hurry up," Chad urged her. "We need to get away from here."

"I'm just getting the clothes I'll need to wear on Monday. I don't want to have to come back here."

She moved into the living room with the open bag, set it on the couch and was suddenly conscious of a heaviness in her head and chest. Allergies. They always hit her when she was nervous. The medicine was on the TV, next to Chiddy's translator. She picked it up, wondering what it was, breaking the silence with a heartfelt, "Damn!"

"What is it?"

"Chiddy's translator. He left it here, I was supposed to turn it on so it could assimilate spoken Spanish. I forgot!"

"Bring it with you," he said impatiently. "We'll speak Spanish to it, wherever we go."

"You speak Spanish?"

"Spanish, German, Arabic, Urdu, Swahili. No Oriental languages yet."

"Yet? You're going to learn what? Chinese?"

"Come on, Benita. Move it." Then, as she went back into the bedroom, he called, "I lust for a job over at State. Besides, I like learning languages. Hurry up, will you!" He

dropped to a chair and put his head in his hands, trying to
remember when he'd last had some sleep.

She turned on the device and dropped it in the left-hand
pocket, along with the nail file and the gun, leaving the
right-hand pocket empty for her wallet, her checkbook, and
her reading glasses snatched up from the bedside table. She
picked up her bag and started for the elevator, calling over
her shoulder, "Okay, I'm ready, let's go."

There was no warning of the attack. Two of the huge
windows along the living room wall burst against the curtains that had been pulled across them. Something very
large came through the curtains. Chad ran for the bedroom
where he thought Benita was. Benita, who had been summoning the elevator on the landing, Sasquatch sniffing at
her heels, heard the crash, dropped her suitcase, turned and
dashed down the fire stairs, slamming the door shut behind
her and barely missing Sasquatch's tail. She was on the second floor. The second floor had windows. Without stopping to think about it, she went on down another flight,
dragged the dog into the supply room, and then checked
both the supply room doors to be sure they were locked.
The doors were steel. According to Simon, they were set in
masonry walls, which might mean they'd be difficult to get
through, though she wouldn't bet on it. She leaned against
the heavy table in the middle of the room, panting. They
must have taken Chad. There was no place to hide up there.
Though, of course, maybe they didn't want him and would
just let him go. Maybe. Or take him and eat him.

She gagged.

Outside the burglar alarm was ringing itself silly, a clangor
one could hear blocks away. Supposedly the alarm was wired
to the police department, and they should come looking.

There were sounds in the stairwell outside the door.
Banging on the door itself.

"We've got your friend," said a mechanical voice from
outside. "We're not going to hurt either of you, though we
might hurt him in order to get you out of there. Either that
or go get your son. He's not far off. We could take him apart.
Like a lobster."

Chad's voice, half muffled, "Don't listen to them, Benita . . ." Then a few mrphls and snrfs, to no purpose.

She listened for the sound of sirens, hearing none, holding her breath. Of course, police didn't have to run their sirens when they were on the way to a burglary, it's just they always did on TV.

"We will now go get your son," said the mechanical voice.

"Grumfissit, quosimik qualad digga," said something from behind Benita. "Likkashiz."

"Don't bother," echoed the translator from Benita's pocket. "I followed her down here. I'll bring her out."

Something invisible grabbed her by her neck, not strangling, just lifting, the door opened and she was thrown through it, to be caught by a bunch of tangled tentacles on the other side. The invisible something buffeted Benita, knocking her down, and a lengthened tentacle seized her and dragged her up two flights of stairs, her legs bumping on each step, then across her living room and out the broken window. Something told her to go to sleep, which she promptly did while the beings retreated, burdened with the two humans. Sasquatch, who had followed Benita up the stairs, ran to the broken windows, thrust his head through the shattered glass and howled. Across the street, a light went on. The burglar alarm continued clanging. The phone rang without stopping.

Some minutes later, Simon, the police, and the FBI, previously alerted by Chad, arrived almost simultaneously.

On Sunday morning, many of the usual religious broadcasts were preempted by news departments who chose to air parts of a tape received from the envoys during the night. This, so said the accompanying letter, explained the fate that had overtaken some notables in and around Washington. It was a tape so packed with scientific jargon that it was unsuitable for broadcast without extensive commentary. Even the newsmen could make little sense of it until biologists and chemists had been called in to interpret.

The experts, more than a little harried looking, appeared on the screen to comment in plain language, though with all the references to "host animals" and "larvae" and so forth, the public was not enlightened at once. The matter became more understandable with the showing of hastily created computer animations of animals being punctured by the Inkleozese, eggs being inserted, eggs hatching into larvae, and larvae growing and ramifying until it was time to chew their way out. The only suitable animals on Earth, so the biologists conceded, were male humans. Part of the tape received from the Pistach listed the names of the hosts chosen on Earth, already impregnated public figures, legislators and media personalities who had publicly espoused the pro-life cause.

Since the larvae now deeply anchored into the torsos of these men had defense mechanisms against being removed, the Inkleozese could have chosen anyone, the tape made clear. Nonetheless, the Inkleozese preferred calm, uninterrupted development of their offspring, and they had therefore chosen only men who could be depended upon not to threaten the lives of the tiny moving, swallowing, heartbeating Inklit babies now snuggled beneath their capacious rib cages. In any case—the tape was specific—trying to remove them would be a very bad thing to do, since it might permanently destroy any chance of Earth's joining the Confederation.

The Pistach apologized for the inconvenience, saying that normally Inkleozese do not travel away from their home world during larval-transfer seasons. This, however, had been an emergency brought about by the unwarranted and unconscionable intrusions of the predators and had been thought acceptable purely because of the pro-life philosophy of the men in question and of those others like them who would be needed as hosts for the eggs of the hundreds of Inkleozese who hadn't laid yet. Since each Inkleozese produced from ten to twenty eggs, a large number of those in the pro-life camp could illustrate their faithfulness to that position.

The preferred hosts would be men of middle age, medium to large size, good health, and temperate habits. Once impregnated, the hosts would find it necessary to stay quietly at home for the following thirteen months—the period of maturation of the larvae—until the larvae began to chew their way out, at which time the Inkleozese would supervise the process in order to minimize any risk to the hosts. The Inkleozese wished to convey their regret that no anesthetic could be used at that time, as it might adversely affect the infant Inklit, but since most Inkliti chewed their way out in from twelve to fifteen hours, the pain, though severe, would not be protracted. Classes in breathing and meditation to assist relaxed larval emergence would be offered to the men in question.

Lupé heard all this on the car radio on her way back from Baltimore, where she had spent the previous day with her mother who was in considerable discomfort but not seriously injured. The break was clean and would heal. Lupé had been greatly relieved about this, though her relief was short-lived. No sooner had she put down her worries about Mama than she had been seized with new concerns about By. Though she had called repeatedly, she had been unable to reach him. She had been trying since Friday night, and he did not answer the phone. On Saturday evening, she had gone so far as to call one of his aides and ask the aide to check the hospitals for possible accident victims. The aide had, instead, checked the house and found the car in the drive, which he had duly reported to Lupé along with his conjecture that By was probably spending the weekend with a golfing buddy.

By played golf rarely and without enthusiasm, and Lupé was unaware that he had any golfing buddies. He did, however, enjoy sailing and he had a few sailing friends. It was possible that with her gone, he might have gone to the shore for the weekend. One thing was certain: he would most annoyed if she raised a fuss trying to find him.

When Lupé heard about the Inkleozese, however, she knew at once that Byron was exactly the kind of person the ETs were selecting. Outspokenly opposed to reproductive choice. Healthy. Of a good size. Of middle age, not too young (too many hormones) or too old (insufficient hormones). She knew in her heart that Byron was one of the selectees, he had to be, and that's why she hadn't been able to reach him!

She also knew, as probably the Inkleozese did not, that Byron was almost psychotic on the subject of pregnancy. If anyone could be said to be phobic about anything, By Morse was phobic about parturition. Not just his bad experiences with Janet, but something that had happened to him in childhood, something he would not talk about.

She got home around noon. Normally By would have been up by now, maybe even have left to have lunch. He wasn't downstairs, however, and his car was still in the drive. She found him still in bed, very soundly asleep. She shook him, and he came groggily out of his doze.

"Ah, Lupé. You back already?"

"It's Sunday noon. I said I'd be back today."

"Sunday? Can't be. What happened to Saturday?"

"It was yesterday. What's . . . what's the matter? What time did you get to bed Friday night? Did you have . . . ah, bad dreams? Something like that?"

"Had a hell of a nightmare," he responded. "That's probably why I overslept. Hey, be a sweetheart and bring me a cup of coffee, will you? I can't get the cobwebs out!"

He went to the shower, pausing to glance at himself in the mirror. He seemed to remember . . . some kind of an injury? No, no injury. A tiny little bruise next to his ribs, with a pimple of scab at its middle. He had probably bumped into something, the car door maybe. He turned on the shower, letting the hot water pour soothingly over him. The bathroom door opened, and Lupé brought him coffee, setting it on the vanity while he dried himself off. The towel wrapped around him, he turned to pick up the cup. She was watching him warily, her eyes roving over him, settling on the little bruise.

"What's that?" she asked, leaning forward to touch it.

The ceiling fell on him. He screamed, threw the coffee cup at her and cowered away from her as though she had been a monster. Scalded, she shrieked back at him as she turned on the cold water and thrust her reddened arms into the flow. Luckily, he'd missed her face.

"What in the hell is the matter with you?" she cried, knowing with sick certainly what was the matter with him.

"I don't know, I don't know, I don't know," he gabbled, slowly pulling himself upright. "When you touched me, the pain went through me like . . . like a knife."

She took a deep breath. "By, sweetie, I think you'd better put your robe on and come watch TV for a little bit."

"My God, woman, you know how I feel about Sunday TV!"

"Yeah," she said. "I know. But you'd still better catch up on what's been happening before you leave the house."

The president appeared on the screen late Sunday afternoon to verify what the ETs had said on their tape.

"Yes, it's true that a number of men have been impregnated. This may be inconvenient for them, but all the men in question have asserted year after year that convenience really isn't the issue. They have told us that the issue is reverence for life, and since these men have gone on record as supporting such reverence, we agree with the Pistach that now is the time for them to put their careers on hold and their bodies on the line, just as they have expected others to do."

"Mr. President, Mr. President." Hands waved. One was selected. "Mr. President, is it mere coincidence that none of the men selected are Democrats?"

The president looked at the ceiling. "Yes. I should think it is purely coincidence."

He got through this without smiling, but some of the reporters in the audience kept holding up their notebooks to hide the fact they were cracking up. In the evening, one of the doctors who'd been involved in treating the pregnant men appeared on a special *Larry King Live* and told why the larvae couldn't be removed. Each growing creature sent extensions of itself into the vital organs, and any attempt to remove them ended up killing the host. These extensions withdrew in the days preceding emergence.

"The Inkleozese furnished us with information regarding the care of the men who are carrying the larvae," the doctor said. "They will need to avoid stress, to get regular exercise, plenty of sleep, plenty of liquids, plus calcium and iron supplements. They must avoid alcohol and tobacco and all drugs except vitamins. We're assured the condition will last for only thirteen months, as with elephants."

CNN Headline News had pictures of Senator Morse being brought by ambulance to a local hospital earlier that day. The screaming, flailing form on the screen bore little resemblance to the dignified and poised Senator Morse with whom his constituents were familiar. Off camera, after everyone had come to his or her wit's end, he had actually been put in restraints, though this was known only to himself, Lupé, and the hospital staff. It had to be restraints because the guidelines from the Inkleozese forbade sedatives. On hastily sought advice of counsel, no hospital was prepared to risk the wrath of the Inkleozese by failure to follow the guidelines.

Lupé stayed at the senator's side until he finally settled down, though it took awhile, and by evening, he had stopped raving. He sent Lupé home to get the car—she had come with him in the ambulance—and his clothing. Upon the arrival of both, he checked himself out of the hospital and stopped at a pay phone on the way home to call McVane.

Chad's cronies at the FBI had been keeping tabs on the senator for some time. The agents following him had a directional microphone that could pick up, so the technician bragged, a gnat fart at half a mile, and they had no trouble recording both sides of the conversation.

Morse yelled, "Call the damned woman, McVane."

"She's not there, Senator. She agreed to testify before your committee on Monday, but we couldn't get hold of you, so the predators have already picked her up."

"Testify? Picked her up? You mean they've kidnapped her? Where is she?"

In the heat of the moment McVane had neglected to arrange contact with the predators, which he admitted to, and the senator subsided into his car in a state of shock. Lupé drove him home while he fumed and snorted and made threats both general and specific about what he would do to this one or that one when this matter was over. On arrival home, he called his secretary and several staff members and dictated a press release to be sent out immediately, charging the president and the intermediary with complicity in the attack upon his body, which, he said, he intended to prove as soon as the intermediary could be found.

SIX SOUTHERN SENATORS SEXUALLY ASSAULTED
ALL SIX MEN PREGNANT, ACCORDING TO PHYSICIANS.
TWO HOSPITALIZED FOR HYSTERIA, POST TRAUMATIC STRESS
SYNDROME

LDS ELDERS REQUIRE RESPECT FOR HUMAN LIFE ONLY
UTAH SENATOR EXCOMMUNICATED
IMMORAL BEHAVIOR WITH ET ALLEGED

"I was raped," he says, denying reports he was on drugs when admitted to hospital.

"He was high as a kite, laughing like a lunatic," reported ER nurse Blanche Smith. "And he was wearing tight jeans. Didn't some judge just recently rule you can't rape somebody wearing tight jeans?"

THIS ISN'T A BABY, SAYS TV PERSONALITY REQUESTING
ABORTION
INFANT ET IMPOSSIBLE TO REMOVE WITHOUT KILLING
OVERWEIGHT HOST

INKLEOZESE THREATEN REPRISAL IF LARVAE INJURED
UNITED NATIONS SECURITY COUNCIL IN EMERGENCY SESSION
ARAB NATIONS DEMAND ACCESS TO INTERMEDIARY,
INSIST ON IMMUNITY FROM PREGNANCY
IMMEDIATE CURE DEMANDED FOR INFECTIOUS UGLY

43

benita, bound

Benita dreamed she was rocking in Mami's hammock, the one on the back portal of the old house, where she and her brothers had sometimes slept during the summer. It was a soothing motion, though subtly wrong, for her legs were rocking much more widely than her head. As though she'd gotten all tangled up in the hammock and one end had come loose, leaving her dangling upright. She heard one of her brothers moan, and she opened her eyes to locate him and tell him to be still, he was making her seasick.

The portal posts were gone. There was no roof. Only the moonlit sky above her, against treetops that bent and swayed in a soft breeze, just as she did. She tried to move her arms and found she couldn't. She was wrapped, not uncomfortably tightly, but tight enough that she couldn't move. She turned her head to see Chad, head on his chest, and beyond him three other figures, long bundles hung in the treetops. And beyond that, heavens, a dozen or more others, just hanging there. Like in the *Hobbit*. Spider food. Rock-a-bye baby, she thought. Rocky-bye. Below her, in a moonlit clearing, stumpy trees wandered about among squat, furry creatures, occasionally turning toward some vacancy and gesturing at it, as though there was someone there.

As, undoubtedly, there was. She remembered at once what had happened. She and Chad had been about to leave, but the Wulivery had bashed in the front windows and grabbed them, and then something had told them firmly to go to sleep. That had to have been a Fluiquosm, one of the vacancies below her in the forest.

She risked another look below. The Wulivery and the Xankatikitiki were busy doing something else and were paying no attention to her. After a time, she realized what it was they were doing and hastily averted her eyes. Evidently they'd stopped somewhere en route in order to hunt. Or maybe they'd just taken something down out of the larder.

Contorting herself, she managed to swing the cocoon until it bumped into Chad. He moaned softly, but did not waken. The membrane that wrapped her was quite elastic. Though her hand was pressed against her side, she could clench her fist, move her fingers, feel with her fingers . . . feel the sharply pointed nail file she had dropped in the large flapped shirt pocket after she had filed down her broken nail. Also in the pocket, yes, by all that was holy, the handgun Chad had given her when he walked in the door. And the translator! She'd pocketed it along with the gun. She'd been all packed. Chad had left the car down below, she was telling him she was ready . . . and that's when the windows fell in.

Moving carefully, inch by inch, she bent her elbow and moved her hand up, over the pocket flap, then fiddled with the flap, rolling it up under her hand so the hand could go down again, into the pocket. Grasp the nail file. Bend the elbow again, bring the file out of the pocket, jab the membrane she was wrapped in. Flexible. Like a rubber balloon. Not infinitely flexible, however, for it punctured very nicely on about the fourth try. Another puncture just below the first one, then a few above and a few more below, working up and down to make a dotted line, tear here, r-r-rip. Actually, it didn't rip, which was lucky, or she might have fallen a considerable distance, but it did loosen. After ten minutes of careful effort, the wrapping was loose enough that she could get the gun out with her left hand and pass it across her body to her right hand. After thumbing off the safety, she put it in the right pocket. Chad had pointed out the safety, first thing in the apartment, or she might not have remembered.

The apartment. Lord, Sasquatch! He'd probably hidden under the bed, and hooray for him, if so. And the alarm had gone off, so her absence wouldn't go unnoticed for long. Not that it would help anything, since no one had a clue where she was, including herself, except that she was hanging in a maple tree. The silhouette of the leaves against the moon was unmistakable. A large maple tree, just starting to shed its leaves, somewhere in a forest which could be anywhere from Maine to Wisconsin, from Canada to Virginia. Probably Virginia or Maryland. Why carry her farther than they needed to?

The branch from which she was hung was only a foot over her head, and another sizeable branch went off to her right, just below shoulder level. After a few moments' rest, she decided the lower one of these was reachable. She passed the file to her right hand and made an arm hole, somewhat easier this time since the membrane was looser, and got her arm out and over the branch. No good. She needed her right hand to work with. She contorted herself to spin the cocoon until she could get her left arm out and over the branch, pulling herself halfway onto it. That was better. Now she could make more holes with her right hand, enough to extricate one leg, an inch at a time, which immediately loosened the wrapper enough that the other leg came out easily and there she was, heaving herself up to lie along the branch, the flaccid wrapper hanging around her like the skin of a sucked grape.

If one of them looked up, they'd see that. Better they didn't see that. Carefully, she gathered the wrapper up onto the branch, stuffing it under her. From below, it shouldn't be evident at all. There'd be one bundle missing, but among so many, maybe they wouldn't notice it.

The branch beneath her was, however, somewhat narrower than her body, which could be noticeable from below. She eased back toward the trunk of the tree, the branch thickening in that direction, until she was totally hidden from below except for one eye and a bit of forehead resting in a fork of the branch to keep watch on what happened down there. Now, if she could just figure out a way to get Chad awake and moving, maybe they could escape . . .

Carlos! She hadn't been thinking at all! The three hanging bundles on beyond Chad had to be her family! Well, two of them, Carlos and Bert, plus the unknown girl. She rested her head on her hands, fighting an insane desire to scream: No way she could get all five of them out and down this tree . . . no, not this tree. The other three weren't even in this tree, they were hung from another tree. It was nearby, but she was no damned flying squirrel!

Chad, then. At least Chad. He had been armed, too, when they were taken. A shoulder holster, with his jacket over it. Perhaps they'd paid no more attention to that than they had the gun in her pocket. Thinking of which, she reached back along her body and carefully buttoned the pocket flap. The gun was a small one. What had Chiddy and Vess said? You shoot a Xankatikitiki in the head. And you shoot a Wulivery just below the tentacles, where the seven eye holes are. Or, shoot the breathing apparatus on top, which would immobilize the creature and eventually kill it. And if you can locate a Fluiquosm, just shoot it anywhere. Any wound of the flight organ pretty well disabled them.

She crawled out on the branch once more, taking another fork that brought her alongside Chad's cocoon. She reached out, pinched his cheek, slapped him lightly, whispered in his ear. No reaction. Either he was unconscious or he'd been . . . whatever the Fluiquosm did to people. Convinced him he was in paradise, maybe. Convinced him he was a baby in Mommy's womb. Maybe if she cut him some slack, he'd suck his thumb. She put her head down again and fought tears. If Chad couldn't help, who the hell could?

Below her, the eerie sound of untranslated alien speech. She had the translator in her pocket, and she knew it had been on in the stockroom because it had translated the speech of whatever had grabbed her. Had it been damaged in transit? She fished it out of her pocket, holding it to her ear to hear it humming. There were no other buttons, no other controls. What had Chiddy said to her . . . yell at it? Not damn likely, here where she was a minute away from being sucked like a orange!

She whispered, "Translate what you hear into English, very softly."

"Is this soft enough?" whispered the translator.

"Very good," she said, fighting an urge to giggle hysterically.

"The Wulivery is saying he sees no reason not to eat Chad now, or if not him, then the girl. The Fluiquosm say they do not want to partake of Bert or Carlos, inasmuch as they both smoke and drink much alcohol which makes the blood taste funny.

"The Xankatikitiki don't mind eating Carlos or Bert, but they're not hungry right now, and besides, they should leave everyone alone until after they have spoken to the humans again. They must not do anything to endanger the pact they hope to make to hunt on this world, as this will give them authority before the Confederation."

Benita put her head on her hands and considered. "Can you speak Fluiquosm?" she asked. "And Wulivery?"

"Of course," said the translator. "Right now one Fluiquosm says she wants to drink your blood because she has smelled you, and you smell very sweet. Someone else has told her to wait until . . . until they talk to someone named . . . M'van?"

"McVane."

"Ah. Would you like me to summon the Pistach?"

"Can you do that? Silently? Without the predators knowing?"

"If you wish it. They are very far away, however, and they cannot travel as quickly on a planet as they can in space."

"Please let them know immediately where we are and what's going on. Now what are they saying?"

"The Wulivery assert their right to eat Chad or the girl now. They are hungry and see no reason to wait."

"Oh, Lord," she sighed. What could she do? Obviously, something was needed by way of a diversion, which she could do better from ground level.

Easing back along the branch, she reached the trunk, the translator keeping up a steady murmur of argument from the creatures below. There were plenty of branches on the back side of the trunk, and she slithered from one to another, taking care not to make any sound. Luckily, she was wearing chinos and a sweater and soft-soled shoes when the attack came. If one had to climb trees, at least it was better to be dressed for it. The argument went on, and on, as she struggled silently downward, arriving finally at the foot of the tree, where, realizing she'd been holding her breath, it took all her willpower not to gasp audibly.

Slow breaths. One, two, three. Again. One, two, three. The pressure in her head and chest eased.

" 'Go ahead and eat him then,' says the Xankatikitiki. 'If you have so little foresight.' " The translator chuckled to itself. "The Wulivery says the man is out of reach, it asks the Fluiquosm to bring him down and the Fluiquosm says no."

Diversion, diversion, Benita thought desperately. Stab something with the nail file? Confuse them with the translator? Shoot them? How about all three?

She leaned from behind the tree to reconnoiter. The woods thinned opposite her, and beyond was a moonlit meadow.

"When you hear a loud bang," she whispered to the translator, "I want you to yell loudly, first in Fluiquosm and then in Xankatikitiki. Yell, 'There it goes, out onto the meadow, get it, get it.' Okay?"

Leaning from behind the tree, Benita sighted the pistol at the nearest Xankatikitiki's head. It was talking with another Xanka, just a foot to the right, so she shot twice, bang, right a notch, another bang. She sagged back behind the tree.

"Qyoxilizimak! Zixit izi. Shamma! Shamma!" yelled the translator. "Gromfrr growrrg glor, Furrgrinnor! Furrgrinnor!"

The creatures turned and made for the meadow, except for two Xankatikitiki, one of whom was still and silent, the other barely moving.

Now what? Benita asked herself. They'd come back. She'd better finish off the moving one. She stepped out into the clearing, moving quickly toward the moving Xanka, gun in pocket, hand on gun. She did not see the stooping form above her until the tentacles closed around her. She was lifted, hoisted, up, up, turned upside down and then swallowed, glurgle, glurgle, glurgle, her way down the long throat oiled by jets of stinking liquid, choking from the stench, dropped into a sac half-filled with stinking ooze.

Gagging, she sagged against one side of the stomach and peered upward, catching a glimpse of light among the tentacles. She thrust the gun up in trembling hands, held her breath and fired. Once, turn slightly, twice. Turn slightly again, three times, then a fourth. She should have pierced the body in several places, right up at the top. The walls of her prison trembled. High above her the tentacles lashed. Then, slowly, slowly, the creature fell, changing from a smokestack to a lengthy culvert, down which Benita began to crawl, sloshing, toward the roots of a tree, barely visible in the moonlight. Around her, the flesh of the creature still shook, and a high keening moved up the scale toward inaudibility.

She arrived at the dead, lax tentacles just as the predators came back from the meadow, talking loudly among themselves. The translator was still giving her the gist of it, still in a whisper.

"Odiferous Tentacle, Oh, Stinky, what's happened to you. Look, look, Stinky's down. Stinky's leaking! Oh, Stinky emits death stenches! Alas, alas! Oh, Mrrgrowr is dead, see him lying there, dead and gone, his strength gone, his proud head fallen low, oh, alas, alas."

"Do they all say alas?" murmured Benita.

"I'm translating freely," admitted the machine. "I lack synonyms for *alas*. The Fluiquosm is asking if it or they got away. The Xankatikitiki say they must depart immediately with their fallen comrades, the burial rituals of their people demand it. The Wulivery say they must also depart, taking their commander with them . . ."

Benita very much wished to exit the commander. Her

legs were beginning to burn, as though they were being digested. The tentacle end lay amid a cluster of evergreens, however, so she took the chance and crawled out beneath the low branches of the nearest. Behind her, the body of the dead Wulivery was tugged into the clearing. There were bustling sounds.

"Quolzikkaz closmmi wozzik."

"The Fluiquosm wonders how many creatures it took to kill three of their group, why they were not seen, and how they got away," murmured the translator. "The Fluiquosm are discussing moving the prey creatures to their own larder, after the Wulivery and the Xankatikitiki leave . . ."

Benita started, gritted her teeth and began to move out of her hiding place. She still had a few shots left. Maybe she could hit a Fluiquosm when it started to move one of the humans. It stood to reason she'd be able to tell where it was from the way the packaged body was moved. . . .

"Shhh," said a voice at her ear.

Slowly, in total terror, she turned her head to confront the huge, compound eyes of . . . an Inkleozese, who spoke at some length, unintelligibly.

"The Pistach are on their way," whispered the translator. "I strongly suggest that you stay here very quietly while we conduct our business. Our being here makes the ensuing time an official matter. It will be tiresome, time consuming, but do be still. They will not speak freely if they know you are listening."

"The others . . ." murmured Benita, gesturing.

"They will not be harmed, and they will not move on their own. Only you were given the ability to shake off the Fluiquosm mindfog. Immunity to common types of predation is a usual gift to give an intermediary. We do not like persons of any planet interfering with official intermediaries." The Inkleozese went up the trunk and out along a branch, where it disappeared among the leaves.

Like a great, big wasp, Benita thought to herself. A huge wasp, going about its business. Except it had more than six legs. However many legs, its presence was reassuring, and the expectation of Chiddy and Vess arriving was even more so. And what was that about who speaking freely? The predators? Who cared if they spoke freely!

In the clearing, a fire had been built, and the Wulivery, some half dozen of them, were gathered around their fallen leader, while a dozen or so Xankatikitiki were busy with their slain comrades. The night was chilly, and she recalled that both the Wulivery and Xankatikitiki had high body temperatures. No doubt they felt the cold, but the Fluiquosm probably did not.

Abruptly, the fire leapt up, a bright light illuminated the clearing, and Chiddy's voice, tight with fury, said in impeccable English, "You will all have the courtesy to stay precisely where you are." His words were followed by loud, simultaneous translations.

There were exclamations of surprise and annoyance. There was movement among the trees, quickly stopped, and several Inkleozese moved into the clearing tugging nets that were full of something invisible. These were pegged down with considerable dispatch under Chiddy's watchful eyes, though they continued to move restlessly as Chiddy spoke angrily.

"Stinky seems to have met with difficulty, and so has 'Growr. Well, they have played games with your membership in the Confederation for many years. The last time you pulled something like this your people paid a monstrous fine. That alone should have been enough to dissuade you from repeating your behavior."

"Oh, end talk, Pistach," said a voice from one of the nets. "This planet is incredibly rich! There's enough here for all of us. You take the western half of it and civilize it. We'll take Asia and Africa and eat them. And the Inkleozese can monitor Europe to their souls' content. We won't even stumble over one another!"

"That may be true," said Chiddy. "But we have rules against involving ourselves in adversarial or factional relationships on new planets. You're working with a rebel force against the legitimate government of this nation."

"You're working with a reactionary element against the best interest of the people of this planet," charged one of the

Wulivery. "And we're prepared to bring it before the Confederation court! These people don't need civilizing! They need weeding out! They need cutting down, losing their flab! Our entire population could dine four meals a day for a century before humans would even notice a drop in their population density!"

"That's true, but irrelevant," said Chiddy, wrathfully. "The humans must come to grips with their own population problem."

"Just like they come to grips with their own drug problem?" cried Odiferous Tentacle. "You're very selective which problems you will solve and which you won't."

"We only solve the ones that affect Neighborliness, and you very well known it," snapped Chiddy. "We solve situations that may lead to general war, situations that cause continuing discontent among populations. In our opinion, drugs do that, and weapons do that and repressions do that. Such things are powderkegs, just waiting to explode! Men with breeding madness versus women. Catholic Ireland versus the northern Protestants! Israel versus the Palestinians! Iraq or the Turks versus the Kurds! Serbia, what's left of it, versus the Universe! Ridiculous. These can be handled with a few suspensions, a few vanishments, without ending in a war that will kill off half the world's population!"

"Enough," said one of the Inkleozese. "We are here to monitor this situation. We have already found the three predatory races to be in contempt of the regulations concerning hunting rights on assisted planets. We find the predatory races were properly informed of the Pistach initiative on Earth. We find the Xankatikitiki, the Fluiquosm, the Wulivery have no right to be here."

"We raise a point of procedure," cried a voice from an empty net.

"State your point," answered the Inkleozese.

"Section 7A of the book of procedures establishes that when an initiative is begun on a false premise, that the initiative may be cancelled when the premise is corrected."

"What false premise?" cried Chiddy.

"You say that Neighborliness will be best assured by eliminating drugs and weapons and by quieting repressions. We, the predators, say that Neighborliness will be best assured when the population of this planet is reduced by at least half and that the best way to do this is to increase drugs and weapons, increase warlike situations, and let the predators have freedom to hunt here as they will."

Hidden behind her tree, Benita shuddered. The world had been repeatedly swept by war and famine and plague when the population had been a quarter of what it was now! Less than a hundred years ago. Sparse population didn't equal peace. It never had. All it meant were fewer casualties.

The agitated net spoke again: "I will quote our Pistach friend who said, on Earthian TV, that it had read in a gardening book that one saved much labor by learning to love weeds. . . ."

"Out of context," cried Vess. "We said allow people to kill themselves if they will. We said nothing about doing the killing for them! We find no fault with suicide! People who risk their own lives or who do not want to live should not be rescued or required to live. We find great fault with murder!"

Three of the Inkleozese put their heads together, their antennas touching. One of them turned to the predators, saying, "You have legitimate points of argument. However, once planetary assistance has begun, points of procedure must be argued before the Council, not on the planet in question. Research into the history of this planet must be done. We will do so, and we will notify you of the hearing. In the meantime, you will return to your ships. You will enter into no further agreements with humans on this planet. The Pistach will continue their efforts for the time being, though those efforts may be set aside if your appeal is granted."

There were howls, chitterings, yips and stinks of annoyance, but within a short time the predators had departed, along with their dead comrades. Then the Inkleozese set about lowering the captives from the trees and stripping off the membrane wrappers. At this point, Chiddy came to Benita.

"Are you all right, dearest Benita?" He morphed into his favorite male human form, one she had become accustomed to, a rather professorial or perhaps wizardly form with gray-ing hair and far-seeing eyes. "Oh, we so deeply regret not being there when these . . . naughty people took you away. There is your friend, Chad. The Inkleozese are helping him, now. It is necessary they work on him a little, wiping out the mind picture put in his head by the Fluiquosm."

"My son ought to be among those prisoners," she mur-mured. "And the girl who was taken at the same time. And Bert."

"What is best to do with them?" Chiddy asked. "We can return them near the place they were taken from. Perhaps that would save much trouble?"

"It would save trouble. I think. Only . . . didn't the cabal ask that they be kidnapped? This has all happened in such a rush. It's hard to think. It's still night, but it's Monday, isn't it? I'm supposed to appear before a committee this morning? And . . . Morse? He believes he still has Bert and Carlos and Angelica, even though it wasn't really Angelica? Maybe we shouldn't let him know what's happened here tonight. Maybe we should let him think he still has them."

"For what reason?"

"I don't know. Just that telling the truth to men like that never does any good. They always deal from a stacked deck."

"Which is cheating?"

"Yes. And the only way to beat a cheater is to cheat bet-ter," she said.

The nearest Inkleozese said, "We will take these people, your son and his father and the female, and we will keep them for a time, while you decide what should be done with them. The others, we will return to the places they were taken from."

"Perhaps that's best," agreed Chiddy. "What is important now is to get you and Chad back to your homes. It is almost dawn."

One thing about Inkleozese, Benita soon understood, was their extreme efficiency. Everything happened with such dispatch that she found it difficult to remember how, ex-actly, she'd gotten home. She'd come in a ship, a very small one, and it had landed outside the back door, and they had let her in even though she hadn't had her keys with her. It was just as she had left it, except that the broken glass had been swept up, the broken windows had been boarded up, and Sasquatch was missing. A howl that came up the firewell from the stockroom told Benita he wasn't far away. She went into the bathroom and looked at herself in the mirror. A mess. She took off her trousers and looked at her legs. Her knees and lower legs were blistered where they'd been in contact with Stinky as she crawled out.

She stripped off the rest of her clothes, took a quick, hot shower, and put on one of her long sleep-tees. As she came out the bathroom door she heard an "Ahem" from the doorway.

Chiddy. He was holding out a small bottle. "Tonic," he said. "To make you feel you have slept well and are unstressed and confident. We sent some home with Chad, as well."

"Is it a drug?" she asked.

He frowned. "You mean, is it addictive? No. Unless you are addicted to staying up all night every night and being frightened out of your wits all the time. Then, I suppose, one might come to rely on it."

She laughed, the laughter becoming almost hysterical, until she found herself sitting on the bed, Chiddy holding a cold washcloth to her head. "Did you think they would eat you?" he asked.

"Chiddy, they did eat me! Or, one of them did. I was inside a Wulivery. My legs, look at them, they're all red and blistered and they burn like fury . . ."

He growled something and disappeared, returning in a moment with another bottle containing a lotion that he spread upon the reddened skin. The relief from pain was immediate. "Twice each day," he muttered angrily, recapping the bottle and setting it beside her. "The Inkleozese didn't tell me. How did you get out?"

"I killed it," she said. "And two Xankatikitiki, as well."

"You killed them! Three of them. Remarkable."

"Oh, yeah. I'm a walking advertisement for the NRA. Where did the Inkleozese take Bert and the kids?"

He shrugged. "Somewhere nearby. They will not suffer, any of them, and Vess and I agree it is best for the cabal not to know what has happened. In a few hours, you must appear before Senator Morse's committee."

"That's right," she sighed.

He stared at her for a time, nodding. "Chad will come get you. Until near the time, perhaps you should sleep."

"If I can, sure."

"Drink the tonic," he said. "You'll find you can."

44

benita

MONDAY

By eight o'clock on Monday morning, Benita felt considerably better. Chiddy's tonic had calmed her down, brightened her eyes, and allowed her to convince herself, as Chiddy suggested, that she was involved in an interesting episode in human history rather than the debacle of the millennium. Shortly after eight, Chad called to say she was to appear before Morse's committee in closed session.

"I don't like that closed session bit."

"Neither do I. We'll see what we can do when we get there."

Chad drove her to the Capitol, where they went down a wide hallway without attracting the least attention. In the committee room, Senator Morse was already seated, glaring at the far end of the table with its empty chair, the one Benita was presumably to occupy. When he looked up and saw her, he started, very much as though her presence was unexpected.

Chad caught the reaction and pressed her arm. Benita murmured, "He thought I wouldn't show up. Now isn't that interesting."

To either side of the table committee members fumbled

papers and murmured to one another, glancing with equal curiosity first at Benita and Chad and then at Morse. Perhaps, Benita thought, they had assumed she would have two heads. Or tentacles. Perhaps they had assumed a pregnant Morse would not appear. Whatever their assumptions, here she was, and here he was, and the one thing that really bothered her was that there were no neutral outside observers in the room. She didn't trust Morse and much preferred that he do nothing to her or with her in private.

"Who are you?" Morse demanded of Chad.

"I'm the intermediary's bodyguard, Senator. I'm an FBI agent, and I'll stay with her during the hearing."

"You will not," said Morse. "This is a private hearing."

Benita felt herself flushing. It was all too, too reminiscent of a former occasion. "I agreed to speak to this committee voluntarily," she said. "However, I will not do so unless Agent Riley is here."

"My dear lady, you will be held in contempt of Congress if you do not do precisely what we order," sneered Morse.

She started to speak, hushing when Chad put his hand on her arm. "Senator, the envoys are not delighted at your demanding the intermediary to be here, and though we do not know how they might react to such an action on your part, we have seen what actions they are capable of. Our agency, at least, feels it is wiser to be cautious."

One of Morse's committee members leaned over and whispered in Morse's ear, his hand over the microphone. Morse's nostrils flared and his mouth twisted unattractively.

Benita distinctly heard the colleague say, "By, you're making an ass of yourself. We don't want to rub the envoys the wrong way and this hearing is all on the record, anyhow."

While Morse, flushing, pretended to look at the papers before him, Benita sat down, her feet together in ladylike fashion, her hands folded in her lap.

The colleague asked her to state her name.

"Your committee knows who I really am," she said. "You were told by Congressman Alvarez. The envoys prefer that my name not be widely used. To protect my privacy and that of my family, and for the purposes of this hearing, I am Jane Doe."

"For the purposes of this hearing," snarled Morse, "you are whoever you are. Give us your name."

"Since this intermediary business has been dumped on me, Senator, and since my family knows nothing about it, it would be polite of the committee to grant my wish for anonymity."

Morse spluttered and boomed, "It will be necessary to question your family in order to ascertain that you are who and what you say you are."

Benita glared at him, feeling her mind slip a gear. "That is utterly specious, Senator. The FBI has already ascertained that I am who I say I am. Why don't you ask your questions, and if you think some particular question isn't answered honestly, we can talk about a polygraph. My intention is to tell the truth, and since I have not been consulted about any decisions the envoys have made or any activity they have engaged in or thought of engaging in, I have no reason whatsoever to lie about it."

Benita had read McIntyre's *FrankenStarr* when it first came out, so she wasn't totally unprepared for the deep-water fishing expedition Morse conducted. Where had she met the aliens? What had they looked like to her? What had she done, where had she gone? When had she met with the president?

"The day after I delivered the cube to Congressman Alvarez."

"Who else was at that meeting?"

"General Wallace."

"Was that the only time you met with the president?"

"That was the only time I have seen the president in person," Benita answered. "Agent Riley was appointed my go-between to the White House, and I have communicated through him."

Her answers obviously displeased Morse. "Aside from that dinner you attended, who have you spoken to about the aliens?"

"The only people I have spoken to about the aliens are Representative Alvarez and General Wallace, and—" she meant to continue with the SOS and the FL, but he interrupted.

"And the president?"

"No, I didn't speak to him about them even when I saw him. The president simply thanked me for my efforts because by that time he'd already seen the envoys for himself."

"What have you done since that time?" asked someone else.

"Once the FBI was involved, I figured the matter was out of my hands. Since then, all I've done is transmit messages from the Pistach to Mr. Riley, who transmits them to whoever needs to know."

"Why was the FBI involved in the first place?" Morse snarled, with a glare at Chad.

Benita pursed her lips, considering. "To do just what you said you wanted to do, Senator. The White House and the Justice Department felt it was wise to check me out and be sure I am who I say I am, to be sure my story is true."

Somebody snapped at Chad, "Is that the case?"

Chad said it was.

At this juncture, Senator Morse snarled at Benita, "This all sounds very innocent, but you and I both know that you and the president and others have conspired to let these predators take over our country, haven't you?"

That came so far from left field that her jaw dropped and the committee members hastily covered microphones and began muttering to one another. While they squabbled lengthily, she decided upon a response, beginning by saying stiffly:

"I'm not aware they're taking over the country, sir. If so, I certainly didn't plan it. I can't speak for the Pistach, though my opinion is they didn't plan it either. They were extremely upset when they learned the predators were here, and they've already given them notice to leave the planet."

She paused, looked thoughtful, shook her head and said, barely audibly, "No, I shouldn't say . . . ."

"Say what?" he pounced. "What were you going to say?"

She bit her lip, hesitated, breathed rapidly to make herself flush. "I'm not sure it's relevant, Senator."

He almost screamed at her. "I'll be the judge of that! Answer the question."

She said, haltingly, as if she hadn't planned it down to every pause and sigh: "I started to say that it . . . ah . . . probably wasn't the envoys or the president who encouraged the predators." Sigh. "It's probable that the predators have sought or even made an agreement with some member or members of the U.S. Congress." Sigh, again, look down, pick at the seam of her skirt, shake her head very slightly. "They do want hunting privileges on Earth very badly."

Morse turned absolutely white.

"Hunt what?" cried one of the members.

"Why, people," she said, looking up innocently. "There are more of us here than anything else."

And at that point the committee room exploded, some yelling, some looking serious, some merely staring angrily at Morse while others focused their suspicion on Benita. There were only men on this committee, loud ones, and Benita put her hands over her ears. Chad leaned over to her and asked her if she wanted to take a break while they ranted at one another. She nodded. He whispered to one of the members, and they went out, Benita to the ladies' room, Chad to a secluded corner of the corridor where he could use his phone. When Benita opened the door to come out, she saw reporters and cameramen in the hallway. She wasn't ready to talk to them yet. They didn't see her, and when she peeked out a bit later, they had gone.

"They'll be downstairs when we're finished," Chad said, looking into her eyes with frank curiosity. "Did you have that bombshell all ready to drop on him?"

"Sort of," she admitted, flushing. "I was angry at being harassed, first off, and when I got here I was even angrier at being accused of things, and I thought, well, that works both ways. Why not be the accuser instead of the accused? That contempt of Congress bit just made me furious, Chad. Just like the judge in Albuquerque. Let Morse be dropped in the you-know-what for a change."

They went back to the committee room. Senator Morse

was pale, his lips pinched, his jaw seeming set in cement, but he managed to speak without yelling.

"Why did you say the predators had already made contact with members of Congress?"

She gave him her innocent look. "I said it was probable, Senator, because the Pistach told me that's the predators' usual mode of action. If they can get some level of government or even some individual associated with the government to make an agreement with them, like a senator or a representative or some member of the staff of a legislator, even if some other level of government or other individuals would oppose such an agreement, the matter then has to be settled in the Confederation courts, and it can take a very long time to sort out. Centuries, even. During which the predators go on hunting. The Pistach told me the predators always record such understandings . . . ."

Morse turned, if possible, even paler.

". . . so they have them for evidence in Confederation courts."

A thoughtful-looking man at the end of the table asked, "Do you, personally, know anyone who might be involved with the predators?"

"I can't swear to it," she said. "But I think General McVane may be involved, along with a man named Dink Dinklemier, a man named Prentice Arthur, and a man named Briess. The man named Arthur approached my husband and the man named Briess evidently threatened my son. I also received an anonymous phone call early this morning threatening to hurt my family if I didn't turn myself over to the person calling. I told the voice on the phone that I couldn't because I'd agreed to appear before this committee."

The place blew up again. The name Dinklemier led them straight to Morse, and he became the immediate focus of their shouted questions. Someone, presumably the vice chairman, grabbed the gavel out of his hand and declared a thirty-minute recess. Chad and Benita left, Chad remarking to the man at the door that they would be in the House gallery. They sat there, watching Congress at work, Benita remarking that on that particular day, it was not exciting.

"I'm not sure it ever is," Chad admitted. "Why did you clue them in on the cabal?"

"Morse knew where I was because Dink knew where I was from the predators. What he was really after was a private inquiry, just him and me, with nobody monitoring it, so he could extort information or misinformation by threatening me or my family." She recalled Morse's face and added, "Or by other means."

"What's his motive?"

"Oh, hell, Chad, I don't know! Maybe he actually believes the president invited the Pistach here, or the predators. Maybe the rest of the cabal didn't tell him they were talking to the predators, so he believes the accusation he just made. Maybe he thinks he can make a name for himself by interrogating the envoys, and he thinks he can get at them through me. Maybe he's just pulling a McCarthy, telling big lies and getting his name in the newspapers. What's your best guess?"

Chad frowned. "It's likely he's known about the predators all along. It's probable he doesn't care whether the information he might get out of you is true or not so long as it includes something he can use. He's part of a small group who would rather get the president than go to heaven. It's deeply personal, it's unabashed hatred, and he keeps yanking at the strings, trying to find something that will come unraveled. It's like the independent prosecutor business. If you don't have a case, just unlimber your fishing poles and go at it until you catch something you can blow up into a case, no matter how irrelevant it is."

She watched him thinking, each separate thought crossing his face like a cloud shadow, darkening and lightening, the way she had seen them do over the canyon lands, revealing, concealing. She wanted to touch his face, and the thought made her bite her lip and clench her hands. He was a married man. With young sons. He was not available. Nor was she. Nonetheless, though the urge had been a very modest one, it was the first honest-to-God even remotely sexual urge she'd had in . . . a very long time!

She switched her mind to another subject. "There have to

be a few honest men on that committee who know we appeared voluntarily and won't let him get away with murder," she murmured.

"You mean literal murder? You think he would kill you?"

"If he wanted to get rid of me and could do it without getting caught. He can still get me arrested on some pretext or other, like that contempt of Congress business. And once I'm in custody, something might happen to me. I'm taking Chiddy's word that I don't have to worry about Bert or Carlos and the girl."

"And you've made it less likely for Morse to take action by implicating a committee staff member."

"I hope I did," she murmured. "Give them all something else to chew on. I was careful to say I couldn't swear to it, so they can't get me on perjury."

"Remind me never to play cards with you," he said.

"I was worried that Morse might talk about the Inkleozese," she murmured. "That really was a conspiracy, of sorts, between the Pistach and the Inkleozese themselves, but Morse is pretending it never happened."

"Right. If he acknowledges they impregnated him, someone may commiserate with him, or grin at him, or laugh behind his back, and he couldn't take that."

"He's going to have to deal with it sooner or later."

"Maybe denial is the only way he can function at all," said Chad. "The whole business has to be pretty traumatic." He got up. "We'd better go back and see if they're continuing or recessing."

They were continuing. Morse was gone, the vice chairman of the committee had taken over, and he did want to know about the Inkleozese.

"I saw them on TV," Benita said. "When everyone else did. Also, the envoys told me about them. Evidently their specialty is to serve as monitors and observers for the Confederation."

"Are they female?" the vice chairman wanted to know. "And if so, why were only females sent here?"

Three members of the committee leaned forward when he asked the question, focused intently on Benita. She said,

"The envoys said all the diplomatic and professional Inkleozese are female. Most of their race's artists and craftsmen are male, however. Males and females in their race have different skills. The females work better with persons and the males with things."

"So they say," snorted a burly committee member.

"Well, it's possible the envoys are prejudiced," she granted. "Or the Inkleozese themselves. For generations, our national legislature was made up of men only, most of whom thought women were brainless. Some of them still think so."

"But the Pistach envoys are male?" the same man asked intently.

"No, sir. They are not. They are nonreproductive members of their race, which has five or six different types or genders in it, like ants, or bees."

"Then they're gay!"

"Sir, a worker bee is not gay. It is simply nonsexual."

"Worker bees are females," asserted a man at the end of the table. "I raise bees, I know."

"Worker bees aren't lesbians, and Pistach aren't gay. They're nonsexual."

They went on, not for long. Several men on the committee seemed to be convinced that God could imagine no more than two sexes, that the devil had come up with a third, that every being in the universe had to be one of those three, and therefore Vess and Chiddy had to be gay. Finally they started asking questions about the Pistach home world and the Pistach themselves, questions that could equally well have been asked about Sodom and Gomorrah. She had to tell them she didn't know the answers.

"They don't talk about their home world a great deal. They mention it from time to time, but I've never gained a clear idea of their world and how it works. Actually, I have a clearer picture of the predator worlds than I do the Pistach, because the envoys talk more about the predators."

The committeemen looked at each other, with no idea what else they might ask her. After a spate of whispering, they excused her and Chad escorted her downstairs where he had asked the aggravation of reporters to wait.

"The senators seem to be stuck on the idea the Pistach are gay, which they're not," she said to the waiting microphones. "Senator Morse seems to be stuck with the idea that I'm part of some conspiracy, which I'm not. The committee became very upset when I told them the predators might have made a side agreement with someone associated with their committee."

"Agreement for what?" called a man from the back of the group.

"A formal agreement to hunt people here on Earth," she said in her most innocent voice. "They could just go on poaching, but they really want a formal agreement for their own legal protection at the Confederation level."

She answered shouted questions for about ten minutes, then Chad got her away with the help of six men in suits who barricaded her from the reporters as they got her out a back door. Then they went to the White House where she was sneaked up the back stairs into the family quarters where the president and First Lady were waiting for them.

"Well," said the president to Benita. "So much for anonymity, Benita."

"And so much for calming the committee down," said the First Lady, shaking her head. "A couple of our party are on the committee. They told us it was quite a show."

Benita said, "Keeping me anonymous was a lost cause from the beginning, Mr. President, ma'am. I got to the point I wasn't interested in calming them down."

"Chad says you've had some personal experience with the predators," murmured the FL.

"Not one I'd care to repeat, ma'am."

Chad took a chair by the window. Benita was gestured to the chair opposite the president, who leaned forward, fixing his eyes on hers.

"Benita, we're in trouble here, and we need your help."

She folded her hands in her lap as he went on:

"We have assumed the Pistach are beneficent. They've told us so; the things they've done for us have measurably helped without harming anyone. We would prefer to believe them, and we've gone along with them when they told us the predators are a separate people, races that eat other intelligent life and who do not, therefore, eat Republicans. Or newsmen."

She laughed dutifully. He was trying to be funny and charming, but his eyes were troubled as he went on.

"If, however, I am coldly rational as my aides suggest is necessary, I have to admit there could be another explanation for what's happening. All these ETs could be one people who are capable of taking different shapes in order to fool us."

"It doesn't sound impossible," Benita said. She didn't believe it, but it wasn't impossible.

"All right. Then let's suppose for a moment they are all one people, and they want to invade Earth and prey on our population. How would they do that?"

She thought for a moment. "They might send envoys to offer us candy and chuck us under the chin and say kootsie-coo."

He actually smiled, though only a little. "They might, yes. Then they could move in and start hunting us while keeping us pacified by telling us the predators are really a different set of people and so on and so on."

"And while this is going on," said the First Lady, "still more of these creatures pick up some of our congressmen and political columnists and impregnate them with what we are told are infant members of their race. The impregnation could just as well be some kind of disease or parasite that will turn us into passive livestock."

"And they're clever," remarked Chad. "They pick only members of the opposition political party so that the administration would be less inclined to object."

The president nodded. "And, by the time we work ourselves around to doing something about it, they have us whipped."

He sat back and stared at her, switching his glance to Chad, who said, "You think Chiddy and Vess are a Trojan horse?"

"Or you think I am?" Benita asked, hearing her voice tremble.

The president shook his head. "You're not a Trojan horse knowingly, Benita. I don't believe for a minute that you could be. But . . . let's say that scenario is correct. What kind of woman would the envoys look for? Someone trusting. Someone . . . ah, patient . . ."

"Long suffering," said the FL pointedly and a little indignantly. "Someone who'd put up with a lot before she got really angry, if ever. Someone who'd go along with the way things were happening, without having hysterics or throwing a fit . . ."

"All the time telling herself it couldn't be true," Benita finished for her, flushing an angry red. "And you really think I'm that kind of person?"

"You've showed endless patience and forbearance in the past," she said. "Although, from what you did today, that may no longer be true. Be that as it may, we've never had a satisfactory answer to the question, why you? Why not General Wallace? Why not the president himself, or, if he's too surrounded by Secret Service people, then why not the Chief Justice or the Speaker of the House?"

"Because those particular people are all men," Benita said angrily. "And the Pistach didn't want a man. They were making a particular point when they chose me, an unknown, because any woman who's known for anything will already have enemies. The minute a woman, including the president's wife, tries to do something significant, even if it's for the good of the citizenry, everybody puts her down as being a woman who doesn't know her place. People love their heroes and heroines, but they love them in their assigned roles. Move outside those roles, and the public loves to make them stumble."

The president frowned. "I had hoped we had grown more tolerant and understanding than that."

Benita shook her head. "We like to think people are tolerant and understanding, but mostly we aren't, and there are a lot of men who think of women as a kind of speaking livestock."

The FL said, "So the Pistach picked you because . . . ?"

"Because nobody knows me, or anything about me. I've

done one really stupid thing in my life, and that was to marry the wrong man. Get past that and I've had an utterly unremarkable and very . . . chaste kind of life. Never used drugs, never smoked. My drinking is limited to an occasional beer in the summertime, or a glass of wine with Thanksgiving or Christmas dinner. I've never been able to afford dissipation. I haven't had the time or the money to support controversial causes. The same goes for love affairs. The only men I've been at all close to over the years are gay, and they were my bosses. Believe me, McVane has known who I am for weeks, and if there were anything in my past to stir a scandal, it would be on the front pages by now, like a Jackson Pollock painting, all squirt and dribble! And if McVane had information he could use, then Morse would have it. There are no issues in my past for me to get past except that I'm a woman."

"I agree with you," agreed the FL. "I've been trying to explain to my husband, that your being a woman is really what sticks in their craw."

"All the people I talk to think the envoys are male," said the president, sitting back and frowning. "Every domestic politico I talk to, every foreign diplomat who calls me, all of them, every damned one says 'him' when he refers to an envoy."

"They aren't male," Benita said, turning to the FL. "That's why they did that Indian woman business at dinner."

"But with you," she said, "what do they appear as?"

They appeared as different things, but she had to admit, Chiddy took his human male form more often than not. She said as much, and the president and FL looked at one another meaningfully.

"What?" she demanded.

"People say that you probably react to them as a woman would to a man. That your relationship with them is subtly different than it would be if they were female, or sexless."

"People?"

He looked uncomfortable. The FL said, "Profilers. Think people. Analysts. FBI."

"Chad's been spying on me?" she said, glaring at him.

"No," he said abruptly.

The FL said, "He refused to spy on you. He has only passed on what you've said about the Pistach. The people over at the FBI who attempt to make—"

"A sow's ear out of a silk purse," Benita interrupted angrily. "They're trying to imply something sexual?"

The president leaned back in his chair. "Quite frankly, I don't think they know what they're trying to imply. They simply have a situation they don't understand, one that won't fit any pattern they're accustomed to, and they can't help me with the current problem!

"We need . . . we're going to have to have something more than just the envoys' word that they're beneficent. You told Chad the Pistach have gone home at least once during their visit here. That means either that home is very close, which we don't believe, or that they have a method of travel . . ."

"Polarized space," she said.

All three of them looked at her in confusion.

"Chiddy told me about it," she said, trying to remember what he'd said. "Space is full of these little tiny thingies—Chiddy calls them umquah—all spread out, evenly distributed, like layers of marbles in a tray, only marbles would have little spaces among them, and the umquah shape themselves to fill all the spaces, and they're infinitely small. All together, they fill the universe, and they repel matter and energy, joining together to squeeze matter or energy out. Chiddy said I should think of it as though gravity wasn't an attractive force but a repulsive force. It's as though matter doesn't attract other matter, it simply gets squeezed together by the umquah, and the more matter there is in one place, the more umquah are displaced to do the squeezing, so they can squeeze harder. When they squeeze out clumps of matter, they become compressed and curved around it, and they're always trying to straighten out and spread out evenly.

"When an umquah gets touched by a photon, say, it and its neighbors squeeze it out, so it gets passed along. Each umquah touches more than one other, of course, so whenever one squeezes something out, it can start up a wave form. Sometimes it just squeezes around and around, in a tiny circle; sometimes it squeezes things across the universe."

"I see," said the president.

"I doubt it," she said. "Because I don't, and neither does Chiddy. He says it's impossible to explain without the math, and he doesn't do that kind of math."

"And you know Chiddy was telling you the truth?"

"No. Of course not, though I can't think why he would lie about it. It's possible they don't know what they're talking about. It's possible I'm not quoting them correctly. I'm not a scientist and neither are they. They're diplomats. Foreign Service types. Maybe Chiddy just made it up when I asked how they travel so quickly."

"String physics?" murmured the FL.

Benita nodded. "Chiddy did mention string physics. He said it's a move in the right direction, because the strings are just lined up—or maybe it was curled up—umquah. Ai is very pleased with our progress."

"You are pleased?" asked the First Lady, puzzled.

"Ai," Benita said. "Ay-eye pronounced Ah-ee. See, that's what I mean about their gender. It's a neutral pronoun. Chiddy and Vess are athyci, fourth caste, and their pronouns are ai, ais, and aisos . . ."

"Benita," interrupted the president, rubbing his forehead wearily. "Would you be willing to do something for us?"

"If I can," she said, suddenly embarrassed at the way she'd been going on and on.

"All my instincts say these people are good people. They have done wonders for us. Drugs, terrorism, the inhumane treatment of women, all being solved."

The FL said, "Forced marriage of young girls has stopped. Selling young women into the sex trade has stopped. Genital mutilation has stopped. The last several days we've been getting reports that some people who try to drive cars are unable to do so. The cars won't start unless the person in question has knowledge equivalent to a GED. It affects all age groups. It's amazing."

The president nodded. "All this . . . it's so valuable to us. The dream of peace. The dream of progress without conflict. We feel, that is, the First Lady and I feel, that if things go on as they are for a while, say a few years, we'll have a breakthrough of expectations. If we did a happiness index here in the U.S., people would be less worried and more contented than they've ever been. You'd think every politician in the country would rejoice, but they claim it's all a hoax, that the real motives behind it are nefarious, and I can't prove they're wrong! We know what they can do, but we know nothing about them as people. Until we know something about them as people, we can't answer the charges that our opponents make against them."

He stopped, leaned forward and took Benita's hand. "Will you ask them to show you their world?"

"Ask them to take me to Pistach-home?" she said, astonished.

"Yes. Ask them if they will. The FBI will provide some small recording devices to take with you, sealed, and when you get back, you can give these recordings to the committees in Congress that are kicking up the worst of it, so it won't be your word alone. We can publicize your findings in the media. Maybe then, they'll quit playing games and let us get on with . . . with . . . Excuse me." He got up hastily and left the room.

The FL got up and went to the window, murmuring, "He thinks the arrival of the Pistach is the most exciting event in the history of mankind, but his own advisors are telling him he's being played for a fool, he ought to order a full-scale mobilization. Congress is like a dozen armed camps, all fighting each other, one side blaming another for defunding NASA just when we need it. American Jewry is furious because of Jerusalem. Some conservative Islamic Americans are furious because of Infectious Ugly. Evidently the ugly-plague has started here, too, among immigrants from Afghanistan and Pakistan and even India. My husband . . . he genuinely likes people. He has a warm and trusting nature toward people, and he wants to trust the envoys, but his own people are making it impossible."

"You want me to ask this favor of Chiddy and Vess?"

"Yes. Please. You shouldn't go alone, though. There are idiots over there on the hill who would probably listen to a man where they wouldn't listen to you."

"Chad could go," Benita said. "We get along well together."

"But not too well," the FL cautioned, giving Benita and Chad a searching look.

"No, ma'am," he responded in an angry tone.

Benita said, "You could always have the CIA design me a chastity belt before I leave, if that's important. Or is my sex life a domestic matter for the FBI?"

"Don't be angry, either of you. You know what we're up against. We've had more than one commentator accuse the president of carrying on with Benita!"

"I've never been alone with him, ma'am."

"Oh, I know that! He's careful these days not to be alone with anyone, regardless of what sex they are. He has a chaperon around when he plays with the dog!"

Benita smiled dutifully, looked at her shoes, then at the ceiling, finding no help either place. She sighed. "I'll do what I can. Really."

She and Chad talked about it on the way home, both of them were in the backseat, behind dark-tinted windows, with someone else doing the driving. Now that the news people had seen her in Chad's company, he was as much fair game as she was.

Halfway home, she started crying. She was too much at the center of things. Without specific reason, the tears welled and spilled over. Chad put his arms around her and they sat that way for a while, just close. He offered her his handkerchief, and she wiped her face. When they got to the apartment, he sent the car away and came upstairs. She opened a bottle of wine, and they sat in the living room, looking between two boarded-up windows through a clear one that showed the Capitol dome.

"How do you get in touch with them?" he asked.

"Usually I just yell. Chiddy, I need you now!" She said it quite loudly. "If he agrees to take me, he may do it all at once, just boom. They do things like that."

"You mean, they might take you suddenly, without me or any of the surveillance stuff?"

"If there is such stuff, you should get it here in a hurry, Chad," she said. "Chiddy and Vess move awfully fast when they're motivated."

He went to the phone and made a call, then several more, taking notes as he did so. His last call was a ten-digit one. He spoke, listened, spoke, then turned to Benita with the phone still in his hand.

"Merilu?" he said. "She hung up on me. She says your husband alleges we're involved sexually, right now, on CNN."

"Bert? I thought the Inkleozese had him!" She turned to CNN, and there was Bert, a bit foggy around the eyes, but by heaven he had on a new suit, he was shaved, and he was being interviewed on national TV, and telling them all about his wife, old moocow Benita, who was being a sex slave to some aliens for the FBI.

She had barely time to get angry when the air turned cold, then warm, then wavy, and Chiddy materialized in a burst of light on the living room rug.

"Dear Benita," ai said, patting her on the shoulder. Ai offered his hand to Chad, who took it. Chiddy was, no need to say, in his masculine human form.

"Look," Benita cried, pointing to the TV. "What's that about?"

"The Fluiquosm," growled Chiddy. "They made that tape several days ago by planting an idea in his head, but they hadn't used it yet. Now they are angry at having to leave Earth, so they sent it out to TV networks in a fit of resentment. It will be necessary to supplant that idea in his mind and then undo this damage."

Chad asked, "Are the predators gone . . . ?"

Chiddy pinched his lips and looked severe. "They have departed. As I said, they were very angry about it, but they have definitely departed. None of them wants to tangle with the Inkleozese." He sat down beside Benita. "What is the emergency?"

She told him, everything tumbling out at once, the committee and Morse and what the president wanted her to do, and why it was necessary.

He stared at both the humans thoughtfully. "Before any of this is taken care of, I *must* go back and finish our discussions with the Inkleozese. They are most annoyed at the ShLQ, as are we, and steps must be taken to keep them in line and to make your former inceptor withdraw his stupidities. While this is being accomplished, we will think on this business of taking you to Pistach-home.

"Mr. Riley, be kind enough to get together whatever you need to take with you. Also, since gender mistrust seems to play a part in this whole matter, we agree it would indeed be wise for you to accompany Benita to my home world. If there is any possibility of their assuming you have a . . . relationship between you that is unacceptable, please recommend a third party to come along as well. A 'chaperon,' I think it is called. Though I would be happy to serve in that capacity, my word might not be trusted. By the way, I assume you are male, in all respects, heterosexual, functioning, and so forth?"

Chad laughed, a real laugh. "When called upon," he said, shaking his head in amazement. "I am still functional, yes. And heterosexual, though I have a past very much like Benita's, remarkably conformist and dull."

"My son," Benita cried, suddenly remembering. "We're forgetting him in the midst of all this! As well as the girl they took instead of Angelica."

"We will see to that, as well," Chiddy said. "We have already assured ourselves that they have not been injured." And ai was gone.

"He seemed very affectionate," said Chad, regarding her with curious eyes.

"I think they probably are an affectionate people," she replied, shaking her head at him. "I know they're a sensual people, too, because Chiddy's mentioned how much he enjoys hot springs and massage and certain earthly scents and flavors. I am fond of ais, and ai may well be fond of me. That doesn't equal an affair. Companionship isn't sexuality."

"Even when he's in human shape?"

"Even when ai looks human. Though, come to think of it, when they take other shapes, I think the shape has different sensory equipment from their own forms. You shake his hand, and Chiddy feels it, even though the real Chiddy doesn't have hands. Maybe that's why they morph so much, because they like the new sensations they get."

"Their morphed selves certainly feel real to the touch," he said. "I purposely bumped them and brushed up against them at that first dinner."

"I know," she said tiredly. "It's very confusing."

He stared at her for a long moment, then patted her, rather as he patted Sasquatch. "Since our previous effort to get away was interrupted, our bags are already packed. Mine's down in the car that's still parked out back. I'll go pick up the stuff from the bureau. Have a nap. I'll be back as soon as I can."

"What about . . . Merilu?"

"Merilu is looking for excuses to end our marriage," he said in a flat, dead voice. "Any excuse will do, even a phony one. Even if I quit the job today and was in Montana by tonight, she'd find some reason. She'll do what your husband is doing, what she started to do on the phone, accuse me of having an affair, or putting my job ahead of the boys, or anything. I've been hoping she'll settle down. I'm not sure she will."

"And she doesn't work?"

"No," he said. "That's part of the problem."

"Do you have a picture of her?" Benita asked curiously.

He dug it out of his wallet. She was blonde, blue-eyed, with a face like an angel. Everyman's everywoman.

"She's beautiful."

"Yes," he said with an aching sigh. "She certainly is. I sometimes look at that face and think I'm the luckiest man in creation. On the phone, however, I sometimes get a more . . . accurate picture."

He went down in the elevator alone. Benita took a few moments to repack the small bag she had packed two days ago, adding casual clothes and another pair of shoes, thinking as she did so that she had never seen any advice about packing for interstellar travel. No raincoat, obviously, or boots. No warm sweaters. No tank tops for sunning. Slacks. Shirts. Sox. Shoes. Underwear. Nightgown. Nothing sexy. Not that she owned any such thing.

While she didn't think she'd sleep, she dozed off as soon as she lay down. She didn't wake up until evening, when Chad rang her on the phone. He'd be over in half an hour.

She called Simon, who was still downstairs in the office doing something or other, and told him she'd be down. When she came in, he was staring at the TV which was re-running her brief interview by the press that morning. He turned from the screen and stared at her.

"So that's what it was all about," he said.

She fumbled for something to say. He shook his head. "The apartment renovation? All the comings and goings?"

She sat down across from him. "Yes, Simon. But, I had no idea all this would happen when I applied for the job."

"I know." He shuffled the papers in front of him. "I was angry at first. Because you didn't tell me. But then, I thought why would you? You wouldn't want to tell anybody, for fear they'd get at you. The press, I mean. Right?"

"Right."

"And you're doing a good job here. The best. I can't imagine where you found the time, with all this going on . . ."

"There was plenty of time, Simon. It doesn't take long to pass on a message or talk to the ETs. Mostly that stuff happens in the evenings, after we're closed."

"Well, everything you've done so far is great. Your files are up to date. Your work is accurate. Are you going to go on working for me?"

"Simon, I would very much like to go on working for you. However, I can't work for you this week. The president has asked me to go to the Pistach home world and look at it. The FBI man who's been guarding me—"

Simon's eyes flickered sideways. "Oh. That's who he is. I wondered."

"He's been working as liaison. He'll go with me on the trip, so he can verify what I see."

"What do they think you'll see?"

"Our government, part of it, anyhow, is worried it's a conspiracy. The predators. The Pistach. The Inkleozese."

"Why doesn't the president go?"

"Who'd believe him? He's trying to work inside the politics of mistrust, Simon. The other side has only one agenda, to discredit him, falsely if necessary, and they don't care if it hurts the country. I have no ax to grind. I'm not a political person. If Bert can be muzzled, they'll have a hard time discrediting me because there's nothing there to discredit."

He nodded sympathetically. "Well, you know, if they can get the public lined up to peek through bedroom windows, it makes it easier for them to rob the rest of the house!"

She smiled. "I'll be away for a few days. I came down to ask if you'll feed Sasquatch."

"I will feed and exercise Sasquatch. And I'll be glad when you come back, Benita." He held out his hand, and she took it. He pulled her across the desk and kissed her cheek, quite gently. "Very glad," he said.

She went back upstairs and waited for Chad, looking out the little window in the elevator hall, her hand on the cheek that Simon had kissed. What a strange man. Or not. He was really very nice, wasn't he? Thoughtful. Considerate. Appreciative. Undemanding.

Chad always parked where she could see him from the elevator hall, so she could come down to unlock the door. He arrived bearing two small suitcases and a paper bag of Chinese takeout. When Benita smelled it, she realized she hadn't eaten all day, not even breakfast, and Chad hadn't either. They set it out on the table in the living room and munched without talking for some time.

"I wonder where Chiddy is?" she said finally, surfeit with sesame shrimp, asparagus and rice.

"On his way, I should imagine," he said, putting down his fork with a sigh. He wiped his mouth thoroughly on a paper napkin. "I wonder what they'll feed us on Pistach-home."

"If they take us," she amended.

"I think they'll take us. If only because they're so embarrassed over this predator business."

"Or over the Inkleozese."

"My guess would be that doesn't embarrass them at all. The envoys took it for granted that intelligent people mean what they say, and somebody who says he's pro-life means it."

"How do we go about finding out whether the Pistach are as represented?" she asked him. "If we depend on them to show us the world, won't they just show us what they want us to see?"

"There are ways," he said. "Dissonances one can listen for. Differences of opinion one can ferret out. Are you frightened, Benita?"

"A little." It was true. But the apprehension was accompanied by a bubbling feeling, as though she'd swallowed a little volcano, something that was building up toward an eruption. The feeling was vaguely familiar, and at last she tracked it back to a day in summer when Mami had taken her to the amusement park for her birthday, and she had ridden the roller coaster. Fear, and pleasure, and joy. Pure joy. It was such a lovely feeling! Why had it been such a rare one?

The evening grew late, and Chad took off his jacket and shoes and lay down on the couch in the living room, while she stretched out on the bed, Sasquatch at her feet. They had both dozed for some little time when Sasquatch roused them with a rumbling growl and a couple of firm woofs. It was Chiddy, back again, and he had Carlos and a girl with him. Of the two, the girl was in better shape. She looked tired, dirty, and a little frightened, but she was very much herself, ready to get angry the moment she thought it wouldn't endanger her life.

Carlos had evidently not been so sensible. He'd been battered here and there. Benita cautioned herself and did not shriek, did not sympathize, did not question. He wasn't hurt any worse than she had been, many times, with similar bruises darkening under his skin, and a black eye beginning to bloom.

"Mom," he cried, making a run for her and half knocking her down in the process. She fended him off, fighting down an urge to say, "Down, heel," except that he'd seldom listened to her in the past and was unlikely to do so now.

She put her hands on his shoulder to hold him up and away—hugs from Carlos had always been rare, usually confined to times he was frightened. "Are you all right, Carlos?"

He blubbered something, "Okay. All right. Not . . . they didn't . . . they were going to!"

She raised her eyebrows at Chiddy, who said with considerable distaste, "The Fluiquosm and Wulivery threatened to eat him. The Wulivery do that sometimes, teasing. I think he believed they would eat him."

"I saw them," he cried. "Eating people. They've got a storage place near the camp, and it's all full of dead people!"

"That's quite true, but they were under instructions not to eat you," said Chiddy, firmly. "Settle down."

"You don't know what they were like," Carlos screamed.

"I know exactly what they were like," snapped Benita. "I was eaten by a Wulivery. Stop dramatizing yourself."

Benita turned from Carlos to the girl, holding out her hand. "I think you were taken because you were mistaken for my daughter."

"Sonia Bigg," she said. "They were determined to make me tell them I was Angelica Shipton, if that's your daughter. As for him," she gestured toward Carlos, "he told them to start with me, if they were going to eat us."

"Sonia . . ." Carlos wailed. "I didn't mean that. I love you, I wouldn't say anything like that."

"You're . . . Carlos's friend?" asked Benita, with a disbelieving glance at her son.

"Was," said Miss Bigg.

"Well, well," Carlos babbled, "if they were going to eat us both anyhow, it didn't make any difference which of us was first, and I was just trying to keep them talking."

Chiddy saw the look of total dismay on her face and patted her shoulder soothingly. "As it happens, the predators did not at that time intend to eat either of them, and Miss Bigg is unhurt."

The girl said in a firm voice, "Unhurt! Hah." She turned to Benita. "May I use your bathroom, please?"

Benita indicated where it was, saying, "I can also lend you a clean shirt." She turned to Chiddy, whispering, "Can you take her back where she was taken from? What about Carlos? Is it safe to send him back?"

"She, yes. Not him, just yet. I spoke previously of needing a chaperon. I should imagine he will serve. If we take him with us, it will keep him out of circulation for a few days."

"What about Bert?"

"The Inkleozese are working on him. Arranging to straighten out the misinformation that was broadcast."

Chad said, "You want me to arrange for Miss Bigg to get back home?"

He accepted Chiddy's nod and began phoning. While he was busy, the girl came out of the bathroom. Benita fetched a clean shirt for her, and by the time they emerged from the bedroom, Chad had arranged for her to be picked up. "If you need anything, a change of clothes or any necessaries, they'll provide it, and you'll be on a flight back to California today."

She thanked him, then turned to Carlos. "If you come back, don't call me."

A car came, the girl departed. Chiddy asked, "Are you and Chad ready to depart?"

Carlos interrupted to whine, "I'm sure as hell not. I don't even have a change of underwear."

"We can provide whatever you need," said Chiddy. "I need to provide proper costumes for all of you, anyhow. It is considered polite to wear garments suitable to one's station in life."

Carlos glowered, obviously getting ready to explode, and Chad took him by one shoulder, asking, "How far do we go to your ship?"

Vess laughed.

Chiddy bowed them into the elevator. "Not far," he said. "Not far at all."

45

in afghanistan

Mustapha ibn Daud shut his door against the noises in the room beneath him where a rancorous debate continued, without letup, as it had for hours.

"If we do not feel lust, it is the will of Allah!" the old imam was still saying, over and over. Likely it had been decades since he had been able to feel anything of the kind, but now he championed the cause of the hideous women. "If these otherworldly afrits have changed our women, then they have done Allah's work whether they know it or not! Nothing happens that is not the will of Allah! We are being rebuked for our lusts, which burned more hotly the more the fuel was hidden!

"Listen to me! We refused to see our women as people like ourselves; we hid them to make them titillating, to think of them only as vessels for our lusts, servants for our kitchens, breeders of our sons! Let us free the women to walk as we do, with their faces uncovered. Let us see if this does not please Allah."

And, as he had done over and over, another, younger man attacked him: "Though he cannot lastingly prevail, Satan can do what Allah does not will! We are being tested! We should never change our ways! In time, Allah will restore our own to us."

"And if He does not?" asked the old man. "If our women continue as they are? If my sons are unable to beget children? Is our lineage to stop with this generation? Do not say we are not changing our ways. It was agreed in the Taliban that we would eschew all modern gadgetry, was it not? And yet now, we have laptops. We have telephones. These things are needed in a modern state. Why should we not have modern women, too? They can be modern and still virtuous . . ."

Mustapha had held up his hand for silence, waiting until it fell. "I disagree. Our wives have been replaced by demons. Since Satan makes it impossible for us to kill these demons who have taken the places of our wives and daughters, let them go where they will! Some of our men have already gone to the Pakistan border to take women from there. We will bring women from elsewhere to serve our needs. Our ways are righteous! Our ways are proper! To protect the purity of our womenfolk—"

"They are pure now," shouted the old man, shaking his fist at Mustapha. "They are not demons. I have talked with them. They are our women, and they are more pure now than they have ever been! When they were hidden, they were lusted after. *Now, no one lusts after them!*"

A murmur of discontent ran through the room. No man here had touched a woman for some time. Every one of them had in his house at least one woman of supreme and utter repulsiveness, a woman he gagged to look at or smell. A woman who was hideous to the senses.

The old man spoke again. "Listen to me. You cannot deny that the women in our houses are pure. Untouched. Let us achieve some consistency. We have said this is what we desire, that our wives and daughters be pure. That they not be raped, that they not be looked upon with lascivious eyes. Well, now they are pure, they are not raped, no one looks at them with desire, yet we complain! This causes me to wonder whether their purity was really our aim. Or did we want something else? By hiding them did we increase their erotic allure? Did we arouse ourselves with the idea of their subjugation? Is this something of which Allah approves?"

That was when Mustapha ibn Daud had left the room in disgust. To hear a teacher of the Koran speak so! To hear their culture so disparaged! He stood in the window looking out at the silent darkness. There was something here he did not understand, an enemy he could not bring down with a gun, and it made him feel trapped and angry.

Someone spoke at the doorway. Ben Shadouf. He came in, was offered a place to sit and did so.

"You have heard, my wife is gone?" he said.

"We do not speak of women," Mustapha answered loftily.

"Oh, but we do," said Ben Shadouf. "We always have. We talk of the dancers we have seen. We go to prostitutes and talk of them to our friends. We talk of women."

"We do not talk of our wives and daughters!"

"True. Except, when we first marry, or when we grow weary of our wives, we ask our friends if they have marriageable daughters. Young ones. Healthy ones. Frightened ones who would be sure to obey." He spoke bitterly and his hands twisted in his lap. "I loved my wife, Mustapha. She was gentle and kind. She cooked well. She was considerate of my feelings and well being. I loved my little daughters. Their faces made a garden in my house."

"You love them even now?" barked Mustapha, with a laugh. "Then you are a saint."

"No. I am not worthy of loving her. I am not even a good man. She was ill, you know. And I would not take her to the clinic. Then the ugliness came, and I told her to go where she would. She had a disease of the lungs, and if they had not given her the medicine, she would have died."

"The clinic is run by foreigners! Evil-doers!"

"Who seem to care more for our wives and our children than we do. They save their lives while we let them die."

Mustapha snarled between his teeth. "Caring about women is not our destiny. Our destiny is to live in accordance with the word and in duty to Allah and follow the teachings of our leaders. Besides, your wife didn't die."

"No. When the clinic had healed her, she took our children and went over the mountains. A traveler brought a letter from her. She is well, but she is staying there for our daughters' sake, so she says, for in that country, women are valued more than they are here."

"Then good riddance," said Mustapha.

Ben Shadouf rose and paced restlessly across the room. "I have been thinking of what she said. Other Muslim nations do not require what we do of women. Other Muslim nations do not use them as we do. Do not make stabled beasts out of them."

"Then those nations are less pure than we."

"You will not reconsider what we demand of them? The chadoor? The sequestration? Forbidding them to work or to learn? Forbidding them to have medical attention? Stoning them to death because they stumble, or do not hold the veil tightly enough when the wind blows?"

Mustapha snorted angrily. "Those prohibitions are the result of days of discussion among the elders. We worked hard to get the wording exactly right. Not one word will be changed. The world may grow ugly, but I will remain constant."

"Then so remain," said Ben Shadouf, leaning toward him with a glittering blade in his hand. Mustapha felt the knife before he realized it was there, felt it run into him like ice, then like fire.

Ben Shadouf withdrew the blade, then leaned forward to speak into the dimming eyes. "So remain forever, Mustapha. I have done as you many times commanded me. I have slain a heretic who disbelieves the true way. Your eyes close as mine are opened by the imam. Now I will go in search of my wife."

46
from chiddy's journal

Dearest Benita, as I write this you are nearby in a rest cubby, soundly sleeping. I amuse myself recalling the surprise on your face when we walked through the back of your elevator and into our ship, your astonishment at learning we had been living just the other side of the wall for all this time. It has been quite convenient and very saving on our power cells. The ship is as morphable as we, and it interpenetrated the third-story offices beside your home with its usual imperturbability. It was the presence of our ship, unfortunately, which brought the Wulivery to your windows. They smelled us out, indeed, and though they did not find our ship, they found you.

We are furious at them, and at the other predators as well. What they did was unethical, though their sins were compounded by humans who see fit to play politics with their fellows' lives. That is a phrase I had never heard before, dear Benita. Playing politics. It is like playing war, a game for degenerates. Statesmen should not "play" politics.

We are at the moment, as I write, scudding along at many times light speed in a tube which is, to all intents and purposes, empty. Behind us, the fabric of space thrusts our material ship on before it, for it seeks always to exclude matter, or at least to clump it insofar as is possible. I could say that space bends behind us to push us. I could say that space ceases to exist in the direction of our movement, lining up on either side in strings of umquah. When we say such things, however, our scientists pish and tush at us, for neither is at all correct.

I confess, I understand neither the universe nor the spacedrive. Only a few of our most intelligent claim to understand the drive, and even they did not invent it. It was made by the Jabal, aeons ago, a people who left the galaxy before our own people existed. We have only the records they left behind on many planets together with plans for their devices: spacedrives, star milkers, fusion generators, morph-engines (tiny implanted ones to change ourselves, large ones to make cities like Jerusalem seem to disappear, though it never really went anywhere) all carefully preserved for whomever came along next. Luckily for us, we emerged originally in a thickly starred part of the galaxy and with even our rather primitive stardrives, we managed to be first in line for a lot of the devices. We moved, later on, to a less thickly settled sector, one quieter, more peaceful, less liable to predatory irruptions. Other races who arrived nearer the center of things profited from discovery, as well. Sometimes we meet during the knitting of the web of universal intelligence into a more durable fabric. This is our purpose and the purpose of all intelligent life. So we believe.

The human recording devices you brought with you are working well. They will keep track of your entire voyage, the interior of the ship, the fact that outside the ship there is nothing, not even light. We move in other dimensions of space and in the null dimension of time. When we draw near our destination, the ship will sense the complex curvature signature, one peculiar to that destination, and the emptiness in which we move will collapse to allow ordinary space-time to curve around us once more.

We intend to take you to several planets besides our own. It will be more convincing to the people of Earth if they see several different races. Your Earth devices will record our arrival on each, our departure from each. When we get to Pistach, the devices will probably note some confusion among the Pistach people, for they do not know we are coming. No message could get to our home sooner than we ourselves will arrive. You will not be the first non-Pistach visitors on Pistach-home, but you will be the first who have not yet been admitted to the Confederation. Vess and I have discussed this. We will have to do some of what you call "fast talking." Still, given the well-known perfidy of the predators, your difficulty will be perfectly understandable, even to the most rigid among us.

I have no trepidation concerning your treatment. Hospitality is a virtue we have polished to a finer sheen than some other of our probities. Though we advocate toleration, we do not do it so well as we do some other things. We are not as unselfish as an advanced race should be. We struggle to burnish all our virtues, but every now and then a rock of reality catches our feet to make us stumble. Though we advocate equality of all intelligences, still we are like most races: happiest among peoples we know well and whose ways we understand.

If the Chapter will allow, you will be welcomed to a guest house of my family, on the Cavita home ground. It is near the House of the Fresco, and we know you will want to see that. Also, it would be pleasant to introduce you to my nootch. She will be most interested in you and in Chad and in the ways of your world. You are, functionally, more nootch than you are receptor, and she will be pleased to recognize someone of like mind and responsibility. I have provided festive red-and-yellow clothing for you, so you will, as you say, "fit in." Chad could be introduced as an inceptor, of course, but since his "job" on Earth is to keep order and allocate responsibility, the tasks performed by our proffi caste—which also includes doctors and scholars—I intend introducing him as a proffe, dressed properly in formal brown. My evaluation of the two of you indicates you are unlikely to break out in a fit of breeding madness partway through the visit, for which I am very grateful.

As for your son, though he is rather too old for it, we

must dress him as an undifferentiated one. As such, he will be regarded with a good deal of tolerance, more than we manage under most other circumstances. Your young are not unlike ours in being demanding, eager, selfish, gauche. As our sages have said, *youth builds a universe with self at the center.* Carlos will not be an asset. Our position would be improved had we been able to bring an Earthian athyco with us, if there had been one who would have been accepted by all the religions, political bodies, racial constituencies and social movements on your world. Such a one could have spoken pointedly to our Confederation ambassadors, calling them to account for the depredations of the Fluiquosm, et al. No such person exists on your world, so it is left to us. Vess and I will speak, but we will have to be diplomatic. The practice of diplomacy, I have found, is sometimes like eating soup with a fork: much activity yielding little nourishment.

However, there is some time before we get to Pistach-home. We have other worlds to visit first. The subjective time lapse from Earth to the first one, Flibotsia, is about two of your days, and you will sleep during all of it. If we could not travel in the null-time dimension, it would take thousands of your years to reach any of our near worlds, but the drive allows us to stand teetering upon a point of time as we plunge onward in several dimensions of space. Indeed, some of the new drives are virtually instantaneous. One begins here, gets in the ship, has a cup of tea, gets out of the ship, and behold, one is there. Poof. Even so, we are far from the intergalactic drive our religion posits as the next necessary step in the evolution of intelligence! Between the galaxies, so our scientists think, the umquah are more evenly spread and less irritable than where matter annoys them constantly.

When we arrive on Pistach-home, I know you will enjoy seeing the House of the Fresco. Oh, I wish it were less obscured by soot, so you could see it as it was when first painted. Though perhaps you would be disappointed. I have seen the Sistine Chapel. I have seen the caves at Lescaux. Your people have an inborn artistry of very high degree. It may be our Fresco would not have impressed you, even when it was new. The Inkleozese agree that this is probable. They, too, deeply admire the artistry of your race.

We must rest now. When we have rested, Vess and I must argue yet again. We have been arguing about Earth for a very long time, now. There is so much to do, and I want to do it all at once while Vess counsels caution, a little at a time. It was I who insisted upon the Ugliness Plague. "An immediate lesson," I cried. Even Vess agrees it is working, though many of the women are simply leaving the countries that mistreated them. Whether they do or not is up to them, the men cannot harm them. The important issue, the question of purity versus lust, is for the first time being put into its proper context. Some of the men prefer to continue in the old mold, of course, by trying to kidnap women from neighboring countries, but that won't work. As soon as a man with that attitude touches a woman, she becomes a hag, though only to others. Her mirror continues to show her real self.

We have also scheduled a lengthy time for discussion about your prisons, which preoccupy your people to an abnormal extent. Unfortunately, your penal system is based on religious notions of penitence and reformation, character emendations which can be evoked only where a sense of shame is present. In a society as mobile as your own, many people are totally anonymous to those around them. They do not care what they do before strangers or to strangers. If one feels no shame, punishment only angers. If one feels shame, punishment is almost unnecessary.

Logically, therefore, your prisons should seek to instill shame, but even if it were possible, it would offend your civil libertarians to do so. "Shaming" others is considered an affront to their dignity. Since shame is essential to remorse, which is the natural punishment for misbehavior—just as gut cramps are the natural punishment for eating unripe thrags—if one cannot evoke shame, then forget about penitence or reformation. It won't happen.

In the place of shame you have substituted a meaningless phrase, "Paying one's debt to society." You send a rapist or murderer to prison for a few years, and then you say he has "paid his debt to society." Of course, he has done no such thing. A term in prison pays for nothing, not if it is for ten years or twenty or fifty! The victim or victims are still violated or dead, and to say that the evildoer has paid his debt is to denigrate the value of the victim! This, in turn, causes anger among the victim's family or friends, who wonder why a beloved wife is worth five years while someone else's daughter is worth twice that. This, in turn, causes disrespect for the law. As Canthorel has written, "If the law does not do justice, the people will mock the law."

Vess is astonished that Earthians define as cruel and unusual many acts that are not unusual and not particularly cruel. Breeding madness is cruel, breeding madness is unusual. Most of your men don't have it. Most of your men wouldn't want it. Castration would remove it from those who have it. What is cruel about that? Is the inceptive organ really more important than the mind? Vess and I find this an extremely exotic notion. In your great documents of national purpose, the right to pursue satisfactions in one's own life is asserted, but not at others' expense. People who misuse the lives of others should not be allowed to repeat the act, but your peculiar ideas about cruelty allow it, time and again.

One of the programs we left to start without us, back on Earth, is the rewording of your newspapers and TV shows. They will no longer be able to use empty language, like "paid his debt to society," or "claimed responsibility" for an act of terrorism. Instead, they must use true words. "He has been sentenced to prison for ten years which will do nothing to ameliorate his urges to molest and mutilate little girls." Or, "The XX faction has asserted that it committed the cowardly atrocity of killing a busload of schoolchildren." Earthians must learn to say truly what has happened and not cover it with easy-speak.

Earthians, or perhaps only Americans, must also realize that some persons cannot be fixed, that nurture can go only so far in changing what people are born to be. Some people are born dangerous. We have a saying, we Pistach: "Some pfiggy can't breed, some pfluggi can't bite, some flosti can't fly, some Pistach are glusi." Pfiggi are small and numerous, Pfluggi are larger and have sharp teeth. Both live in swamps. In essence, the saying means that we must accept the reality of persons, not what they should be or we wish they were, but what they are. Someone may be born of humans and look like a human without having humanity. Someone may be born of kind parents and raised with kindness and be unkind, just as someone may be born crippled or dwarfed to people who are neither. The biological body may not manifest the psychological quality of humanity, and if it does not, it is not human. We Pistach know what it takes to mend people, and it takes a good deal more than you are willing to do.

Vess and I will also talk about your reproductive habits. Your people have learned a great deal about the subject, but you have applied little sense to it, even yet. Now you are begetting children scientifically, and great law courts grind to stillness on the issues of who owns the resultant child. Is it the donor of sperm or the donor of egg; is it the womb that bears, the person who paid, the doctor who was instrumental, the legal wife of the sperm donor, the legal husband of the egg donor, the legal husband of the womb, the legitimate previous children of the womb, the mate of the person who paid, the person who signed the contract?

We have another saying, "Those who cause, pay." It is a simple rule, but it has been very, very effective in bringing order to our lives. If a physician helps a woman bear eight children at once, then that doctor must support seven of them! If your congressmen will not vote to control guns, if your NRA fights against gun control, then your congressmen and the members of the NRA must individually help pay for medical care and wrongful deaths and funeral expenses for every accidental shooting death. We will figure out a way to do this. Vess and I have had several good ideas.

Oh, Vess and I have much, much to argue about. Your world has so many difficulties to be straightened out, though it is my belief that many of them will submit to simple cures, forcefully applied and diligently monitored. So many little glitches, and yet . . . as my nootch said of me, long and long ago, we have such hopes for you, dearest

Benita, such hopes, dear Chad. Such hopes your people will be another node in the weaving of intelligence among the worlds. When I am arguing with Fluiquosm, when I am listening to ego-wrangles on your TV or in my own Chapter House, when I must consider disorders like those on Assurdo and Quo-Tem, even I sometimes lose sight of what we are truly doing. We are spreading throughout all space and time, weaving a mind to the edges of the galaxy, and in time, in time perhaps throughout the universe. So I remember and keep firmly in my mind when I say, dearest Benita, we have such hopes for you.

47
benita

JOURNEY OUT OF TIME

Benita woke in a coffinlike cubby hung on the hull of the ship. She was not conscious of time having passed, not even of a night gone by, as she usually was in the morning when she woke. She'd simply lain down and slept and now was awake, without any sense of laterness at all. When she lay down, she was still in a state of speechless surprise about where the ship had been all that time. They had walked into the elevator, and suddenly the back of it opened up like a buttonhole and they slipped through, bag and baggage, into the ship. Chiddy explained that it was coexistent with the entire third floor of the building, wall to wall, and that what Benita had thought of as the lower roof was also the outer integument of the ship.

Her first thought was Sasquatch. He had committed indecencies on the ship, time after time. Chiddy didn't mention it or seem concerned, however, so she decided it was not worth mentioning.

They came aboard, Carlos, thank God, sufficiently impressed to be silent. They drank a glass of something celebratory (and quite likely sedative) with the two Pistach, they lay down in the allocated cubbies. Later, Chiddy told

Benita's cubby to wake her, and also Chad's, though he let Carlos remain asleep.

Without asking, Benita knew why Chiddy left Carlos asleep. There was no point in waking him any earlier than needful. She started to go through her usual Carlos litany, all the things she might have done differently, the help she might have sought, the influences she might have brought to bear. If there had been more time. If there had been more money. If she had not been so young. In the current surroundings, however, the litany of self-blame lacked force and conviction. Carlos had been a petulant, screaming, stubborn baby; a whiny little boy; a bully in the playground. He had been a slacker at school. He had never been abused, not even by Bert, in any physical sense. He could be charming, when he thought it would get him something, but most of the time he was not. She decided not to play the game with herself anymore. Mother bears didn't play such games. They knew their cubs had to go. So, let him go.

Once awake, Chad and Benita were told they had arrived near Flibotsia, which they admired through a suddenly opened view screen. Chiddy spoke to someone on the ground, and then the ship went down, light as a bubble.

Chad made himself responsible for the recording equipment. When they stepped outside the ship it was like stepping into a meadow full of huge butterflies that smelled like flowers. Several of them, larger and more brightly colored than the others, approached at once, clustering around Chiddy and Vess to thank them for some event in the past when the Pistach had solved a great problem, or so Benita inferred from the slightly embarrassed expressions on the Pistach faces.

"What was that about?" asked Benita, during a hiatus while the Flibotsi prepared a festive meal to be laid out, picnic style, in the grassy clearing near the ship.

"A fertility problem," said Chiddy. "Those larger beings are empresses of this world, their home world, and some years ago, they were becoming infertile. Vess and I found out why and fixed it for them."

"They seemed very grateful," said Chad.

Chiddy nodded. "They are. Even though it was more by luck than skill that we figured it out."

The banquet was duly provided, tiny containers of various syrups and pastes, to be drunk or spread on sweet crackers or just sniffed, for all of them smelled as marvelous as they tasted. Chiddy whispered that many of them were euphorics, as well. It was, Benita thought, rather like being happily drunk. She felt jolly and joyous, with no thoughts of problems or pains, and also, Chiddy assured her, no need to worry about a possible hangover later.

When they parted from the Flibotsi with mutual expressions of regard, and while they were on their way to the next stop, Chad asked Chiddy about the fertility problem the two Pistach had solved, and after hemming and humming for a time, Chiddy agreed to tell them about it.

"The Flibotsi are trisexual, with a few breeding females—the empresses—a few more breeding males—the consorts—and many unsexed ones who do a little work but mostly just enjoy life. When I read your fairy tales of little winged people, I think of the Flibotsi. Of course, as you have seen, they are not small. Indeed they are larger than we, but they are also more fragile, since their planets are low-gravity ones."

"I didn't notice," said Chad.

"The ship projected a field around each of us that prevented our doing so," said Vess. "We weren't staying long enough for you to acclimate, and we did not wish to run the risk of gastric upset. It would have offended our hostesses."

Nodding agreement, Chiddy went on. "The worker Flibotsi are excellent gardeners, and they eat many types of flowers which gives each of them a lovely and quite particular scent. The filaments that grow on their heads and down their backs, their breath, indeed, even their skin smells of flowers, and as you have experienced, being in the midst of a hovering group of Flibotsi is an olfactory delight.

"We were called in because the empresses were becoming unable to produce male offspring, a certain number of whom are needed to continue the race. Vess and I asked at once if males from some of the other Flibotsi settled worlds couldn't simply be reassigned to the home world. This would be by far the easiest way to make up the lack, but the empress told us how difficult interstellar travel is for them. It is more than mere dislike of being shut up in close quarters; it amounts almost to terror. Also, they told us, the cost is great. They must pay huge amounts to starship owners whenever they decide to establish a new colony.

"They have no ships of their own. They do not, as a matter of fact, manufacture many artifacts of any kind, which explains their lack of exchangeable currency. Their entire off-world economy is supported by their trade in botanicals and perfumes. The few artifacts they make include writing implements, of course, as poetry and song are important to them, and musical instruments, mostly stringed ones that are either bowed or plucked, plus drums and chimes. They construct many shrines, small ones, exquisitely made, and they plant gardens and groves everywhere. All this work is done by the unsexed ones, the neuters.

"Males grow up in the homes of their empress mothers, then are traded to other empresses in the general vicinity when they reach breeding age. Since their aptitudes are more or less the same as those of a registered male poodle on your world, they are pampered and well groomed, and also, for the most part, amusing, affectionate, and capable of sustained sexual activity.

"All the nonsexual eggs are parthenogenically produced as sterile copies of the empress herself. Both empress and male eggs, however, are fertilized by the male. Following mating flights, during which a supply of sperm is inserted into the empress's vlasiput, a kind of internal purse or sac, the sperm is very slowly leaked into the oviduct, male eggs being laid at the rate of about one per two hundred sexless ones, and female empress eggs at the rate of one or two per thousand. In the recent past, the rate of male eggs, distinguishable through color and size, had fallen to a level so low that there were some mature empresses who had had no males when they were ready for their maiden flights.

"The Flibotsi live in *flissits*, which are built high around the trunks of great trees, roofed with thatch and caulked with fresh moss that takes root on the sides of the structure and soon covers the entire flissit, making it both weather-tight and cushiony. When well sheathed by moss, the flissits completely disappear into the forest scene, small ones for one Flibot, larger ones for two or three or even more, so that nothing intrusive or untidy mars the beauty of the landscape. Though there were a hundred flissits within seeing distance of the glade where we feasted, I doubt that you noticed even one of them, for the Flibotsi have a horror of what I have heard you, Benita, refer to as 'tackiness.'

"Very large flissits in giant trees provide apartments for the empresses and their consorts as well as for hatcheries, brooders, and nurseries for the young. The moss covering royal flissits is of a different sort, a paler green, and it grows down the trunk of the tree and then spreads radially, though very slowly, bits of it running off in all directions, like the spokes of a wheel. It has a strong, pungent, though not unpleasant odor.

"Vess and I, together with a consultant committee of proffi—scientists, physicians, and the like—set about determining why male eggs were not being laid. The cause was not environmental; the soil and water and air had no poisons in them. We found no inimical radiation, nothing in the food or drink. It wasn't genetic. It wasn't the weather or the climate or some new cultural habit that had recently begun. In fact, everything we postulated failed to prove out.

"When everything else had been exhausted as a possibility, Vess and I decided to go on to our last resort: hanging about and chatting with people. No matter how pleasant, one must put this off, as otherwise one might be misled. Once there is no other recourse, however, one may relax and enjoy it.

"So we talked to the empresses, who are rather complacent and preoccupied with their sex lives. And to the unsexed ones, who are mostly delightful. And to the male partners, who are the only Flibotsi to demonstrate what you on Earth call *angst*. We asked all kinds of questions. We chatted with aged brooder and incubator managers, with ancient gardeners, one of whom actually gave us the first clue.

" 'In my day,' it said, 'when I was under-gardener to old

Flargee at Empress Magh's, there wasn't another empress within flying distance. Now, well, now, there's Empress Irin, Empress Flitch, Empress Moggys, Empress Tryff, Empress (so on and so on, as the gardener listed a dozen or more) all within a bit of a fly, and many close enough to walk to!'

'This rang a bell with me, and with Vess. Something we had heard or seen or read about. We sat up late that night, in a visitors' flissit, thinking and chatting, hoping some idea would pop out of the moss walls. In fact, I said at one point, 'Some idea should pop out of the moss walls,' and Vess said, 'That's it.' "

"Vess reminded me that there are certain trees and mosses and other plants that make a kind of herbicide in their roots or leaves, and this chemical keeps other trees or bushes or mosses from growing in their immediate vicinity. Sometimes it keeps all growth away, sometimes only certain growths. You have such trees on Earth, dear Benita. The black walnut tree, I believe is one. Such a compound would not be something one would look for when seeking pollutants or poisons.

"So, we sent for moss samples from the flissits of the Empresses in the neighborhood. We found that each moss was slightly different, each exuding a slightly different pheromone, each one lethal to the male sperm in any vlasiput except that of the local empress. We sent for samples of the moss in the wild and found it exuded no pheromones at all.

"This was interesting. We obtained samples of skin and flesh and fluids from the empresses and immediately hit, as you say, pay dirt. The empresses have highly individual attractant odors that are produced during their first mating flights and continue to exude during their lives, a kind of olfactory fingerprint. During the mating flights, the particular scent is fixated upon by the males. Thereafter, a mated male cannot be utilized by any other empress. It would do no good, as that empress would not have the proper pheromone.

"The odors emanate, we found, from waxy secretions created by bacteria living in pores in the empresses' skins. The bacteria are subject to constant mutation, and thus each population of bacteria is unique. The bacteria rub off on the moss, the moss incorporates them into its own structure where they reproduce and spread radially, creating an area that is recognizable to all as the territory of that particular Empress because it smells like her.

"However, when empresses are crowded together, one empress's scent actually abuts and interpenetrates the moss spread of one or more neighboring empresses. Inimical scents are picked up by worker Flibotsi and carried into the vicinity of the empress and the male sperm in the vlasiput are affected.

"Once we were sure how it happened, we didn't take time to investigate the biology of the situation. It was enough to know where the problem lay, and we had no wish to infringe further upon the privacy of the Flibotsi empresses."

"They needed to move farther apart," suggested Chad.

Chiddy nodded. "As you saw, however, when we were orbiting the planet, the forest lands cover only a small portion of Flibotsia. The Flibotsi cannot live in the sea or on the deserts or even in the great prairies which, so we were told, had been forested until several centuries ago, when the Flibotsi sold the timber to alien lumbermen in return for transport to new colonies."

"So there was no room for them to separate, was there?" said Benita.

"You are correct. In order to make more room between empresses, new empresses could not be allowed to mature until several old empresses had died, opening up a space. Any new empresses for which there was no vacant slot had to settle off planet, no matter how traumatic they found the journey. We also suggested that they begin reforestation of the plains to provide for future living space. Until this is well underway, the population must be very strictly controlled.

"We also suggested the immediate retirement of the more aged empresses and the roll-back of their mosses."

"Did it work?" asked Chad.

"As you saw," said Chiddy, "they have reduced the number of empresses by half. Each time we return, they thank us again and again for our intervention."

The next planet was Vixbotine, a desert world full of dunes and tormented stone, interrupted here and there by fertile oases and permeated by caverns which were cool, moist, and sheltered from the sun and everlasting winds. They landed near one such cavern, were welcomed by several small, slender persons who seemed to be hollow. Their living parts, so Chiddy informed the humans in an aside, were just beneath the skin, as in a tree on Earth, while the center portion was a sound box that grew longer and larger as the Vixbot aged.

"They are, I suppose, as much vegetable as animal," Vess said. "Those lacy things around their heads are not quite ovaries—the eggs are in the fringe—and the long leafy part on top is the flower that sheds not-quite pollen into the wind. When the pollen hits the ovary, it makes seeds, of course, and the ripened seeds have little wings that let the wind spread them to some welcoming cavern entrance. That is, unless the Vixbot wishes to plant them somewhere in particular, as many do. Between the inner cavity and the outer integument there are pump chambers which suck air in and direct it through various openings to the sound cavity, thus making both single tones and harmonics.

"The young ones are supersonic, but they are merely high pitched by the age of two, becoming soprano, alto, tenor, baritone and finally basso profundo as they age and become less and less mobile. The very oldest ones have taken root and grown long, leafy hair, so most of the truly great chorales are built around a copse of aged Vixbot who sing down to your subsonic range."

"Will we get to hear them?" Benita asked, amazed.

"Oh, indeed. That's why we landed here. Those great huge tree-looking things over there at the edge of the cavern are bassos profundissimos. You may not even hear the tones they sing, but you'll feel them through your feet."

Chad fussed with the sound recorder, setting it to record even the subsonics, and they sat in awed astonishment, not moving, barely breathing, while the concert took place. They were treated to everything from what Chiddy called a simple summer pastoral song, rather fluty, to a lament on the fall of a great ancestor, extremely profound, full of aching chords and fleeting dissonances. At various points during the music, the

Vixbot struck themselves with their arms, accompanying their harmonies with percussion in complex rhythms. Chiddy had said the Vixbot choirs created the universe's most marvelous sounds, and when Benita managed to achieve some degree of self-awareness once more—which was long after the ship had taken off again—she knew ai was right.

Chiddy gave them the choice of visiting the Thwakians or the Oumfuz, or both, explaining rather apologetically that since the Oumfuz were swamp livers, visiting them entailed unavoidable exposure to muck and fetid aromas. They chose the Thwakians, and were next plunged deep into a violet ocean dotted with verdant islands. Through the view screen they were shown the undersea tunnels, accretions like vast cables of sand netting the bottoms of the planetary sea, outside the portals of which were gardens of seaweed and small, immobile creatures. They followed one of the tunnels to its emergence on an island, where Benita and Chad were introduced to two Thwakians who emerged only partially from the tunnel, rather in the manner of hermit crabs emerging partially from their borrowed shells.

Their foreparts seemed armored, though what could be seen of the nether parts seemed naked and fragile. Chiddy explained that they ate both flora and fauna of the ocean, going out through sea locks to harvest their crops and flocks. The Thwakians explained, through Vess, that the only time they were endangered was when they emerged onto dry land, which was necessary only at the time of egg laying. Since the ocean-living form had descended from a land-living one, the young still had to hatch in the sands, under the orange sun. Once hatched, they skittered into the nearest tunnel and were thereafter quite safe.

"What danger is there?" Chad asked.

Chiddy said, "A large winged thing, analogous to your osprey or albatross. It spends most of its life in the air, coming to ground only when it, too, needs to feed or reproduce. Usually it eats fish, but it is also willing to dine on a Thwakian or a clutch of Thwaki eggs."

The two representatives of their race were thanked for their time and trouble, and the visitors returned to their ship.

"No trouble admitting them to the Confederation," Chiddy remarked. "They are the single intelligent race on the planet, they inhabit the entire planet, and except for recurrent arguments over nest space, they are almost totally peaceable."

Their final stop was Pistach-home, swimming in air, with its own green oceans and greener mountains and chains of silver lakes and vast ocher prairies and sparkling little cities.

"Beautiful," breathed Benita, Chad nodding seriously at her side. Even from this distance, it was attractive, and as they came closer, it was obvious that it was consistently lovely. They saw deserts but no desolations, and nowhere did any fog of despoilment spew from chimneys to hang loathsomely over the land.

When they were quite near the surface on the night side, they saw three moons, one largish silvery one, two much smaller greenish-blue ones, all more or less spherical, all bearing clusters of domes, like drops of dew. Chiddy mentioned that there were also three other occupied planets in the system, one very warm and fertile farm planet in the next orbit toward the sun, one completely domed laboratory and light industry planet so far from the sun the atmosphere was frozen, and one dead rock planet, even farther out, on which all system heavy industry and asteroid smelters were located. Since all work was done by robots and no one lived there except temporary supervisors and inspectors, and since they had completely enclosed quarters with gardens attached and even a little aviary and zoo, so as not to lose track of their place in the natural world, the need for extensive antipollution programs was lessened. There were such programs, Chiddy said, even there, but they were concerned with storing dangerous substances so they should never threaten living things. Each inbound ship carried a load of disposables which was at some point released on a trajectory that would carry it into the sun.

Carlos would, so Chiddy informed them, be awakened when they were ready to leave the ship, and in the meantime he suggested that Chad and Benita should change into the appropriate caste clothing. Then they could have coffee and watch the scenery. While they were so employed, Chiddy and Vess talked unintelligibly to the authorities on their planet. It was the first time Benita had heard Pistach spoken at length, and she thought it an interesting language, full of sibilant stretches and lots of Kwa and Wak and Foum sounds. She heard their names, Benita Alvarez and Chad Riley, coupled with the terms nootch and proffe, and assumed they were being introduced prior to arrival.

Came a hiatus, during which they ate breakfast, taking their time about it, and then the conversation with the ground began again, being conducted this time, evidently, with ultimate authority.

Benita and Chad both detected concern in Chiddy's voice, as though he did not know or recognize the voice or person he was dealing with. Benita asked Vess if anything was wrong, and he shrugged, insofar as his normal shape could shrug. The Pistach didn't have shoulders that could go up and down. Their pseudo shrug was a kind of sideways nod accompanied by a slightly raised upper limb on that side.

As Chiddy spoke, more and more worriedly, his color betraying increasing concern, Vess, with an equally worried expression, unpacked clothing they had prepared for Carlos. He suggested that Benita get him up and dressed, which she did, though awkwardly, and with bad grace and much complaint on Carlos's part. This ship was not as tiny as the first one she had seen—one they called a quimish, a word that means, so said Vess, to scoot or buzz about—but still tiny so far as crew space went. Chad remarked that it was a good thing trips didn't last very long, because one could severely injure oneself trying to change trousers.

By the time Carlos was dressed, permission had been granted for the ship to land near the little community where Chiddy's family had lived for generations. Benita asked who was meeting them, and Chiddy replied that the Pistach regarded it as the height of arrogance and rudeness to confront a newly arrived person, or one who has just been given news of a possibly disrupting happening, or one who has suffered loss. "Your newsmen on Earth," said Chiddy, making a face, "would be regressed and reselected here on Pistach-home. I have seen them sticking their microphones into the faces of the bereaved and of the assaulted and of persons just arrested or survivors of disasters asking them how they feel, as though that were news! It is incivility of the worst sort. We would not tolerate it. One should be met, of course, and welcomed, but quietly, discreetly."

48

on pistach home

They expected modest if any greeting, in keeping with Chiddy's explanations of Pistach manners. Chiddy blanked the view ports and set down. They arranged themselves to depart. The outer hull split vertically, the opening widened, and they walked out into a numerous assembly: a double rank of large Pistach in an arc around the ship, several even larger ones standing close, one particularly large one coming forward, his pincers extended. Chiddy stopped dead in his tracks, staring, his mouth parts slightly agape, and murmured in a shocked voice, "T'Fees!"

Chad gave Benita a quick look. They had heard much about T'Fees. His being here, at this time, with this number of quite large and able-looking Pistach did not bode well for their mission.

T'Fees spoke. Chiddy spoke. Vess murmured to the humans:

"T'Fees is telling him not to be frightened, he intends no harm. Chiddy is asking if T'Fees will respect your status as visitors to whom hospitality is due. T'Fees says he is a rebel, not a barbarian, of course he will."

T'Fees came forward and bowed, announcing his name,

which sounded just as Chiddy had said it, Tuh-FEEZ. Without prompting, Chad pronounced Benita's name, gesturing toward her, then introduced Carlos, then himself. As the highest caste among the three, this was proper etiquette, according to instructions before landing, given by Vess, who now suggested they bow, which they did, Chad dragging Carlos down by the arm.

T'Fees spoke, evidently questioning. Vess said he asked what the humans hoped to see while on Pistach.

Chad said they hoped to see the Fresco and the people of Pistach-home.

T'Fees spoke again, at length, and Chiddy turned pale. Pallor among the Pistach was a very light and sickish sort of green and was quite unmistakable. Chiddy was shaken.

"What?" Benita demanded of Vess.

"He says it is a good time for you to see the Fresco, for he and his people have come to clean it!"

Benita looked helplessly at Chad and he at her. At first it meant nothing to either of them, but then the words *fresco* and *cleaning* clicked in Benita's mind, reminding her of how Chiddy had reacted when she had spoken of cleaning the Sistine Chapel, removing, in the process, interpolations that Michelangelo had never put there.

She whispered to Chad, telling him about it. "Chiddy turned quite pale at the time. Could this threatened cleaning bode something similar? Some unexpected change?"

"How long," Chad murmured to Vess, "since the Fresco has been cleaned?"

"It has never been cleaned," he gargled, looking down toward his lower appendages. "It is too holy to clean."

"And do the people light candles before it?" Benita asked, still with the Sistine Chapel in mind.

"Oh," he moaned. "Yes. Yes. Quiria of candles; veritable jecaloms of candles, over ocalecs and ocalecs of years."

Chad didn't get it. He bent toward her, and she whispered again. He straightened up, looking stern. "If it cleans up saying something different than they've always thought . . . ?"

"Chiddy and Vess evidently think something like that could

happen," Benita muttered. "Remember the fuss over the Dead Sea Scrolls? There was all that secrecy and tabooing, remember? Because the orthodox religions were scared to death the scrolls might say something contrary to accepted theology!"

"I remember," he muttered out of the side of his mouth. "It might be taken as a desecration. Remember what happened to Indira Gandhi after the attack on the Sikh Temple. And all the recent Moslem–Hindu riots . . ."

"I know," she murmured.

T'Fees spoke again. Chiddy approached him, and the two of them moved away, talking together. Vess told the humans to stay where they were, beside the ship, as details of the visit were being worked out, then he went to join the discussion. Carlos had been standing mulishly between Chad and Benita, thus far silent but glowering with evident distaste at everyone and everything.

"I'm not going to waste my time standing around here," he muttered at his mother. "All these bugs can just stuff it."

Chad turned toward him, saying almost in a whisper, "The big one is a rebel, Carlos. The other big ones are soldiers. I'm sure they have weapons. If you do something out of hand, they will probably kill you."

Carlos tried to sneer, swiveling his eyes between Benita and Chad. Though Benita saw no reason for T'Fees to kill him, she knew the temptation. "He's right, Carlos. If we play it cool, nobody gets hurt and we'll be going home in a few days." She swallowed, hoping she was right.

"All this is your fault," he snarled angrily. "If you hadn't gotten me mixed up in this, I wouldn't even be here."

Benita moved to put herself between Carlos and the multitude, keeping her voice low. "Carlos, listen. We're not in control here. The people in control are the people you're getting ready to insult. You can be charming when you choose to be. It would be a good idea to be charming now."

"Or what?" he growled.

Chad said quietly, over her shoulder, "When we return, those of us on this trip will be very important people. The TV shows will be bidding for us. The publishers will want to ghostwrite books for us. If you're smart, if you play it right and get in good with these people, you'll end up making a lot of money."

Carlos's face slowly changed, and Benita kept her face perfectly empty. Why hadn't she thought of that? Being a VIP would suit Carlos to a tee. Couple that with money, and it would be his idea of paradise! Being important, being first in line, had been on Carlos's agenda since he learned to walk and talk.

Benita turned her face away to hide her expression. Chad reached out and squeezed her hand.

Chiddy and Vess returned. The welcoming party gathered around the tall figure of T'fees and then they strolled off, in no particular order.

"We have gained some time," said Chiddy, drawing Benita away from Carlos and Chad. "One has told them of the predators, of your son's capture, of your fear for his life. One has begged tolerance for his lack of manners, saying that time is needed for balance, for regaining equanimity. Please, Benita, may one speak to you sincerely?"

She nodded. He took her a step or two farther from the others and said, "T'Fees notwithstanding, Benita, one can help you with your boy, if you like."

"What do you mean?"

"One's hearing is keen. One heard his comments and saw his comportment. Such a demeanor is injudicious at this juncture."

"That's true," she admitted. "But he's still frightened. We gave him no time to get his balance after you saved him from the Fluiquosm."

"One knows. So one offers a way of rebalancing. It's a kind of therapy. A way of changing behaviors. It does work. Would you like one to try?"

She wanted to say yes. She wanted to say, he's broken, fix him. She couldn't. Suppose it made him happier? Suppose it made him a nicer person? Perhaps he enjoyed being unhappy, some people did. Perhaps he *chose* to be miserable! She shook her head, whispering, "Not just yet, Chiddy. Give him a chance on his own . . ."

"One understands, dear Benita. Individuality is very important to your people. Vess and I have seen that some humans think of their pain as their own, whereas they think of happiness as something they should have been given and did not receive. They do not know that happiness comes from within. They rant at the world for not providing it while they keep it from ever emerging. Your son would rather play tragedy than comedy. It is an individual choice."

She wiped her eyes surreptitiously. "I do feel guilty. I should have controlled it, Chiddy. If I had married someone else, if I had not been impetuous, if I had waited until my judgment was better, maybe he wouldn't be like this. It makes me sorrowful."

"Ha. And would some other choice have produced some other result? Perhaps not. Your son would not have been like this, true. Also, he would not have been this son. Another son could have been happier only if this one had not existed. This argument is futile and silly. We will not discuss it further."

She flushed and nodded.

Chiddy said, "This idea of cleaning of the Fresco is more dangerous than I can say. If we had known T'Fees was here, we would not have brought your son with us. Now, Carlos is, as you say, a loose cannon, and we cannot risk his crashing about. Will you allow me to give him a slight euphoric? One that will keep him happy and quiet?"

"Of course, Chiddy. I don't want him to upset things. He just seemed to be so . . . useless, and it hurts!"

Chiddy patted her arm. "Don't be so sure he is useless. The Pistach have a little saying: 'Goff requos bemin pequos.' *From this shit may verdure come.* All kinds of people turn out to have a use." He patted her again. "Enough of sadness. Welcome awaits at the guest house of the Cavita family."

The house was small and elegant. It reminded Benita of pictures she had seen of Japanese houses: sliding screens instead of walls, simple surfaces, beautifully finished, only necessary furniture, a few storage chests, a few mats. Obviously the Pistach did not use chairs, but they did have slanting boards they could lean their ventral sides on, leaving their arms free on each side. There were three sleeping areas, separable each from the others, with soft mats on the floors, and each human adopted one, putting their belongings on the simple chests.

The sanitary arrangements were out back, so to speak, except for the bath, an anteroom leading to a tiled booth with nozzles in every direction. A carved chest in the anteroom attracted Benita's attention, and without thinking she opened the lid. Something flew out of the chest and covered her, crawling under her clothing, into every seam and crease of her body. She screamed, and things crawled into her mouth. She gurgled, hearing the rattle of Chiddy's feet on the floor.

Chiddy whistled, and the stuff came off her, rushing back into the box. It was . . . insects. Beetles or something. She leaned against the wall, shuddering. "What . . . what . . ."

"So very sorry," said Chiddy, his mouth parts shivering. "Oh, so very sorry. The iglak was supposed to be removed. I told them twice. Remove the iglak."

"What in hell is it?" asked Chad, standing wide-eyed behind him.

"They," said Chiddy. "A small life form that lives on the shed skin of other life forms. You have dust mites, too small to see. We have iglak, necessary to get under the carapace and around all the joints where water may not take away the soil. We open the box, they come out and go all over us, eating every dead flake of integument, then we whistle and they go back to the box, then we shower in water. Oh, I am so sorry you were frightened, dear Benita."

He left her there, and she took the opportunity to undress and shake her clothing. The iglak had all gone, but she still felt itchy. She put her clothes in a cabinet, stepped into the booth and turned on the water, if it was water. When she turned it off, it dried, almost at once, no towels needed. She realized for the first time that the Pistach were far lighter than water. They would float in a tub.

That evening, several members of the family came to the house to wish the visitors well. They stayed only briefly except for Chiddy's nootch, Varsi, who lingered to talk with Benita through her own translation device. She was very proud of Chiddy; Benita heard it in every word she said. "Ai has gone far," ke said. "Ai is the best one I have nootched, ever. Needed so little, ke did! Only a word, now and then. No sleep teaching. No removals of bad traits."

"You can remove bad traits?"

"Some. If they have not gone too deep. Nootchi in your race cannot do this?"

"Regrettably, no. I wish we could."

Benita was so touched by Varsi that she gave her the scarf from her own outfit, a red one, knowing this color could be worn by a second-level Pistach.

Each Pistach who came brought something pleasant to eat or drink. As the evening wore on, Benita guessed that Chiddy had spiked Carlos's tea with the proposed euphoric, for he became mild and mannerly, even seeming to be interested in what was going on.

"Are those iglak things trained?" he asked Chiddy. "I mean, do you train them to answer the whistle that way?"

Chiddy made his negative gesture, his half headshake, half lowered shoulder. "It is the sound their nootchi make, from the nest, recalling the workers. The box is their nest. Inside it is very complicated, with many chambers. Are you interested in such things?"

Carlos nodded. "I was just thinking, that'd go over great on Earth. At a spa, like. You'd have to have a cabinet that left people's heads out, though."

Chiddy said thoughtfully, "You may be right. They are very easy to breed and control. Perhaps we will attempt to export them."

Vess announced that they were invited to the House of the Fresco on the following morning, to see the cleaning, which was likely to take all day.

"You're terribly worried about it," Benita said to Chiddy. "Aren't you?"

"I have reason to believe," he murmured, "that the actual paintings may differ in details from what we have learned of the content."

"Would this be a tragedy? Which takes precedence, your teachings, or the content of the Fresco?"

"Ah, Benita. I have asked myself that question, over and over. The Fresco has given us legitimacy, the way your holy scriptures give you legitimacy. How often have I heard your legislators quoting Scripture to prove almost anything. I have heard your people speak of 'two millennia of tradition,' or even, 'four millennia of culture.' Unlike your Scripture, the Fresco does not govern our belief about the universe, for Aiton is Aiton, no matter what being paints what or what writer writes what or what philosopher says what. In the nebulae, in the clusters, in the spaces between the galaxies, no matter what persons think, Aiton is still Aiton.

"But, the Fresco does define our belief about ourselves and our worlds. Your Scripture defines men and women as unique children of God and it defines the world as the center of God's attention. Because of your Scripture, you behave as though that is true, unfortunately from our point of view, for it leads you to destructive, hurtful excesses. Our Fresco defines us as a people who amend other worlds and bring them to peace, but I confess, we are that people only because the Fresco says so."

Chad said, "I'm a student of languages, and in our world, seminal works of ethics are almost always written. In fact, I know of no culture in which moralities are conveyed by picture, though certainly many histories are memorialized in that way. What is it that makes you so concerned?"

Chiddy came close and confided in them, telling them all about the dropped cleaning rag and the flap that followed. He told them about Glumshalak and the Compendium. He told them how the Chapter had refused to look any deeper at the Fresco itself.

"How far back does the cleaning taboo go?" Chad asked.

"To the time of Glumshalak," Chiddy said. "It was that athyco who forbade us to fiddle with the Fresco evermore. We have always believed that Glumshalak considered the possibility the Fresco might be changed by some political or tribal faction to gain power for themselves, and so ai forbade it."

Chad nodded, asked a few more questions, and looked exceeding thoughtful.

"Do you understand what's going on?" Benita asked him when they were alone.

"You reminded me about the Dead Sea Scrolls. The reason there was such a tizzy was that many religious groups really don't worship God, they worship the Scriptures. Christians,

Jews, they both do it. So do the Moslems. Even though the commandment says 'You shall have no other God before me,' the Scripture worshippers put the writings ahead of God. Instead of interpreting God's actions in nature, for example, they interpret nature in the light of the Scripture. Nature says the rock is billions of years old, but the book says different, so even though men wrote the book, and God made the rock and God gave us minds that have found ways to tell how old it is, we still choose to believe the Scripture.

"The Pistach could be like that. Totally governed by what's on that wall."

"That's a happy thought," said Benita, finding it anything but. If anything, the discussion amplified the atmosphere of pending danger, one sufficiently disturbing that none of them, except for Carlos, slept really well that night.

In the morning they were given a meal of tea and a fruit that looked like a spherical, faceted eggplant and tasted like nothing they had ever tasted before. Rhubarb, maybe, Benita suggested. Chad thought sweetened asparagus. Carlos merely smiled and ate it without complaint. Even as they climbed the stairs to the House of the Fresco, Carlos had a smile on his face and was humming under his breath. The stairway was wide and gracefully curved, with flowers growing along the edges of the terraces and flat areas where Pistach gathered and sang. Their singing, Benita thought, was like an evening chorus of crickets and night birds and frogs, repetitive and soothing and, after a time, so subliminal as to be totally disregarded. The House at the top of the stairs rose in a lovely domed line, like the breast of a young girl. They went through the center one of three bronze doors.

She had expected dirtiness, dark colors, ominous shadings something akin to the look of the Sistine Chapel murals before they were cleaned, but it was far worse than she had imagined. The room was lofty, well proportioned and clean, but the painted panels were only dark smears, shapes barely discernable through a varnish of soot. Above the Fresco was a narrow circular gallery on which a number of Pistach were gathered. Though she wasn't sure what old age looked like among the Pistach, she got the immediate impression that these were very old ones. Perhaps it was the way Chiddy and Vess bowed to them and walked with their eyes down beneath the gaze of those above.

The humans were led to the center of the room, to the "Ground of Canthorel," a plot of fragrant leafed plants where a bench had been provided for them.

"The plants are actually grown in a greenhouse," whispered Vess. "They bring in fresh ones each morning, take the bottoms off the pots so the roots can actually touch the Ground of Canthorel, which is where his ashes were spread, thus sanctifying the plants. Visitors nip off a leaf as a remembrance. There'd be nothing left unless they put new ones in each day."

Several Pistach carrying buckets and mops were gathered between the center door and the one to the right, and a tall Pistach in blue apron and hood (a curator, they were told) stood behind a lectern. Benita thought he looked nervous, though she couldn't tell why she thought so until she noticed the tiny fringy bits around his mouth trembling, as though he had Parkinson's disease. T'Fees emerged from the group with the mops and signaled the curator, who began to read. Chiddy, beside her, translated.

"Panel number one," he said. *"The Meeting.* This panel portrays the welcoming of Mengantowhai by the Jaupati. We see the ship in the background, and in the foreground several of the Jaupati, gazing with wonder at the great vessel. In the middle distance, we see Mengantowhai approaching, carrying his staff. Stepping forward from among the Jaupati is the person of Bendangiwees, leader of the Jaupati and first friend of the Pistach. To the rear, right, we see three amorphous figures assaulting wine jars. This is a teaching against drunkenness."

At this point in the reading, T'Fees shouted a command, and his minions began sloshing liquid over the amber/ocher haze that hid the subject matter. As the curator went on with the details of commentary, the liquid ran down the wall, carrying the soot away, disclosing the bright colors of the wall. Runnels of dark cleanser gathered on the floor to be sponged up by the cleaners and squeezed into empty buckets. Again and again the mops stroked fresh cleanser across the panel between the doors, and the cleaning Pistach moved back and forth, taking buckets away and bringing new ones.

On the gallery, the old Pistach murmured among themselves, sometimes crying out in feeble voices. Benita saw them point and shiver and point again, as though they saw some great disaster they were impotent to avert.

Since the cleaners worked from the top down, the first part of the picture to emerge was an expanse of bluish violet sky. The ship emerged next, coming out of the sooty haze as a great lumpy thing with what looked like gun turrets all over it. Next was Mengantowhai, a strong, stern-looking Pistach carrying . . . well, the curator had called it a staff, but it was obviously a weapon. The huddled things in the middle right background were not wine jars or any kind of vessels, but people, presumably Jaupati, who were being beaten by uniformed Pistach.

Finally, they saw the foreground Jaupati emerge from the veil, a furry people rather like large six-legged cats. Their mobile faces showed expressions of terror and loathing of the Pistach. Their gestures were aversive, and their leader, Bendangiwees, thrust out his four-fingered forehands, warningly.

"Look at it, curator!" called T'Fees, when the last of the mopping and sponging had been done. "What does it show?"

"As I said," the curator intoned, his voice shaking only slightly. "It shows Mengantowhai's first meeting with the Jaupati. The Jaupati were afraid, at first, but this emotion was soon replaced with gratitude."

"And the ones being beaten?"

"Probably . . . criminals. People . . . who had attempted to disrupt the order of the meeting ceremony . . ."

"Or perhaps simple citizens who didn't get out of the way fast enough," trumpeted T'Fees. "Second panel! Read, curator!"

The curator looked at the page before him, hesitantly, letting his eyes drift upward to the aged Pistach on the gallery.

"Read!" demanded T'Fees again.

He read.

"*The Descent of the Steadfast Docents*. We see the docents descending into the society of the Jaupati, spreading through-

out their society in order to civilize them and make them
orderly. . . ."

This time the sloshing was done more quickly, the wiping away more efficiently. This panel was not crowded between bronze pillars, more cleaners could work at once, and they were falling into the routine of it. Everyone saw armored figures moving out from the ship, crushing any who stood in their path. In the picture, one of the Pistach carried a lance with a Jaupati head on it, and when he saw this, Chiddy stopped translating. He was shaking. The Pistach do not weep outwardly, Benita knew, but something very similar was going on with him.

"Third panel," cried T'Fees. "Read!"

"*The Uniting of the Tribes*," read the curator. "Seeing the peaceful Pistach willing to help them, the tribes voluntarily gave up their independence to join into a union . . ."

On the wall, they saw the tribes united, by force, and marched off into the next three panels, *Peaceful Work, Civilization* and *The Offerings*, where they saw slaves laboring for the Pistach to build mighty monuments and estates and finally a great palace. *The Offerings* was panel number six, and it purported to show the voluntary offerings of the Jaupati to King Mengantowhai at the time of his crowning. It was, however, the Jaupati who were being offered up, and in panel seven, *The Adoration*, the Jaupati were being slain at Mengantowhai's feet. Among the slain was the leader Bendangiwees, and dragged along to observe his murder was his obviously pregnant mate.

Panel eight was the *Birth of Kasiwees*. The mother was the same female as in the preceding panel (the Jaupati had distinctive skin markings that enabled one to identify individuals). When the soot was removed, they saw the gifts brought to the child by his family; many types of blades and weapons, sharp edges to turn against the conquerors who had murdered his father. Panel nine, *The Evangelism of Kasiwees* could have been better named the Vengeance of Kasiwees for it showed the young Kasiwees raising up a rebel force under a banner bearing the word *UmaPokoti*, or Avengers.

"We were told the Pokoti were another people entirely,

whispered Chiddy in a depressed and horrified voice. "We have been taught they were envious of the peaceful Jaupati."

"It looks like to me they were simply fighting against invaders," said Chad. "But that was centuries ago. Many races begin as warlike."

Chiddy was not comforted. And so it went through panels showing the kidnapping of Mengantowhai, the rescue of Mengantowhai by Canthorel, the reprimands given to Mengantowhai by several of his own aged athyci who told him slavery and murder were wrong. It was impossible to misunderstand the panels, for many of them contained written quotations of those pictured.

In Panel fourteen, *The Fearful Faithless*, the abolitionists left the planet at the head of a schism that erupted over the question of slavery. The teaching of the panel had always been that these were traitorous Pistach, afraid of the Pokoti. In Panel fifteen, *The Blessing of Canthorel*, which was supposed to show Mengantowhai's work affirmed and blessed by Canthorel, it actually showed him confessing to Canthorel that he had underestimated the Jaupati's desire for freedom, that more force and greater atrocities would be needed to put down the rebellion. This was clearly conveyed by a transcript of their conversation written down the sides of the panel, no interpretation needed. In panel sixteen, *Departure of Canthorel*, Canthorel left the planet after telling the Jaupati they had been greatly wronged. And, in the final panel, between the left and center doors, the one called the *Martyrdom of Kasiwees*, they saw Kasiwees being murdered yes, but by Mengantowhai himself. Around Kasiwees were scattered the stones and arrows of his battle, and he held a long dagger in his hand. In the upper left, they could see the last of the Pistach flying away, and in the middle foreground stood a device easily identifiable as a *planet stripper*, one that would destroy all life upon the Jaupati world.

This was the story Canthorel had painted in the House of the Fresco. No matter how one looked at it, it was an accusation and a warning. It said as clearly as paint could say, "Woe and Tribulation, this is an offense before the universe, do not do this again!"

revelation

The curator had long since given up reading the orthodox version. The room was as hushed as a tomb. Only T'Fees trumpeted on, "You see, you see, you damned interfering blobs of worthless guts! You had no right! You have no right! Pistach peace is based on a lie!"

He threw open the bronze door and stormed out into the light of a bloody sunset, his minions behind him, leaving the observers among the guttering candles.

"I'm hungry," said Carlos.

Vess rose, saying in a toneless voice, "I'll take you back to the guest house. There'll be food there." They went out, soundlessly.

Benita stood wearily and turned, looking upward at the gallery. Many of the old Pistach still leaned upon the railing, their normally bright green-, yellow-, and red-colored bodies pale.

"They had no idea, did they?" Benita asked, almost whispering.

Chiddy did the little rotation of the upper body that passed for a negative headshake. "We thought . . . we knew some things would be different. We thought they would be matters of interpretation. A wine jar versus another kind of vessel. A springtime symbol versus an autumnal one. But not this. None of us thought this." He made the sound of Pistach laughter, harshly rasping.

"Benita, athyci give sermon cycles at the great festivals, seventeen sermons on seventeen days, to accord with the number of panels, one sermon on each panel subject. I have done it myself. I have quoted Glumshalak's Commentaries to explain why we do what we do. And now . . . now, what can I base my beliefs upon?"

He turned and walked sadly toward the door. She started to follow him, but then detoured to her left, toward panel thirteen. Something had been bothering her about the panel in which Mengantowhai was reprimanded by his athyci. The counselors were gathered beneath a tree that had a few bare branches but was mostly leafy, with both blossoms and fruit. There were words along the bottom of the panel. She took out her little notepad and copied the words down, being thankful Pistach lettering was phonetic, not ideographic.

She noticed there was a similar tree in the panel to the left, *The Rescue*, in which Mengantowhai was rescued from the Pokoti. It was the same tree, same number of branches, same shape of trunk, but this tree was completely dead. She turned to the right, to panel fourteen, *The Fearful Faithless*. The same tree was there as well, partly alive.

"Chad," she called. "Come look."

He came over and they walked back, counterclockwise, around the House of the Fresco. Every single panel had the same tree in it, either dead or leafing out, or in flower or fruit.

"The two growing trees are in panels where Pistach people disdained Mengantowhai," she said.

Chad murmured, "And they were painted after the rest of the Fresco. See, the overlap here? You can see what was painted underneath. That's why most of the trees are small, they're fitted into whatever vacant space was left."

They had come to the first panel, and even there they found a tree. Chad shrugged and she returned the gesture. It was interesting, but they didn't know what it meant, if anything. They went out onto the terrace where Chiddy waited in morose silence.

"What does a fruiting tree symbolize?" she asked.

Chiddy looked at her, sighing. "Well, it's a sign of fruition, of course. Of something long in growth that has ripened. Like a head of grain. Or a pomego, like the ones you had for breakfast."

"Is that an accepted meaning among Pistach?"

"Oh, yes. The Pistach revere edible fruit. They regard it as a great gift. The fruiting tree is carved on some of our most ancient monuments, some that go back long before the House of the Fresco was built."

They went back to the guest house, to an evening meal that none of them tasted, and then to another restless night. Sometime in the dark house, Benita got up to find Chad wandering about, at loose ends, as she was. They went out into the dark drenched garden, following the firefly glow of tiny lanterns to a bench that had been put there for them, one of the Pistach leaning boards laid across two stones to make it flat and low enough to sit on.

"You know what I think," she said to Chad. "I think that historian, Glumshalak, purposely changed the Fresco in his Compendium, diametrically changed it. And he forbid the Pistach to clean the Fresco so they'd never know."

"Why would he have done that?"

"Do you ever go to church, Chad?"

"Not often. My parents were Methodists, at least at Christmas and Easter. Merilu was reared Episcopalian, but that was more a social thing with her parents than it was religious."

"My mother was Catholic for weddings and burials and funerals. At other times she was a pagan I guess. She believed in spirits of the trees and mountains and rivers, not that they would do anyting for her, rather that she should be protective of them. Her father was a history professor, in Mexico. He wrote several books about the bloody gods of Mexico, and she read them all. When I was a kid, Mami told me the Mexican gods weren't the only bloody ones, and we should never serve gods that had been invented to take the blame for everything bloody, painful, primitive and unenlightened that people wanted to do. *Why did we Israelites kill every man, woman, child and beast in that city? Why, the Lord Jehovah commanded it. Why do we Spaniards steal food from these Indian people, and mutilate them, and use them as slaves? Why, we do it so they will love Christ! Why do we Aztecs torture and sacrifice people? Huitzilopotchli demands it!*

"Whether it was the Israelites invading Canaan or the Spanish invading the Southwest, or one Mexican tribe warring against another, the answer was always the same. *We enslave and torture and mutilate and kill in the name of our god.*

"My grandfather said people who can learn, learn morality the way they learn everything else, by building on history. He also said that some people cannot learn from history, so they cannot change. For them, there's only one book or tradition or whatever it's called in their religion, and in that book God is eternal and whatever the book says God commanded two or three or four thousand years ago, God still commands today. That may be kill homosexuals or kill nonbelievers. It may say enslave your enemies. It may say mutilate or sequester women, or sell your ten-year-old daughter for somebody's third wife.

"But suppose back in A.D. two or three hundred, we had had a Glumshalak, and he had blanked out all the Old Testament. Suppose he had written a commentary that purported to tell us what was in the book, but the book itself was eliminated. Suppose the commentary was devoted to tolerance and persuasion, suppose it forbade violence. We wouldn't have a god who kicked Adam and Eve out of the garden for intellectual curiosity, or the destruction of the whole world by flood, or the slaughtering of innocents right and left. The commentary would tell us about a God who triumphed through peace and paying attention to history instead of bloodshed and horror."

"You think we'd have sweetness and light?" asked Chad.

"Maybe, if there was no bloody scripture for the evangelists to quote."

"It would make a big dent in self-righteousness, but it wouldn't change human nature."

"It might not change human nature, but it would eliminate a whole set of alibis. I think that's what Glumshalak did. He didn't want his people to be bound by the cruelty and violence in their history. He wanted his people to *believe* they were good. So he destroyed all the records that said what was really there . . ."

"How do you know?"

"He had to have done, otherwise they'd have turned up before now. He certainly didn't repaint the Fresco, he didn't have the talent. That's obvious. He forbade anybody cleaning the Fresco, and he wrote down what he thought should have been there. I think Glumshalak's commentary made the Pistach the people they are. A good people. Not perfect, but good, because they've been selecting toward goodness for generations and generations. When the president told me not to let anything interfere with their coming back and finishing the job, he was saying that they're a good people."

"You think the Pistach won't go back to Earth?"

"You heard T'Fees. I think this throws their whole interventionist policy into the toilet and leaves us at the mercy of the Fluiquosm, the Wulivery, the Xankatikitiki and the American Congress." Her voice shook a little as she remembered the Wulivery and Morse trying to devour her. Not a good experience, either of them.

"I hadn't thought that far," he said in a hollow voice.

"There's a problem," she said. "You haven't been around the Pistach as much as I have, but one thing is very clear to me and it frightens me. They're selected for their jobs, and when one of them is selected to do a certain specific job, that one has little or none of the flexibility a generalist would bring to the same job. The Pistach pretty much go by the book."

"By the Fresco."

"Right."

He sighed. "What's the significance of the tree?"

"Just what Chiddy said: fruition, growth, change. In our Bible, Jesus says you know trees by their fruits. I think Glumshalak realized someday people might clean that Fresco. He put the trees there, to indicate why he was doing what he was doing, showing what incidents were deadly and which ones were fruitful, coding the history they should put behind them, in order that they might grow up and bear good fruit."

She leaned wearily on his shoulder and he put his arm around her. They sat there, deep in thought, sharing their mutual humanity in a place far, far from home.

"Oh, that's really nice," said a sarcastic voice behind them. Carlos.

She got up without haste and turned to face him. "We think there's a tragedy coming, Carlos. Human companionship helps when contemplating tragedy."

"What tragedy?"

"The possibility that the Pistach may not return to Earth."

"So long as they get me home, I should give a shit?" he commented.

"You know," said Chad, in a conversational voice, "I really don't like your son, Benita."

"I know," she said, looking into Carlos's surprised face. "I don't like him either."

"What d' you . . ." Carlos gargled. "You're still . . ."

"Go to bed, Carlos," said Chiddy, from the open door.

Carlos made a threatening move, there was a spark, and he fell down. Chiddy said, "The euphoric wore off. His manner is partly a reaction to that fact. Put him in the ship, in the cubby." He came to the bench. "I've been listening."

"We were talking about the Bible," Benita said, her voice trembling a little. Her first instinct had been to go to Carlos, then to yell at Chiddy for hurting him, even though she knew Chiddy hadn't hurt him. The Pistach lugging him away weren't hurting him either. "What did you do to him?"

"Silenced him for the moment," said Chiddy. "It's something we do with our own children occasionally. Shut their bodies down to let their minds calm themselves. I don't have time to deal with him now. Neither do you."

"What's going on?" asked Chad.

"The Chapter have been meeting. They are adrift. They lack any sense of direction. I wish you could come talk to them, dear Benita, but they won't listen to a nootch! Oh, if only you could say to them what I have just heard you saying . . ."

"Then tell them I am an athyco in disguise," she said. "Hell, tell them we're both athyci. Appointed by our government to assess the help you're giving us!"

"They have already seen," he said. "Your clothing. Your manner. It . . . they wouldn't accept it. I can tell which way the decision is going. I came tonight, because if I wait for morning, they will have decided I may not return to Earth at all. They will have decided on nonintervention. They will forget Tassifoduma. There is something base in each of us, something we keep hidden and quiet. Now it will bubble up, like tar in a pit, and people will say to themselves, well, we are something other than we thought. We are violent, we are conquerors. We will return to the time of weapons, the time of disorder, the time of slavery. They are already saying that is what we are, and we can't fight what we are!"

"What you are is what you choose to be," Benita cried.

He choked with bitter laughter. "Oh, Benita, even as tiny ones, we are taught not to choose, not to want. Choosing is not what we do."

She fumbled about for a reason, finally suggesting, "But you have to take us back, Chiddy!"

"I know. That's what I'm saying. I have to take you back."

"And you have to stay on Earth a while . . ."

"No, I must return at once. They won't let—"

"The Inkleozese! They're still on Earth, awaiting the emergence of their larvae! They have no spaceships. You have to wait and bring them back. Otherwise you're intervening, aren't you?"

"This is true," he said haltingly. "I had forgotten the Inkleozese."

"And Vess has to come with you, just in case something goes wrong." Over Chiddy's shoulder she saw T'Fees approaching.

"A little redundancy," said Chad. "Every venture requires a little redundancy. She's right."

T'Fees came within hearing distance. "What are you discussing?"

"Benita says we have to go back and pick up the Inkleozese," said Chiddy. "We really are committed to doing so."

"Benita is correct," said T'Fees, after a moment's thought. "But we will insist upon holding a hostage, just to be sure Chiddy and Vess return to their home!"

The large Pistach came closer, peering into Benita's face. "It is true that you must be returned to your homes and the Inkleozese must be fetched, but now that we have proved Pistach interventionism to be nonhistoric, we have no intention of letting it start up again."

"What do you mean, hostage?" she asked.

"We will keep your son," said T'Fees. "He is not essential to anything, so far as we can see. We will hold him here until Chiddy and Vess return. Then we will send him home by some other means. A Credon ship can be paid to take him as a passenger."

"They won't hurt him," murmured Chiddy, close to Benita's ear. "Really."

"I know," she murmured in return. "But he'll try their patience severely."

"One will ask to'eros nootch to see to your son's welfare," said Chiddy. "All nootchi have the power of silencing children."

She turned and went into the room where Carlos had been deposited on a sleeping mat. His face was peaceful, like a child's. She had not seen that expression in a long, long time. For several years now, whenever she'd seen him awake, she had seen only discontent and rancor. There was no reason not to leave him. Missing school was no reason. According to Angelica, he'd been cutting classes. Relationships was no reason. Miss Bigg was no longer interested.

She sighed, wiped her eyes, and returned to Chiddy. "Let him stay here if it will help matters," she said.

Their preparations for departure were sketchy and urgent. Vess came scrambling through the shadows, Chad and Benita took their little bags and plodded toward the ship, T'Fees following closely behind them with several of his burlier rebels.

As they started to board the ship, T'Fees grasped Benita by the shoulder and turned her to face it. Him. Ter. She didn't know what it was or how to refer to it.

"We know how long the Inkleozese take to pupate," T'Fees said. "Do not keep Chiddy and Vess past that time, or your son will be worse for it."

"Would you hurt him, T'Fees?" she asked, gently. "Would you really?"

For a moment, it looked startled, as though it had not thought what it would do. Then it looked crafty. "You have seen on the Fresco what we are capable of."

Two of T'Fees's aides handed Carlos out like a bale of fiber. Chad and Benita got into the ship. With a sound that was suspiciously like a sob, Chiddy closed the portholes and started them on their journey home.

50
benita

---

hortly after they left Pistach-home, Chiddy offered Chad
nd Benita the sedative food and drink they had taken dur-
ng the trip from Earth. Both refused.

"We have a lot of thinking to do," Benita said. "You and
ess are obviously upset; I know our president is going to be
ry upset. I wouldn't feel I had done my utmost unless Chad
nd I had talked this matter over from end to end. Somehow,
omeone must come up with some way to prevent tragedy
om happening to your people and ours!"

Chiddy didn't reply. Instead he went over to Vess, who
as dithering about in an agitated manner. Chiddy put his
and on Vess's upper thorax, and the two of them simply
ood there, unmoving, saying nothing, as though they had
eparated from the reality of now.

Chad whispered, "They don't learn how to cope with
nique challenges in their own lives. They only learn the
stems, and how to make the systems work."

"They have that saying, emergencies make their own
les."

"Even so, the rules will be things they've done before,
ough perhaps in a different context." He raised his voice.

"I wish to hell I had something written about the Pistach people. Something that would give me some insight . . ."

Chiddy heard him and turned toward the two humans. He did it jerkily, reluctantly. "One . . . well, one has a journal that one began when one first talked with Benita. In it one has expressed thoughts and feelings about humankind and Pistach. One cannot say if these ideas are representative of Pistach people as a whole, but if you think they would help . . ."

"Oh, yes," Benita cried. "Do let us see it, Chiddy. Or . . is it written in Pistach?"

He made the expression she had grown to know as a smile, rather than as an expression of dismay or threat. "Oh no, dearest Benita. One wrote it for you, so certainly it was written in a language you can understand. Otherwise one would be a mythologizer, a mystifier, no? Making mystic marks on sheets of precious metal or scribbling prophecies in languages long forgotten, to make oneself feel arcane and esoteric! If it is important to communicate, one does so in the language of the people."

"Some fairly important religious messages have had to be deciphered on Earth," Chad muttered.

"Nothing prevents a mythologizer from discovering a truth," Chiddy said sadly, "or from misrepresenting it once he has done so, but one has always thought to find real truth emanating from many sources, written in multiple places, so to speak. Why would a communicator choose to speak or write a truth in only one place, in a language people could not understand?"

Chad cocked his head as Benita had seen him do when he was getting ready to debate a point, something he much enjoyed. "All that doesn't matter," Benita interrupted hastily. "You wanted something written; Chiddy has something written. So let's read it."

"One . . . wasn't going to give it to you until your people had qualified for membership in the Confederation," Chiddy confessed. "Strictly speaking, one shouldn't be giving it to you at all, now. Nonmembers are not supposed to receive much information about the peoples of the Confederation, but . . . considering the way things are . . ."

He sighed heavily, the gill covers under his thorax plates fluttering in a soft chatter, like a winter wind moving through a last few dried leaves at the tip of a branch. Chiddy fetched a folder out of a cupboard and gave it to Chad, who sat down next to Benita to read it. The individual pages looked like handmade paper, and though the writing was a perfectly legible English cursive, it was somewhat crabbed and the spelling, though quite accurate phonetically, was highly original. Accordingly, the reading went slowly, and Chad and Benita grew quieter and quieter as they read on.

Chiddy's journal made it clear why membership in the Confederation was important. They could not join without assifoduma, and if Earth didn't get to that point, it was at the mercy of the predators. Not only the Wulivery, the Kankatikitiki and the Fluiquosm, but dozens of others, also, who lived farther toward the center of the galaxy but who would undoubtedly make the trip for such a very, very rich hunting ground.

"Remember the meeting before we left for Pistach," Benita whispered to Chad, while Chiddy was concentrating on his dials and buttons, "when the president told me that it was of the utmost importance the envoys continue their work. He said most of the world leaders, the responsible ones, anyway, were agreed that this firm, outside pressure was bringing the positive changes no one had been able to bring about in the past."

Chad murmured, "I was also told, confidentially, that in an environmental sense, even the predators were working to our eventual advantage. Habitat destruction is way, way down and people are talking about reclaiming eroded land rather than wiping out the last few forests in places like Madagascar. There has also been a renewed interest in population limitation, and that's something I didn't think we'd see in my lifetime."

They went on reading, making notes, until they had to rest because it was becoming impossible to go on. Their eyes wouldn't focus. Their attention wavered.

Chiddy made his sighing sound again, which he had been doing a good deal of. "Normally the umquah push bod-

ies together, just as they push planets and stars together, bu
when bodies move in total emptiness, the ship must gener
ate forces to help the bodies resist disintegration. It is easie
when bodies are at rest, not laboring either mentally o
physically. It would be sensible to rest."

Benita agreed. She and Chad ate something and slept
long time, and read a bit more, and slept a bit more, an
conferred with one another in whispers, and read parts o
the journal over again, until suddenly and all at once the hu
window opened or transmuted or whatever it did, as Benit
thought, and they got a look at the Earth from space.

"It's like a sapphire pendant around the throat of the sky
so beautiful," said Benita, thinking of predators and peopl
she cared about and all the threats and commotions tha
were sure to come. The hull went solid again. In only a mo
ment, they heard Sasquatch woofing, and they were home

Benita asked what day it was.

Chiddy referred to a complicated little device hanging o
the wall or bulkhead or hull and pronounced it to be Tues
day, at eight o'clock in the morning. They had been gon
only a week.

Chad left immediately, in pursuance of the plans they ha
made during the journey. Benita took a few moments to as
sure Sasquatch that she was home, that she still loved him
and that he was a good dog, then went downstairs to than
Simon for taking care of him and to ask what had happene
while they'd been away.

"For five days, zip, zilch, nada, nil," he said. "No mor
mysterious deaths. No more countries or cities disappearing
No shootings, no turf wars, no nothing. Peace and tranqui
ity." He gave her a piercing look. "Then, suddenly, two day
ago, all hell broke loose."

"What?" she cried. "What do you mean?"

"The newspapers had blanks in them. That was the firs
thing. Certain phrases just didn't appear!"

"Like?"

"Like 'paid his debt to society,' or 'took responsibility fo
the bombing.' Or in a quote from some prominent church
man—I forget who—talking about famines, 'We have t

provide for the millions who are yet to be born.' I mean, that's what he said on TV, but when it came out in the paper, it was a blank except for the words, 'We have to? Why?' in parentheses. Well, everyone was in fits about that, claiming government censorship or political interference with the free press, and then to top the day off, the predators came back. They announced it on TV. They said the Confederation would shortly confirm their right to be here. They told us they were hunting, starting now. They said the Pistach no longer have the moral authority to keep them out. There've been . . . well, you can imagine what there've been. Political fallout is the worst of it. The actual deaths don't amount to many, but my God, Benita . . ."

"Oh, Lord," she whispered. "Those races . . . they knew. They were all primed to return, weren't they? I just know they were helping T'Fees all along. Chiddy wondered how in heaven they got access to all the ships and weapons they had. I'll bet T'Fees promised them he would cause a revolution on Pistach!"

Simon stared at her, owl eyed. "I have no idea what you're talking about, though I'm sure it must be extremely interesting. Are you allowed to tell me anything about *your* last few days?"

His eyebrows were up to his hairline with curiosity, but she begged off. "When it's over, I'll take you to lunch, Simon, and then I'll tell you everything. Literally, everything."

Back upstairs, she called Angelica. Since it was apparent Benita might be outed at any moment, during the journey she had decided to tell her daughter the truth about the intermediary.

Angelica, of course, already knew, because she'd seen the news conference after the committee hearing. She had a hundred questions, which Benita answered, and a hundred more, which she couldn't.

When told that Carlos had been taken to Pistach-home and left there, she cried, "Mother! You left him there!"

"He's a hostage. Frankly, Angelica, it's difficult to think of any other role he could play as well. It doesn't require him to do anything, not even to be pleasant, and he would complain no matter where he was. What my . . . colleagues and I have to do in the next few days is extremely sensitive, and Carlos is in as disruptive mood as I've ever seen. The girl who was kidnapped with him, by the way, was his girlfriend. A Miss Sonia Bigg."

"You're kidding."

"I'm not in a jovial mood. Actually, it's fortunate the Pistach accepted him as a hostage, rather than insisting on one of the other of us. They won't hurt him, not at all, and we'll get him back as soon as the envoys go home."

"They're going home?" She seemed shocked by this.

"Well, not right away. Maybe soon."

"Oh, *no*, Mom, they've *got* to stay. They've got to get rid of those predators, and you have no idea how much things have improved. At the school! At the housing development by the bus stop! People keep talking about it! They want them to stay."

"That's what the president told me, too. I don't have time to explain just now, because we're terribly busy. I wanted you to know I'm all right because you may not hear from me for a while."

"Did you see Dad on TV?" she demanded.

"Yes. Just before I left," Benita said, flushing. "He was claiming I was a sex slave to the ETs."

"He is *so* stupid! It's embarrassing!"

"Those men you mentioned to me, Angelica? The ones who were hanging around out there? They're part of a group made up of political opponents of the president. They will do literally anything to bring him down, including making an alliance with the predators, or the Devil, if it came to that! Your father was only a minor bargaining chip in the process, a way of getting at me, and it didn't work out the way they planned. So, either they were paying him to spread around dirty misinformation, or they were paying the predators to plant ideas in his head."

"I think it's rotten. Will you call me back when you know something? And you're telling me the truth about Carlos? I don't have to worry about him? He's all right where he is?"

"He's perfectly all right where he is."

"I just . . . I think about him all the time. When we were little, you know, and you were at work, he was sort of my responsibility. Sometimes he was nice."

Benita took a deep breath. "Angelica, I wasn't going to mention this to you, but when you and Carlos left home, I went into sort of a funk. Depression, I guess. You know that Goose and Marsh paid for good health insurance for our family, so I decided to use it and go to a shrink. We had just a few sessions."

"You never told me . . ."

"I'm telling you now. Just listen. This psychologist asked me to visualize my trying to save someone who was drowning. She said to visualize the drowning person pulling my head under. She said to imagine that I struggled, and struggled, getting my head up just enough to gulp some air, but every time I did, the drowning person pulled my head under again.

"She said living with someone like your dad is like trying to save someone from drowning when what the person really wants is to drown you with him. He wants to go, but he doesn't want to go alone. She said the drowner's strongest motivation is to 'miserate his companions,' to pull your head under, over and over until all your strength is gone and you die."

"Mom!"

"Listen. She said once you've done everything you can to get help for the person, once the drowner has firmly or repeatedly rejected that help, the drowner has made his choice. He's deciding to be where he is, when he is, as he is. If you choose not to drown, at that point, you quit trying to save the person. You leave him where he wants to be and you stand back from him far enough he can't drag you in. That may mean far away."

"You're talking about my brother . . ."

"I'm talking about Bert. I'm talking about me. I'm telling you what the psychologist told me. You haven't heard the end of it. The psychologist said that sometimes when the constant rescuer walks away, the drowner decides to swim to shore. I'm suggesting you remember it. That's all."

"Well, I'm not giving up on Carlos."

"You're grown up too, dear. You can make your own choices."

She had no sooner hung up than the phone rang. Chad, saying she was expected at the White House in forty-five minutes. She took a quick shower, dug out some clean clothing, and was downstairs waiting by the time Chad arrived to pick her up.

"You suggested his wife sit in?" she asked.

"He said she would. He made it clear he's not inclined to have any private meetings with anyone. He's been walking on eggs since we've been gone. Things were in delicate balance until this predator thing—can you believe those people?—Morse is working up to some blatant, McCarthyesque attack, issuing little news bulletins that gain credence because of the source rather than the facts. I can honestly remember a time when people who worked for major news organizations had some pride in getting the story right. Now all they seem to care about is getting any story first, true or false. Morse is pretending to be outraged by it all, and by the way, he's still pretending he isn't pregnant."

Chad might think it was pretence, but Benita thought it was more probably denial, helped along by frantic, distractive activity.

They arrived at the White House and went upstairs where the president and the First Lady were waiting, both of them looking drawn and harassed. They talked about religion for a while, then about culture, then about how the Earth could meet the challenge of the predators, then about ways to prevent the predators staying. Between spates of talk, Benita or Chad, as they had planned to do, read sections of Chiddy's journal aloud and showed scenes from the tapes recorded on the journey. Chad had delivered the devices to the FBI, where they'd been examined in front of unimpeachable witnesses who would testify they hadn't been tampered with. The contents had been developed and copied before still other witnesses who could testify they had not been changed in any way.

They broke for lunch—a meal that no one really ate—

during which Benita mentally ordered everything that had been said into one, understandable package. When the meal was over, she said she had a suggestion. The others listened, at first with incredulity, Chad no less than the FL and president, as she briefly restated where they were and then went on to suggest what they could do about it. All three of them brought up objections. Benita countered the objections, soon joined in the effort by Chad, who had begun to see the possibilities.

"But can we get the kind of help we'd need?" he cried, at one point.

"I think we can probably manage that," said the president. "What I'm doubtful about managing is my being gone without the whole world knowing about it."

"Go on a religious retreat," suggested Benita. "With your spiritual advisor." She stopped, thinking. "Actually, it would be a good idea to have someone like that along. To lend us . . . respectability."

"You mean the Reverend?" he asked. "He might really enjoy that. The first evangelist on Pistach-home! I think the press would try to observe even a spiritual retreat. And, of course, I've got the Secret Service hanging around, ready to testify to everything I do."

"I think it's manageable," said the FL. "We'll figure out a way to duck the Secret Service. And I agree with you, the Reverend would enjoy it very much." She turned to Benita. "Do you think you can get the envoys to go along with this?"

"I don't know," Benita admitted. "Though I think Chiddy was leaning in that direction. I'll have to talk fast, but if they will . . ."

By the time all four of them had agreed on a plan of action, Chad and Benita were exhausted, though the president seemed remarkably energized by the whole thing. Chad drove Benita home, asking if she wanted him to come in.

"No, Chad. I've got things to do, and so have you, and best we get at them as soon as we can. If we pull this off, it'll be the coup of the century, and we'll never be able to tell a soul."

Upstairs, she stayed in the elevator and screamed loudly, "Chiddy, I need you and Vess!"

The buttonhole opened in the back of the elevator and they came out in their natural forms.

"Have you heard," whispered Chiddy. "The Shalaquah has returned. They had a spy on Pistach-home . . ."

"And his name was T'Fees," said Benita. "T'Fees has been working with the predators. It's as clear as your . . . mandibles on your face. T'Fees couldn't have mounted that campaign on his own. He needed help. T'Fees is a rebel against Pistach order, and so are the predators. They want to do what they like, when they like, and the predators want to hunt what they like, where they like. They're all in it!"

"I never thought of that," cried Vess, in a voice that was stridently shrill, like a cricket chirp in the middle of the night. "But you're right. He couldn't have done that without help . . ."

Benita said firmly, "Vess, now is not the time to discuss it. We have an emergency on our hands, and we need you to round up the Inkleozese and bring them to my apartment, this afternoon if possible, or tonight, or failing that, tomorrow morning."

Chiddy started to argue, but she took his pincers in her hands and looked straight into all his eyes. "Chiddy, you came here to help us. You were helping us. You are good people, and you were doing a good thing. Now your help is being threatened, and despite what you believe you can or cannot do, Chad and I have an ethical imperative to do what we can to prevent harm to our people."

"But, our people—" murmured Chiddy.

She interrupted, "What is happening to your people should not determine what happens to ours, and you're too ethical a person to interfere with our efforts. The predators found us originally by following you here, which means you're responsible for the trouble we're in. I'm not blaming you, but you have a responsibility to cooperate in solving the problem. Now, please, do as we ask. Chad and I have talked it all out, and we think we have a plan."

Chiddy stared at his feet, as though marshaling arguments, but Vess pulled him away, muttering, "Gefissit molt-plat gom," which sentiment Benita recognized. She and Chad had discussed just that point.

She figured she had a least an hour before Chiddy would manage to get the Inkleozese moving, assuming they would move at all. She took fruit juice from the freezer, made a pitcherful and put in the fridge. That left her time for a shower and hair wash, a change of clothes, time to run the clothes she'd worn on Pistach-home through the washer. Every time she put them on, she felt iglak crawling out of the seams!

Chad called twice, to ask what had happened. The first time, nothing had. The second time she told him that Vess had called to say the Inkleozese were on their way.

"Do you need my help?" he asked.

"Better not, Chad. They might take one good look at you and decide you'd make a good brooder."

He laughed, not an amused laugh, and remarked that he was glad to be relieved of the duty, as the rest of his phone calls would keep him busy for hours.

Benita set out little glasses for the fruit juice, the Inkleozese beverage of choice. She heard movement in the elevator hall, and Chiddy and Vess came in, escorting ten of the tall, angular Inkleozese.

Chiddy and Vess introduced her to the ladies, except for the one who had saved her life. To that one Benita bowed very low and gave heartfelt thanks. Once they had all been served little glasses of fruit juice along with a honey jar to pass around among themselves, Benita asked Chiddy and Vess to excuse themselves as she had a message from the president for the Inkleozese ears alone. They had tympanum, not ears, but everyone knew what she meant. The Inkleozese had translator machines, just as Chiddy and Vess did, so she knew she and they could make themselves mutually understood.

The High Assessor, one K'tif'kt'hmm (who was to be addressed as Your Exactitude) leaned on the back of a chair, her entourage found other places to perch comfortably, and Benita laid out the problems, first of the Pistach, then of Earth, then of Earth and the Pistach and the Inkleozese. She had organized it in her head while in the shower, and was able to talk for about thirty minutes without losing track of

where she was going or repeating herself. Through it all, a
small part of herself stood to one side, listening in amazement, for Benita had never thought of herself as a speaker,
but her presentation was fluent and sensible. Her voice was
hoarse by the time she had finished.

Her Exactitude asked a few questions, very politely.
Benita was able to answer most of them, and those she
could not answer, the other Inkleozese were able to help
her think out.

"It does not seem impossible," murmured Her Exactitude.
"Moreover, it accords with our ethical imperative. Luckily,
our imperative is based upon experience, rather than upon
artifacts or scriptures, so we are not likely to be thrown into
disorganization by judgments made centuries ago. We do
not assert as true anything which we have not proven or
seen proven by others. Thus, we never claimed that we were
the center either of the universe or of a deity's attention.
While we do not deny deity, we do not presume to understand it, plea bargain with it, or tell others what shape it
takes. It does make life easier."

"I am extremely grateful for your attention," murmured
Benita. "I have told you the only solution we can think of,
unless you, yourselves . . ."

The High Assessor made a negating gesture. "No, your
idea is quite good. Besides, we monitor, we do not labor. We
judge, we do not devise. In this case, doing the right thing
is its own reward and makes your gratitude unnecessary.
Shall we summon the envoys?" She turned her head and
looked around the group, all of whom raised a front leg, sig-
nifying assent.

Her Exactitude spoke rapidly into her translation device-
transmitter, and in a few moments, Chiddy and Vess came
in, looking rather like boys who have been summoned to the
principal's office.

Her Exactitude held up a pincer. "Pistach athyci, attend.
We speak on a matter of morality. Your race has encountered
a philosophical abyss. Your beliefs are threatened. Because
of this and others of your actions, another race has become
threatened. We speak with authority. Before you attend to

the crisis of your people, you must attend to the crisis of this people, for you have reached out your manipulators and cannot withdraw them in good conscience."

Chiddy bowed and said something to the effect that he was always at the command of the monitors.

"Pistach athyci, attend! This country has a chieftain, this chieftain has spiritual advisors. This man and his advisors must be taken to Pistach-home, at once. There they must see the great Fresco and spend a time in meditation, enabling the chieftain to return and explain to his people what has transpired. We, the Inkleozese, approve this journey and its objective. The chieftain and his people, however, cannot be taken in a tiny ship. A large ship is necessary."

Chiddy hemmed and hawed and stuttered and thought there might be a Pistach colonial ship on Inkleoza. Or maybe on Gofar or Faroff.

Her Exactitude agreed. "This assumption has high likelihood of being accurate. We ourselves desire concurrent transport to Inkleoza, together with all the human brooders we will have impregnated by that time, in order to supervise their health. The ship must be large enough for both groups. We will need a dozen more brooders in the next few days, but this concludes the current breeding cycle. When the Inkleti have emerged, prior to pupation, the brooders will be returned to Earth."

Chiddy was still dithering, shifting weight from one set of legs to another, upper body twisting, eyes swiveling.

Benita took Chiddy's pincers in her hands, got his full attention and told him that both he and Vess must depart immediately. Chiddy finally focused on her and agreed, though he wasn't his usual self at all.

"Pistach selves will find a large ship somewhere and commandeer it in the name of the Inkleozese!" said Her Exactitude, sounding very magisterial and imperative. "What time will this take?"

"Four days, minimum," said Chiddy. "Four Earth days."

The ladies bowed, Benita bowed, everyone bowed, Chiddy left, the ladies left, except for Her Exactitude.

This personage came to Benita's side. "Aside from our

providing you with the recorded voice you require, is there anything else we can do to assist you, Benita? You bear much responsibility of a suddenly imposed sort. Such surprising burdens are sometimes difficult to uphold."

Benita thanked her and started to say, no, nothing you can do for me right now, but then she thought of something.

"Ma'am, Your Exactitude, I apologize if what I am about to ask is rude or impossible or simply undesirable on aesthetic grounds—" She stopped, clenched her jaw, sighed deeply and went on to make her request.

She seemed amused as she responded, "I will take it up with my people. If they have no objection, we will be happy to grant your plea."

They made mutual farewells. The Inkleozese vanished just as Chiddy and Vess often did, no beam-me-up sparkles, no dissolving into space, just poof, gone. Benita had decided it was some sort of transport commonly used in the Confederation. She did not spend much time thinking about it, however, for it was ten o'clock, she had had little lunch and no supper and was desperate for both food and sleep. Sleep aboard the ship had not been restful. She thought it possible that she had dreamed during much of it: conflict dreams, terror dreams, like those she had had long ago, as a young wife, when she would wake with her heart thundering in her ears, so frightened she couldn't move. Night terrors, the doctor said. Fairly common. Meaningless, so far as anyone knew.

Well. A lot of things were meaningless so far as anyone knew. A year before, what would she have thought of an ancient invasion of the lands of the Jaupati? Would she have cared at all? If she had heard of a rebellion among the critters of Quirk, or of a Fresco cleaning, or if someone had foreseen her being selected as an intermediary . . .

Before she lay down, she called Chad, who sounded every bit as weary as she did.

"Well?" she asked.

"We've got seven definite yesses so far. A whole bunch of others will call back. The best ones tell us we'll need at least eighteen or twenty, and a few more wouldn't hurt. The pre got the preacher."

"The right one?"

"Yes, the right one, plus a pinch hitter, just in case. The preacher was a little worried about the language barrier, but I said we will overcome, one way or another."

"Don't forget emergency rations, supplies, you know. We won't be eating Pistach food or using Pistach beds, and we'll be there at least a day, maybe longer."

"I know. Are they getting a ship?"

"The Inkleozese told them they had to."

"How long before it gets here?"

"Four days, minimum, and I'm going to sleep two of them," she said.

"Both of us," groaned Chad.

When she lay down on her bed, Sasquatch curled up next to her, his back against her legs, just to be sure she didn't wander off again. She fell asleep thinking of Carlos out there among the stars. Maybe he'd decide since nobody cared, he'd swim to shore.

And, she thought, firmly, decisively, without her usual vacillation, it wasn't up to her whether he did or not.

51
the cabal

A day or so after Benita left for Pistach-home, the members of Morse's cabal, sans Morse himself, had taken themselves down to the farm in Virginia where they'd set up camp in the house and waited for word from the predators. It was their opinion that though the predators had pretended to leave Earth, they wouldn't go far, and the best thing to do was wait at the farm for them to show up. They had been waiting for almost a week, and were not the better tempered for it.

"Nothing," Dink said in an aggrieved tone, coming in from his tenth circuit of the surrounding area. "No sign of them at all."

"Any word from NASA?" asked Briess, who was stretched on a cot by the window.

Dink hung up his jacket and slumped into the nearest chair. "The surveillance satellite that was kicked into a moon-loop got a clear picture of what are obviously ships, three of them, one big and two small. The satellite was a quick and dirty job, one loop only, so we don't know if they're still there."

"Are there more of them, that's what I want to know," said

McVane. "We got damn little information for all that money." He was slumped in a chair by the empty fireplace, his usually impeccable uniform rumpled, his tie loose, an open beer can at his elbow.

Dink shook his head ponderously. "Be thankful we got what we did. For such a hasty modification, we're doing well to get any pictures at all. The ships are huge. They could hold a lot more than we ever saw here on the ground."

"I wonder what the hell they're playing at!" growled McVane. "They've obviously pulled some stunt with the Pistach, for they now say the Confederation has no right to stop them coming here. They've been seen hunting and eating people all over the world, or at least the results have been seen, if not the critters themselves. What happened to the agreement we were supposed to have with them?"

"Could be they've decided they don't need us anymore," murmured Arthur. "If the Pistach have no authority to stop them, what do they need us for?"

Dink nodded. "Or maybe the Pistach weren't as bamboozled as they thought. We haven't heard anything about them recently, either."

"My understanding was that even if the Confederation does anything about the predators being here, it would take forever," commented Briess.

"Unless it's a unilateral action," said McVane. "Maybe the Pistach went on the warpath all by themselves."

"Our profilers say no," said Arthur. "They read the Pistach as nonviolent and conformist. Though they're criticism proof when they start working with new races, when they're finished their work is subject to review, and it seems they really care what other races think and say about them. They're not likely to risk unpopular action."

"Maybe those others, those what-you-call-'ems," murmured Briess. "Maybe they've stepped in. The ones that got Morse pregnant."

"Morse claims he's not pregnant," reminded Arthur.

"Yeah, well, he claims he's a Christian, too," said Briess, "but last time I looked, Christians don't assault their wives."

"Lupé?" asked Dink. "I didn't know that."

"Not Lupé, the ex-Mrs. Morse. You should read the medical reports." Briess sniggered.

"Let that alone," said McVane. "It's past. Focus on the current rapes and assaults, by the Inkleozese, even though it's only pro-life politicians and preachers they've done it to so far."

"Be thankful for small mercies," said Briess.

"You're pro-life," Dink commented.

Briess widened the slit of his mouth into an excruciating smile. "No, my friend, I'm merely anti-woman. I was born in the wrong system. Once female life expectancy exceeded that of men in the U.S., it was obvious we were doing something wrong."

"What you got against old ladies?" asked Dink. "Your mother was probably an old lady."

"Bingo," said Briess, with a chilly smile. "Let's change the subject, if you don't mind. Since it's obvious we're not getting anywhere waiting here, let's leave them a message and get back to Washington. Morse has already subpoenaed the so-called intermediary for another inquiry before his committee, and once he starts in on her sexual habits, with her husband testifying to her depravity, people will assume it's true that she had a relationship with the president and the ETs and possibly her dog."

"I don't like this," murmured Prentice Arthur. "It smacks too much of McCarthyism."

Dink snorted. "You wanna grow corn, somebody's got to turn over the dirt, Arthur! Now that we don't have independent counsels with unlimited budgets to do it, we'll have to pick up the spades ourselves. I suggest we get back and start digging."

"I hope you've got Bert dried out enough to be believable," said McVane. "When I saw him on 20/20 he certainly wasn't!"

"We've got him stashed away," said Dink, with a feral smile. "I'm told he responds well to pain."

They were interrupted by the blink of a red light and a hesitant beeping from a metal box by the window.

"There they are," breathed Briess. "Better late than never."

McVane was already on his feet beside the machine. "It doesn't read their signatures," he said doubtfully. "Too hot for a Wulivery or Fluiquosm, too cool for a Xankatikitiki. Too many for any of 'em."

"Where are they?" asked Dink, peering out the window.

"Over to our left, among the trees," muttered McVane.

Dink picked up his glasses, put on his jacket, and went out onto the rickety porch. From the end of it he had a good view of the trees. McVane and Arthur came out onto the porch behind him as Dink spoke over his shoulder. "Must be the invisible Fluiquosm wearing heated suits!"

A faint yelp came from behind him, and he turned to find himself alone on the porch. He went to the door and looked in to see Briess still hovering over the machine.

He knocked on the door frame. Briess looked up, and not seeing anyone, went out onto the porch himself. Nobody there but him. Very shortly thereafter, nobody there at all.

52
benita

Benita had thought there might be a quiet interlude before
the large ship arrived, but the morning after her return she
received a subpoena, dated several days before and routed
through the White House. She was to testify that day before
Morse's committee, this time about her sexual involvement
with the ETs and any current members of government. Even
though the president had told her to expect it, it made her
furious. It was all part of Morse's choreography, of course,
part of the shit ballet he hoped to stage.

Chad picked her up, as before, and they arrived at the
hearing chamber at the time specified to find the inquiry in
some disarray because Morse wasn't there. The vice chairman wasn't there. Several of Morse's staffers weren't there.
Eventually, someone was appointed to be chairman pro tem,
and Benita swore to tell the truth and was then accused of
sexual contact with the ETs and/or the president, et al.

"Where on earth did you hear such a thing?" she asked,
affronted.

"We ask the questions," muttered the senator, slightly red
in the face.

"Well, all I can say is that if you listen to alcoholics like my husband, from whom I am separated, he'll say anything anyone tells him to say for ten dollars or a drink, whichever is closest."

"Are you denying these allegations?"

"Of course I'm denying these allegations. They're ridiculous."

There was muttering, leaning, whispering. The interrogator, face rather red, leaned into his microphone. "Do you have any knowledge of where your . . . husband is, Mrs. Alvarez?"

She answered honestly. "I couldn't tell you where he is, sir. He's been working for Senator Morse for some time, so maybe the senator can tell you."

More consternation.

"Why do you claim he works for Senator Morse?"

"With the envoys here, it's almost impossible to do anything secretly, sir. According to the envoys, a Mr. Dinklemier and a Mr. Arthur have been paying Bert Shipton to make up stories about me on instructions from Senator Morse."

Whispers, covered mikes, people turning redder.

"Perhaps you can tell us about your relationship with the president?"

"We covered this ground previously, gentlemen, but I'll refresh your memories. I first saw the president in his office on the day after I delivered the envoys' message to Congressman Martinez. We talked for five or ten minutes, during which time he thanked me for my efforts. The door to the outer office was open during my visit, and General Wallace was standing in the doorway. The second time I met the president, his wife was there, and that was when he asked me to see if the envoys would take me to their planet for a firsthand view. I have just returned from there."

Consternation. Someone got up hastily and left the room.

"And since then?" asked the man with the gavel, his mouth remaining open as she replied.

"Since then, I have seen and talked with the president and his wife in company with Mr. Riley, who accompanied me on the expedition to Pistach-home and other worlds. During that journey we saw and were greeted by three other races besides the Pistach. These were the Flibotsi, the Thwakians, and the Vixbot. Our entire journey was recorded, and when the security people are through with the recordings, I'm sure they'll be shown to the American people, and to the world."

There was more whispering, more running back and forth, and finally the senator who had assumed the chair decided he didn't want it anymore. Sounding as severe and threatening as he was able to manage around the distractions, the chairman pro tem told her she was still under subpoena and would have to appear again later.

The big talk on the TV blather shows that night concerned the disappearance of all the pregnant men plus some others who had worked for them. Among them, it was alleged, was the intermediary's husband. Much was made of the fact that Bert had been scheduled to appear before the same committee Benita had been subpoenaed for, that she had denied his allegations, and that he himself had disappeared. Benita smiled at this, saying a brief litany of thanks to the Inkleozese, who had removed him even though he wouldn't be useful as a breeder. Getting Bert out of circulation relieved her mind a good deal. If he couldn't get a drink for a year or two, it should do him a world of good!

Some TV channels were still showing interviews with him, but they were obviously old ones. Though he didn't look drunk, precisely, he was definitely glassy eyed from something. The only hopeful item reported was that no further hearings were planned until Senator Morse could be found. Benita felt that by that time the situation would be either improved or lost. Either way, it would be long past crying about.

Next morning, the disappearances were still in the news. The Senate demanded an investigation. Lupé Roybal-Morse suggested that Morse may have been so upset by being pregnant that he simply went off to be alone. His colleagues pretended to believe that was impossible, though she knew him better than they did. Within a few hours, it was reported on CNN that every man used as a brooder had vanished. The president issued a statement saying he had been informed the Inkleozese had wanted to take them to a safe place, where they would not be harassed by the news media, that he was assured they would be returned.

Surprisingly, except for the religious far right (those who were left) nobody screamed much about it. Comics had a field day, of course. Jay Leno did a Morse-travelogue, to Bee or not to Bee. Actually, Benita thought, the Inkleozese looked more like wasps, but it was close enough to be funny.

Benita called Angelica, who seemed to be coping all right, though she wanted to know where her father was. Benita said she didn't know where he was being taken, which was true, astronomy not being her forte. "However, I'm assured he's safe, just as Carlos is safe. You don't have to worry about either of them."

"I haven't been. But then, I feel guilty because I haven't been. You know?"

"Remember what I told you about drowning, Angel. Try to keep your head above water."

The following day the disappearances were replaced in the headlines by reports of massive slaughters in Northern Ethiopia, coastal Bangladesh, and among the Chinese settlers in Tibet, with lots and lots of gory pictures, enough to keep the media scrambling for the next few weeks, even if nothing else happened at all.

Chiddy and Vess took five days to make their trip, arriving back on Earth in what *Star Trek* would call a shuttle, except that it was morphable. The big ship, they said, was on the back of the moon, a considerable distance from those of the predators. Benita phoned Chad, as arranged, and within the hour a parade of long black limousines bearing dark-suited "spiritual advisors" began to arrive at Benita's back door. Benita didn't see any of them. They came in the door, got into the elevator, and vanished. The Reverend—the president's spiritual advisor, the Big SA—wasn't scheduled to arrive until the President did.

The Inkleozese arrived by their usual form of transport: abrupt materialization. Her Exactitude arrived first. She provided Benita with both a tape and a disc of the recorded voice Benita had asked for, then suggested Benita go to the bathroom and stay there while they and their "baggage" transitted the living room. Since no one was willing to gamble on how things would turn out, everyone was being very careful of what Benita saw and didn't see, just in case she had to testify about it. She took the opportunity for a long, luxurious shower while poor Sasquatch, who'd tried a sniff at one of the Inkleozese and had been abruptly flattened for it, lay on the bathroom rug whining at her. Poor dog, he didn't know what to think or who to bark at or even who to smell.

Late that evening, right after the arrival of the Big SA and the president, it was Chad and Benita's turn. Benita had already arranged for Simon to do dog duty again, and he'd wished her well. She had hinted to him that something epochal was happening, so he'd feel better about all the bother she was causing him. She really didn't want to get back and find she had no job. She liked her job. Besides, if they were successful in their efforts, things would go back to more or less normal, on its way to being forgotten except by historians, and nobody would give her a pension for her part in it.

The shuttle delivered the last few of them to the larger ship on the moon, pausing there while the Inkleozese delivered cease and desist documents to the predator ships, denying their right to stay on Earth without decision by the Confederation. While they were waiting, all the Earthians had their pictures taken in front of the window wall of the big ship. The little "SAs" had been promised they could use the trip as a CV item later on, so pictures were absolutely essential, that and bits of moon rock and certificates signed by the president and by Chiddy or Vess. Chiddy protested at putting himself in the position of seeming to endorse the Earthian visit, when it was being required by the Inkleozese, so Chad suggested he write "Real moon rock, best wishes" in Pistach. It was doubtful anyone would ever know the difference.

While everyone slept a good bit of the time, all the waking hours were spent working. Half a dozen animatronics people were working with the recorded voice Benita had obtained from the Inkleozese, and all the artists (who would pretend to be little SAs, when they arrived at Pistach-home) had copies of a Fresco panel or panels, copies that had been enhanced, enlarged, and had the colors corrected by the FBI labs from those Chad had recorded during the previous trip. The conversation that went on about them was constant and fascinating, or so Benita thought. She wouldn't have dreamed there were that many things to say about artworks that all the little "SAs" agreed could be compared, at best, to Grandma Moses on a very bad day. The talk about color and composition and message went on, deep into every "night" that they were aboard. (Both Chad and Benita were grateful that the larger ship was able to prevent the exhaustion they'd felt in the smaller one.)

Though the humans occasionally encountered Chiddy and Vess, nothing was discussed where they would be able to hear it. The Inkleozese had assured Benita the Earthian quarters were strictly private, and the ship was large enough that the Pistach were encountered only at meals.

Each member of the group had been given a copy of Chiddy's journal also, as a guide to Pistach thought. At one point in the journey, the Big SA, looking very stern, asked Benita just what Chiddy meant when he wrote "dearest" Benita.

"Chiddy's an affectionate sort of person," she answered, after a moment's thought. "I assume he, or it, or ai, feels toward me pretty much the same way I feel about my dog, or perhaps, my dog about me, when I come home from work. I mean, that's a cross-species relationship, but we both have a sense of security and pleasure in it, and perhaps even rapture. Sasquatch does act rapturous sometimes."

"There is no physical . . . ah . . . ?"

"There is no physical ah," Benita confirmed. "Beyond what might amount to a scratch behind the ears. Not that intimacy would be impossible. Chad says he's fairly well convinced there's a point to point correspondence between their actual forms and any morphed form they adopt. Morphing isn't natural to them, you know. It's something they've discovered how to do, and it takes some kind of implanted electronic assist."

"Why do they do it?" he demanded.

"I think it has to do with exploration. If you're going to a planet that's all water, you need gills. If you're going to one that's all desert, you need a body that conserves moisture. And on any new planet, you need to be able to look like the natives while you're finding things out."

Though the Big SA had a very odd look on his face when she finished, Benita was quite satisfied with her analysis. It was probably as close to the truth as she could get.

The Big SA went on to ask her what she knew about the Pistach religion.

"Chiddy calls the Pistach god, Aitun. It means 'The one who is.' Chiddy says the Pistach don't presume to know what Aitun is up to or desires. They have a duty, however, to infer purpose from what they see and discover. They have inferred that as an intelligent race who can see that intelligence is a rarity among the stars, they must help spread intelligence throughout the galaxy. They read this as Aitun's possible intent without ever unequivocally saying it is Aitun's intent. They avoid saying what God wants or means. They regard races who do as prideful and arrogant.

"Chiddy also says there are over five thousand picky little gods among the races ai knows of," she said. "A lot of them inceptorish . . ."

"Inceptorish?"

"You've read the journal, Reverend. Inceptorish. Virile. Arbitrary, egocentric, and often belligerent. Anyhow, Chiddy says none of the five thousand have sufficient universality to be the god of everyone. Chiddy includes our Earthian gods in the five thousand."

"There is only one Earthian God," said the SA, in a ponderous tone.

"You are no doubt correct," said Benita. "But Chiddy says none of the ones humans talk about in the Western world are it, and none of the hundreds they talk about in the Eastern and undeveloped worlds are it, either."

They stopped on Inkleoza, to drop off the Inkleozese and their brooders and to pick up a couple of replacement assesors who were beyond breeding age. Chiddy said Inkleozese were needed on board, as they were the Confederation's accepted witnesses and attestors, but he thought the president and the male members of his entourage would be more relaxed with nonbreeding Inkleozese. Even though the Inkleozese and their brooders had stayed in a separate section of the ship, Benita and Chad noticed a definite lowering of tension when they were in transit again. The new Inkeleozese were very jolly, fatter than their predecessors and much less austere.

The balance of the trip was over far too soon. Each one of those playing the part of a little SA complained that he or she wasn't ready. Each one dithered, getting all his or her supplies packed into the smallest possible volume. When everyone was ready to disembark, each took his or her predetermined place in the procession. First the two Inkleozese, escorting the president, who was robed in blue with a blue headdress, looking like someone on a Mardi Gras float, but very dignified. Then Chiddy and Vess, escorting the Big SA, also clad in blue, also dignified, though more meditative. Then the little SAs in robes of a lighter and less piercing sapphire, two by two, thirty-six of them—including the specialists from Hollywood, carrying their special paraphernalia—all looking solemn and dedicated, some of them bearing "altars," large chests that held the equipment. Blue was a high caste color on Pistach planets, so Chiddy had told them, and the plan required that the Pistach realize these Earthians were very high caste and dead serious about the whole thing. Chad and Benita, being of infinitely lower rank, brought up the rear.

T'Fees and his group were there to meet them. Chiddy spoke to him while Vess translated to the humans. Then the Inkleozese spoke, very dignified, very stern. Then Chiddy spoke again. The gist of the whole thing was that T'Fees's interference with the way of life on Pistach-home was a matter for the Pistach to handle among themselves, but any philosophical changes that impacted upon the human race were outside Pistach's sole authority. Now that the members of the Confederation were involved, the Inkleozese were there to supervise the human race's attempt to get a grip on the situation.

T'Fees asked what they wanted.

The humans, said the lead Inkleoza, wanted to spend a night of meditation in the House of the Fresco, in the hope this would give them insight to aid their world in facing the grave tragedies which might be in the offing.

Benita was watching T'Fees. He turned slightly ocher.

"What tragedies are those?" he boomed.

"If the Pistach withdraw, Earth will be at the mercy of the predators, and Earth's leaders need to prepare for that eventuality," said the Inkleozese. "Certain other worlds, such as Pistach-home and Quirk, may also be at the mercy of the predators."

T'Fees looked startled. Benita thought he was surprised, as though aware for the first time that his own actions had consequences he might not have thought of. The surprise carried over to the crowd of his supporters, where there was a good deal of expostulation back and forth.

This was followed by a lengthy argument between the curators and the Inkleozese. Then the Big SA asked to speak, translated by Chiddy. He spoke of the necessity of working in accord with the single spirit of universal life and intelligence, but what he conveyed was mostly rhythm and elation. Vess had had an advance copy, so the translation was well worked out, and the humans had been coached. As the Big SA stayed strictly away from anything that could be considered a reference to any picky, inceptorish little Earth god, by the time he was finished, he had the whole crowd swaying and shouting either "Amen, hallelujah," or "Shavil, dashavil," which meant "Amen, hallelujah" in Pistach.

When that died down, the president spoke, again translated by Chiddy, saying that he and his advisors intended to pray for clarification of both the Earthian and the Pistach role in the galaxy. More talk followed, quite subdued, ending with the curators' permission to spend the night with the Fresco. A half dozen of them—not including Chiddy or Vess—would have to stay with the humans, however, just to be sure the Fresco came to no harm. T'Fees would come with them to be sure they were really interested in meditating, and the two Inkleozese would accompany the group. The humans bowed, the Pistach bowed, the Inkleozese bowed, T'Fees and his people bowed, and the whole procession went off up the stairs toward the House of the Fresco, lugging the altars containing, so Chiddy had informed the Pistach, their ritual materials. They had timed their arrival to coincide with the sunset, so they had to move very quickly.

Once inside, Benita and Chad shut the tall doors while the little SAs set up their altars, large carved wooden ones, upon which a ritual meal of cookies and root beer was set out in silver plates and faux crystal chalices. The Inkleozese and the Pistach, including T'Fees, joined in the ritual repast to be polite, for Chiddy had told them that human foods were all quite harmless. Which they were, of course, if one didn't count sarsaparilla-induced unconsciousness as a harm.

Benita and Chad watched both the Pistach and the Inkleozese. Within moments, T'Fees and the Pistach elders were nodding on their reclining boards, and shortly they were completely out of it. The Inkleozese were still quite wide awake.

"Not as close physiologically as we hoped," murmured Chad.

"Maybe even less close psychologically," murmured Benita in return. "It's a gamble, but they've cooperated so far. Let's get on with it."

The battery packs came out of the hollow altars, and bright lamps illuminated every line and surface of the Fresco. Powerful projectors were adjusted to show new outlines on each panel; the "spiritual advisors" took off their robes and put on their smocks; drop cloths were spread beneath the panels; and paint odors filled the House. There was at least one painter for each panel, more on the panels that needed the most help, and while Chad and Benita played endless rounds of poker with the president and the Big SA, all the artists who had pretended to be SAs went at the business of painting over the old Fresco to make it show precisely what the Pistach had thought it showed prior to the cleaning. The Inkleozese, without a word of protest, wandered around behind them, watching the work go on.

They used fast-drying paints. There was no display of artistic temperament. Each one of them was a professional artist who could work to a deadline, and each had already figured out exactly how he or she would proceed. They had agreed on a consistent style—more Diego Rivera than Michelangelo—and each artist had a predrawn overlay for his or her particular panel plus "character studies" of the main characters, so they'd be consistent from panel to panel. A great deal of attention had been paid to the figure of Canthorel, and great trouble was taken everywhere it appeared. Canthorel became three-dimensional, individual, recognizable. Since every painter had a fortune in spray cans and mini-rollers and a huge selection of sponges and brushes, large sections of the surfaces were covered quickly. Meantime, the group of puppeteers put together their apparatus and began rehearsing.

When the four nonartists/nonactors got tired of poker (the Big SA was the big winner, fourteen dollars and twenty cents, and the president accused him of having had help), they watched, fascinated, as weapons disappeared from the Fresco to be replaced by symbols of peaceful progress, as Mengantowhai became a sage and guide instead of a bloodthirsty oppressor, and as the Pokoti race was differentiated from the Jaupati race. Since both races were extinct, it didn't really matter what they'd looked like so long as they were different from one another. Kasiwees was murdered all over again, this time by a vengeful Pokoti. Mengantowhai passed on his virtue and power to Canthorel, who now had a very high-caste blue aura painted around him. The wine jars that had turned into assaulted Jaupati turned back into wine jars being virtuously fractured by abstemious Pistach.

The level of artistry exhibited that night was very, very high—a little slick, Chad murmured—but very high. Chiddy had been quite right when he said humans excel in artistry. There was simply no comparison between these painters and the original painter of the Fresco. The earlier panels had had no composition, no perspective, they were deficient in color, and no Pistach had ever heard of chiaroscuro. Perhaps it was the way the Pistach eyes interpreted their world, or perhaps representational art just wasn't their thing. Whatever talent the Pistach lacked, human people had had it from their infancy. Benita found herself imagining all those old Cro Magnons sitting around the fire talking about Ugh's lampsoot technique with mastodons, and how beautifully Glub used ocher to shade the flanks of the horse.

She also wondered what Chiddy would say when he saw it, as he eventually would. The president asked, "Will they understand what they see, or are their eyes too different?"

"They'll understand," Benita murmured. "They've been raving about the Sistine Chapel ever since they arrived."

Along a couple of hours before sunrise, the artists finished up their panels and began circulating, critiquing one another's work, catching little bits of this and that, symbols that weren't clear, and so forth. Oddly enough, the Inkleozese did a fair bit of this too, suggesting a change here, an emphasis there. Benita watched them closely, and if she had had to say what they were thinking, she would have guessed they were amused, interested, and approving.

When everyone was finished, anyone would swear the Fresco had always been that way. Panel number sixteen, where Canthorel leaves Jaupat, had been considerably modified. He still left Jaupat, but with him went a winged symbol of the future, fluttering at his shoulder, and from the winged figure's mouth came a ribbon lettered with the Pistach words that meant, *In time I will return.* There were also ideograms for the name Glumshalak, which Chiddy had included in his journal. As foreshadowing, it was neatly done.

It was, all in all, an excellent job, one so far above the original that its divine inspiration could hardly be doubted, particularly by Pistach who had never seen Earthly art. There was still a final step, however. When all the supplies had been put away, Chad unpacked a sprayer that contained a mix of soot, grease, and odds and ends of other pollutants mixed with a chemical dispersant. Standing well back, he went from panel to panel, spraying goop into the air until they were all just slightly hazed, nothing completely veiled, but nothing looking new, either, about the way they would have been in a few more weeks of candle smoke. A second spray gun contained piñon smoke mist, to eliminate any lingering paint smells. Benita had suggested piñon smoke, because it was one totally unfamiliar to the Pistach, or so Chiddy had told her.

When all the equipment was packed up, everyone got back into his or her robes. The actors assembled their devices and the Pistach were nudged into wakefulness among smells of incense and sounds of drums and chimes. The room was dimly candlelit.

"Oh, Canthorel, come to us," intoned the Big SA, in passable Pistach. "Show us the truth!"

T'Fees pushed himself higher on his legs. The Pistach elders shifted, staring at one another. One of them asked Chad, through his translator, "Is this evocation of the sacred persons of other races customary?"

"Only after hours of meditation," Chad responded. "Oh. Look there!" He pointed into the gloom.

In the dim glow of the candle flames the figure of Canthorel emerged from the darkness, garbed in a radiant blue aura, taller than a normal Pistach, an absolute replica of the Canthorel figures in the Fresco. The figure bowed, only slightly, gestured widely, then opened its mouth and cried, in Pistach:

"I have returned to restore my work and to reestablish the teachings of Mengantowhai."

The Pistach opened their eyes wide. T'Fees muttered in an ugly voice, and three of the more robust elders silenced him.

The image of Canthorel went on. "Into this place came an evil-doer to change my works and cast doubt upon our purpose. The infamy of this evil-doer was foreseen. Glumshalak came to cover the false works so they might not hinder the spiritual progress of my people. Into this place, another evil-doer has come, and there the miscreant stands, the one who wished to negate Glumshalak's virtuous deeds. Now, I have returned to reassert the value of Pistach life, the work they do, the order they bring. Go forth and assist the worlds of the galaxy, remembering always the commandments given me by Mengantowhai:

"Where you see an unfruitful tree, make it bear.

"Do as little as possible.

"Do it as painlessly as possible.

"Be responsible for having done it."

The voice dwindled away, the aura faded, the figure moved toward the altar. A smoke lit from within, as by blue fire, exploded in the House, and Chad and Benita ran to thrust open the doors to let in the first pale rays of dawn. When the smoke cleared, Canthorel was gone.

Half a dozen Earthians went about the room, extinguishing the few candles, leaving it virtually dark. Tambourines and drums continued their tinka-tinka-tinka, bom bom bom.

The Pistach were soundless, speechless. T'Fees struggled with the three elders who were holding him down. The humans chanted, swaying in time to the drums, giving the Pistach time to recover.

Eventually, the leader of the Pistach elders asked the president, "Did you see Canthorel? Was he indeed present among us?"

The president nodded, saying truthfully, "I saw a marvelous figure emerge from the Ground of Canthorel. One moment he was not there, the next moment, he was."

"Did you hear him speak?"

The president said yes, he had heard the figure speak, but he was not sure he understood all that Canthorel had said. Would the elders explain it to him?

"Later," murmured the elder. "Oh, yes, but later."

The sounds of drums and tambourines faded. The Pistach rose from their reclining boards, all of them still staring at the place Canthorel had been, before he disappeared. Since their sleeping position was no different from their resting or sitting position, there was no indication they had drifted off. Even T'Fees seemed unaware of having done so.

Through her own translator, Benita heard one say to another, "I'm afraid I dozed off there for a moment. Did I miss anything?"

The other answered, "Just sitting and meditating until Canthorel came. You saw that!"

"Oh, yes. I saw that."

The room was dim, the darkness broken only near the top of the dome where the clerestories admitted a pale glow. All the Pistach, including T'Fees, were so occupied with the vision of Canthorel that none of them glanced at the walls, and had they done so, it was still too dim to see anything. Benita remembered Chiddy's description of the first time he had seen it. People came in and went out, they didn't really look.

As the Pistach moved toward the door, she wandered toward the wall, peering at the Fresco, reaching with tentative fingers to stroke the dim figures that bright morning would disclose. The True Fresco of Canthorel.

53

the morning after

The Pistach elders were on the stairs before the humans emerged in the same order as they had gone in, followed by the Inkleozese. All of them moved slowly downward toward T'Fees's supporters, who were gathered below. As T'Fees neared them, he hastened his steps to join his colleagues. The rest of the group paused not far away.

The elder Inkleozese, the Assessor Emeritus, turned to face the human delegation and cried:

"Do you consider that your meditation has been successful?"

The crowd grew silent as Chiddy translated this question. The president nodded, smiled, and intoned, "We spent the night praying the meaning of the Fresco would be clear to us. When morning came, we saw a vision of Canthorel. All of us saw it. The human race is very grateful for Canthorel's return."

Chiddy turned pale green. His mouthparts trembled, as did his voice as he translated this statement. The crowd around T'Fees stirred ominously. Several of them cried out in objection, but an elder silenced them with a sharp reproof, as though to say the translation was accurate.

When the crowd stilled, the president continued. "We are reassured that the Pistach may go on assisting the human race. As Canthorel said, it is their job. We are reassured to know that the previous misunderstanding was caused by an evil-doer in an attempt to obscure both Canthorel's great artistry and the authority that had been passed through him to the current athyci in a direct line of descent from Mengantowhai.

"The Fresco makes it perfectly clear," the president concluded. "There can be no question about it."

Chiddy, who was by now almost ashen, translated once more.

Confusion. Consternation. Pallor. Babble.

"Heads up, people," said Chad, tapping the president on the arm. "To the ship, now."

As the Earthians started for the ship, a mob of Pistach with T'Fees in the vanguard surged up the stairs toward the House of the Fresco at an eight-legged gallop, all shrilling at one another like locusts. The humans ignored this rather ostentatiously, as they strode confidently toward the ship with heads up, drums beating, tambourines chinking, and the president reaching out to shake the manipulators of every Pistach that he passed while the Big SA God-blessed them right and left. While the others blocked the doorway, the artists went aboard, opened up the altars and took out all the paint cartons, brushes, rollers, smocks, projectors, and drop cloths and put them down the conversion chutes along with the lighting equipment and the elaborate animatronic figure of Canthorel, complete with aura. Also down the chutes went the voice recording in Pistach provided earlier by the Inkleozese. It had been done, so the Assessor Emeritus had told Benita, by a Pistach actor who happened to be on tour in Inkleoza. He had been well paid for the work, and for keeping his mouthparts fastened thereafter.

Robes, candles, bells, drums and other ritual impedimenta went into the altars, which were left conveniently close to the loading ramp, wide open, so anyone could see the contents. The artists split off, some toward food, some toward beds, while the president, the Big SA, Chad and

Benita went into the dining room, which was near the hatch. The first two nonhumans into the ship were the Inkleozese, who also entered the salon.

"I take it you don't disapprove of our actions," said the president to the elder one, the Assessor Emeritus, as he led the way to the kitchen where Chad was starting a pot of coffee.

The assessor rubbed her forelegs together, pondering. "I am not appointed to approve or disapprove of human conduct. I merely observe. What you have done breaks no rule of our people. Because this effort of yours aligns the Pistach with their traditional inclinations, those of self-approving benignity, and because we owed a debt to the intermediary, we cooperated in this effort. We are unaware that it disrupts any galactic trend."

A few other weary humans trickled into the dining room, broke out Earthian stores and began fixing breakfast. Through the view screen they could see arguments erupting all up and down the Fresco stairs. After about an hour, Chiddy came trudging up the ramp into the ship, along with a few of T'Fees's followers, who stopped just inside the door to run their pincers through the stuff inside the hollow altars, chattering in confusion. Eventually Chiddy came to the dining area.

"There has been a miracle," Chiddy said, giving Benita a strange, almost doleful look.

"Oh?" she asked. "What miracle was that."

"The Fresco changed, overnight."

"That couldn't be," the president said. "It was dark when we went in last night, so we couldn't really see the Fresco, but we were there the whole time and we didn't see a miracle. When daylight came this morning, the Fresco was exactly as Glumshalak's Compendium describes it, though far better done, of course. I'm afraid Glumshalak was no artist."

"Canthorel spoke to you!"

The president said, "We saw a figure who resembled the Canthorel in the Fresco, though ai offered us no proof of identity. The figure said it had come to repeat aisos message to the Pistach people. Presumably Canthorel's Fresco is as it is by the will of Aitun."

"It could be any way at all by the will of Aitun," snapped Chiddy. "Aitun lets everything happen that can happen! It is up to intelligence to select!"

"Well, then," said the Big SA, "*Something* selected it the way it is. Something that we know is very good because it chooses to avoid death and pain and horror and hurting creatures, which the false Fresco certainly would have caused. I can't imagine Canthorel being on the side of predators eating humans, or eating Pistach, can you? On Earth we say, don't look a gift horse in the mouth."

"It wasn't the way we remembered it from when T'Fees cleaned it," mumbled Vess. "Benita and Chad were there, they know!"

"Well," Benita said, with considerable hauteur, "what I remember most about the way it was before was that there was a tree in every panel, and there's still a tree in every panel. And I saw the form of Canthorel in a burst of smoke and light saying the work was originally beautiful."

"So I had always believed," said Chiddy.

"Well, the one I saw when I was here before wasn't all that beautiful, which means some evil-doer must have come along and painted over it. That was when Canthorel inspired Glumshalak to provide the Compendium in its place. And when Glumshalak's efforts were thwarted by T'Fees, someone—and I'd like to believe it was Canthorel—put it back the way it was supposed to be."

"The way it was at first?" said Chiddy, still sounding somewhat indignant.

"Well, Chiddy," she said, "it certainly didn't make sense the way it was when T'Fees cleaned it. Would you choose to put something like that on your walls to guide your people?"

Chiddy gestured, no.

"And it was badly painted, too," said the president thoughtfully. "Chad took pictures of it, and it was quite dreadful. If I had been Canthorel, I'd have been as upset at the lack of artistry as at the misrepresentation of what I was teaching! We feel so fortunate that Canthorel came to set things right. Even T'Fees saw it happen!"

Chad voiced agreement, backed by all the little SAs.

"T'Fees did see it happen," Chiddy agreed. "T'Fees just isn't willing to believe any of his own eyes!"

The Big SA took this as a cue to speak at length on the subject of belief, quoting Scripture to the point, citing several of the Fresco panels as exemplary. Benita thought he should have been an actor instead of an SA, though maybe one had to be an actor to be a Big SA. In any case, Chiddy had to stand there listening out of Pistach politeness, until the president whispered in the SA's ears, and he let Chiddy escape dazedly back down the exit ramp.

Benita watched Chiddy go. He seemed depressed. She felt a little sorry for him, the way she had felt sorry for the children, sometimes, when she had had to say "no playing until homework" or go "write your spelling words." One had to do it, but one still regretted the sadness it caused. Of course later, at least in Angelica's case, there had been the jubilation at getting an A, so it was all worth it. She wondered when Chiddy would realize he was getting an A.

He evidently passed along the comment that T'Fees had wilfully chosen to restore an evil version of the Fresco, for a little later they saw T'Fees led by in shackles. Benita said she hoped they wouldn't hurt him, and was assured they intended only to regress him to age twelve, select him as a quality improvement consultant—for which job they already knew he had skills—and provide him with rigorous training.

Despite the combined feelings of weariness, relief, and subdued elation that most of the humans felt, there was also unspoken agreement among them that getting out before too many questions could be asked might be an excellent idea. Chad saw a number of the Chapter members standing at the foot of the stairs, and he walked over to suggest the immediate departure of the Earthians. The Chapter members seemed more than willing to see them go as soon as possible. It was obvious that the members needed to get their heads together and talk about what had happened. They were shifting from one set of feet to another, twitching their mouthparts, exhibiting all the signs of distraction. They were not too distracted, however, to summon Chiddy and Vess and the two Inkleozese, who seemed even jollier than usual as they agreed it was time to leave Pistach-home.

Benita and Chiddy were standing beside the ramp when Carlos came from the direction of the village, walking beside a Pistach whom Benita thought she knew. As they came closer, she identified Chiddy's nootch, Varsi, the one she'd given the scarf to on her first trip to Pistach-home. Varsi, the nice one.

"Ke greets someone," called the nootch.

"Mother," said Carlos. "It's wonderful to see you. Is everything working out well? Varsi tells me there's been a miracle."

Benita took a deep breath and held it, then blinked a time or two. "Carlos?" she said, uncertainly.

"It's been fun here," he said, smiling. "But I'm dying to get back to school. I've really let things slide there, and it's going to take major effort to get back on track." He moved past her, holding his hand out to Chiddy. "Chiddy, good to see you again. Your nootch has told me so many stories about you . . ."

"Wha . . . ?" Benita said to the nootch, as Carlos moved on toward the ramp.

"For someone, a gift," warbled the nootch, through her translator device. "In return for a gift received. A small expression of esteem."

Ke bowed, and moved toward the ramp, following Carlos.

Benita turned to glare at Chiddy. "You *did* it."

"I did not," he said, moving his shoulders from side to side in Pistach negation. "You told me not to. I wouldn't have gone against your will, Benita. You know I respect you too much to do that."

"Then who?" she demanded.

"Varsi," he confessed, almost in a whisper. "Ke told me when we got here. It was while we were gone. Ke couldn't bear to let him be so unhappy. Not even if he wished it."

"What did she . . . I mean it . . . I mean the nootch, do?"

"Not much, really," Chiddy said, looking anywhere but at her.

"But, is that really him?"

"Are you really you?"

"What do you mean?"

"Varsi did Carlos a welcome reversal, as ton'i, Vess and I, did for you when ton'i first met. Someone had . . . ghosts. Someone had troubles. Ghosts and troubles were sent away."

"That's all?"

"Yes. My nootch says it didn't take a lot. Not a regression, which ke would not have had the authority to do, anyhow. Ke told me it was just a little envy removal. Just enough so Carlos did not measure everything against some other person. Plus just enough forgetting not to resent the world. And then, too, ke has been giving him sleep lessons in good manners." He frowned, or did with his face what Pistach do when they are troubled. "Do you want to report ker to the athyci? Do you want ker to be punished? If so, Vess and Chiddy should also be punished."

Wordless, Benita shook her head. No. No. Punished for what?

They boarded the ship, and she went on down a main gangway into her own roomlet, where she found Carlos reading a book that he said the "reverend with the president" had given him.

"It looks interesting," he remarked. "Will we sleep on the flight home, like we did before?"

She shook her head, still wordless. He looked different. It was in the eyes, the muscles around the mouth. He looked at her, not past her, as though he saw her.

"We won't have to sleep so much, no. It's a big ship, and evidently being on a big ship is less tiring. There's an empty room next door to this one, that you can have."

"Hey," he said. "Cool. It'll be fun hearing about what happened on the way."

And without fuss, he departed to the next roomlet, taking the book with him.

During the trip, Carlos was charming. He was respectful to Chad, boyishly awed by the president, sincere and intent with the Big SA. He talked art endlessly with the artists, asking intelligent questions. During the trip, Benita watched him, bouncing back and forth between awe and jealousy. A nootch! Who wasn't even human! And look what she'd managed to do!

During the trip, Chiddy and Vess stayed away from the humans and busied themselves ostentatiously with running the spaceship, though both Benita and Chad knew it hardly took any effort to run.

At breakfast on the first "day" of the journey, they asked one of the Inkleozese what the feeling had been on Pistachhome about what had happened.

"Yes, please tell us," murmured the president. "How were they reacting?"

The Inkleozese made a chuckling sound. "The majority of the people of Pistach have decided it was a miracle. The Chapter closed the House of the Fresco after T'Fees's people cleaned it, so few if any of the Pistach actually saw it the way it was, though rumors flew, of course. Since any wise government knows it is best to go along with the majority of the people, it is very likely that the curators will confirm that it was a miracle and leave well enough alone. There is precedent for this. On a former occasion, as Chiddy may have told you, the Chapter decided not to upset the status quo by inquiring into the real content of the Fresco. Since the current Fresco maintains that status quo, they will no doubt come to a like conclusion.

"Of course," and she actually laughed, "they have never seen human art. Our sisters who visited you on Earth have seen it. They have told us all about the remarkable talents of humans. It was amusing to see the Chapter members teetering on their ethical slide, deciding whether to inquire about or even mention the artistry of Earthians. Several of them finally got up the courage to ask me if I had seen Earthian art. Of course, I had to be honest. I told them, no, I had not."

Then she turned to the president and asked softly, "Have the Pistach really done so much for your people?"

"They really have," he murmured. "A lot of things they speak of doing are things many humans have wanted to do but have never been able to muster a mandate to get them done. Things like legalizing drugs to take out the profit motive. Or paying teachers the way we do athletes, depending on how effective they are. Or getting rid of weapons whose only purpose is to kill people."

"Is a mandate necessary?"

"If you're going to overcome an economic incentive, yes."

"Logic has no part?"

"No part at all. People can see the problem, they're not stupid, but they can't influence the legislators the way money can. Even when bad situations go on and on until the people are desperate for a correction, even when they threaten legislators with voting them out, the money still prevails."

"It is hard for me to see how this could happen."

Chad said, "The legislators react to a problem by writing a law, let's say to put repeat drunk drivers in jail. The liquor industry objects, because they don't like a lot of discussion about drunkenness, it hurts their image. The legislators react by amending the law to create a commission to study how best to jail drunk drivers. Then, when the budget bills come along, they fund only the commission. The appointees to the commission include representatives of the liquor industry.

"This allows the legislators to claim success, because the law got voted in. The liquor industry also claims success, because they made sure the law won't work.

"The next step is to hire a lot people to work for the commission, many of whom are also liquor industry supporters, and the commission begins to issue long, complicated, vaguely pointless reports. Now, however, there are jobs involved, and legislators can't get rid of jobs, even useless ones.

"Then, repeatedly, the lawmakers amend the law further, tweaking this and changing that, but always adding more jobs—until we have a bureaucratic monstrosity that's in the business of helping the liquor industry prevent legislation against drunk drivers. That's the way our Forestry Service got to be owned by the lumbermen, and our DEA got to be owned by the drug cartels, welfare got to be owned by a social work hierarchy, and schools got to be owned by professional educationalists. None of them work, because that's not what they're designed to do."

The Inkleozese nodded. "I see. The Pistach wouldn't accept that, of course. It's ineffectual."

The president nodded. "The Pistach don't have opposing political parties shooting one another out of the sky just for the fun of it, or legislators who sell their votes. The Pistach are way ahead of us technologically, and they're blessed pragmatists, and we need them. We really, really do."

"And you think you'll achieve Tassifoduma?" She cocked her head at him.

Benita, watching, saw something of the praying mantis in her stance and realized with a shock that if they didn't achieve Tassifoduma, all the men on Earth would be useable as brooders by the Inkleozese. The Assessor Emeritus turned her slightly mocking gaze on Benita, who flushed and looked at her feet.

The president murmured, "Nothing is ever sure in the world . . . in the galaxy, but we'll certainly come closer with the Pistach than we would without."

Benita and Chad went with the Inkleozese as she left the room.

"And how do you rationalize this little . . . joke you played on the Pistach?" the Inkleozese asked, staring at Benita and Chad.

Benita looked at Chad, and then at the ceiling.

He said, "I've heard Benita quote her grandfather about civilized people trying to cope with the problems caused by belief in savage gods left over from barbaric yesterdays. It seemed to us that since Chiddy and Vess have been helping us with that problem, it's only right we should help them with similar problems in our turn. They don't tell us everything while they're helping us—Chiddy's journal made that clear—so it would be quid pro quo if we didn't tell them everything while we're helping them."

The Assessor Emeritus was dropped off on Inkleoza, still laughing every time she looked at the president, and after that, the humans went on home.

Chiddy and Vess joined Benita as she was leaving the ship, the last human to do so but Carlos. Before the Pistach took the large ship back to Inkleoza, Carlos was getting a lift to California so he could make his apologies to the foundation.

"We'll be back in a few days," said Chiddy, rather formally. "You can take a few days to figure out what you're going to tell me," he said. "About what happened."

She gave him a long, level look. "I don't need a few days, Chiddy. Do you respect the Inkleozese?"

"You know we do."

"If the Inkleozese approve of what happened, why would you expect me to tell you anything?"

"I don't know," he said, making his peculiar, not-human shrug.

"You and Vess were very selective about what you told us, but I don't hold it against you."

"Um," he said, giving her a strange look.

When he returned in a much smaller ship, several days later, she asked, "How are things back on Pistach-home?"

He said thoughtfully, "Very . . . settled. They've decided to take images of the Fresco. And every planet is going to have a set of the images on the walls of its Fresco House. That way, no evil-doer can corrupt us just by repainting one set. And they'll put them behind glass and clean them every season, so everyone can see them, and there won't be any doubt that we're good people . . ."

"I never had any doubt," she said, adding, not quite truthfully, "Neither did the president."

54

on inkleoza

SOMETIME

Senator Byron Morse, together with the members of his cabal, plus several hundred other pregnant men, spent the last months of their confinement in idle luxury at a rest home, high in the hills of a lovely forested area on Inkleoza. Fed and massaged and petted, they awaited deliverance, which, when it came, was far worse than anything they had ever experienced. Far, far worse, though it was over in a few hours, more or less, except for the few who didn't survive, Briess among them. When the chewing started, Briess had committed suicide, something the Inkleozese had never thought to guard against.

Afterward, temporarily tranquilized and permanently traumatized, they spent a brief convalescence in somewhat modified luxury before being returned home, along with Bert Shipton, who had been fed and housed in much less luxury during his stay on the planet.

Senator Byron Morse, Dink Dinklemier, and Prentice Arthur were dropped off on Morse's doorstep shortly after Christmas, a little over a year after they left home. They entered to find the house empty and dusty. A note on the coffee table was dated a full year before:

"By . . . don't know when you're getting back. The Pistach say when you've had a baby. I thought we covered that in prenup! Funny, huh? The governor appointed a replacement for you in the Senate since you had less than two years and were going to be gone over a year of it. She's a Democrat, wouldn't that frost you? When those Inkleo-whatsits said they'd be using you and the other pro-life people as brooders whenever they needed to, most states chose pro-choice or women candidates instead. Like you always used to say, motherhood and careers don't mix!

"Still, it's not the end of the world. Your old law partner called. He's wanting you to come back to work, filing class actions against the Pistach. Guns have taken to shooting the shooter instead of the shootee—usually some guy trying to rob a liquor store, though the other day it was some high school kid trying to knock off his teachers—and some munitions people are claiming interference with trade. I'm going down to Mexico for the holidays, with Mama. Acapulco, maybe. Get a little sun, a little relaxation. I'll go on back to Baltimore with her. No point my staying here all alone in this house. When you come in, call me. Let me know how you are. Love, Lupé."

He poured himself a scotch, and invited the others to partake while he went back to the kitchen to call Janet and ask about the boys.

"I just got back," he said.

"I figured it would be any time now," she said in a dry voice, totally unlike herself. "It must have been a terrible experience for you."

"I don't remember anything about it," he lied.

"Lucky you," she remarked. "I remember all about my pregnancies, one right after the other. I had no rest between times at all, even though you hated it when I was pregnant! It really surprised me when you let that ET get to you."

"I didn't let her. That's not true! I was raped," he cried.

"Oh, come on, By. Raped? Did you call for help? Did you fight?"

He snarled, "I was in no condition to do either. You think

I'd have done this willingly? My life has been completely disrupted."

She chuckled, a totally unfamiliar sound. "Well, so was mine, over and over."

"No, Janet, it's not the same thing, that was your duty, but I've been robbed of my life. I've been forced to continue a pregnancy I didn't want."

"It was only an inconvenience, By." She laughed. "You wouldn't let me have that excuse."

"Janet, damn it, stop laughing! I want to talk to the boys."

"Stop laughing? By, when I heard you were pregnant, the load seemed to drop from my shoulders. You know, I giggled for two solid days, and I haven't been hungry since. I've dropped fifty pounds, I've got a good job, and the boys tell me I look great. I'll ask the boys to call you, By, but they were so embarrassed, your being pregnant by an ET, I'm not sure they'll do it anytime soon. I sent you a letter. Lupé said she put it on your bedside table."

Before he could bellow, she had hung up on him. He went upstairs, found the dusty letter and opened it: just a line of text and a photograph. He stared at it.

Dink called from the foot of the stairs. "By? You all right?"

"Get out," the senator yelled. "You and Arthur get out of here. I want to be by myself!"

He heard the door shut behind them. Janet looked marvelous in the picture. God, he didn't remember she'd ever looked like that. And the boys . . . the two boys. They looked so much like her. They didn't look anything like him. Why hadn't he seen that? They didn't look anything like him at all! And that horrible squirming thing on Inkleoza hadn't looked like him either!

Bert Shipton was dropped off at his home in Albuquerque. He had forgotten it was being repossessed, a fact of which he was forcefully apprised by the new owners when they found him ransacking the kitchen for beer. He'd been keeping himself sane by anticipating the beer he would drink when he got back to Earth, and now here he was, and there wasn't any. At loose ends, he wandered down the street,

inking he'd stop in to see Larry Cinch. Larry was out in the
lley, fixing his car.

"Well, stranger," said Larry, wiping his hands on a greasy
g. "Haven't seen you in a year or better. Thought you'd
ied. Say, isn't that a kick about Benita?"

"What about her?" Bert wanted to know.

"She's some high mucky-muck in Washington. Special at-
aché for something or other to the U.N. Sorry about the
ee-vorce, but you're prolly better off."

"What dee-vorce?"

"She married somebody else. Since nobody could find
ou, and the ETs said you'd prolly been eaten, the president
ot you declared dead by special act of Congress. Part of a
ompensation package for the intermediary."

"Hell, I'm not dead. Never was dead!"

"I'll bet nobody knows you're alive! If that don't frost the
ake. Here, have a beer. Any man just recent dead deserves
 beer."

Bert took it in hand and drank deeply. His face turned
:d, he choked, then spewed the contents across the fence
ith a cough that reached down into his thighs. He felt as
ough his insides were coming out. Another sip brought
e same reaction.

"You're one, huh," said Larry, with a sympathetic shake of
e head. "That's too bad."

"I'm one what?" gasped Bert.

"One of those that shouldn't drink. The ETs, they've put
me stuff in the air. It's to keep people from endangering
ther people. People who get nasty when they drink can't
rink. They heave it up. People who can't drive safely can't
rive. They forget how. Simple, huh? Nobody can smoke
ntil they're eighty-five, and people who plan to shoot
ther people go into screaming fits if they touch a gun. Ei-
er that or the gun shoots them. Gun sales are down over
 ghty percent.

"Funny how we didn't know that most people who
ought guns were really thinking about killing people?
urns out they were, though. Even me. I have this kind of
ntasy about killin' my wife an' her mother. Didn't ever take

it serious, but got to admit, I'd thought about it. So, I can't
buy a gun, but I can drink, so long as it's no more than one
beer an hour, no more than five in any one day."

After a few minutes of watching Larry enjoying his beer,
Bert decided to go see if he could find somebody else to talk
to. He wandered down to the police station. Though he'd
spent some time locked up, he also had friends there.
Sergeant Wilkes and Joe Keene and . . . lots of people.

The place was like a graveyard.

"Hey," he yelled. "Gimme a little service here."

Wilkes came out of the office and stared at him in astonishment. "Bert? I thought you was dead."

"I'm not dead, Jim," Bert replied testily, repeating: "Never
was dead."

"Well, I be damned," said the sergeant. "Hey, you hear
about Benita?"

"Larry tole me."

"That was somethin, wasn't it? Remember how she used
to go down to the shelter to hide out when you was on a
rampage? Boy, you two used to get into it. You used to
whack her a good one, ever now and then." He shook his
head sadly. "None of that stuff happens anymore."

"Whatta you mean, none of that stuff? Wives don't drive
men crazy anymore? That'd be the day."

The sergeant shook his head. "Hardly ever. It just don
happen like it used to. I think it's something in the air, yo
know. Like the antidrunk dust." He rearranged some paper
on the desk, raising a cloud of ordinary dust in the proces
"Heard your house got sold."

"Damn Benita! She didn't pay the mortgage."

"You know, if you need a job or a place to sleep, yo
should go down to that shelter where she used to go. It's no
for women anymore. They call it a Glusi Center now. Like
homeless shelter. Got some real good programs for peop
sort of . . . at loose ends, you might say."

Bert figured he was at loose ends. Until he could get hol
of Benita. Make her pay him some alimony or somethin
He'd have to think about that.

His feet remembered the way to the shelter, even if h

rain didn't. It was still right where it had been, in back of
he old Methodist church, but it had a new sign.

Glusi Center
Life Plans for the Needy

Inside, a pleasant young woman helped him fill out a
questionnaire, had him hold his ideogram in front of a ma-
hine, then gave him a card that told him where to get his
lothes washed, where to get dinner that night, and a bed to
leep in, where to breakfast tomorrow, and where to go to
vork the next morning. "Free." She smiled. "All the services
re free. And when you go to work tomorrow, you'll get an-
ther card with the next day's schedule on it, and on week-
nds, you get weekend cards for recreation activities,
novies, or sports. All free."

"Wha'f I don't feel like working?" he asked, summoning
ruculence.

"That's fine. You do what you like. If you'd rather lie
round all day, you can do that, but it gets pretty boring,
ou know, when you can't drink or smoke and there's no TV
ntil evening and you can't loiter."

"Whadda you mean, can't loiter?"

"Loitering isn't allowed. Streets are for transit. Everyone
s happier if he's going somewhere and doing something. If
ne isn't working, one should be enjoying life, meditating,
ecreating, relaxing in some appropriate place. If you'd
ather meditate or relax than work, that's fine, here's a list of
neditation and relaxation centers."

"And if I don't want to meditate?" he cried, outraged.

"That's fine," she said. "That's perfectly fine. We'll find
omething else for you to do."

Bert wandered out, feeling aimless. He should, he felt, be
eally angry about moocow, but somehow, it was all too
nuch effort. The streets were empty except for people ob-
iously going somewhere. And he couldn't drink beer, or
nything alcoholic. And he couldn't smoke, he wasn't even
fty yet.

The address sheet said there was a meditation center a

block away. He turned left and found the entrance, a plai
door with a symbol on the doorway that looked like a hea
with rays coming out of it. He remembered the building firs
as a warehouse and then later as a place where Larry's frien
used to store bales of marijuana. Now, however, rows of pil
lows were lined up on the floor, a few of them occupied b
quiet people. Bert sat down.

A voice spoke to him, very softly. "Let's think abou
things," it said. "Let's decide what we can do today that wi
be useful. . . ."

Bert tried to get up, but his legs wouldn't work, and th
voice in his head said, "That's fine, we can go when we'v
finished, but we don't want to go just yet, do we? No. W
want to think about being useful . . ." And the voice went or
and on, and on, until it was time for lunch.

"That's fine," said the smiling lady at the lunch counte
when he complained about too much salad. "Tomorrow, yo
choose something else."

"That's fine," said the man at the shelter that nigh
"Here's your card for tomorrow and a list of other shelters.

"That's fine," said the boss the next morning, when Be
reported and said he didn't want to work. "You can go to th
meditation center."

"That's fine," said Bert a week or so later, looking at him
self in the mirror of the room that had his name on it, roo
502 at Glusi Housing Center #10. His boss on the paintin
crew had told him he was doing really well. The food at th
center tasted better all the time. "That's just fine," he saic
trying to identify the strange feeling he had. Really weir
After a while, he decided he felt contented.

55
benita

About a year later, Benita was in her new office in Washington, D.C., talking to her assistant, Jewel.

"Did you get monthly reports from the Glusi Centers?" she asked, checking a previous item off her list.

Jewel referred to her notebook. "Finished this afternoon, Bennie. Leonard says he'll bring them up as soon as they're printed. Preliminary indications were, glusi population requiring assistance was down maybe three percent."

"Three percent down," she breathed. "That's a first! That's wonderful. We started with four percent of the total population as glusi, and Chiddy said the total shouldn't exceed one percent of the population, so we're on our way down. Great!"

"Let's hope Chiddy was right. Can I get you some coffee, Bennie?"

"I'm fine, thanks. Have we had any more media fallout from the lawsuits those pregnant guys brought?"

"Not particularly. There was some case law involving rapists who'd been sued, but the courts just won't call what the Inkleozese did rape. There've been a few columns advocating recompense for their time and trouble, or in the case of the guys who didn't make it, payment to families. All the survivors are back now, all in good health, all returned to their homes. Of course, a number of their wives went elsewhere during their absence."

"The wives surely didn't blame their husbands."

"As a matter of fact, some of them did. In the morning paper, Mrs. Morse was quoted as saying her husband asked for it, talking the way he did. If he didn't want to be raped, he should have been more careful what he said."

"Which Mrs. Morse was that?" Benita asked.

"The first one. The second one was nicer. She seemed to be really fond of him."

"Lupé?"

"Right."

"Well, Lupé has always been said to be fond of a lot of people. She's a very . . . gregarious person. Anything else?"

"Your daughter called. She says she hasn't seen her brother in weeks, and have you heard from him?"

"Oh, my goodness, yes. Jewel, I'm such an idiot. I should have let her know. He called me three months ago to ask if I'd recommend him for the patterner's job. He got through the interviews, last time I talked to him, and then Vess called me to say he'd been selected! I'll call Angelica the minute I get home. Is that it?"

"That's it. No reason you can't take off for the weekend with a clear conscience."

Benita nodded, tucked some of the paperwork on her desk into the top drawer, put on her jacket, and left, turning in the doorway to admire the office. It was a splendid office. The furniture was elegant, all in Pchar wood, from the planet of the Vixbot. The rug was soft and beautifully colored, woven from the wooly integument of Oumfuzzian swamp plants. The plants in the window were from half a dozen different planets, all of them in gorgeous bloom, and the Confederation changed them for new ones, every few days.

Being Confederation Link wasn't a *big* job yet. Important, but not *big*. Once Earth was a full member of the Confederation—which seemed certain now, so much progress had been made—the Link liaison job would be a big, big job concerned with making import-export regulations, inter-species employment agreements, passport restrictions, all kinds of things. She was working closely with the new president, and she still saw the old president and First Lady every now and then. He was writing a book, and she was running for office. They both kept very busy and, like Benita, looked forward to the future with great anticipation. As for Benita's future, since she'd been appointed as Link by Confederation ETs on terms no other person was able (or maybe willing) to meet, it wasn't a political thing and she could look forward to being Link for life, if she liked.

Home was still the apartment above the bookstore. It was convenient and efficient, though it wouldn't be long before they'd need a larger place. She really wanted more country around her. Entertaining was part of the job, and having a buffet for fifty, mixed human and alien, wasn't something easily done in an apartment on the third floor with a wheezy elevator. They needed a place with a yard, with a big patio, maybe even a swimming pool.

When she parked behind the bookstore and opened the back door, the stockroom door was open. Hearing Simon's voice, she leaned in and cried, "Hi, Simon. See you later?"

"I'll be up in a bit," he yelled from behind a pile of books.

She took the elevator up, thinking that when they moved, she'd really miss the creaky old elevator. It rather punctuated her days, creak in the morning, creak in the evening, creak when anyone came or went. She dropped her things on the couch and sat down by the phone and called Angelica.

"Hi, Mom. Sorry to bother you, calling you at work, but I haven't been able to reach Carlos. He hasn't . . . reverted or anything, has he?"

"Angel, no. No, he's on top of the world. He called me about three months ago to ask if I'd recommend him for a job with the Confederation. Evidently, he'd discussed it with Chiddy and Vess before they dropped him off in California after we got back from Pistach-home last year."

"What Confederation job? He never mentioned it to me."

"There are two Confederation jobs that have to be filled

by Earthians. One is the Link job, that's the one I'm doing. The other one they call the Pattern job. It only opened up a few months ago, after we met the preliminary requirements for membership."

She smiled, thinking about it. American culture was indeed tasty and catching. What started in the U.S. had rapidly spread across the world. Conflict was down. Destruction of habitat was down. Incivility was down. All schools had classes on good citizenship and polite conduct, and if a student failed that class, they went to remedial school until they passed it, and if they acted out after passing it, they went back into class again. Freedom of speech was unabridged, but one could not yell in other people's faces, harass them, or use easy-speak to cover up unpleasant facts. Food distribution systems had been worked out to minimize famines; a new pregnancy immunization process was being distributed worldwide, making women increasingly infertile the more pregnancies they had. Gender selection had been perfected, so everyone could have the gender child they wanted, which had made Chiddy exult. In many countries everyone would have boys, by preference; the number of boys would exceed the number of girls by up to a third, and that would really drop the population during the next generation. World human population was too high, everyone agreed, but individual choice had to be respected.

The Inkleozese had petitioned formally for a meeting with the UN, during which they had said how gratified they were at the progress Earth had made and pointed out that in order to join the Confederation, Earth was required to provide two humans to work with the Confederation, and the first one had been selected, someone with intimate knowledge of and feelings of kinship for alien peoples, Benita Alvarez.

Previous to the announcement, Benita had been asked to take the job by the Confederation ambassador, another jolly Inkleozese, and after considering the requirements for a week or so, she had agreed. She had become quite uniquely qualified, after all. At least, so the Inkleozese had told her.

Now Carlos had been approved for the other position.

"I'm surprised he didn't talk to you before he left, Angelica."

"He left a message, but it was all garbled. And I've had finals. I guess I was too busy to worry about him until now."

"Well, you needn't worry at all. He's got the job."

Angelica asked, "What is the job? I don't get it."

"The Confederation needs one of us to travel among the Confederation worlds for the other races to study. The rules provide that new planets shouldn't submit anyone who has family because the job will take a large chunk of their lives. They like to have someone young, who isn't involved in professional work or some long-planned career."

"Travel around the galaxy?" Angel said. "Carlos?"

"That's right. So that all the races out there can record our parameters so that our people won't get into situations that are dangerous for them. If we have limited ability to withstand deterioration during long flights, the Confederation needs to know that. If our race has an adverse reaction to some botanical found on Vixbot, they need to know that."

"A lab rat!" exclaimed Angelica.

"Not really, Angelica. Chiddy says Patterns have a wonderful time. They have people paying attention to them all day, every day. They get to see things other people of their races may never see. They get the best of everything, amusements, housing, food . . ."

"How long will he be gone?"

"He should be back within two to four years. And he'll be in demand, Angel. I should imagine he'll be offered a book deal, at the very least. You may expect to see him on 20/20 or *Primetime*."

"Wow," she said doubtfully. "I can't believe it'll be Carlos."

"I can tell you're glad for him. Ah . . . I've got some news. Your father's back. He's in a glusi support program back in Albuquerque. I've got the number, if you want to call him."

"A program for the needy? Oh, Mom, that's sad."

"Well, so far as I'm concerned, he always was in a program for the needy, and I was it! I could go back to supporting him, I suppose, Angelica. I can't see that it did him any good before."

"Oh, no, no. Don't you dare! I'm just . . . sorry for him, that's all. My father in a program for the needy! Well."

So far as Angelica and the rest of the human race was concerned, glusi meant "needy" or "homeless." That's what Chiddy had defined it as, and only Chad and Benita and the people who'd read Chiddy's journal knew it had ever meant anything different. Everyone knew, of course, that glusi included former drunks who couldn't drink anymore and former nutters who had been smoothed out enough not to be agonized or dangerous, but otherwise left to do precisely what they chose. It included the occasional displaced person, for whom assistance could be both immediate and effectual, and also the occasional tormented eccentric for whom some form of mediation with the world was necessary, though the attempt was always made to ease the pain without interfering with creativity. The Confederation had a high regard for Earthian creativity, particularly in the graphic, musical and theater arts, and though suffering as a way of life was foreign to the Pistach, they had accepted that a certain amount of excruciation often went along with imagination.

Glusi also included runaway children, a no-longer-frequent category, along with women whom Chiddy still called "erotic stimulators for hire," who wished to do something else. Erotic stimulators for hire who liked their work, however (and a surprising number did), had their own support network offering medical and social benefits and assistance.

Angelica and Benita talked a while longer, though Angelica seemed unconvinced about Carlos, still finding it hard to believe he was doing anything important.

Benita had no sooner hung up than the phone rang. Chad.

"How are you?" she cried, joyously. "Haven't seen you in . . . weeks."

"Well, I've been . . . occupied," he said in a strained voice. "Merilu decided to come back. With the boys."

She took a deep breath. "Well . . . Chad. That's . . . what is that? Wonderful?"

"Ah . . . yes, in a way. She's written herself a new life-script, and it fits her to a tee. You know, behind every famous man there's a woman? Well, she's it."

"And you're the famous man?"

"If she has her way, I will be. As she keeps pointing out, I'm one of only two people who've ever seen a number of other planets. Since we have a ten-year probationary period before humans will be allowed to travel to other worlds, except the patterner, that is, no other human will see other planets for at least that long, and she's working on a book deal for me. 'Chad Riley as told to Merilu Riley.' Either that, or she wants to go to Pistach-home so we can write it together. She thinks with my influence, the Pistach would be happy to take us there. I've tried to explain, but she's not listening."

"Tell her about the toilets."

"The ones on Pistach-home?"

"Right. And tell her about the iglak, and what the food is like. All those squirmy things you have to eat to be polite. And how they won't let her wear anything but caste clothes, and how receptors are rather low caste . . . you get the idea."

"Benita, you're a lifesaver."

"Is it still worth it?"

Long silence. Sigh. "You pointed out to me once that she's a very beautiful woman."

"I did that," she admitted, wondering how long that would be enough for him. "Of course, the Pistach won't think so. They think all humans are odd looking. Tell her that, too."

"What have you heard from Carlos?" he asked.

"Well, you know he got the patterner job. Vess is with him, kind of a troubleshooter–escort. Vess said Carlos is on his way, enjoying himself, learning a lot, becoming quite the diplomat. You told me once you hankered for a job at State. I'm coming to believe Carlos may get one. He always loved the sound of his own voice. You better write your book before he gets back, or you'll have competition."

She hung up. Sasquatch stuck his nose in her lap and whined. He smelled something lovely emanating from the kitchen, as did she, so they went to see what was cooking. Her husband was at the stove, juggling several pans at once.

"Hi," glancing at her briefly. "Don't interrupt. I'm sautéing fin-zannels, and they mustn't burn."

"I don't think I've tasted fin-zannels."

"The Inkleozese brought in a case. I had to promise to give them a beef roast in return for these."

"Beef?"

"Any red meat. I don't think they care what. They say they'll label it as Earth meat and trade it to the Wulivery for flamsit eggs."

"The Wulivery got a taste for Earth flesh, hmm."

"Allegedly. They're still not speaking to the Inkleozese. They claim the assessors used unethical means to get them off Earth."

The sauté pan received a final, quite professional flip that emptied the whatsits onto a plate that was thrust into the warm oven.

"Bert showed up," Benita said.

"Ah."

"He's in a glusi center in Albuquerque."

"Good, good," distractedly as hands busily grated an onion, which was added to the plate in the oven before Benita was seized in an enormous hug. Certain pressure points were touched, tiny electric shocks went down particular muscles, all of it infinitely warm and loving. The room spun agreeably. It wasn't sex, but it was very, very nice.

"What's the occasion?" she asked, somewhat breathlessly.

"We're having a guest for dinner, and it's our six-month anniversary." A small box materialized before her nose. "Six months since you agreed to meet the Confederation guidelines for liaison officers and ally yourself with an otherworldly person."

She opened it. A pair of earrings. Not gold, something else, very light and lacy, set with gorgeous green stones. What a dear spouse, no matter what shape!

"Oh, they're lovely," she cried. "You're so wonderful to me!"

"As I should be," ai said. "Dearest, dearest Benita."

THE FRESCO
by
Sheri S. Tepper

The art world of Santa Fe was recently hurled into conflict. One set of people called other sets of people hypocritical and disrespectful of religion. Other sets brandished the freedom of speech banner in response. The cause? A Hispanic woman artist from California, whose work was included in a recent exhibit at the Museum of International Folk Art, displayed a representation of the Lady of Guadalupe wreathed in roses. I say wreathed, because that's what the picture looks like, a by-no-means sexy woman surrounded by roses with bands of the flowers amply covering breasts and thighs, but with nude legs and a midriff showing.

Someone who saw this artwork howled that it showed the Lady of Guadalupe in a bikini. Others, most of whom had not seen the art work, picked up the cry. Hundreds of petitioners showed up at the hearing to voice their opinion on the disrespect and lack of sensitivity displayed both by the artist and by those whose job it is to schedule and mount exhibitions. The fact that the artist herself was of the same heritage and possibily the same sensitivity as the complainers cut no ice. Meetings were scheduled. Hundreds of hours and thousands of dollars of public moneys were spent in an effort to be "sensitive" to the issue. In the end, the body responsible for the show allowed it to continue throughout its scheduled time, but the cries of protest still go on. . . .

The Lady of Guadalupe is a dark-skinned Virgin identified with Mary, the mother of Jesus. Her legend began in Mexico, and she is worshipped by many Mexicans as their own particular goddess. She is pictured as a dark-skinned

woman, robed and draped, usually with roses, and alway
backed by a many-tongued aureole of flame from head t
foot. As such she appears among the carved *santos* and *bulto*
(religious carvings and paintings) for which Santa Fe is wel
known, but also, and without criticism, as plastic models o
the dashboards of cars, on woven "throws," on T-shirts, an
in many other cheap, mass-produced and, to my mind, to
tally irreverent and totally disrespectful forms.

One of the leading firebrands in this issue is a priest wh
was removed from Santa Fe a year or so ago for stirring u
another such conflict. The old Sanctuary of Guadalupe, a
adobe church of some historic significance, had been fo
some time falling into ruin. Adobe structures are of the eartl
and to earth return unless rigorously, one might say reli
giously, maintained. The congregation has long since move
to new quarters nearby; the old sanctuary has been unsancti
fied; and the incipient ruin lay quiescent, awaiting the notic
of do-gooders of any faith who might stop decay in its track

As a number did. People interested in the architecture c
historic Santa Fe, both Catholic and non-Catholic, gav
contributions. Some money was given by local governmen
and some was obtained from the federal government, to re
store the old building as a community center where meet
ings might be held and art might, on occasion, be displaye
In time, with much effort and expenditure, this goal wa
achieved, the old sanctuary was turned over to a non-sectaria
group for management, and also, in time, art was displaye
there of which the young priest at the adjacent church dis
approved. He invaded the exhibit with a goodly number c
followers. Signs were waved, chants were chanted, fist
were no doubt brandished, all demanding that the offend
ing art be removed and the sanctuary be returned to it
sacred purpose.

No one opted for the simplest solution, which woul
have been to advise the group that the sanctuary could b
returned if the group paid back all the money and time sper
on its resurrection. Being expected to pay money for some
thing often resolves the question of its real value. This, how
ever, would have been practical, and Santa Fe is not know

for its practicality. Instead, the newspaper featured each day the latest outrage, the newest demand, the most recent attempt to mollify or negotiate. Eventually the matter was resolved when the archbishop moved the priest to a remote parish in less sensitive surroundings. That is, until the Lady in the Bikini episode.

All of the people involved in these skirmishes are sincere. They really believe that an unfamiliar image—which by being unfamiliar must be insensitive or disrespectful—has a mystic power beyond the print on the page or the paint on the canvas to besmirch the holy reality. In similar fashion, some of the local Native American pueblo peoples are deeply offended by the creation and sale of *kachina* figures, believing this dissemination of the image has the power to devalue the actual divinity.

It is the ability of the sacred image to control the thought, the actions, and the self-esteem of those invested in it that forms the framework of *The Fresco*. In the book, the painter is an ET, and a long dead one at that, but the observers include those among us who may find the image a matter of life and death.

We hope you've enjoyed this Eos book. As part of our mission to give readers the best science fiction and fantasy being written today, the following pages contain a glimpse into the fascinating worlds of a select group of Eos authors.

Join us as beloved sf author Sheri S. Tepper recounts an intelligent, witty, and deeply human tale of first contact. As fantasy author Sharon Green reveals the true fates of the Chosen Blending, six courageous men and women whose talents stand between the evil and the innocent. As Holly Lisle introduces a magical world so close to our own that both destiny and disaster spill through the world gates. And as acclaimed editor David G. Hartwell brings us the very best science fiction stories of the year.

Eos. Out of this World.

THE FRESCO
BY Sheri S. Tepper
Available in February 2002

Along the Oregon coast an arm of the Pacific shushes softly
against rocky shores. Above the waves, dripping silver in the
moonlight, old trees, giant trees, few now, thrust their heads
among low clouds, the moss thick upon their boles and
shadow deep around their roots. In these woods nights are
quiet save for the questing hoot of an owl, the satin stroke
of fur against a twig, the tick and rasp of small claws climbing up clambering down. In these woods bear is the big boy,
the top of the chain, but even he goes quietly and mostly by
day. It is a place of mosses and liverworts and ferns of filmy
green that curtains the branches and cushions the soil, a wet
place, a still place.

A place in which something new is happening. If there
were eyes to see, they might make out a bear-sized shadow
agile as a squirrel, puckering the quiet like an opening zipper, rrrrip up rrrrip down, high into the trees then down
again, disappearing into mist. Silence intervenes, then another seam is ripped softly on one side, then on the other
followed by new silences. Whatever these climbers are,
there are more than a few of them.

The owl opens his eyes wide and turns his head backwards, staring at the surrounding shades. Something new,

something strange, something to make a hunter curiou
When the next sound comes, he launches himself into th
air, swerving silently around the huge trunks, as he do
when he hunts mice or voles or small birds, following th
pucker of individual tics to its lively source, exploring int
his life's darkness. What he finds is nothing he might hav
imagined, and a few moments later his bloody feathe
float down to be followed by another sound, like a sati
fied sigh.

Near the Mexican border, rocky canyons cleave th
mountains, laying them aside like broken wedges of gra
cheese furred with a dark mold of pinon and juniper th
sheds hard shadows on moon glazed stone, etched lithe
graphs in gray and black, taupe and silver.

Beneath feathery chamisa a rattlesnake flicks his tongu
following a scent. Along a precarious rock ledge a ring-taile
cat strolls, nose snuffling the cracks. At the base of the sto
a peccary trots along familiar foot trails, toward the toes
a higher cliff where a seeping spring gathers in a rocky go
let. In the desert, sounds are dry and rattling: pebbles toe
into cracks, hoofs tac-tacking on stone, the serpent ratt
warning the wild pig to veer away, which she does with
grunt to the tribe behind her. From the rocky scrap the rin
tailed cat hears the whole population of the desert pa
about its business in the canyon below.

A new sound comes to this place, too. High in the air,
chuff, chuff, chuff, most like the wings of a monstrous cro
crisp and powerful, enginelike in their regularity. Then a cr
eerie and utterly alien, not from any native bird ever hea
in this place.

The peccary freezes in place. The ring-tailed cat lea
into the nearest crevice. Only the rattler does not hear do
not care. For the others staying frozen in place seems the a
propriate and prudent thing to do as the chutt, chutt, chu
moves overhead, another cry and an answer from places ea
and west and north as well. The aerial hunter is not alon

and its screams fade into the distance, the echoes still, and the canyon comes quiet again.

And farther south and east, along the gulf in the wetland that breeds the livelihood of the sea, in the mangrove swamps, the cypress bogs, the moss-lapped, vine-twined, sawgrass-grown, reptile-ridden mudflats, night sounds are continuous. Here the bull gator bellows, swamp birds call, insects and frogs whir and buzz and babble and creak. Fish jump, huge tails thrash, wings take off from cover to silhouette themselves on the face of the moon.

And even here comes strangeness, a great squadge, sqaudge, sqaudge, as though something walks through the deep muck in giant boots on ogre legs, squishing feet down and sucking them up only to squish them down once more. Squadge, squadge, squadge, three at a time, then a pause, then three more.

As in other places, the natives fall silent. The heron finds himself a perch and pulls his head back on his long neck, letting it rest on his back, crouching a little, not to be seen against the sky. The bull gator floats on the oily surface like a scaly buoy, fifteen feet of hunger and dim thought, an old man of the muck, protruding eyes seeing nothing as flared nostrils taste something strange. He lies in his favorite resting place near the trunk of a water-washed tree. There was no tree in that place earlier today, but the reptilian mind does not consider this. Only when something from above slithers sinuously onto the top of his head does he react violently, his body bending, monstrous tail thrashing, huge jaws gaping wide . . .

Then nothing. No more from the gator until morning, when the exploring heron looks along his beak to find an intaglio of strange bones on the bank, carefully trodden into the muck, from the fangs at the front of the jaw to the vertebra at the tip of the tail. Like a frieze of bloody murder, carefully displayed.

DESTINY

Book Three of The Blending Enthroned

BY Sharon Green

Available in April 2002

"What's happenin' now?" Vallant asked, and there was almos
accusation in his tone. "I leave the bunch of you alone for no
more than five minutes, and you find somethin' else to worry
about as soon as my back is turned. So what is it now, and
just how dangerous will it turn out to be?"

"A flux has been keeping me from seeing more than bits
and snatches," Naran said with a sigh. "I'm being surprised
by everything but what we absolutely have to know."

"You know, that's exactly the way it *has* been," I said, hi
by a flash of revelation. "You haven't been able to see much
of anything beyond the completely essential, and that can'
possibly be a coincidence either. Someone has to be delib
erately blocking you."

"Could the enemy really be strong enough to reach al
the way here to block Naran without us being aware of it?
Lorand asked, worry widening his eyes. "If they are, we have
even more trouble than we thought."

"It can't possibly be the invaders," I said while everyone
else just came up with exclamations of worry and startle
ment. "Naran's had this trouble since before we left Gar
Garee, and if the invaders are *that* strong we might as wel
just stand here and let them take us over. No, someone else

is responsible for blindfolding us, and I'd really like to know who that is."

"Who *could* it be?" Vallant countered, but not in a challenging way. "I'd be willin' to believe that Ristor Ardanis, leader of those with Sight magic, is behind the blockin', but he and most of his people are a long way away from here. Naran, are you absolutely certain that the people in your link groups are workin' *with* you rather than against your breakin' through?"

"Normally I might not be absolutely certain, but once I'm part of the Blending there's no doubt," Naran answered with a nod. "My people are trying as hard as I am, but something is keeping us from breaking through."

"It certainly can't be the Gracelians," Jovvi said, her distracted gaze saying that her mind searched for an answer. "The Gracelians don't *have* anyone with Sight magic, so they can't possibly affect it. Who does that leave?"

"No one but the Highest Aspect," I said, finding it impossible to keep the dryness from my tone. "If the enemy isn't doing it, the Gracelians aren't doing it, and Ristor Ardanis's people aren't doing it, there's no one left."

"But there *is* someone left," Rion disagreed slowly, his gaze as distracted as Jovvi's had been. "We haven't mentioned the fact in quite some time, but there's still a mystery in our lives that we haven't solved. Those 'signs' the Prophecies spoke of . . . We've denied that they ever happened, but they did happen and we still don't know who was responsible for causing them."

"And we don't know who was responsible for bringing us all together," Lorand took his turn to point out. "A minute or two ago we were refusing to accept all those dreams as a coincidence, but we never questioned the even bigger coincidence that we all ended up in the same residence. We are each of us the strongest practitioner of our respective talents, and we all just *happened* to end up in the same residence and made into a Blending? If you can believe *that*, then you must also believe that the Highest Aspect leaves a copper coin under our pillows as a reward for having gone through the five-year-old tests successfully."

"It looks like someone's been makin' a *lot* of things happen around us," Vallant observed, vexation showing on his face as strongly as I felt it inside me. "So there's some group, large or small, makin' these things happen, but we don't know i they're friend or foe. Until we find out just what their aim is we can't call them one or the other."

"Well, one of their aims *was* to bring us together," I suggested, thinking about it even as I spoke. "If they're friend of ours, they did it so that we could win the throne and ge rid of the nobility. If they're enemies, they did it to put us al in the same place so we could be gotten rid of with a single effort. If *we* get taken down, everyone knows that no one else is as strong as we are and so they might not even put up a token struggle. By winning over us, the enemy would win over everyone else at the same time."

"I see a flaw in that logic," Lorand said, another of us al most lost to distraction. "These unknown someones have obviously known about us since before we got together in Gan Garee. Putting us all together just to conquer us at the same time makes no sense, not when they could have killed us one at a time before we knew what we were doing. If they had, there would *be* no 'others' to worry about, only the Middle Seated Blending the nobles picked out. Even an arrogan enemy would never go to such lengths just to best six people."

"I'm forced to agree with that," Vallant said even as Jovv nodded her own agreement. "What's the sense in havin' al most a dozen more enemies, when killin' a few people wil give you no enemies to speak of at all? These invader leaders just rolled over all opposition until it was crushed, and then it took over the people and used them for their own purposes. That means there's definitely someone else in the game."

MEMORY OF FIRE
Book One of the World Gates
BY Holly Lisle
Available in May 2002

Molly McColl woke to darkness—and to men dragging her from her bed toward her bedroom door. The door glowed with a terrifying green light.

She didn't waste her breath screaming; she attacked. She kicked upward, and felt like she'd kicked a rock—but she heard the satisfying crack of bone under her bare heel, and the resulting shriek of pain. She snapped her right elbow back into ribs and gut, and her hand broke free from the thin, hot, strong fingers that clutched at it. She twisted and bit down on the fingers holding her left wrist, and was rewarded with a scream. She clawed at eyes, she kneed groins, she bit and kicked and fought with every trick at her disposal, with every ounce of her strength and every bit of her fear and rage.

But they had her outnumbered, and even though she could make out the outlines of the ones she'd hurt curled on the floor, the rest of her assailants still dragged her into that wall of fire. She screamed, but as the cluster of tall men around her forced her into the flames, her scream—and all other sounds—died.

No pain. No heat. The flames that brushed against her didn't hurt at all—instead, the cold fire felt wonderful, energizing, life-giving; as her kidnappers dragged her clawing and kicking into the curving, pulsing tunnel, something in her mind whispered "yes." For the instant—or the eternity— in which she hung suspended in that place, no one held her, no one was trying to hurt her, and for the first time in a long time, all the pain in her body fell away.

She had no idea what was going on; she felt on the one hand like she was fighting for her life, and on the other hand like she was moving into something wonderful.

And then, out of the tunnel of green fire, she erupted into a world of ice and snow and darkness, and all doubts vanished. The men still held her captive, and one of them shouted, "Get ropes and a wagon—she hurt Paith and Kevrad and Tajaro. We're going to have to tie her." She was in trouble—nothing good would come of this.

"It's only two leagues to Copper House."

"She'll kill one of us in that distance. Tie her."

"But the Imallin said she's not to be hurt."

Other hands were grabbing her now—catching at her feet, locking on to her elbows and wrists, knees and calves.

"Don't *hurt* her," said the one closest to her head. "Just tie her so she can't hurt us, damnall. And where's that useless Gateman the Imallin found to make the gate? We still have people back there! Send someone to get them out before he closes it!"

Molly fought as hard as she could, but the men—thin and tall, but strong—forced her forward, adding hands to hands on her arms and legs until she simply couldn't move.

When she couldn't fight, Molly relaxed her body completely. First, she wasn't going to waste energy uselessly. Second, if she stopped fighting, she might catch them off guard and be able to escape.

Someone dragged a big, snorting animal through the dark toward her, and rattling behind the animal was a big wooden farm-type wagon. But what the hell was the thing pulling it? It wasn't a horse and it wasn't any variety of cow—it had a bit of a moose shape to it, and a hint of cari bou, and some angles that suggested bones where bones didn't belong in any beast of burden Molly had ever seen. And its eyes glowed hell-red in the darkness.

The whole mob of them picked her up and shoved her into the back of the wagon, and most of them clambered up there with her—bending down to twist soft rope around her ankles, and then around her wrists. When they had her bound, they wrapped blankets around her, and tucked her deep into bales of straw. Instantly, she was warmer. Hell, she was warm. But as the wagon lurched and creaked, and began to rattle forward, she heard lines of marching feet forming on either side of the wagon. She knew the creak of boots and pack straps, the soft bitching, the sound of feet moving in rhythm while weighted down by gear and weapons. She remembered basic training all too well—and if Air Force basic was pretty easy compared to the Army or the Marines, she'd still got enough of marching to know the drill. She had a military escort.

What the hell was going on?

But the people who had come to get her weren't soldiers. They were too unprepared for resistance, too sure of themselves. Soldiers knew that trouble could be anywhere, and took precautions. More than that, though, she couldn't get over the feel of those hands on her—hot, thin, dry hands.

She decided she wasn't going to just wait for them to haul her where they were going and then . . . do things to her. She'd learned in the Air Force that the best way to survive a hostage situation was to not be a hostage. She started to work on the rope on her wrists, and managed by dint of persistence and a high tolerance to pain to free her hands. She'd done some damage—she could feel rope burns and scratches from metal embedded beneath the soft outer strands, and the heat and wetness where a bit of her own blood trickled down her hand—but she wasn't worried about any of that.

Fold and wrap a blanket around each foot and bind it in place with the rope, she thought. It won't make great boots, but it will get me home. Turn the other blankets into a pon-

cho, get the hell out of this place and back home. She could
follow the tracks in the snow.

Except there were the niggling details she hadn't let her
self think about while she was fighting, while she was get
ting her hands and then her feet untied, while she wa
folding boots out of blankets and tying them in place. She
hadn't heard an engine since she came out of the tunnel o
fire; she hadn't heard a car pass, or seen anything that migh
even be mistaken for an electric light; nor had she heard a
plane fly over. In the darkness, she could make out the vague
outlines of trees overhead, but not much else—not a sta
shone in the sky, which felt close and pregnant with more
snow.

She had the bad feeling that if she managed to escape the
soldiers that marched to either side of the wagon and suc
ceeded in tracing the wagon tracks back to the place where
she'd come through the tunnel of fire, that tunnel wouldn'
be there anymore. And she was very, very afraid that there
would be no other way to get home.

She listened to the speech of the men who drove the
wagons, and she could understand it flawlessly—but if she
forced herself to listen to the words, they were vowel-rich
and liquid, and they didn't have the shape of English. The
hands on her arms had felt wrong in ways besides their heat
their dryness, their thinness. When she closed her eyes and
stilled her breath and forced herself to remember, those
hands had gripped her with too many fingers. And when
she'd been fighting, her elbows had jammed into ribs that
weren't where ribs were supposed to be.

When the sun came up or they got to a place with lights
Molly had a bad feeling that she wasn't going to like getting
her first clear look at her kidnappers. Because when she le
herself really think about it, she had the feeling that she
wasn't on Earth anymore—and that her captors weren'
human.

YEAR'S BEST SF 7

EDITED BY David G. Hartwell

The tradition continues! The YEAR'S BEST SF 7 collects the best science fiction stories of 2001, never before published in book form, in one easy-to-carry volume. Previous volumes have included stories by Ray Bradbury, Joe Haldeman, Ursula K. Le Guin, Kim Stanley Robinson, Robert Silverberg, Bruce Sterling, Gene Wolfe, and many more.

With tales from both the grand masters of the field and the rising new stars, the YEAR'S BEST SF is rapidly becoming the indispensable guide to science fiction today.

Praise for the YEAR'S BEST series:

"Impressive."
Locus magazine

"The finest modern science fiction writing,"
Pittsburgh Tribune